A FALLEN SPY

A MISSING MASTERPIECE

A DARING MISSION

THE HEIST

Praise for *The Heist*

"Magnificent ... This book has all the elements you love about Silva's writing—his way with a plot, his incomparable characters, and the range of emotions he piles into his pages."

Huffington Post

"Ingenious."
Fort Worth Star Telegram

"Silva is a true genius with his portrait of the Israeli assassin-art restorer facing new, real-world complexities."

Bob Woodward, *Politico*

"*The Heist* by Silva is nothing short of phenomenal. It is his best work to date. And that is a huge statement since each novel has been unique and marvelous."

Naples Daily News

"As always, Silva doesn't disappoint. The Ian Fleming of our generation is a master storyteller who touches on political and moral issues of our time, while pulling us into the web he has spun."

The Jewish Journal

"A non-stop romp."
Suspense Magazine

"In erudition, action, and temperament, Silva has made Allon the modern-day covert warrior extraordinaire."

Kirkus

"Silva has weaved together a story with intrigue, insight, and suspense."

Crimespree Magazine

By Daniel Silva

Daniel Silva

The Heist

HARPER

An Imprint of HarperCollinsPublishers

This is a work of fiction. Names, characters, places, and incidents are products of the author's imagination or are used fictitiously and are not to be construed as real. Any resemblance to actual events, locales, organizations, or persons, living or dead, is entirely coincidental.

HARPER

An Imprint of HarperCollins*Publishers*
195 Broadway
New York, New York 10007

Copyright © 2014 by Daniel Silva
ISBN 978-0-06-232006-3

First Harper premium printing: March 2015
First Harper mass market international printing: January 2015
First Harper paperback international printing: July 2014
First Harper hardcover printing: July 2014

HarperCollins ® and Harper ® are registered trademarks of Harper-Collins Publishers.

Printed in the United States of America

Visit Harper paperbacks on the World Wide Web at
www.harpercollins.com

10 9 8 7 6 5

As always, for my wife, Jamie, and my children, Nicholas and Lily

Most stolen art is gone forever. . . . The lone bit of good news is that the better the painting, the better the odds it will someday be found.

—EDWARD DOLNICK, *THE RESCUE ARTIST*

He that diggeth a pit shall fall into it; and who so breaketh a hedge, a serpent shall bite him.

—ECCLESIASTES 10:8

O N October 18, 1969, Caravaggio's *Nativity with St. Francis and St. Lawrence* vanished from the Oratorio di San Lorenzo in Palermo, Sicily. The *Nativity*, as it is commonly known, is one of Caravaggio's last great masterworks, painted in 1609 while he was a fugitive from justice, wanted by papal authorities in Rome for killing a man during a swordfight. For more than four decades, the altarpiece has been the most sought-after stolen painting in the world, and yet its exact whereabouts, even its fate, have remained a mystery. Until now . . .

PART ONE

CHIAROSCURO

ST. JAMES'S, LONDON

IT BEGAN WITH an accident, but then matters involving Julian Isherwood invariably did. In fact, his reputation for folly and misadventure was so indisputably established that London's art world, had it known of the affair, which it did not, would have expected nothing less. Isherwood, declared one wit from the Old Masters department at Sotheby's, was the patron saint of lost causes, a high-wire artist with a penchant for carefully planned schemes that ended in ruins, oftentimes through no fault of his own. Consequently, he was both admired and pitied, a rare trait for a man of his position. Julian Isherwood made life a bit less tedious. And for that, London's smart set adored him.

His gallery stood at the far corner of the cobbled quadrangle known as Mason's Yard, occupying three floors of a sagging Victorian warehouse once owned by Fortnum & Mason. On one side were the London offices of a minor Greek shipping company; on the other was a pub that catered to pretty office girls who rode motor scooters. Many years earlier, before the successive waves of Arab and Russian money had swamped London's real estate market, the gallery had been located in stylish New Bond Street, or New Bondstrasse, as it was known in the trade. Then came the likes of Hermès, Burberry, Chanel, and Cartier, leaving Isherwood and others like him—independent dealers specializing in museum-quality Old Master paintings—no choice but to seek sanctuary in St. James's.

It was not the first time Isherwood had been forced into exile. Born in Paris on the eve of World War II, the only child of the renowned art dealer Samuel Isakowitz, he had been carried over the Pyrenees after the German invasion and smuggled into Britain. His Parisian childhood and Jewish lineage were just two pieces of his tangled past that Isherwood kept secret from the rest of London's notoriously backbiting art world. As far as anyone knew, he was English to the core—English as high tea and bad teeth, as he was fond of saying. He was the incomparable Julian Isherwood, Julie to his friends, Juicy Julian to his partners in the occasional crime of drink, and His Holiness to the art historians and curators who routinely made use of his infallible eye. He was loyal as the day was long, trusting to a fault, impeccably mannered, and had no real enemies, a singular achievement given that he had spent two lifetimes navigating the treacherous waters of the art world. Mainly, Isherwood was decent—decency being in short supply these days, in London or anywhere else.

Isherwood Fine Arts was a vertical affair: bulging storage rooms on the ground floor, business offices on the second, and a formal exhibition room on the third. The exhibition room, considered by many to be the most glorious in all of London, was an exact replica of Paul Rosenberg's famous gallery in Paris, where Isherwood had spent many happy hours as a child, oftentimes in the company of Picasso himself. The business office was a Dickensian warren piled high with yellowed catalogues and monographs. To reach it, visitors had to pass through a pair of secure glass doorways, the first off Mason's Yard, the second at the top of a narrow flight of stairs covered in stained brown carpeting. There they would encounter Maggie, a sleepy-eyed blonde who couldn't tell a Titian from toilet paper. Isherwood had once made a complete ass of himself trying to seduce her and, having no other recourse, hired her to be his receptionist instead. Presently, she was buffing her nails while the telephone on her desk bleated unanswered.

"Mind getting that, Mags?" Isherwood inquired benevolently.

"Why?" she asked without a trace of irony in her voice.

"Might be important."

She rolled her eyes before resentfully lifting the receiver to her ear and purring, "Isherwood Fine Arts." A few seconds later, she rang off without another word and resumed work on her nails.

"Well?" asked Isherwood.

"No one on the line."

"Be a love, petal, and check the caller ID."

"He'll call back."

Isherwood, frowning, resumed his silent appraisal of the painting propped upon the baize-covered easel in the center of the room—a depiction of Christ appearing before Mary Magdalene, probably by a follower of Francesco Albani, which Isherwood had recently plucked for a pittance from a manor house in Berkshire. The painting, like Isherwood himself, was badly in need of restoration. He had reached the age that estate planners refer to as "the autumn of his years." It was not a golden autumn, he thought gloomily. It was late autumn, with the wind knife-edged and Christmas lights burning along Oxford Street. Still, with his handmade Savile Row suit and plentiful gray locks, he cut an elegant if precarious figure, a look he described as dignified depravity. At this stage of his life, he could strive for nothing more.

"I thought some dreadful Russian was dropping by at four to look at a painting," said Isherwood suddenly, his gaze still roaming the worn canvas.

"The dreadful Russian canceled."

"When?"

"This morning."

"Why?"

"Didn't say."

"Why didn't you tell me?"

"Did."

"Nonsense."

"You must have forgotten, Julian. Been happening a lot lately."

Isherwood fixed Maggie with a withering stare, all the while wondering how he could have been attracted to so repulsive a creature. Then, having no other appointments on his calendar, and positively nothing better to do, he crawled into his overcoat and hiked over to Green's Restaurant and Oyster Bar, thus setting in motion the chain of events that would lead him into yet another calamity not of his own making. The time was twenty minutes past four. It was a bit too early for the usual crowd, and the bar was empty except for Simon Mendenhall, Christie's permanently suntanned chief auctioneer. Mendenhall had once played an unwitting role in a joint Israeli-American intelligence operation to penetrate a jihadist terror network that was bombing the daylights out of Western Europe. Isherwood knew this because he had played a minor role in the operation himself. Isherwood was not a spy. He was a helper of spies, one spy in particular.

"Julie!" Mendenhall called out. Then, in the bedroom voice he reserved for reluctant bidders, he added, "You look positively marvelous. Lost weight? Been to a pricey spa? A new girl? What's your secret?"

"Sancerre," replied Isherwood before settling in at his usual table next to the window overlooking Duke Street. And there he ordered a bottle of the stuff, brutally cold, for a glass wouldn't do. Mendenhall soon departed with his usual flourish, and Isherwood was alone with his thoughts and his drink, a dangerous combination for a man of advancing years with a career in full retreat.

But eventually the door swung open, and the wet darkening street yielded a pair of curators from the National Gallery. Someone important from the Tate came next, followed by a delegation from Bonhams led by Jeremy Crabbe, the tweedy director of the auction house's Old Master paintings department.

Hard on their heels was Roddy Hutchinson, widely regarded as the most unscrupulous dealer in all of London. His arrival was a bad omen, for everywhere Roddy went, tubby Oliver Dimbleby was sure to follow. As expected, he came waddling into the bar a few minutes later with all the discretion of a train whistle at midnight. Isherwood seized his mobile phone and feigned an urgent conversation, but Oliver was having none of it. He made a straight line toward the table—like a hound bearing down on a fox, Isherwood would recall later—and settled his ample backside into the empty chair. "Domaine Daniel Chotard," he said approvingly, lifting the bottle of wine from the ice bucket. "Don't mind if I do."

He wore a blue power suit that fit his portly frame like a sausage casing and large gold cuff links the size of shillings. His cheeks were rounded and pink; his pale blue eyes shone with a brightness that suggested he slept well at night. Oliver Dimbleby was a sinner of the highest order, but his conscience bothered him not.

"Don't take this the wrong way, Julie," he said as he poured himself a generous measure of Isherwood's wine, "but you look like a pile of dirty laundry."

"That's not what Simon Mendenhall said."

"Simon earns his living by talking people out of their money. I, however, am a source of unvarnished truth, even when it hurts." Dimbleby settled his gaze on Isherwood with a look of genuine concern.

"Oh, don't look at me like that, Oliver."

"Like what?"

"Like you're trying to think of something kind to say before the doctor pulls the plug."

"Have you had a peek in the mirror lately?"

"I try to avoid mirrors these days."

"I can see why." Dimbleby added another half inch of the wine to his glass.

"Is there anything else I can get for you, Oliver? Some caviar?"

"Don't I always reciprocate?"

"No, Oliver, you don't. In fact, if I were keeping track, which I am not, you would be several thousand pounds in arrears."

Dimbleby ignored the remark. "What is it, Julian? What's troubling you this time?"

"At the moment, Oliver, it's you."

"It's that girl, isn't it, Julie? That's what's got you down. What was her name again?"

"Cassandra," Isherwood answered to the window.

"Broke your heart, did she?"

"They always do."

Dimbleby smiled. "Your capacity for love astounds me. What I wouldn't give to fall in love just once."

"You're the biggest womanizer I know, Oliver."

"Being a womanizer has precious little to do with being in love. I love women, *all* women. And therein lies the problem."

Isherwood stared into the street. It was starting to rain again, just in time for the evening rush.

"Sold any paintings lately?" asked Dimbleby.

"Several, actually."

"None that I've heard about."

"That's because the sales were private."

"Bollocks," replied Oliver with a snort. "You haven't sold anything in months. But that hasn't stopped you from acquiring new stock, has it? How many paintings have you got stashed away in that storeroom of yours? Enough to fill a museum, with a few thousand paintings to spare. And they're all burned to a crisp, deader than the proverbial doornail."

Isherwood made no response other than to rub at his lower back. It had replaced a barking cough as his most persistent physical ailment. He supposed it was an improvement. A sore back didn't disturb the neighbors.

"My offer still stands," Dimbleby was saying.

"What offer is that?"

"Come on, Julie. Don't make me say it aloud."

Isherwood swiveled his head a few degrees and stared directly into Dimbleby's fleshy, childlike face. "You're not talking about buying my gallery again, are you?"

"I'm prepared to be more than generous. I'll give you a fair price for the small portion of your collection that's sellable and use the rest to heat the building."

"That's very charitable of you," Isherwood responded sardonically, "but I have other plans for the gallery."

"Realistic?"

Isherwood was silent.

"Very well," said Dimbleby. "If you won't allow me to take possession of that flaming wreck you refer to as a gallery, at least let me do something else to help lift you out of your current Blue Period."

"I don't want one of your girls, Oliver."

"I'm not talking about a girl. I'm talking about a nice trip to help take your mind off your troubles."

"Where?"

"Lake Como. All expenses paid. First-class air-fare. Two nights in a luxury suite at the Villa d'Este."

"And what do I have to do in return?"

"A small favor."

"How small?"

Dimbleby helped himself to another glass of the wine and told Isherwood the rest of it.

It seemed Oliver Dimbleby had recently made the acquaintance of an expatriate Englishman who collected ravenously but without the aid of a trained art adviser to guide him. Furthermore, it seemed the Englishman's finances were not what they once were, thus requiring the rapid sale of a portion of his holdings. Dimbleby had agreed to have a quiet look at the collection, but now that the trip was upon him, he couldn't face the prospect of getting on yet another airplane. Or so he claimed. Isherwood suspected Dimbleby's true motives for backing out of the trip resided elsewhere, for Oliver Dimbleby was ulterior motives made flesh.

Nevertheless, there was something about the idea of an unexpected journey that appealed to Isherwood, and against all better judgment he accepted the offer on the spot. That evening he packed lightly, and at nine the next morning was settling into his first-class seat on British Airways Flight 576, with nonstop service to Milan's Mal-pensa Airport. He drank only a single glass of wine during the flight—for the sake of his heart, he told himself—and at half past twelve, as he was climbing into a rented Mercedes, he was fully in command of his faculties. He made the drive northward to Lake Como without the aid of a map or navigation device. A highly regarded art historian who specialized in the painters of Venice, Isherwood had made countless journeys to Italy to prowl its churches and museums. Even so, he always leapt at the chance to return, especially when someone else was footing the bill. Julian Isherwood was French by birth and English by upbringing, but within his sunken chest beat the romantic, undisciplined heart of an Italian.

The expatriate Englishman of shrinking resources was expecting Isherwood at two. He lived grandly, according to Dimbleby's hastily drafted e-mail, on the southwestern prong of the lake, near the town of Laglio. Isherwood arrived a few minutes early and found the imposing gate open to receive him. Beyond the gate stretched a newly paved drive, which bore him gracefully to a gravel forecourt. He parked next to the villa's private quay and made his way past molded statuary to the front door. The bell, when pressed, went unanswered. Isherwood checked his watch and then rang the bell a second time. The result was the same.

At which point Isherwood would have been wise to climb into his rented car and leave Como as quickly as possible. Instead, he tried the latch and, regrettably, found it was unlocked. He opened the door a few inches, called a greeting into the darkened interior, and then stepped uncertainly into the grand entrance hall. Instantly, he saw the lake of blood on the marble floor, and the two bare feet suspended in space, and the swollen blue-black face staring down from above. Isherwood felt his knees buckle and saw the floor rising to receive him. He knelt there for a moment until the wave of nausea had passed. Then he rose unsteadily to his feet and, with his hand over his mouth, stumbled out of the villa toward his car. And though he did not realize it at the time, he was cursing tubby Oliver Dimbleby's name every step of the way.

VENICE

EARLY THE FOLLOWING morning, Venice lost yet another skirmish in its ancient war with the sea. The floodwaters carried marine creatures of every sort into the lobby of the Hotel Cipriani and inundated Harry's Bar. Danish tourists went for a morning swim in the Piazza San Marco; tables and chairs from Caffè Florian bobbed against the steps of the basilica like debris from a sunken luxury liner. For once, the pigeons were nowhere to be found. Most wisely fled the submerged city in search of dry land.

There were portions of Venice, however, where the *acqua alta* was more a nuisance than a calamity. In fact, the restorer managed to find an archipelago of reasonably dry land stretching from the door of his apartment in the *sestiere* of Cannaregio to Dorsoduro, at the southern end of the city. The restorer was not a Venetian by birth, but he knew its alleyways and squares better than most of the natives. He had studied his craft in Venice, loved and grieved in Venice, and once, when he was known by a name not his own, he had been chased from

Venice by his enemies. Now, after a long absence, he had returned to his beloved city of water and paintings, the only city where he had ever experienced anything like contentment. Not peace, though; for the restorer, peace was only the period between the last war and the next. It was fleeting, a falsehood. Poets and widows dreamed of it, but men such as the restorer never allowed themselves to be seduced by the notion that peace might actually be possible.

He paused at a kiosk to see whether he was being followed and then continued on in the same direction. He was below average in height—five foot eight perhaps, but no more—and had the spare physique of a cyclist. The face was long and narrow at the chin, with wide cheekbones and a slender nose that looked as though it had been carved from wood. The eyes that peered from beneath the brim of his flat cap were unnaturally green; the hair at his temples was the color of ash. He wore an oilskin coat and Wellington boots but carried no umbrella against the steady rain. Out of habit, he never burdened himself in public with any object that might impede the swift movement of his hands.

He crossed into Dorsoduro, the highest point of the city, and made his way to the Church of San Sebastiano. The front entrance was tightly sealed, and there was an official-looking notice explaining that the building would be closed to the public until the following autumn. The restorer approached a smaller doorway on the right side of the church and opened it with a heavy skeleton key. A breath of cool air from the interior caressed his cheek. Candle smoke, incense, ancient mildew: something about the smell reminded the restorer of death. He locked the door behind him, sidestepped a font filled with holy water, and headed inside.

The nave was in darkness and empty of pews. The restorer trod silently over the smooth timeworn stones and slipped through the open gate of the altar rail. The ornate Eucharistic table had been removed for cleaning; in its place rose thirty feet of aluminum scaffolding. The restorer scaled it with the agility of a house cat and slipped through a tarpaulin shroud onto his work platform. His supplies were precisely as he had left them the previous evening: flasks of chemicals, a wad of cotton wool, a bundle of wooden dowels, a magnifying visor, two powerful halogen lamps, a paint-smudged portable stereo. The altarpiece—*Virgin and Child in Glory with Saints* by Paolo Veronese—was as he had left it, too. It was just one of several remarkable paintings Veronese had produced for the church between 1556 and 1565. His tomb, with his glowering marble bust, was on the left side of the presbytery. At moments like these, when the church was empty and dark, the restorer could almost feel Veronese's ghost watching him as he worked.

The restorer switched on the lamps and stood motionless for a long moment before the altarpiece. At the apex were Mary and the Christ Child, seated upon clouds of glory and surrounded by musician angels. Beneath them, gazing upward in rapture, was a group of saints, including the patron saint of the church, Sebastian, whom Veronese depicted in martyrdom. For the past three weeks, the restorer had been painstakingly removing the cracked and yellowed varnish with a carefully calibrated mixture of acetone, methyl proxitol, and mineral spirits. Removing varnish from a Baroque painting, he liked to explain, was not like stripping a piece of furniture; it was more akin to scrubbing the deck of an aircraft carrier with a toothbrush. He first had to fashion a swab with cotton wool and a wooden dowel. After moistening the swab with solvent, he would apply it to the surface of the canvas and twirl, gently, so as not to cause any additional flaking of the paint. Each swab could clean about a square inch of the painting before it became too soiled to use. At night, when he was not dreaming of blood and fire, he was removing yellowed varnish from a canvas the size of the Piazza San Marco.

Another week, he thought, and then he would be ready to move on to the second phase of the restoration, retouching those portions of the canvas where Veronese's original paint had flaked away. The figures of Mary and the Christ Child were largely free of damage, but the restorer had uncovered extensive losses along the top and bottom portion of the canvas. If everything went according to plan, he would finish the restoration as his wife was entering the final weeks of her pregnancy. If everything went according to plan, he thought again.

He inserted a CD of *La Bohème* into the stereo, and a moment later the sanctuary was filled with the opening notes of "Non sono in vena." As Rodolfo and Mimi were falling in love in a tiny garret studio in Paris, the restorer stood alone before the

Veronese, meticulously removing the surface grime and yellowed varnish. He worked steadily and with an easy rhythm—*dip, twirl, discard . . . dip, twirl, discard*—until the platform was littered with acrid balls of soiled cotton wool. Veronese had perfected formulae for paints that did not fade with age; and as the restorer removed each tiny patch of tobacco-brown varnish, the colors beneath glowed intensely. It was almost as if the master had applied the paint to the canvas only yesterday instead of four and a half centuries ago.

The restorer had the church to himself for another two hours. Then, at ten o'clock, he heard the clatter of boots across the stone floor of the nave. The boots belonged to Adrianna Zinetti, cleaner of altars, seducer of men. After that it was Lorenzo Vasari, a gifted restorer of frescoes who had almost single-handedly brought Leonardo's *Last Supper* back from the dead. Then came the conspiratorial shuffle of Antonio Politi, who, much to his annoyance, had been assigned the ceiling panels instead of the main altarpiece. As a result, he spent his days sprawled on his back like a modern-day Michelangelo, glaring resentfully at the restorer's shrouded platform high above the chancel.

It was not the first time the restorer and the other members of the team had worked together. Several years earlier, they had carried out major restorations of the Church of San Giovanni Crisostomo in Cannaregio and, before that, at the Church of San Zaccaria in Castello. At the time, they had known the restorer as the brilliant but intensely private Mario Delvecchio. Later, they would learn, along with the rest of the world, that he was a legendary Israeli intelligence officer and assassin named Gabriel Allon. Adrianna Zinetti and Lorenzo Vasari had found it in their hearts to forgive Gabriel's deception, but not Antonio Politi. In his youth, he had once accused Mario Delvecchio of being a terrorist, and he regarded Gabriel Allon as a terrorist, too. Secretly, he suspected it was because of Gabriel that he spent his days in the upper reaches of the nave, supine and contorted, isolated from human contact, with solvent and paint dripping onto his face. The panels depicted the story of Queen Esther. Surely, Politi told anyone who would listen, it was no coincidence.

In truth, Gabriel had had nothing to do with the decision; it had been made by Francesco Tiepolo, owner of the most prominent restoration firm in the Veneto and director of the San Sebastiano project. A bearlike figure with a tangled gray-and-black beard, Tiepolo was a man of enormous appetites and passions, capable of great anger and even greater love. As he strode up the center of the nave, he was dressed, as usual, in a flowing tunic-like shirt with a silk scarf knotted around his neck. The clothing made it seem as though he were overseeing the construction of the church rather than its renovation.

Tiepolo paused briefly to cast an admiring glance at Adrianna Zinetti, with whom he had once had an affair that was among the worst-kept secrets in Venice. Then he scaled Gabriel's scaffolding and barged through the gap in the tarpaulin shroud. The wooden platform seemed to bow under the strain of his enormous weight.

"Careful, Francesco," said Gabriel, frowning.

"The floor of the altar is made of marble, and it's a long way down."

"What are you saying?"

"I'm saying that it might be wise for you to lose a few kilos. You're starting to develop your own gravitational pull."

"What good would it do to lose weight? I could shed twenty kilos, and I'd still be fat." The Italian took a step forward and examined the altarpiece over Gabriel's shoulder. "Very good," he said with mock admiration. "If you continue at this pace, you'll be finished in time for the first birthday of your children."

"I can do it quickly," replied Gabriel, "or I can do it right."

"They're not mutually exclusive, you know. Here in Italy, our restorers work quickly. But not you," Tiepolo added. "Even when you were pretending to be one of us, you were always very slow."

Gabriel fashioned a fresh swab, moistened it with solvent, and twirled it over Sebastian's arrow-pierced torso. Tiepolo watched intently for a moment; then he fashioned a swab of his own and worked it against the saint's shoulder. The yellowed varnish dissolved instantly, exposing Veronese's pristine paint.

"Your solvent mixture is perfect," said Tiepolo.

"It always is," replied Gabriel.

"What's the solution?"

"It's a secret."

"Must everything be a secret with you?"

When Gabriel made no reply, Tiepolo glanced down at the flasks of chemicals.

"How much methyl proxitol did you use?"

"Exactly the right amount."

Tiepolo scowled. "Didn't I arrange work for you when your wife decided she wanted to spend her pregnancy in Venice?"

"You did, Francesco."

"And do I not pay you far more than I pay the others," he whispered, "despite the fact that you're always running out on me every time your masters require your services?"

"You've always been very generous."

"Then why won't you tell me the formula for your solvent?"

"Because Veronese had his secret formula, and I have mine."

Tiepolo gave a dismissive wave of his enormous hand. Then he discarded his soiled swab and fashioned a new one.

"I got a call from the Rome bureau chief of the *New York Times* last night," he said, his tone offhand. "She's interested in doing a piece on the restoration for the Sunday arts section. She wants to come up here on Friday and have a look around."

"If you don't mind, Francesco, I think I'll take Friday off."

"I thought you'd say that." Tiepolo gave Gabriel a sidelong glance. "Not even tempted?"

"To what?"

"To show the world the *real* Gabriel Allon. The Gabriel Allon who cares for the works of the great masters. The Gabriel Allon who can paint like an angel."

"I only talk to journalists as a last resort. And I would never dream of talking to one about myself."

"You've lived an interesting life."

"That's putting it mildly."

"Perhaps it's time for you to come out from behind the shroud."

"And then what?"

"You can spend the rest of your days here in Venice with us. You always were a Venetian at heart, Gabriel."

"It's tempting."

"But?"

With his expression, Gabriel made it clear he wished to discuss the matter no further. Then, turning to the canvas, he asked, "Have you received any other phone calls I should know about?"

"Just one," answered Tiepolo. "General Ferrari of the Carabinieri is coming into town later this morning. He'd like a word with you in private."

Gabriel turned sharply and looked at Tiepolo. "About what?"

"He didn't say. The general is far better at asking questions than answering them." Tiepolo scrutinized Gabriel for a moment. "I never knew that you and the general were friends."

"We're not."

"How do you know him?"

"He once asked me for a favor, and I had no choice but to agree."

Tiepolo made a show of thought. "It must have been that business at the Vatican a couple of years ago, that girl who fell from the dome of the Basilica. As I recall, you were restoring their Caravaggio at the time it happened."

"Was I?"

"That was the rumor."

"You shouldn't listen to rumors, Francesco. They're almost always wrong."

"Unless they involve you," Tiepolo responded with a smile.

Gabriel allowed the remark to echo unanswered into the heights of the chancel. Then he resumed his work. A moment earlier, he had been using his right hand. Now he was using his left, with equal dexterity.

"You're like Titian," Tiepolo said, watching him. "You are a sun amidst small stars."

"If you don't leave me in peace, the sun is never going to finish this painting."

Tiepolo didn't move. "Are you sure you're not him?" he asked after a moment.

"Who?"

"Mario Delvecchio."

"Mario is dead, Francesco. Mario never was."

THE REGIONAL HEADQUARTERS of the Carabinieri, Italy's national military police force, was located in the *sestiere* of Castello, not far from the Campo San Zaccaria. General Cesare Ferrari emerged from the building promptly at one. He had forsaken his blue uniform with its many medals and insignia and was wearing a business suit instead. One hand clutched a stainless steel attaché case; the other, the one missing two fingers, was thrust into the pocket of a well-cut overcoat. He removed the hand long enough to offer it to Gabriel. His smile was brief and formal. As usual, it had no influence upon his prosthetic right eye. Even Gabriel found its lifeless, unyielding gaze difficult to bear. It was like being studied by the all-seeing eye of an unforgiving God.

"You're looking well," said General Ferrari. "Being back in Venice obviously agrees with you."

"How did you know I was here?"

The general's second smile lasted scarcely longer than his first. "There isn't much that happens in Italy that I don't know about, especially when it concerns you."

"How did you know?" Gabriel asked again.

"When you requested permission from our intelligence services to return to Venice, they forwarded that information to all relevant ministries and divisions of law enforcement. One of those places was the palazzo."

The palazzo to which the general was referring overlooked the Piazza di Sant'Ignazio in the ancient center of Rome. It housed the Division for the Defense of Cultural Patrimony, which was better known as the Art Squad. General Ferrari was its chief. And he was right about one thing, thought Gabriel. There wasn't much that happened in Italy the general didn't know about.

The son of schoolteachers from the impoverished Campania region, Ferrari had long been regarded as one of Italy's most competent and accomplished law enforcement officials. During the 1970s, a time of terrorist bombings in Italy, he helped to neutralize the Communist Red Brigades. Then, during the Mafia wars of the 1980s, he served as a commander in the Camorra-infested Naples division. The assignment was so dangerous that Ferrari's wife and three daughters were forced to live under twenty-four-hour guard. Ferrari himself was the target of numerous assassination attempts, including the letter-bomb attack that claimed his eye and two fingers.

The posting to the Art Squad was supposed to be a reward for a long and distinguished career. It was assumed Ferrari would merely follow in the footsteps of his lackluster predecessor, that he would shuffle papers, take long Roman lunches, and, oc-

casionally, find one or two of the museum's worth
of paintings that were stolen in Italy each year.
Instead, he immediately set about modernizing a
once-effective unit that had been allowed to atro-
phy with age and neglect. Within days of his arrival,
he fired half the staff and quickly replenished the
ranks with aggressive young officers who actually
knew something about art. He gave them a simple
mandate. He wasn't much interested in the street-
level hoods who dabbled in art theft; he wanted the
big fish, the bosses who brought the stolen goods
to market. It didn't take long for Ferrari's new approach to pay dividends. More than a dozen important thieves were now behind bars, and statistics for
art theft, while still astonishingly high, were beginning to show improvement.

"So what brings you to Venice?" Gabriel asked as
he led the general between the temporary ponds in
the Campo San Zaccaria.

"I had business in the north—Lake Como, to be
specific."

"Something got stolen?"

"No," replied the general. "Someone got murdered."

"Since when are dead bodies the business of the
Art Squad?"

"When the decedent has a connection to the art
world."

Gabriel stopped walking and turned to face the
general. "You still haven't answered my question,"
he said. "Why are you in Venice?"

"I'm here because of you, of course."

"What does a dead body in Como have to do
with me?"

"The person who found it."

The general was smiling again, but the prosthetic eye was staring blankly into the middle distance. It was the eye of a man who knew everything, thought Gabriel. A man who was not about to take no for an answer.

They entered the church through the main doorway off the *campo* and made their way to Bellini's famed San Zaccaria altarpiece. A tour group stood before it while a guide lectured sonorously on the subject of the painting's most recent restoration, unaware that the man who had performed it was among his audience. Even General Ferrari seemed to find it amusing, though after a moment his monocular gaze began to wander. The Bellini was San Zaccaria's most important piece, but the church contained several other notable paintings as well, including works by Tintoretto, Palma the Elder, and Van Dyke. It was just one example of why the Carabinieri maintained a dedicated unit of art detectives. Italy had been blessed with two things in abundance: art and professional criminals. Much of the art, like the art in the church, was poorly protected. And many of the criminals were bent on stealing every last bit of it.

On the opposite side of the nave was a small chapel that contained the crypt of its patron and a canvas by a minor Venetian painter that no one had bothered to clean in more than a century. General Ferrari lowered himself onto one of the pews, opened his metal attaché case, and removed a file folder.

Then, from the folder, he drew a single eight-by-ten photograph, which he handed to Gabriel. It showed a man of late middle age hanging by his wrists from a chandelier. The cause of death was not clear from the image, though it was obvious the man had been tortured savagely. The face was a bloody, swollen mess, and several swaths of skin and flesh had been carved away from the torso.

"Who was he?" asked Gabriel.

"His name was James Bradshaw, better known as Jack. He was a British subject, but he spent most of his time in Como, along with several thousand of his countrymen." The general paused thoughtfully. "The British don't seem to like living in their own country much these days, do they?"

"No, they don't."

"Why is that?"

"You'd have to ask them." Gabriel looked down at the photograph and winced. "Was he married?"

"No."

"Divorced?"

"No."

"Significant other?"

"Apparently not."

Gabriel returned the photograph to the general and asked what Jack Bradshaw had done for a living.

"He described himself as a consultant."

"What sort?"

"He worked in the Middle East for several years as a diplomat. Then he retired early and went into business for himself. Apparently, he dispensed advice to British firms wishing to do business in the Arab world. He must have been quite good at his job," the general added, "because his villa was among the most expensive on that part of the lake. It also contained a rather impressive collection of Italian art and antiquities."

"Which explains the Art Squad's interest in his death."

"Partly," said the general. "After all, having a nice collection is no crime."

"Unless the collection is acquired in a way that skirts Italian law."

"You're always one step ahead of everyone else, aren't you, Allon?" The general looked up at the darkened painting hanging on the wall of the chapel. "Why wasn't this cleaned in the last restoration?"

"There wasn't enough money."

"The varnish is almost entirely opaque." The general paused, then added, "Just like Jack Bradshaw."

"May he rest in peace."

"That's not likely, not after a death like that." Ferrari looked at Gabriel and asked, "Have you ever had occasion to contemplate your own demise?"

"Unfortunately, I've had several. But if you don't mind, I'd rather talk about the collecting habits of Jack Bradshaw."

"The late Mr. Bradshaw had a reputation for acquiring paintings that were not actually for sale."

"Stolen paintings?"

"Those are your words, my friend. Not mine."

"You were watching him?"

"Let us say that the Art Squad monitored his activities to the best of our ability."

"How?"

"The usual ways," answered the general evasively.

"I assume your men are doing a complete and thorough inventory of his collection."

"As we speak."

"And?"

"Thus far they've found nothing from our database of missing or stolen works."

"Then I suppose you'll have to take back all the nasty things you said about Jack Bradshaw."

"Just because there's no evidence doesn't mean it isn't so."

"Spoken like a true Italian policeman."

It was clear from General Ferrari's expression that he interpreted Gabriel's remark as a compliment. Then, after a moment, he said, "One heard other things about the late Jack Bradshaw."

"What sort of things?"

"That he wasn't just a private collector, that he was involved in the illegal export of paintings and other works of art from Italian soil." The general lowered his voice and added, "Which explains why your friend Julian Isherwood is in a great deal of trouble."

"Julian Isherwood doesn't trade in smuggled art."

The general didn't bother to respond. In his eyes, all art dealers were guilty of something.

"Where is he?" asked Gabriel.

"In my custody."

"Has he been charged with anything?"

"Not yet."

"Under Italian law, you can't hold him for more than forty-eight hours without bringing him before a judge."

"He was found standing over a dead body. I'll think of something."

"You know Julian had nothing to do with Bradshaw's murder."

"Don't worry," the general replied, "I have no plans to recommend charges at this time. But if it were to become public that your friend was meeting with a known smuggler, his career would be over. You see, Allon, in the art world, perception is reality."

"What do I have to do to keep Julian's name out of the papers?"

The general didn't respond immediately; he was scrutinizing the photograph of Jack Bradshaw's body.

"Why do you suppose they tortured him before killing him?" he asked at last.

"Maybe he owed them money."

"Maybe," agreed the general. "Or maybe he had something the killers wanted, something more valuable."

"You were about to tell me what I have to do to save my friend."

"Find out who killed Jack Bradshaw. And find out what they were looking for."

"And if I refuse?"

"The London art world will be abuzz with nasty rumors."

"You're a cheap blackmailer, General Ferrari."

"Blackmail is an ugly word."

"Yes," said Gabriel. "But in the art world, perception is reality."

GABRIEL KNEW A good restaurant not far from the church, in a quiet corner of Castello where tourists rarely ventured. General Ferrari ordered lavishly; Gabriel moved food around his plate and sipped at a glass of mineral water with lemon.

"You're not hungry?" inquired the general.

"I was hoping to spend a few more hours with my Veronese this afternoon."

"Then you should eat something. You need your strength."

"It doesn't work that way."

"You don't eat when you're restoring?"

"Coffee and a bit of bread."

"What kind of diet is that?"

"The kind that allows me to concentrate."

"No wonder you're so thin."

General Ferrari went to the antipasti trolley and filled his plate a second time. There was no one else in the restaurant, no one but the owner and his daughter, a pretty dark-haired girl of twelve or thirteen. The child bore an uncanny resemblance to the daughter of Abu Jihad, the second-in-command of the PLO whom Gabriel, on a warm spring evening in 1988, had assassinated at his villa in Tunis. The killing had been carried out in Abu Jihad's second-floor study, where he had been watching videos of the Palestinian intifada. The girl had seen everything: two immobilizing shots to the chest, two fatal shots to the head, all set to the music of Arab rebellion. Gabriel could no longer recall the death mask of Abu Jihad, but the young girl's portrait, serene but seething with rage, hung prominently in the exhibition rooms of his memory. As the general retook his seat, Gabriel concealed her face beneath a layer of obliterating paint. Then he leaned forward across the table and asked, "Why me?"

"Why *not* you?"

"Shall I start with the obvious reasons?"

"If it makes you feel better."

"I'm not an Italian policeman. In fact, I'm quite the other thing."

"You have a long history here in Italy."

"Not all of it pleasant."

"True," agreed the general. "But along the way, you've made important contacts. You have friends in high places like the Vatican. And, perhaps more importantly, you have friends in low places, too. You know the country from end to end, you speak our language like a native, and you're married to an Italian. You're practically one of us."

"My wife isn't Italian anymore."

"What language do you speak at home?"

"Italian," admitted Gabriel.

"Even when you're in Israel?"

Gabriel nodded.

"I rest my case." The general lapsed into a thoughtful silence. "This might surprise you," he said finally, "but when a painting goes missing, or someone gets hurt, I usually have a pretty good idea who's behind it. We have more than a hundred informants on our payroll, and we've tapped more phones and e-mail accounts than the NSA. When something happens in the criminal end of the art world, there's always chatter. As you say in the counterterrorism business, nodes light up."

"And now?"

"The silence is deafening."

"What do you think it means?"

"It means that, in all likelihood, the men who killed Jack Bradshaw were not from Italy."

"Any guess as to where they're from?"

"No," the general said, shaking his head slowly, "but the level of violence concerns me. I've seen a lot of dead bodies during my career, but this one was different. The things they did to Jack Bradshaw were . . ." His voice trailed off, then he said, "Medieval."

"And now you want *me* to get mixed up with them."

"You strike me as a man who knows how to take care of himself."

Gabriel ignored the remark. "My wife is pregnant. I can't possibly leave her alone."

"We'll keep a close eye on her." The general lowered his voice and added, "We already are."

"It's good to know the Italian government is spying on us."

"You didn't really expect otherwise, did you?"

"Of course not."

"I didn't think so. Besides, Allon, it's for your own good. You have a lot of enemies."

"And now you want me to make another one."

The general laid down his fork and peered contemplatively out the window in the manner of Bellini's *Doge Leonardo Loredan*. "It's rather ironic," he said after a moment.

"What's that?"

"That a man such as yourself would choose to live in a ghetto."

"I don't actually live in the ghetto."

"Close enough," said the general.

"It's a nice neighborhood—the nicest in Venice, if you ask me."

"It's filled with ghosts."

Gabriel glanced at the young girl. "I don't believe in ghosts."

The general dabbed his napkin skeptically at the corner of his mouth.

"How would it work?" asked Gabriel.

"Consider yourself one of my informants."

"Meaning?"

"Go forth into the nether regions of the art world and find out who killed Jack Bradshaw. I'll take care of the rest."

"And if I come up empty?"

"I'm confident you won't."

"That sounds like a threat."

"Does it?"

The general said nothing more. Gabriel exhaled heavily.

"I'm going to need a few things."

"Such as?"

"The usual," replied Gabriel. "Phone records, credit cards, e-mails, Internet browsing histories, and a copy of his computer hard drive."

The general nodded toward his attaché case. "It's all there," he said, "along with every nasty rumor we've ever heard about him."

"I'll also need to have a look around his villa and his collection."

"I'll give you a copy of the inventory when it's complete."

"I don't want an inventory. I want to see the paintings."

"Done," said the general. "Anything else?"

"I suppose someone should tell Francesco Tiepolo that I'm going to be leaving Venice for a few days."

"And your wife, too."

"Yes," said Gabriel distantly.

"Perhaps we should share the labor. I'll tell Francesco, you tell your wife."

"Any chance we can do it the other way around?"

"I'm afraid not." The general raised his right hand, the one with the two missing fingers. "I've suffered enough already."

Which left only Julian Isherwood. As it turned out, he was being held at the Carabinieri's regional headquarters, in a windowless chamber that was not quite a holding cell but not a waiting room, either. The handover took place on the Ponte della Paglia, within sight of the Bridge of Sighs. The general did not seem at all displeased to be rid of his prisoner. He remained on the bridge, with his ruined hand tucked into his coat pocket and his prosthetic eye watching unblinkingly, as Gabriel and Isherwood made their way along the Molo San Marco to Harry's Bar. Isherwood drank two Bellinis very fast while Gabriel quietly saw to his travel arrangements. There was a British Airways flight leaving Venice at six that evening, arriving at Heathrow a few minutes after seven. "Thus leaving me plenty of time," said Isherwood darkly, "to murder Oliver Dimbleby and still be in bed for the *News at Ten*."

"As your informal representative in this matter," said Gabriel, "I would advise against that."

"You think I should wait until morning before killing Oliver?"

Gabriel smiled in spite of himself. "The general has generously agreed to keep your name out of this," he said. "If I were you, I wouldn't say anything in London about your brief brush with Italian law enforcement."

"It wasn't brief enough," said Isherwood. "I'm not like you, petal. I'm not used to spending nights in jail. And I'm certainly not used to stumbling upon dead bodies. My God, but you should have seen him. He was positively filleted."

"All the more reason you shouldn't say anything when you get home," Gabriel said. "The last thing you want is for Jack Bradshaw's killers to read your name in the papers."

Isherwood chewed his lip and nodded slowly in agreement. "The general seemed to think Bradshaw was trafficking in stolen paintings," he said after a moment. "He also seemed to think I was in business with him. He gave me quite a going-over."

"Were you, Julian?"

"In business with Jack Bradshaw?"

Gabriel nodded.

"I won't dignify that with a response."

"I had to ask."

"I've done many naughty things during my career, usually at your behest. But I have never, and I mean *never*, sold a painting that I knew was stolen."

"What about a smuggled painting?"

"Define *smuggled*," said Isherwood with an impish smile.

"What about Oliver?"

"Are you asking whether Oliver Dimbleby is flogging stolen paintings?"

"I suppose I am."

Isherwood had to think it over for a moment before answering. "There's not much I would put past Oliver Dimbleby," he said finally. "But no, I don't believe he's dealing in stolen pictures. It was all a case of bad luck and timing."

Isherwood signaled the waiter and ordered another Bellini. He was finally beginning to relax. "I have to admit," he said, "that you were the absolute last person in the world I expected to see today."

"The feeling is mutual, Julian."

"I take it you and the general are acquainted."

"We've exchanged business cards."

"He's one of the most disagreeable creatures I've ever met."

"He's not so bad once you get to know him."

"How much does he know about our relationship?"

"He knows we're friends and that I've cleaned a number of pictures for you. And if I had to guess," Gabriel added, "he probably knows about your links to King Saul Boulevard."

King Saul Boulevard was the address of Israel's foreign intelligence service. It had a long and deliberately misleading name that had very little to do with the true nature of its work. Those who worked there referred to it as the Office and nothing else. So did Julian Isherwood. He was not directly employed by the Office; he was a member of the *sayanim*, a global network of volunteer helpers. They were the bankers who supplied Office agents with cash in emergencies; the doctors who treated them in secret when they were wounded; the hoteliers who gave them rooms under false names, and the rental car agents who supplied them with untraceable vehicles. Isherwood had been recruited in the mid-1970s, during a wave of Palestinian terrorist attacks against Israeli targets in Europe. He'd had but one assignment—to assist in building and maintaining the operational cover of a young art restorer and assassin named Gabriel Allon.

"I suppose my release didn't come free of charge," Isherwood said.

"No," replied Gabriel. "In fact, it was rather pricey."

"How pricey?"

Gabriel told him.

"So much for your sabbatical in Venice," said Isherwood. "It seems I've ruined everything."

"It's the least I can do for you, Julian. I owe you a great deal."

Isherwood smiled wistfully. "How long has it been?" he asked.

"A hundred years."

"And now you're going to be a father again, twice over. I never thought I'd live to see the day."

"Neither did I."

Isherwood looked at Gabriel. "You don't sound thrilled about the prospect of having children."

"Don't be ridiculous."

"But?"

"I'm old, Julian." Gabriel paused, then added, "Perhaps too old to be starting another family."

"Life dealt you a lousy hand, my boy. You're entitled to a bit of happiness in your dotage. I must admit I envy you. You're married to a beautiful young woman who's going to bear you two beautiful children. I wish I were in your shoes."

"Be careful what you wish for."

Isherwood drank slowly of his Bellini but said nothing.

"It's not too late, you know."

"To have children?" he asked incredulously.

"To find someone to spend the rest of your life with."

"I'm afraid I'm past my expiration date," Isherwood answered. "At this point, I'm married to my gallery."

"Sell the gallery," said Gabriel. "Retire to a villa in the south of France."

"I'd go mad in a week."

They left the bar and walked a few paces to the Grand Canal. A sleek wooden water taxi gleamed at the edge of the crowded dock. Isherwood seemed reluctant to board it.

"If I were you," said Gabriel, "I'd get out of town before the general changes his mind."

"Sound advice," replied Isherwood. "May I give you some?"

Gabriel was silent.

"Tell the general to find someone else."

"I'm afraid it's too late for that."

"Then watch your step out there. And don't go playing the hero again. You have a lot to live for."

"You're going to miss your plane, Julian."

Isherwood teetered aboard the water taxi. As it eased away from the dock, he turned to Gabriel and shouted, "What do I say to Oliver?"

"You'll think of something."

"Yes," said Isherwood. "I always do."

Then he ducked into the cabin and was gone.

5

VENICE

G ABRIEL WORKED ON the Veronese until the
windows of the nave darkened with dusk.
Then he rang Francesco Tiepolo on his
telefonino and broke the news that he had to run a
very private errand for General Cesare Ferrari of
the Carabinieri. He didn't go into any of the details.

"How long will you be gone?" asked Tiepolo.

"A day or two," replied Gabriel. "Maybe a month."

"What shall I say to the others?"

"Tell them I died. It will lift Antonio's spirits."

Gabriel straightened his work platform with
more care than usual and went into the cold evening. He followed his usual route northward, across
San Polo and Cannaregio, until he came to an iron
bridge, the only iron bridge in all of Venice. In the
Middle Ages there had been a gate in the center of
the bridge, and at night a Christian watchman had
stood guard so that those imprisoned on the other
side could not escape. Now the bridge was empty
except for a single gull that glared at Gabriel ma-
levolently as he trod slowly past.

He entered a darkened *sottoportego*. At the end of

the passageway a broad square opened before him, the Campo di Ghetto Nuovo, the heart of the ancient ghetto of Venice. He crossed the square and stopped at the door of Number 2899. A small brass plaque read *COMUNITÀ EBRAICA DI VENEZIA*: JEWISH COMMUNITY OF VENICE. He pressed the bell, then, instinctively, turned his face away from the security camera.

"Can I help you?" a familiar female voice asked in Italian.

"It's me."

"Who's me?"

"Open the door, Chiara."

A buzzer howled, a deadbolt snapped open. Gabriel entered a cramped passage and followed it to another door, which unlocked automatically as he approached. It gave onto a small office, where Chiara sat primly behind an orderly desk. She wore a sweater of winter white, fawn-colored leggings, and a pair of leather boots. Her riotous auburn hair fell across her shoulders and upon a silk scarf that Gabriel had purchased on the island of Corsica. He resisted the impulse to kiss her wide mouth. He didn't think it proper to express physical affection toward the receptionist of the chief rabbi of Venice, even if the receptionist also happened to be the rabbi's devoted daughter.

Chiara was about to address him but was interrupted by the ringing of the telephone. Gabriel sat on the edge of her desk and listened as she dispensed with a small crisis afflicting a shrinking community of believers. She looked astonishingly like the beautiful young woman he had first encountered, ten years earlier, when he had come calling on Rabbi Jacob Zolli for information on the fate of Italy's Jews during the Second World War. Gabriel had not known then that Chiara was an agent of Israeli intelligence, or that she had been assigned by King Saul Boulevard to watch over him during the restoration of the San Zaccaria altarpiece. She revealed herself to him a short time later in Rome, after an incident involving gunplay and the Italian police. Trapped alone with Chiara in a safe flat, Gabriel had wanted desperately to touch her. He had waited until the case was resolved and they had returned to Venice. There, in a canal house in Cannaregio, they made love for the first time, in a bed prepared with fresh linen. It was like making love to a figure painted by the hand of Veronese.

On the day of their first meeting, Chiara had offered him coffee. She no longer drank coffee, only water and fruit juice, which she sipped constantly from a plastic bottle. It was the only outward sign that, after a long struggle with infertility, she was finally pregnant with twins. She had vowed not to resist the inevitable weight gain with dieting or exercise, which she regarded as yet another obsession inflicted upon the world by the Americans. Chiara was a Venetian at heart, and Venetians did not flail on cardio contraptions or lift heavy objects to build their muscles. They ate and drank well, they made love, and when they required a bit of exercise, they strolled the sands of the Lido or walked down to the Zattere for a gelato.

She hung up the telephone and settled her playful gaze upon him. Her eyes were the color of caramel and flecked with gold, a combination that Gabriel had never been able to render accurately on canvas. At the moment, they were very bright. She was happy, he thought, happier than he had ever seen her before. Suddenly, he didn't have the heart to tell her that General Ferrari had appeared like the flood to spoil everything.

"How are you feeling?" he asked.

She rolled her eyes and sipped from her plastic water bottle.

"Did I say something wrong?"

"You don't have to ask me how I'm feeling *all* the time."

"I want you to know that I'm concerned about you."

"I know you're concerned, darling. But I'm not terminally ill. I'm just pregnant."

"What should I ask you?"

"You should ask me what I want for dinner."

"I'm famished," he said.

"I'm always famished."

"Should we go out?"

"Actually, I feel like cooking."

"Are you up to it?"

"Gabriel!"

She began to needlessly straighten the papers on her desk. It wasn't a good sign. Chiara always straightened things when she was annoyed.

"How was your work?" she asked.

"It was a thrill a minute."

"Don't tell me you're bored with the Veronese."

"Removing dirty varnish isn't the most rewarding part of a restoration."

"No surprises?"

"With the painting?"

"In general," she answered.

It was a peculiar question. "Adrianna Zinetti came to work dressed as Groucho Marx," Gabriel replied, "but otherwise it was a normal day at the Church of San Sebastiano."

Chiara frowned at him. Then she opened a drawer with the toe of her boot and absently inserted a few papers into a manila folder. Gabriel wouldn't have been surprised if the papers bore no relation to the others already in the file.

"Is there something bothering you?" he asked.

"You're not going to ask me how I'm feeling again, are you?"

"I wouldn't dream of it."

She closed the drawer with more force than necessary. "I stopped by the church at lunchtime to surprise you," she said after a moment, "but you weren't there. Francesco said you had a visitor. He claimed not to know who it was."

"And you knew Francesco was lying, of course."

"It didn't take a trained intelligence officer to see that."

"Go on," said Gabriel.

"I called the Operations Desk to see whether anyone from King Saul Boulevard was in town, but the Operations Desk told me that no one was looking for you."

"For a change."

"Who came to see you today, Gabriel?"

"This is beginning to sound like an interrogation."

"Who was it?" she asked again.

Gabriel held up his right hand and then lowered two of the fingers.

"General Ferrari?"

Gabriel nodded. Chiara stared at her desk as if searching for something out of place.

"How are you feeling?" asked Gabriel quietly.

"I'm fine," she replied without looking up. "But if you ask me that question one more time . . ."

It was true that Gabriel and Chiara did not actually live in the ancient ghetto of Venice. Their rented apartment was on the second floor of a faded old palazzo, in a quiet quarter of Cannaregio where Jews never had been forbidden to enter. On one side was a quiet square; on the other was a canal where King Saul Boulevard kept a small, fast boat, lest Gabriel had need to flee Venice for the second time in his storied career. Tel Aviv had good reason to be mindful of his security; after many years of resistance, he had agreed to become the next chief of the Office. A year remained until his term was to begin. After that, his every waking moment would be devoted to protecting the State of Israel from those who wished to destroy it. There would be no more restorations or extended stays in Venice with his beautiful young wife—at least, not without an army of bodyguards watching over them.

The apartment had been fitted with a sophisticated security system, which chirped benignly when Gabriel pushed open the door. Entering, he removed the cork from a bottle of Bardolino and sat at the kitchen counter, listening to the news on the

BBC, while Chiara prepared a platter of bruschetta. A UN panel had predicted an apocalyptic warming of the global climate, a car bomb had killed forty in a Shiite neighborhood of Baghdad, and the Syrian president, the butcher of Damascus, had once again used chemical weapons against his own people. Chiara frowned and switched off the radio. Then she looked longingly at the open bottle of wine. Gabriel was sorry for her. Chiara had always loved to drink Bardolino in the springtime.

"It won't harm them if you take just a sip," he said.

"My mother never touched wine when she was pregnant with me."

"And look how you turned out."

"Perfect in every way."

She smiled and then placed the bruschetta in front of Gabriel. He selected two slices—one with chopped olives, the other with white beans and rosemary—and poured some of the Bardolino. Chiara peeled the skin from an onion and with a few quick thrusts of her knife turned it into a pile of perfect white cubes.

"You'd better be careful," said Gabriel, watching her, "or you'll end up looking like the general."

"Don't give me any ideas."

"What was I supposed to say to him, Chiara?"

"You might have told him the truth."

"Which version of the truth?"

"You have one year until you take your oath, darling. After that, you'll be at the prime minister's beck and call, and the security of the state will be your responsibility. Your life will be one long meeting interspersed with the occasional crisis."

"Which is why I turned down the job several times before finally accepting it."

"But now it's yours. And this is your last chance to take some well-deserved time off before we go back to Israel."

"I tried to explain that to the general without going into all the sordid details. That's when he threatened to leave Julian rotting in an Italian jail cell."

"He had nothing on Julian. He was bluffing."

"He might have been," Gabriel conceded. "But what if some enterprising British reporter decided to do a little digging into Julian's background? And what if the same enterprising reporter somehow discovered he was an asset of the Office? I would have never forgiven myself if I'd allowed him to be dragged through the mud. He's always been there when I needed him."

"Do you remember the time you asked him to take care of that Russian defector's cat?"

"How could I forget? I never knew Julian was allergic to cats. He had a rash for a month."

Chiara smiled. She placed the onion in a heavy skillet with olive oil and butter, quickly chopped a carrot, and added it, too.

"What are you making?"

"It's a local meat dish called *calandraca*."

"Where did you learn to make it?"

Chiara glanced at the ceiling, as if to say such knowledge was to be found in the air and the water of Italy. It wasn't far from the truth.

"What can I do to help?" asked Gabriel.

"You can stop hovering over me."

Gabriel carried the platter of bruschetta and the wine into the small sitting room. Before lowering himself onto the couch, he removed the gun from the small of his back and placed it carefully on the coffee table, atop a pile of bright magazines having to do with pregnancy and childbirth. The gun was a Beretta 9mm, and its walnut grip was stained with paint: a dab of Titian, a bit of Bellini, a drop of Raphael and Tintoretto. Soon he would no longer carry a weapon; others would carry weapons on his behalf. He wondered how it was going to feel to walk through the world unarmed. It would be akin, he thought, to leaving home without first putting on a pair of trousers. Some men wore neckties when they went to the office. Gabriel Allon carried a gun.

"I still don't understand why the general needs *you* to find out who killed Jack Bradshaw," Chiara called from the kitchen.

"He seems to think they were looking for something," replied Gabriel, leafing through the pages of one of the magazines. "He'd like me to find it before they do."

"Looking for what?"

"He didn't go into specifics, but I suspect he knows more than he's saying."

"He usually does."

Chiara placed cubes of lightly floured veal in the pan, and soon the apartment was filled with the savor of the browning meat. Next she added a few ounces of tomato sauce, white wine, and herbs that she measured out in the palm of her hand. Gabriel watched the running lights of a boat moving slowly over the black waters of the canal. Then, cautiously, he told Chiara he planned to leave for Lake Como first thing in the morning.

"When will you be back?" she asked.

"That depends."

"On what?"

"On what I find inside Jack Bradshaw's villa."

Chiara was chopping potatoes on a wooden cutting board. As a result, her declaration that she intended to accompany Gabriel was scarcely audible over the clatter of the knife. Gabriel turned from the window and fixed her with a reproachful stare.

"What's wrong?" she asked after a moment.

"You're not going anywhere," he replied evenly.

"It's Lake Como. What could possibly happen?"

"Shall I give you a few examples?"

Chiara was silent. Gabriel turned to watch the boat moving up the canal again, but in his thoughts were images of a long and turbulent career. It was a career, oddly enough, that had played itself out in some of Europe's most glamorous settings. He had killed in Cannes and Saint-Tropez and fought for his life on the streets of Rome and in the mountains of Switzerland. And once, many years earlier, he had lost a wife and son to a car bomb on a quaint street in the elegant First District of Vienna. No, he thought now, Chiara would not be coming with him to Lake Como. He would leave her here in Venice, in the care of her family and under the protection of the Italian police. And God help the general if he allowed anything to happen to her.

She was singing softly to herself, one of those silly Italian pop songs she so adored. She added the chopped potatoes to the pot, lowered the heat, and then joined Gabriel in the sitting room. General Ferrari's file on Jack Bradshaw lay on the coffee table, next to the Beretta pistol. She reached for it, but Gabriel stopped her; he didn't want her to see the mess that Jack Bradshaw's killers had made of his body. She placed her head against his shoulder. Her hair smelled of vanilla.

"How long before the *calandraca* is ready?" asked Gabriel.

"An hour or so."

"I can't wait that long."

"Have another bruschetta."

He did. So did Chiara. Then she lifted the glass of Bardolino to her nose but did not drink from it.

"It won't hurt them if you take only a small sip."

She returned the wineglass to the table and placed her hand over her womb. Gabriel placed his own hand next to hers, and for an instant he thought he could detect the hummingbird flutter of two fetal heartbeats. They're mine, he thought, holding them tightly. And God help the man who ever tries to harm them.

6

LAKE COMO, ITALY

NEXT MORNING, RESIDENTS of the United Kingdom awoke to the news that one of their countrymen, the expatriate businessman James "Jack" Bradshaw, had been found brutally murdered at his villa overlooking Lake Como. The Italian authorities offered up robbery as a possible motive, despite the fact that they had no evidence that anything at all had been stolen. General Ferrari's name did not appear in the coverage; nor was there any mention that Julian Isherwood, the noted London art dealer, had discovered the body. All of the newspapers struggled to find anyone who had a kind word to say about Bradshaw. The *Times* managed to dredge up an old colleague from the Foreign Office who described him as "a fine officer," but otherwise it seemed Bradshaw's life was deserving of no eulogy. The photograph that popped up on the BBC looked at least twenty years old. It showed a man who did not like to have his picture taken.

There was another crucial fact missing from the coverage of Jack Bradshaw's murder: Gabriel Allon,

the legendary but wayward son of Israeli intelligence, had been quietly retained by the Art Squad
to look into it. His investigation commenced at half
past seven when he inserted a high-capacity flash
drive into his notebook computer. Given to him
by General Ferrari, the drive contained the contents of Jack Bradshaw's personal computer. Most
of the documents dealt with his business, the Meridian Global Consulting Group—a curious name,
thought Gabriel, for Meridian appeared to have no
other employees. The drive contained more than
twenty thousand documents. In addition, there
were several thousand telephone numbers and e-
mail addresses that had to be checked out and cross-
referenced. It was far too much material for Gabriel
to review alone. He needed an assistant, a skilled re-
searcher who knew something about criminal matters and, preferably, about Italian art.

"*Me?*" asked Chiara incredulously.

"Do you have a better idea?"

"Are you sure you want me to answer that?"

Gabriel made no reply. He could see there was
something about the idea that appealed to Chiara.
She was a natural solver of puzzles and problems.

"It would be easier if I could run the phone numbers and e-mail addresses through the computers of
King Saul Boulevard," she said after a moment of
thought.

"Obviously," replied Gabriel. "But the last thing I
intend to do is tell the Office that I'm investigating
a case for the Italians."

"They'll find out eventually. They always do."

Gabriel copied Bradshaw's files onto the hard

drive of the notebook computer and kept the flash drive for himself. Then he packed a small overnight bag with two changes of clothing and two sets of identity while Chiara showered and dressed for work. He walked her to the ghetto and on the doorstep of the community center placed his hand on her abdomen one last time. Leaving, he couldn't help but notice the young, good-looking Italian man drinking coffee at the kosher café. He rang General Ferrari at the palazzo in Rome. The general confirmed that the young Italian was an officer of the Carabinieri who specialized in personal protection.

"Couldn't you have found someone to watch my wife who didn't look like a film star?"

"Don't tell me the great Gabriel Allon is jealous."

"Just make sure nothing happens to her. Do you hear me?"

"I only have one eye," replied the general, "but I still have both my ears, and they function quite well."

Like many Venetians, temporary or otherwise, Gabriel kept a car, a Volkswagen sedan, in a garage near the Piazzale Roma. He headed across the causeway to the mainland and then made his way to the autostrada. When the traffic thinned, he pressed his foot to the floor and watched the needle of the speedometer creep toward one hundred. For weeks he had strolled and floated through life at a crawl. Now, the rumble of an internal combustion engine was suddenly a guilty pleasure. He pushed the car to the limit and saw the flatlands of the Veneto sweep past his window in a satisfying green-and-tan blur.

He sped westward, past Padua, Verona, and Bergamo, and arrived at the outskirts of Milan thirty minutes earlier than he had anticipated. From there, he headed north to Como; then he followed the winding shore of the lake until he arrived at the gate of Jack Bradshaw's villa. Through its bars he could see an unmarked Carabinieri car parked in the forecourt. He rang the general in Rome, told him where he was, and then quickly severed the connection. Thirty seconds later, the gate swung open.

Gabriel slipped the car into gear and eased slowly down the steep drive, toward the home of a man whose life had been summarized in a single hollow line. *A fine officer* . . . He was certain of only one thing, that Jack Bradshaw, retired diplomat, consultant to firms doing business in the Middle East, collector of Italian art, had been a liar by trade. He knew this because he was a liar as well. Therefore, as he stepped from his car, he felt a certain kinship with the man whose life he was about to ransack. He came not as an enemy but as a friend, the perfect implement for an unpleasant job. In death there are no secrets, he thought, crossing the forecourt. And if there was a secret hidden in the beautiful villa by the lake, he was going to find it.

A Carabinieri officer in plain clothes waited in the entrance. He introduced himself as Lucca—no last name or rank, just Lucca—and offered Gabriel nothing but a pair of rubber gloves and plastic shoe covers. Gabriel was more than happy to put them on. The last thing he needed at this stage of his life was to leave his DNA at yet another Italian crime scene.

"You have one hour," the Carabinieri man said. "And I'll be coming with you."

"I'll take as long as I need," replied Gabriel. "And you're staying right here."

When the officer offered no response, Gabriel pulled on the gloves and shoe covers and entered the villa. The first thing he noticed was the blood. It was hard not to; the entire stone floor of the entrance foyer was black with it. He wondered why the murder had occurred here rather than in a more secluded section of the house. It was possible Bradshaw had confronted his killers after they broke into the residence, but there was no evidence of forcible entry on the door or at the gate. The more logical explanation was that Bradshaw had admitted his assailants. He had known them, thought Gabriel. And, foolishly, he had trusted them enough to let them into his home.

From the entrance hall, Gabriel moved into the great room. It was elegantly furnished in silk-covered couches and chairs, and adorned with expensive tables, lamps, and trinkets of every kind. One wall was given over entirely to large windows that overlooked the lake; the others were hung with Italian Old Master paintings. Most were minor devotional pieces or portraits churned out by journeymen or followers of well-known painters from Venice and Florence. One, however, was a Roman architectural *capriccio* that clearly was the work of Giovanni Paolo Panini. Gabriel licked his gloved fingertip and dragged it across the surface. The Panini, like the other paintings displayed in the room, was sorely in need of a good cleaning.

Gabriel wiped the surface grime onto the leg of his jeans and walked over to an antique writing desk.

On it were two silver-framed photographs of Jack Bradshaw in happier times. In the first he was posed before the Great Pyramid of Giza, a boyish forelock falling across a face that was full of hope and promise. In the second the backdrop was the ancient city of Petra in Jordan. It had been snapped, Gabriel supposed, when Bradshaw was serving at the British embassy in Amman. He looked older, harder, perhaps wiser. The Middle East was like that. It turned hope to despair, idealists into Machiavellians.

Gabriel opened the drawer of the writing table, found nothing of interest, then scrolled through the directory of missed calls on the telephone. One number, 6215845, appeared seven times—five times before Bradshaw's death, and twice after. Gabriel lifted the receiver, pressed the autodial, and a few seconds later heard the distant tone of a telephone. After several rings came a series of clicks and rattles indicating that the person at the other end of the line had picked up the call and quickly hung up. Gabriel dialed the number again with the same result. But when he tried the number a third time, a male voice came on the line and in Italian said, "This is Father Marco. How can I help you?"

Gabriel gently replaced the receiver without speaking. Next to the phone was a message pad. He tore away the top page, jotted the phone number on the adjoining page, and slipped both into his coat pocket. Then he headed upstairs.

Paintings lined the wide central corridor and covered the walls of two otherwise empty bedrooms.

Bradshaw had used a third bedroom for storage. Several dozen paintings, some in frames, some on their stretchers, leaned against the walls like folding chairs after a catered affair. Most of the paintings were Italian in origin, but there were several works by German, Flemish, and Dutch artists as well. One, a genre painting of Dutch washerwomen working in a courtyard, probably by an imitator of Willem Kalf, appeared as though it had recently been restored. Gabriel wondered why Bradshaw had decided to have the painting cleaned while others in his collection, some more valuable, languished beneath coats of yellowed varnish—and why, having done so, he had left it leaning against a wall in a storage room.

On the opposite side of the center hall were Bradshaw's bedroom and office. Gabriel quickly searched them with the thoroughness of a man who knew how to hide things. In the bedroom, concealed beneath a Gatsbyesque pile of colorful shirts, he found a wrinkled manila envelope stuffed with several thousand euros that had somehow escaped the attention of General Ferrari's men. In the office, he found file folders swollen with business papers, along with an impressive collection of monographs and catalogues. He also discovered documentation suggesting that Meridian Global Consulting had rented a vault in the Geneva Freeport. He wondered whether the documents had escaped the attention of the general's men, too.

Gabriel slipped the Freeport documentation into his coat pocket and crossed the hallway to the room Bradshaw had used for storage. The three

Dutch washerwomen were still toiling away in their cobblestone courtyard, oblivious to his presence. He crouched before the canvas and examined the brushwork carefully. It was quite obviously the work of an imitator, for it lacked any trace of confidence or spontaneity. Indeed, in Gabriel's learned opinion, it had a paint-by-numbers quality to it, as if the artist had been staring at the original while he worked. Perhaps he had been.

Gabriel headed downstairs and, under the watchful gaze of the Carabinieri man, retrieved a handheld ultraviolet lamp from his overnight bag. When trained on an Old Master canvas in a darkened room, the lamp would reveal the extent of the last restoration by making the retouching appear as black blotches. Typically, a Dutch Old Master painting from that period had suffered minor to moderate losses, which meant the retouching—or inpainting, as it was known in the trade—would appear as speckles of black.

Gabriel returned to the room on the second floor of the villa, closed the door, and drew the blinds tightly. Then he switched on the ultraviolet lamp and pointed it toward the painting. The three Dutch washerwomen were no longer visible. The entire canvas was black as pitch.

7

LAKE COMO, ITALY

A T A CHEMICAL supply company in an industrial quarter of Como, Gabriel purchased
acetone, alcohol, distilled water, goggles, a
glass beaker, and a protective mask. Next he stopped
at an arts-and-crafts shop in the center of town where
he picked up wooden dowels and a packet of cotton
wool. Returning to the villa by the lake, he found the
Carabinieri man waiting in the entrance with fresh
gloves and shoe covers. This time, the Italian didn't
make any noises about a one-hour limit. He could see
Gabriel was going to be a while.

"You're not going to contaminate anything, are
you?"

"Only my lungs," replied Gabriel.

Upstairs he removed the canvas from its frame,
propped it on an armless chair, and illuminated its
surface with as much light as he could find. Then
he mixed equal amounts of acetone, alcohol, and
distilled water in the beaker and fashioned a swab
using a dowel and cotton wool. Working quickly,
he removed the fresh varnish and inpainting from a
small rectangle—about two inches by one inch—at

the bottom left corner of the canvas. Restorers referred to the technique as "opening a window." Usually, it was done to test the strength and effectiveness of a solvent solution. In this case, however, Gabriel was opening a window in order to strip away the surface layers of the painting to see what lay beneath. What he discovered were the lush folds of a crimson garment. Clearly, there was an intact painting beneath the three Dutch washerwomen working in a courtyard—a painting that, in Gabriel's opinion, had been produced by a true Old Master of considerable talent.

He quickly opened three more windows, one at the bottom right of the canvas and two more across the top. At the bottom right, he found additional fabric, darker and less distinct; but at the top right, the canvas was nearly black. At the top left, he found a tawny-colored Roman arch that looked as though it was part of an architectural background. The four open windows gave him a rough sense of how the figures were arrayed upon the canvas. More important, they told him that, in all likelihood, the painting was the work of an Italian rather than an artist from the Dutch or Flemish schools.

Gabriel opened a fifth window a few inches below the Roman arch and discovered a balding male pate. Expanding it, he found the bridge of a nose and an eye that was staring directly toward the viewer. Next he opened a window a few inches to the right and found the pale, luminous forehead of a young female. He expanded that window, too, and found a pair of downward-cast eyes. A long nose emerged next, followed by a pair of small red lips and a delicate chin. Then, after another minute of work, Gabriel saw the outstretched hand of a child. *A man, a woman, a child* . . . Gabriel studied the hand of the child—specifically, the way the thumb and forefinger were touching the chin of the woman. The pose was familiar to him. So was the brushwork.

He crossed the hall to Jack Bradshaw's office, switched on the computer, and went to the Web site of the Art Loss Register, the world's largest private database of stolen, missing, and looted artwork. After a few keystrokes, a photograph of a painting appeared on the screen—the same painting that was now propped on a chair in the room across the hall. Beneath the photo was a brief description:

The Holy Family, oil on canvas, Parmigianino (1503–1540), stolen from a restoration lab at the historic Santo Spirito Hospital in Rome, July 31, 2004.

The Art Squad had been searching for the missing painting for more than a decade. And now Gabriel had found it, in the villa of a dead Englishman, hidden beneath a copy of a Dutch painting by Willem Kalf. He started to dial General Ferrari's number but stopped. Where there was one, he thought, there would surely be others. He rose from the dead man's desk and started looking.

Gabriel discovered two additional paintings in the storeroom that, when subjected to ultraviolet light, were totally black. One was a Dutch School coastal scene reminiscent of the work of Simon de Vlieger; the other was a vase of flowers that appeared to be a copy of a painting by the Viennese artist Johann Baptist Drechsler. Gabriel began opening windows.

Dip, twirl, discard . . .

A swollen tree against a cloud-streaked sky, the folds of a skirt spread across a meadow, the naked flank of a corpulent woman . . .

Dip, twirl, discard . . .

A patch of blue-green background, a floral blouse, a wide, sleepy eye above a rose-colored cheek . . .

Gabriel recognized both paintings. He sat down at the computer and returned to the Web site of the Art Loss Register. After a few keystrokes, a photograph of a painting appeared on the screen:

Young Women in the Country, oil on canvas, Pierre-Auguste Renoir (1841–1919), 16.4 x 20 inches, missing since March 13, 1981, from the Musée de Bagnols-sur-Cèze, Gard, France. Estimated current value: unknown.

More keystrokes, another painting, another story of loss:

Portrait of a Woman, oil on canvas, Gustav Klimt (1862–1918), 32.6 x 21.6 inches, missing since February 18, 1997, from the Galleria Ricci Oddi, Piacenza, Italy. Estimated current value: $4 million.

Gabriel placed the Renoir and the Klimt next to the Parmigianino, snapped a photograph with his mobile phone, and quickly forwarded it to the palazzo. General Ferrari rang him back thirty seconds later. Help was on the way.

Gabriel carried the three paintings downstairs and propped them on one of the couches in the great room. *Parmigianino, Renoir, Klimt* . . . Three missing paintings by three prominent artists, all concealed beneath copies of lesser works. Even so, the copies had been of extremely high quality. They were the work of a master forger, thought Gabriel. Perhaps even a restorer. But why go to the trouble of commissioning a copy in order to conceal a stolen work? Clearly, Jack Bradshaw was connected to a sophisticated network that dealt in stolen and smuggled art. Where there were three, thought Gabriel, looking at the paintings, there would be more. Many more.

He picked up one of the photographs of a youthful Jack Bradshaw. His curriculum vitae read like something from a lost age. Educated at Eton and Oxford, fluent in Arabic and Persian, he had been sent into the world to do the bidding of a once-mighty empire that had fallen into terminal decline. Perhaps he had been an ordinary diplomat, an issuer of visas, a stamper of passports, a writer of thoughtful cables that no one bothered to read. Or perhaps he had been something else entirely. Gabriel knew a man in London who could put flesh on the bones of Jack Bradshaw's dubiously thin résumé. The truth would not come without a price. In the espionage business, truth rarely did.

Gabriel set aside the photograph and used his mobile phone to book a seat on the morning flight to Heathrow. Then he picked up the slip of paper on which he'd written the number from the dialing directory of Bradshaw's phone.

6215845 . . .

This is Father Marco. How can I help you?

He dialed the number again now, but this time it rang unanswered. Then, reluctantly, he forwarded it securely to the Operations Desk at King Saul Boulevard and asked for a routine check. Ten minutes later came the reply: 6215845 was an unpublished number located in the rectory of the Church of San Giovanni Evangelista in Brienno, which was located a few kilometers up the lakeshore.

Gabriel picked up the slip of paper that had been at the top of Jack Bradshaw's telephone message pad on the night of his murder. Tilting it toward the lamp, he studied the indentations that had been left by Bradshaw's fountain pen. Then he removed a pencil from the top drawer of the desk and rubbed the tip gently across the surface until a pattern of lines emerged. Most of it was an impenetrable mess: the numeral 4, the numeral 8, the letters C and V and O. At the bottom of the page, however, a single word was clearly visible.

Samir . . .

8

STOCKWELL, LONDON

THE ROAD WAS called Paradise, but it was a paradise lost: tattered blocks of redbrick council flats, a patch of trampled grass, a childless playground where a merry-go-round rotated slowly in the wind. Gabriel lingered there only long enough to make sure he was not being followed. He pulled his coat collar around his ears and shivered. Spring had not yet arrived in London.

Beyond the playground a dirty passageway led to Clapham Road. Gabriel turned to the left and walked through the glare of the oncoming traffic to the Stockwell Tube station. Another turn brought him to a quiet street with a terrace of sooty postwar houses. Number 8 had a crooked black fence of wrought iron and a tiny cement garden with no decoration other than a royal blue recycling bin. Gabriel lifted the lid, saw the bin was empty, and climbed the three steps to the front door. A sign stated that solicitations of any kind were unwelcome. Ignoring it, he placed his thumb atop the bell push—two short bursts, a longer third, just as he had been told. "Mr. Baker," said the man who appeared in the doorway. "So good of you to come. I'm Davies. I'm here to look after you."

Gabriel entered the house and waited for the door to close before turning to face the man who had admitted him. He had soft pale hair and the guiltless face of a country parson. His name was not Davies. It was Nigel Whitcombe.

"Why all the cloak-and-dagger stuff?" asked Gabriel. "I'm not defecting. I just need a word with the boss."

"The Intelligence Service frowns on the use of real names in safe houses. Davies is my work name."

"Catchy," said Gabriel.

"I chose it myself. I was always fond of the Kinks."

"Who's Baker?"

"You're Baker," replied Whitcombe without a trace of irony in his voice.

Gabriel entered the small sitting room. It was furnished with all the charm of an airport departure lounge.

"You couldn't find a safe house in Mayfair or Chelsea?"

"All the West End properties were taken. Besides, this one's closer to Vauxhall Cross."

Vauxhall Cross was the headquarters of Britain's Secret Intelligence Service, also known as MI6. There was a time when the service operated from a dingy building in Broadway and its director-general was known only as "C." Now the spies worked in one of London's flashiest landmarks, and their boss's name appeared regularly in the press. Gabriel liked the old ways better. In matters of intelligence, as in art, he was a traditionalist by nature.

"Does the Intelligence Service allow coffee in safe houses these days?" he asked.

"Not real coffee," replied Whitcombe, smiling. "But there might be a jar of Nescafé in the pantry."

Gabriel shrugged, as if to say one could certainly do worse than Nescafé, and followed Whitcombe into the galley kitchen. It looked as though it belonged to a man who was recently separated and hoping for a quick reconciliation. There was indeed a container of Nescafé, along with a tin of Twinings that looked as though it had been there when Edward Heath was prime minister. Whitcombe filled the electric kettle with water while Gabriel searched the cabinets for a mug. There were two, one with the logo of the London Olympic Games, the other with the face of the Queen. When Gabriel chose the mug with the Queen, Whitcombe smiled.

"I never realized you were an admirer of Her Majesty."

"She has good taste in art."

"She can afford to."

Whitcombe offered this assessment not as a criticism but merely an observation of fact. He was like that: careful, shrewd, opaque as a concrete wall. He had started his career at MI5, where he had cut his operational teeth working with Gabriel against a Russian oligarch and arms dealer named Ivan Kharkov. Soon after, he became the primary aide-de-camp and runner of off-the-record errands for Graham Seymour, MI5's deputy director-general. Seymour had recently been named the new chief of MI6, a move that surprised everyone in the intelligence trade except Gabriel. Whitcombe was now serving his master in the same capacity, which explained his presence in the Stockwell safe house. He spooned the Nescafé into the mug and watched the steam rising from the spout of the kettle.

"How's life at Six?" asked Gabriel.

"When we first arrived, there was a great deal of suspicion among the troops. I suppose they had a right to be uneasy. After all, we were coming across the river from a rival service."

"It's not as if Graham was a total outsider. His father was an MI6 legend. He was practically raised within the service."

"Which is one of the reasons any concerns were short-lived." Whitcombe drew a mobile device from the breast pocket of his suit and peered at the screen. "He's pulling up now. Can you manage the coffee on your own?"

"Pour in the water, then stir, right?"

Whitcombe departed. Gabriel prepared the coffee and went into the sitting room. Entering, he saw a tall figure clad in a perfectly fitted charcoal-gray suit and a striped blue necktie. His face was fine boned and even featured; his hair had a rich silvery cast that made him look like a male model one might see in ads for costly but needless trinkets. He was holding a mobile phone to his ear with his left hand. The right he stretched absently toward Gabriel. His handshake was firm, confident, and appropriate in duration. It was an unfair weapon to be deployed against inferior opponents. It said he had attended the better schools, belonged to the better clubs, and was good at gentlemanly games like tennis and golf, all of which happened to be true. Graham Seymour was a relic of Britain's glorious past, a child of the administrative classes who had been bred, educated, and programmed to lead. A few months earlier, weary after years of trying to protect the British homeland from the forces of Islamic extremism, he had privately told Gabriel of his plans to leave the intelligence trade and retire to his villa in Portugal. Now, unexpectedly, he had been handed the keys to his father's old service. Gabriel suddenly felt guilty about coming to London. He was about to hand Seymour his first potential crisis at MI6.

Seymour murmured a few words into the mobile phone, severed the connection, and handed it to Nigel Whitcombe. Then he turned toward Gabriel and regarded him curiously for a moment. "Given our long history together," Seymour said finally, "I'm a bit reluctant to ask what brings you to town. But I suppose I have no choice."

Gabriel responded by telling Seymour a small portion of the truth—that he had come to London because he was looking into the murder of an expatriate Englishman living in Italy.

"Does the expatriate Englishman have a name?" asked Seymour.

"James Bradshaw," replied Gabriel. He paused, then added, "But his friends called him Jack."

Seymour's face remained a blank mask. "I think I read something about that in the papers," he said. "He was former Foreign Office, wasn't he? Did some consulting work in the Middle East. He was murdered at his villa in Como. Apparently, it was quite messy."

"Quite," agreed Gabriel.

"What does any of this have to do with me?"

"Jack Bradshaw wasn't a diplomat, was he, Graham? He was MI6. He was a spy."

Seymour managed to maintain his composure for a moment longer. Then he narrowed his eyes and asked, "What else have you got?"

"Three stolen paintings, a vault in the Geneva Freeport, and someone named Samir."

"Is that all?" Seymour shook his head slowly and turned to Whitcombe. "Cancel my appointments for the remainder of the afternoon, Nigel. And find us something to drink. We're going to be a while."

9

STOCKWELL, LONDON

WHITCOMBE WENT OUT to fetch the makings of a gin and tonic while Gabriel and Graham Seymour settled into the charmless little sitting room. Gabriel wondered what sort of intelligence debris had floated through this place before him. A KGB defector willing to sell his soul for thirty pieces of Western silver? An Iraqi nuclear scientist with a briefcase full of lies? A jihadist double agent claiming to know the time and place of the next al-Qaeda spectacular? He looked at the wall above the electric fire and saw two horsemen in red jackets leading their mounts across a green English meadow. Then he glanced out the window and saw a portly lawn cherub keeping a lonely vigil in the darkening garden. Graham Seymour seemed oblivious to his surroundings. He was contemplating his hands, as if trying to decide where to begin his account. He didn't bother to delineate the ground rules, for no such disclaimer was necessary. Gabriel and Seymour were as close as two spies from opposing services could be, which meant they distrusted each other only a little.

"Do the Italians know you're here?" asked Seymour at last.

Gabriel shook his head.

"What about the Office?"

"I didn't tell them I was coming, but that doesn't mean they aren't watching my every move."

"I appreciate your honesty."

"I'm always honest with you, Graham."

"At least when it suits your purposes."

Gabriel didn't bother to offer a retort. Instead, he listened intently while Seymour, in the beleaguered voice of a man who would rather be discussing other matters, recounted the brief life and career of James "Jack" Bradshaw. It was familiar territory for a man like Seymour, for he had lived a version of Bradshaw's life himself. Both were products of moderately happy middle-class homes, both had been shipped off to costly but coldhearted public schools, and both had earned admission to elite universities, though Seymour had been at Cambridge while Bradshaw had landed at Oxford. There, while still an undergraduate, he came to the attention of a professor who was serving on the Faculty of Oriental Studies. The professor was actually a talent spotter for MI6. Graham Seymour knew him, too.

"The talent spotter was your father?" asked Gabriel.

Seymour nodded. "He was in the twilight of his career. He was too worn out to be of much use in the field, and he wanted nothing to do with a job at headquarters. So they packed him off to Oxford and told him to keep an eye out for potential recruits. One of the first students he noticed was Jack Bradshaw. It was hard not to notice Jack," Seymour added quickly. "He was a meteor. But more important, he was seductive, naturally deceptive, and without scruples or morals."

"In other words, he had all the makings of a perfect spy."

"In the finest English tradition," Seymour added with a wry smile.

And so it was, he continued, that Jack Bradshaw set out along the same path that so many others had taken before him—the path that led from the tranquil quads of Cambridge and Oxford to the cipher-protected doorway of the Secret Intelligence Service. It was 1985 when he arrived. The Cold War was nearing its end, and MI6 was still searching for a reason to justify its existence after being destroyed from within by Kim Philby and the other members of the Cambridge spy ring. Bradshaw spent two years in the MI6 training program and then headed off to Cairo to serve his apprenticeship. He became an expert in Islamic extremism and accurately predicted the rise of an international jihadist terror network led by veterans of the Afghan war. Next he went to Amman, where he established close ties with the chief of the GID, Jordan's all-powerful intelligence and security service. Before long, Jack Bradshaw was regarded as MI6's top field officer in the Middle East. He assumed he would be the next division chief, but the job went to a rival who promptly shipped Bradshaw to Beirut, one of the most dangerous and thankless posts in the region.

"And that," said Seymour, "is when the trouble began."

"What kind of trouble?"

"The usual kind," replied Seymour. "He started drinking too much and working too little. He also developed a rather high opinion of himself. He came to believe he was the smartest man in any room he entered and that his superiors in London were utter incompetents. How else to explain that he had been passed over for promotion when he was clearly the most qualified candidate for the job? Then he met a woman named Nicole Devereaux, and the situation went from bad to worse."

"Who was she?"

"A staff photographer for AFP, the French news service. She knew Beirut better than most of her competitors because she was married to a Lebanese businessman named Ali Rashid."

"How did Bradshaw meet her?" asked Gabriel.

"A Friday-night mixer at the British embassy: hacks, diplomats, and spies swapping gossip and Beirut horror stories over warm beer and stale savories."

"And they began an affair?"

"A quite torrid one, actually. By all accounts, Bradshaw was in love with her. Rumors started to swirl, of course, and before long they reached the ears of the KGB *rezident* at the Soviet embassy. He managed to snap a few photographs of Nicole in Bradshaw's bedroom. And then he made his move."

"A recruitment?"

"That's one way of putting it," said Seymour. "In reality, it was good old-fashioned blackmail."

"The KGB's specialty."

"Yours, too."

Gabriel ignored the remark and asked about the nature of the approach.

"The *rezident* gave Bradshaw a simple choice," Seymour replied. "He could go to work as a paid agent of the KGB, or the Russians would quietly give the photos of Nicole Devereaux in flagrante delicto to her husband."

"I take it Ali Rashid wouldn't have reacted kindly to the news that his wife was having an affair with a British spy."

"Rashid was a dangerous man." Seymour paused, then added, "A connected man, too."

"What kind of connections?"

"Syrian intelligence."

"So Bradshaw was afraid Rashid would kill her?"

"With good reason. Needless to say, he agreed to cooperate."

"What did he give them?"

"Names of MI6 personnel, current operations, insight into British policy in the region. In short, our entire playbook in the Middle East."

"How did you find out about it?"

"*We* didn't," Seymour said. "The Americans discovered that Bradshaw had a bank account in Switzerland with half a million dollars in it. They revealed the information with great fanfare during a rather horrendous meeting at Langley."

"Why wasn't Bradshaw arrested?"

"You're a man of the world," Seymour said. "You tell me."

"Because it would have led to a scandal that MI6 couldn't afford at the time."

Seymour touched his nose. "They even left the money in the Swiss bank account because they couldn't figure out a way to seize it without raising a red flag. It was quite possibly the most lucrative golden parachute in the history of MI6." Seymour shook his head slowly. "Not exactly our finest hour."

"What happened to Bradshaw after he left MI6?"

"He hung around Beirut for a few months licking his wounds before returning to Europe and starting his own consulting firm. For the record," Seymour added, "British intelligence never thought much of the Meridian Global Consulting Group."

"Did you know Bradshaw was dealing in stolen art?"

"We suspected he was involved in business ventures that were not exactly legal, but for the most part we averted our eyes and hoped for the best."

"And when you learned he'd been murdered in Italy?"

"We clung to the fiction he was a diplomat. The Foreign Office made it clear, however, that they would disown him at the first hint of trouble." Seymour paused, then asked, "Have I left anything out?"

"What happened to Nicole Devereaux?"

"Apparently, someone told her husband about the affair. She disappeared one night after leaving the AFP bureau. They found her body a few days later out in the Bekaa Valley."

"Did Rashid kill her himself?"

"No," replied Seymour. "He had the Syrians do it for him. They had a little fun with her before hanging her from a lamppost and slitting her throat. It was all rather gruesome. But I suppose that was to be expected. After all," he added gloomily, "they were Syrians."

"I wonder if it was a coincidence," said Gabriel.

"What's that?"

"That someone killed Jack Bradshaw in the exact same way."

Seymour made no response other than to ponder his wristwatch with the air of a man who was running late for an appointment he would rather not keep. "Helen is expecting me for dinner," he said with a profound lack of enthusiasm. "I'm afraid she's on an African kick at the moment. I'm not sure, but it's possible I may have eaten goat last week."

"You're a lucky man, Graham."

"Helen says the same thing. My doctor isn't so sure."

Seymour put down his drink and got to his feet. Gabriel remained motionless.

"I take it you have another question," Seymour said.

"Two, actually."

"I'm listening."

"Is there any chance I can have a look at Bradshaw's file?"

"Next question."

"Who's Samir?"

"Last name?"

"I'm working on that."

Seymour lifted his gaze to the ceiling. "There's a Samir who runs a little grocery around the corner from my flat. He's a devout member of the Muslim Brotherhood who believes Britain should be governed by shari'a law." He looked at Gabriel and smiled. "Otherwise, he's a rather nice chap."

The Israeli embassy was located on the other side of the Thames, in a quiet corner of Kensington just off the High Street. Gabriel slipped into the building through an unmarked door in the rear and made his way downstairs to the lead-lined suite of rooms reserved for the Office. The station chief was not present, only a young field hand called Noah who leapt to his feet when his future director came striding through the door unannounced. Gabriel entered the secure communications pod—in the lexicon of the Office it was referred to as the Holy of Holies—and sent a message to King Saul Boulevard requesting access to any files related to a Lebanese businessman named Ali Rashid. He didn't bother to state the reason for his request. Impending rank had its privileges.

Twenty minutes elapsed before the file appeared over the secure link—long enough, Gabriel reckoned, for the current chief of the Office to approve its transmission. It was brief, about a thousand words in length, and composed in the terse style demanded of Office analysts. It stated that Ali Rashid was a known asset of Syrian intelligence, that he served as a paymaster for a large Syrian network in Lebanon, and that he died in a car bombing in the Lebanese capital in 2011, the authorship of which was unknown. At the bottom of the file was the six-digit numerical cipher of the originating officer. Gabriel recognized it; the analyst had once been the Office's top expert on Syria and the Baath Party. These days she was noteworthy for another reason. She was the wife of the soon-to-be-former chief.

Like most Office outposts around the world, London Station contained a small bedroom for times of crisis. Gabriel knew the room well, for he had stayed in it many times. He stretched out on the uncomfortable single bed and tried to sleep, but it was no good; the case would not leave his thoughts. A promising British spy gone bad, a Syrian intelligence asset blown to bits by a car bomb, three stolen paintings covered by high-quality forgeries, a vault in the Geneva Freeport . . . The possibilities, thought Gabriel, were endless. It was no use trying to force the pieces now. He needed to open another window—a window onto the global trade in stolen paintings—and for that he needed the help of a master art thief.

And so he lay sleepless on the stiff little bed, wrestling with memories and with thoughts of his future, until six the following morning. After showering and changing his clothes, he left the embassy in darkness and rode the Underground to St. Pancras Station. A Eurostar was leaving for Paris at half past seven; he bought a stack of newspapers before boarding and finished reading them as the train eased to a stop at the Gare du Nord. Outside, a line of wet taxis waited under a sky the color of gunmetal. Gabriel slipped past them and spent an hour walking the busy streets around the station until he was certain he was not being followed. Then he set out for the Eighth Arrondissement and a street called the rue de Miromesnil.

10

RUE DE MIROMESNIL, PARIS

I N THE INTELLIGENCE business, as in life, it is sometimes necessary to deal with individuals whose hands are far from clean. The best way to catch a terrorist is to employ another terrorist as a source. The same was true, Gabriel reckoned, when one was trying to catch a thief. Which explained why, at 9:55, he was seated at a window table of a rather good brasserie on the rue de Miromesnil, a copy of *Le Monde* spread before him, a steaming café crème at his elbow. At 9:58 he spotted an overcoated, hatted figure walking briskly along the pavement from the direction of the Élysée Palace. The figure entered a small shop called Antiquités Scientifiques at the stroke of ten, switched on the lights, and changed the sign in the window from FERMÉ to OUVERT. Maurice Durand, thought Gabriel, smiling, was nothing if not reliable. He finished his coffee and crossed the empty street to the entrance of the shop. The intercom, when pressed, howled like an inconsolable child. Twenty seconds passed with no invitation to enter. Then the deadbolt snapped open with an inhospitable thud and Gabriel slipped inside.

The small showroom, like Durand himself, was a model of order and precision. Antique microscopes and barometers stood in neat rows along the shelves, their brass fittings shining like the buttons of a soldier's dress tunic; cameras and telescopes peered blindly into the past. In the center of the room was a nineteenth-century Italian terrestrial floor globe, price available upon request. Durand's tiny right hand rested atop Asia Minor. He wore a dark suit, a candy-wrapper gold necktie, and the most insincere smile Gabriel had ever seen. His bald pate shone in the overhead lighting. His small eyes stared straight ahead with the alertness of a terrier.

"How's business?" asked Gabriel cordially.

Durand moved to the photographic devices and picked up an early-twentieth-century camera with a brass lens by Poulenc of Paris. "I'm shipping this to a collector in Australia," he said. "Six hundred euros. Not as much as I would have hoped, but he drove a hard bargain."

"Not that business, Maurice."

Durand made no reply.

"That was a lovely piece of work you and your men pulled off in Munich last month," Gabriel said. "An El Greco portrait disappears from the Alte Pinakothek, and no one's seen or heard of it since. No ransom demands. No hints from the German police that they're close to cracking the case. Nothing but silence and a blank spot on a museum wall where a masterpiece used to hang."

"You don't ask me about my business," said Durand, "and I don't ask you about yours. Those are the rules of our relationship."

"Where's the El Greco, Maurice?"

"It's in Buenos Aires, in the hands of one of my best customers. He has a weakness," Durand added, "an insatiable appetite that only I can satisfy."

"What's that?"

"He likes to own the unownable." Durand returned the camera to the display shelf. "I assume this isn't a social call."

Gabriel shook his head.

"What do you want this time?"

"Information."

"About what?"

"A dead Englishman named Jack Bradshaw."

Durand's face remained expressionless.

"I assume you knew him?" asked Gabriel.

"Only by reputation."

"Any idea who cut him to pieces?"

"No," said Durand, shaking his head slowly. "But I might be able to point you in the right direction."

Gabriel walked over to the window and turned the sign from OUVERT to FERMÉ. Durand exhaled heavily and pulled on his overcoat.

They were as unlikely a pairing as one might have found in Paris that chill spring morning, the art thief and the intelligence operative, walking side by side through the streets of the Eighth Arrondissement. Maurice Durand, meticulous in all things, began with a brief primer on the trade in stolen art. Each year thousands of paintings and other objets d'art went missing from museums, galleries, public institutions, and private homes. Estimates of their value ranged as high as $6 billion, making art crime the fourth most lucrative illicit activity in the world, behind only drug trafficking, money laundering, and arms dealing. And Maurice Durand was responsible for much of it. Working with a stable of Marseilles-based professional thieves, he had carried off some of history's greatest art heists. He no longer thought of himself as a mere art thief. He was a global businessman, a broker of sorts, who specialized in the quiet acquisition of paintings that were not actually for sale.

"In my humble opinion," he continued without a trace of humility in his voice, "there are four distinct types of art thieves. The first is the thrill seeker, the art lover who steals to attain something he could never possibly afford. Stéphane Breitwieser comes to mind." He cast a sidelong glance at Gabriel. "Know the name?"

"Breitwieser was the waiter who stole more than a billion dollars' worth of art for his private collection."

"Including *Sybille of Cleves* by Lucas Cranach the Elder. After he was arrested, his mother cut the paintings into small pieces and threw them out with her kitchen garbage." The Frenchman shook his head reproachfully. "I am far from a perfect person, but I have never destroyed a painting." He cast another glance at Gabriel. "Even when I should have."

"And the second category?"

"The incompetent loser. He steals a painting, doesn't know what to do with it, and panics. Sometimes he manages to collect a bit of ransom or reward money. Oftentimes he gets caught. Frankly," Durand added, "I resent him. He gives people like me a bad name."

"Professionals who carry out commissioned thefts?"

Durand nodded. They were walking along the avenue Matignon. They passed the Paris offices of Christie's and then turned into the Champs-Élysées. The limbs of the chestnut trees lay bare against the gray sky.

"There are some in law enforcement who insist I don't exist," Durand resumed. "They think I'm a fantasy, that I'm wishful thinking. They don't understand that there are extremely wealthy people in the world who lust after great works of art and don't care whether they're stolen or not. In fact, there are some people who want a masterpiece *because* it's stolen."

"What's the fourth category?"

"Organized crime. They're very good at stealing paintings but not so good at bringing them to market." Durand paused, then added, "That's where Jack Bradshaw entered the picture. He was a middleman between the thieves and the buyers—a high-end fence, if you will. And he was good at his job."

"What sort of buyers?"

"Occasionally, he sold directly to collectors," Durand replied. "But most of the time he funneled the stolen works into a network of dealers here in Europe."

"Where?"

"Paris, Brussels, and Amsterdam are excellent dumping grounds for stolen art. But Switzerland's property and privacy laws still make it a mecca for bringing hot property to market."

They made their way across the Place de la Concorde and entered the Jardin des Tuileries. On their left was the Jeu de Paume, the small museum that the Nazis had used as a sorting facility when they were looting France of its art. Durand appeared to be making a conscious effort not to look at it.

"Your friend Jack Bradshaw was in a dangerous line of work," he was saying. "He had to deal with the sort of people who are quick to resort to violence when they don't get their way. The Serbian gangs are particularly active in Western Europe. The Russians, too. It's possible Bradshaw was killed as a result of a deal gone bad. Or . . ." Durand's voice trailed off.

"Or what?"

Durand hesitated before answering. "There were rumors," he said finally. "Nothing concrete, mind you. Just informed speculation."

"What sort of speculation?"

"That Bradshaw was involved in acquiring a large number of paintings on the black market for a single individual."

"Do you know the individual's name?"

"No."

"Are you telling me the truth, Maurice?"

"This might surprise you," Durand replied, "but when one is acquiring a collection of stolen paintings, one tends not to advertise what one is doing."

"Go on."

"There were rumors of another sort swirling around Bradshaw, rumors he was brokering a deal for a masterpiece." Durand made an almost imperceptible check of his surroundings before continuing. It was a move, thought Gabriel, worthy of a professional spy. "A masterpiece that has been missing for several decades."

"Do you know which painting it was?"

"Of course. And so do you." Durand stopped walking and turned to face Gabriel. "It was a nativity painted by a Baroque artist at the end of his career. His name was Michelangelo Merisi, but most people know him by the name of his family's village near Milan."

Gabriel thought of the three letters he had found on Bradshaw's message pad: *C* . . . *V* . . . *O* . . .

The letters weren't random.

They were Caravaggio.

11

JARDIN DES TUILERIES, PARIS

TWO CENTURIES AFTER his death, he was all but forgotten. His paintings gathered dust in the storerooms of galleries and museums, many misattributed, their dramatically illuminated figures receding slowly into the emptiness of their distinctive black backgrounds. Finally, in 1951, the noted Italian art historian Roberto Longhi assembled his known works and displayed them for the world at the Palazzo Reale in Milan. Many of those who visited the remarkable exhibit had never heard the name Caravaggio.

The details of his early life are sketchy at best, faint lines of charcoal on an otherwise blank canvas. He was born on the twenty-ninth day of September in 1571, probably in Milan, where his father was a successful mason and architect. In the summer of 1576, plague returned to the city. By the time it finally abated, one-fifth of the Milan diocese had perished, including young Caravaggio's father, grandfather, and uncle. In 1584, at the age of thirteen, he entered the workshop of Simone Peterzano, a dull but competent Mannerist who claimed to be a pupil of Titian. The contract, which survives, obligated Caravaggio to train "night and day" for a period of four years. It is not known whether he lived up to its terms, or even if he completed his apprenticeship. Clearly, Peterzano's limp, lifeless work had little influence on him.

The exact circumstances surrounding Caravaggio's departure from Milan are, like almost everything else about him, lost to time and shrouded in mystery. Records indicate his mother died in 1590 and that, from her modest estate, he claimed an inheritance equal to six hundred gold scudi. Within a year the money was gone. There is no suggestion, anywhere, that the volatile young man who had trained to be an artist ever placed a brush to canvas during his final years in Milan. It seems he was too busy with other pursuits. Giovanni Pietro Bellori, author of an early biography, suggests Caravaggio had to flee the city, perhaps after an incident involving a prostitute and a razor, perhaps after the murder of a friend. He traveled eastward to Venice, wrote Bellori, where he fell under the spell of Giorgione's palette. Then, in the autumn of 1592, he set out for Rome.

Here Caravaggio's life comes into sharper relief. He entered the city, like all migrants from the north, through the gates of the Porto del Popolo and made his way to the artists' quarter, a warren of filthy streets around the Campo Marzio. According to the painter Baglione, he shared rooms with an artist from Sicily, though another early biographer, a physician who knew Caravaggio in Rome, records that he found lodgings in the home of a priest who forced him to do household chores and gave him only greens to eat. Caravaggio referred to the priest as Monsignor Insalata and left his home after a few months. He lived in as many as ten different places during his first years in Rome, including the workshop of Giuseppe Cesari, where he slept on a straw mattress. He walked the streets in tattered black stockings and a threadbare black cloak. His black hair was an unruly mess.

Cesari allowed Caravaggio to paint only flowers and fruit, the lowliest assignment for a workshop apprentice. Bored, convinced of his superior talent, he began to produce paintings of his own. Some he sold in the alleyways around the Piazza Navona. But one painting, a luminous image of a well-to-do Roman boy being cheated by a pair of cardsharps, he sold to a dealer whose shop was located across the street from the palazzo occupied by Cardinal Francesco del Monte. The transaction would dramatically alter the course of Caravaggio's life, for the cardinal, a connoisseur and patron of the arts, admired the painting greatly and purchased it for a few scudi. Soon after, he acquired a second painting by Caravaggio depicting a smiling fortune-teller stealing a Roman boy's ring as she reads his palm. At some point, the two men met, though at whose initiative remains unclear. The cardinal offered the young artist food, clothing, lodgings, and a studio in his palazzo. All he asked of Caravaggio was that he paint. Caravaggio, then twenty-four, accepted the cardinal's proposal. It was one of the few wise decisions he ever made.

After settling in to his rooms at the palazzo,

Caravaggio produced several works for the cardinal and his circle of wealthy friends, including *The Lute Player*, *The Musicians*, *Bacchus*, *Martha and Mary Magdalene*, and *St. Francis of Assisi in Ecstasy*. Then, in 1599, he was awarded his first public commission: two canvases depicting scenes from the life of Saint Matthew for the Contarelli Chapel in the Church of San Luigi dei Francesi. The paintings, while controversial, instantly established Caravaggio as the most sought-after artist in Rome. Other commissions soon followed, including *The Crucifixion of St. Peter* and *The Conversion of St. Paul* for the Cerasi Chapel of the Church of Santa Maria del Popolo, *The Supper at Emmaus*, *John the Baptist*, *The Betrayal of Christ*, *Doubting Thomas*, and *The Sacrifice of Isaac*. Not all his works met with approval upon delivery. *Madonna and Child with St. Anne* was removed from St. Peter's Basilica because the church hierarchy apparently did not approve of Mary's ample cleavage. Her bare-legged portrayal in *Death of the Virgin* was considered so offensive that the church for which it was commissioned, Santa Maria della Scala in Trastevere, refused to accept it. Rubens called it one of Caravaggio's finest works and helped him to find a buyer.

Success as a painter did not bring calm to Caravaggio's personal life—indeed, it remained as chaotic and violent as ever. He was arrested for carrying a sword without a license in the Campo Marzio. He smashed a plate of artichokes against a waiter's face at the Osteria del Moro. He was jailed for throwing stones at the *sbirri*, the papal police, in the Via dei Greci. The stone-throwing incident occurred at half past nine on an October evening in 1604. By then, Caravaggio was living alone in a rented house with only Cecco, his apprentice and occasional model, for company. His physical appearance had deteriorated; he was once again the unkempt figure in tattered black clothing who used to sell his paintings on the street. Though he had many commissions, he worked fitfully. Somehow he managed to deliver a monumental altarpiece called *The Deposition of Christ.* It was widely regarded as his finest painting.

There were more brushes with the authorities—his name appears in the police records of Rome five times in 1605 alone—but none more serious than the incident that took place on May 28, 1606. It was a Sunday, and as usual Caravaggio went to the ball courts at the Via della Pallacorda for a game of tennis. There he encountered Ranuccio Tomassoni, a street fighter, a rival for the affections of a beautiful young courtesan who had posed for several of Caravaggio's paintings. Words were exchanged, swords were drawn. The details of the mêlée are unclear, but it ended with Tomassoni lying on the ground with a deep wound to his upper thigh. He died a short time later, and by that evening Caravaggio was the target of a citywide manhunt. Wanted for murder, a crime with only one possible punishment, he fled into the Alban Hills. He would never see Rome again.

He made his way south to Naples, where his reputation as a great painter preceded him, the murder notwithstanding. He left behind *The Seven Acts of Mercy* before sailing to Malta. There he was admitted into the Knights of Malta, an expensive honor for which he paid in paintings, and for a brief time he lived as a nobleman. Then a fight with a fellow member of his order led to yet another spell in prison. He managed to escape and flee to Sicily where by all accounts he was a mad, deranged soul who slept with a dagger at his side. Even so, he managed to paint. In Syracuse he left *The Burial of St. Lucy*. In Messina he produced two monumental paintings: *The Raising of Lazarus* and the heartbreaking *Adoration of the Shepherds*. And for the Oratorio di San Lorenzo in Palermo he painted *The Nativity with St. Francis and St. Lawrence*. Three hundred and fifty-nine years later, on the night of October 18, 1969, two men entered the chapel through a window and cut the canvas from its frame. A copy of the painting hung behind General Cesare Ferrari's desk at the palazzo in Rome. It was the Art Squad's number-one target.

"I suspect the general already knows about the connection between the Caravaggio and Jack Bradshaw," Maurice Durand said. "That would explain why he was so insistent you take the case."

"You know the general well," said Gabriel.

"Not really," replied the Frenchman. "But I did meet him once."

"Where?"

"Here in Paris, at a symposium on art crime. The general was on one of the panels."

"And you?"

"I was in attendance."

"In what capacity?"

"A dealer of valuable antiques, of course." Durand smiled. "The general struck me as a serious fellow, very capable. It's been a long time since I've stolen a painting in Italy."

They were walking along the gravel footpath of the *allée centrale*. The leaden clouds had drained the gardens of color. It was Sisley rather than Monet.

"Is it possible?" asked Gabriel.

"That the Caravaggio is actually in play?"

Gabriel nodded. Durand appeared to give the question serious consideration before answering.

"I've heard all the stories," he said at last. "That the collector who commissioned the theft refused to accept the painting because it was so badly damaged when it was cut from the frame. That the Mafia bosses of Sicily used to bring it out during meetings as a kind of trophy. That it was destroyed in a flood. That it was eaten by rats. But I've also heard rumors," he added, "that it's been in play before."

"How much would it be worth on the black market?"

"The paintings Caravaggio produced while he was on the run lack the depth of his great Roman works. Even so," Durand added, "a Caravaggio is still a Caravaggio."

"How much, Maurice?"

"The rule of thumb is that a stolen painting retains ten percent of its value on the black market. If the Caravaggio were worth fifty million on the open market, it would fetch five million dirty."

"There is no open market for a Caravaggio."

"Which means it's truly one of a kind. There are some men in the world who would pay almost anything for it."

"Could you move it?"

"With a single phone call."

They arrived at the boat pond where several min-iature sailing vessels were careening about a tiny storm-tossed sea. Gabriel paused at the edge and ex-plained how he had found three stolen paintings—a Parmigianino, a Renoir, and a Klimt—concealed beneath copies of lesser works at Jack Bradshaw's villa on Lake Como. Durand, watching the boats, nodded thoughtfully.

"It sounds to me as though they were being read-ied for transport and sale."

"Why paint over them?"

"So they could be sold as legitimate works." Durand paused, then added, "Legitimate works of lesser value, of course."

"And when the sales were complete?"

"A person like you would be hired to remove the concealing images and prepare the paintings for hanging."

A pair of tourists, young girls, posed for a photo-graph on the opposite side of the boat pond. Gabriel took Durand by the elbow and led him toward the Louvre Pyramid.

"The person who painted those fakes was good," he said. "Good enough to fool someone like me at first glance."

"There are many talented artists out there who are willing to sell their services to those of us who toil at the dirty end of the trade." The Frenchman looked at Gabriel and asked, "Have you ever had occasion to forge a painting?"

"I might have forged a Cassatt once."

"For a worthy cause, no doubt."

They walked on, the gravel crunching beneath their feet.

"And what about you, Maurice? Have you ever required the services of a forger?"

"We are getting into sensitive territory," Durand cautioned.

"We crossed that border a long time ago, you and I."

They came to the Place du Carrousel, turned to the right, and made for the river.

"Whenever possible," Durand said, "I prefer to create the illusion that a stolen painting hasn't actually been stolen."

"You leave behind a copy."

"We call them replacement jobs."

"How many are hanging in museums and homes across Europe?"

"I'd rather not say."

"Go on, Maurice."

"There's one man who does all my work for me. He's fast, reliable, and quite good."

"Does the man have a name?"

Durand hesitated, then answered. The forger's name was Yves Morel.

"Where did he train?"

"The École Nationale des Beaux-Arts in Lyon."

"Very prestigious," said Gabriel. "Why didn't he become an artist?"

"He tried. It didn't work out as planned."

"So he took his revenge on the art world by becoming a forger?"

"Something like that."

"How noble."

"People in glass houses."

"Is your relationship exclusive?"

"I wish it was, but I can't give him enough work. On occasion he accepts commissions from other patrons. One of those patrons was a now-deceased fence named Jack Bradshaw."

Gabriel stopped walking and turned to face Durand. "Which is why you know so much about Bradshaw's operation," he said. "You were sharing the services of the same forger."

"It was all rather Caravaggesque," replied Durand, nodding.

"Where did Morel do his work for Bradshaw?"

"In a room at the Geneva Freeport. Bradshaw had a rather unique art gallery there. Yves used to call it the gallery of the missing."

"Where is he now?"

"Here in Paris."

"Where, Maurice?"

Durand removed his hand from the pocket of his overcoat and indicated that the forger could be found somewhere near Sacré-Cœur. They entered the Métro, the art thief and the intelligence operative, and headed for Montmartre.

12

MONTMARTRE, PARIS

Yves Morel lived in an apartment building on the rue Ravignon. When Durand pressed the intercom button, there was no answer.

"He's probably in the Place du Tertre."

"Doing what?"

"Selling copies of famous Impressionist paintings to the tourists so the French tax authorities think he has a legitimate income."

They walked to the square, a jumble of outdoor cafés and street artists near the basilica, but Morel wasn't in his usual spot. Then they went to his favorite bar in the rue Norvins, but there was no sign of him there, either. A call to his mobile phone went unanswered.

"Merde," said Durand softly, slipping the phone back into his coat pocket.

"What now?"

"I have a key to his apartment."

"Why?"

"Occasionally, he leaves things in his studio for me to collect."

"Sounds like a trusting soul."

"Contrary to popular myth," said Durand, "there is indeed honor among thieves."

They walked back to the apartment house and rang the intercom a second time. When there was no response, Durand fished a ring of keys from his pocket and used one to unlock the door. He used the same key to unlock the door of Morel's apartment. Darkness greeted them. Durand flipped a light switch on the wall, illuminating a large open room that doubled as a studio and living space. Gabriel walked over to an easel, on which was propped an unfinished copy of a landscape by Pierre Bonnard.

"Does he intend to sell this one to the tourists in the Place du Tertre?"

"That one's for me."

"What's it for?"

"Use your imagination."

Gabriel examined the painting more closely. "If I had to guess," he said, "you intend to hang it in the Musée des Beaux-Arts in Nice."

"You have a good eye."

Gabriel turned away from the easel and walked over to the large rectangular worktable that stood in the center of the studio. Draped over it was a paint-spotted tarpaulin. Beneath it was an object approximately six feet in length and two feet across.

"Is Morel a sculptor?"

"No."

"So what's underneath the tarp?"

"I don't know, but you'd better have a look."

Gabriel lifted the edge of the tarpaulin and peered beneath it.

"Well?" asked Durand.

"I'm afraid you're going to have to find someone else to finish the Bonnard, Maurice."

"Let me see him."

Gabriel drew back the top of the tarpaulin.

"Merde," said Durand softly.

PART TWO

SUNFLOWERS

13

SAN REMO, ITALY

GENERAL FERRARI WAITED near the walls of the old fortress in San Remo at half past two the following afternoon. He wore a business suit, a woolen overcoat, and dark glasses that shielded his all-seeing prosthetic eye from view. Gabriel, dressed in denim and leather, looked like the troubled younger sibling, the one who had made all the wrong choices in life and was once again in need of money. As they walked along the grimy waterfront, he briefed the general on his findings, though he was careful not to divulge his sources. The general didn't seem surprised by anything he was hearing.

"You left out one thing," he said.

"What's that?"

"Jack Bradshaw wasn't a diplomat. He was a spy."

"How did you know?"

"Everyone in the trade knew about Bradshaw's past. It was one of the reasons he was so good at his job. But don't worry," the general added. "I'm not going to make things difficult for you with your friends in London. All I want is my Caravaggio."

They left the waterfront and headed up the slope of the hill toward the center of town. Gabriel wondered why anyone would want to holiday here. The city reminded him of a once-beautiful woman gathering herself to have her portrait painted.

"You misled me," he said.

"Not at all," replied the general.

"How would you describe it?"

"I withheld certain facts so as not to color your investigation."

"Did you know the Caravaggio was in play when you asked me to look into Bradshaw's death?"

"I'd heard rumors to that effect."

"Had you also heard rumors about a collector on a shopping spree for stolen art?"

The general nodded.

"Who is it?"

"I haven't a clue."

"Are you telling me the truth this time?"

The general placed his good hand over his heart. "I do not know the identity of the person who's been buying every piece of stolen art he can lay his hands on. Nor do I know who's behind the murder of Jack Bradshaw." He paused, then added, "Though I suspect they're one and the same."

"Why was Bradshaw killed?"

"I suppose he'd outlived his usefulness."

"Because he'd delivered the Caravaggio?"

The general gave a noncommittal nod.

"So why was he tortured first?"

"Perhaps his killers wanted a name."

"Yves Morel?"

"Bradshaw must have used Morel to knock the

painting into shape so it could be sold." He looked at Gabriel gravely and asked, "How did they kill him?"

"They broke his neck. It looked like a complete transection of the spinal cord."

The general grimaced. "Silent and bloodless."

"And very professional."

"What did you do with the poor devil?"

"He'll be taken care of," said Gabriel quietly.

"By whom?"

"It's better if you don't know the details."

The general shook his head slowly. He was now a party to a felony. It wasn't the first time.

"Let us hope," he said after a moment, "that the French police never discover that you were in Morel's apartment. Given your track record, they might get the wrong impression."

"Yes," said Gabriel morosely. "Let us hope."

They turned into the Via Roma. It reverberated with the buzz of a hundred motor scooters. Gabriel, when he spoke again, had to raise his voice to be heard.

"Who had it last?" he asked.

"The Caravaggio?"

Gabriel nodded.

"Even I'm not sure," the general admitted. "Every time we arrest a mafioso, no matter how insignificant, he offers us information on the whereabouts of the *Nativity* in exchange for a reduced prison sentence. We call it the Caravaggio card. Needless to say, we've wasted countless man-hours chasing down false leads."

"I thought you came close to finding it a couple of years ago."

"So did I, but it slipped through my fingers. I was

beginning to think that I would never get another opportunity to recover it." He smiled in spite of himself. "And now this."

"If the painting's been sold, it's probably no longer in Italy."

"I concur. But in my experience," the general added, "the best time to find a stolen painting is immediately after it's changed hands. We have to move quickly, though. Otherwise, we might have to wait another forty-five years."

"We?"

The general stopped walking but said nothing.

"My involvement in this affair," said Gabriel over the drone of the traffic, "is now officially over."

"You promised to find out who killed Jack Bradshaw in exchange for keeping your friend's name out of the newspapers. The way I see it, you haven't completed your commission."

"I've given you an important lead, not to mention three stolen paintings."

"But not the painting I want." The general removed his sunglasses and fixed Gabriel with his monocular stare. "Your involvement in this case isn't over, Allon. In fact, it's just beginning."

They walked to a small bar overlooking the marina. It was empty except for two young men who were grousing about the sad state of the economy. It was a common sight in Italy these days. There were no jobs, no prospects, no future—only the beautiful reminders of the past that the general and his team at the Art Squad were sworn to protect. He ordered a coffee and a sandwich and led Gabriel to a table outside in the cold sunlight.

"Frankly," he said when they were alone again, "I don't know how you can even think about walking away from the case now. It would be like leaving a painting unfinished."

"My unfinished painting is in Venice," replied Gabriel, "along with my pregnant wife."

"Your Veronese is safe. And so is your wife."

Gabriel looked at an overflowing rubbish bin at the edge of the marina and shook his head. The ancient Romans had invented central heating, but somewhere along the line their descendants had forgotten how to take out the trash.

"It could take months to find that painting," he said.

"We don't have months. I'd say we have a few weeks at most."

"Then I suppose you and your men better get moving."

The general shook his head slowly. "We're good at tapping phones and making deals with mafioso scum. But we don't do undercover operations well, especially outside Italy. I need someone to toss some bait into the waters of the stolen art market and to see if we can tempt Mr. Big into making another acquisition. He's out there somewhere. You just have to find something to interest him."

"One doesn't *find* multimillion-dollar masterpieces. One steals them."

"In spectacular fashion," added the general. "Which means it shouldn't be something from a home or a private gallery."

"Do you realize what you're saying?"

"Yes, I do." The general gave a conspiratorial smile. "Most undercover operations involve sending a fake buyer into the field. But yours will be different. You'll be posing as a thief with a hot piece of canvas to sell. The painting has to be real."

"Why don't you let me borrow something lovely from the Galleria Borghese?"

"The museum will never go for it. Besides," the general added, "the painting can't come from Italy. Otherwise, the person who has the Caravaggio might suspect my involvement."

"You'll never be able to prosecute anyone after something like this."

"Prosecution is definitely second on my list of priorities. I want that Caravaggio back."

The general lapsed into silence. Gabriel had to admit he was intrigued by the idea. "There's no way I can front the operation," he said after a moment. "My face is too well known."

"Then I suppose you'll have to find a good actor to play the role. And if I were you, I'd hire some muscle, too. The underworld can be a dangerous place."

"You don't say."

The general made no reply.

"Muscle doesn't come cheap," Gabriel said. "And neither do competent thieves."

"Can you borrow some from your service?"

"Muscle or thieves?"

"Both."

"Not a chance."

"How much money do you need?"

Gabriel made a show of thought. "Two million, bare minimum."

"I might have a million in the coffee can under my desk."

"I'll take it."

"Actually," said the general, smiling, "the money's in an attaché case in the trunk of my car. I also have a copy of the Caravaggio case file. It will give you something to read while you're waiting for Mr. Big to put his oar into the water."

"What if he doesn't bite?"

"I suppose you'll have to steal something else." The general shrugged. "That's the wonderful thing about stealing masterpieces. It's really not all that difficult."

The money, as promised, was in the trunk of the general's official sedan—a million euros in very used bills, the source of which he refused to specify. Gabriel placed the attaché case on the passenger seat of his own car and drove away without another word. By the time he reached the fringes of San Remo, he had completed the first preparatory sketches of his operation to recover the lost Caravaggio. He had funding and access to the world's most successful art thief. All he needed now was someone to take a stolen painting to market. An amateur wouldn't do. He needed an experienced operative who had been trained in the black arts of deception. Someone who was comfortable in the presence of criminals. Someone who could take care of himself if things got rough. Gabriel knew of just such a man across the water, on the island of Corsica. He was a bit like Maurice Durand, an old adversary who was now an accomplice, but there the similarities ended.

14

CORSICA

I T WAS APPROACHING midnight when the ferry drew into the port of Calvi, hardly the time to be making a social call in Corsica, so Gabriel checked into a hotel near the terminal and slept. In the morning he had breakfast at a small café along the waterfront; then he climbed into his car and set out along the rugged western coastline. For a time the rain persisted, but gradually the clouds thinned and the sea turned from granite to turquoise. Gabriel stopped in the town of Porto to purchase two bottles of chilled Corsican rosé and then headed inland along a narrow road lined with olive groves and stands of laricio pine. The air smelled of *macchia*—the dense undergrowth of rosemary, rockrose, and lavender that covered much of the island—and in the villages he saw many women cloaked in the black of widowhood, a sign they had lost male kin to the vendetta. Once the women might have pointed at him in the Corsican way in order to ward off the effects of the *occhju*, the evil eye, but now they avoided gazing at him for long. They knew he was a friend of Don

Anton Orsati, and friends of the don could travel anywhere in Corsica without fear of reprisal.

For more than two centuries, the Orsati clan had been associated with two things on the island of Corsica: olive oil and death. The oil came from the groves that thrived on their large estates; the death came at the hands of their assassins. The Orsatis killed on behalf of those who could not kill for themselves: notables who were too squeamish to get their hands dirty; women who had no male kin to do the deed on their behalf. No one knew how many Corsicans had died at the hands of Orsati assassins, least of all the Orsatis themselves, but local lore placed the number in the thousands. It might have been significantly higher were it not for the clan's rigorous vetting process. The Orsatis operated by a strict code. They refused to carry out a killing unless satisfied the party before them had indeed been wronged, and blood vengeance was required.

That changed, however, with Don Anton Orsati. By the time he gained control of the family, the French authorities had eradicated feuding and the vendetta in all but the most isolated pockets of the island, leaving few Corsicans with the need for the services of his *taddunaghiu*. With local demand in steep decline, Orsati had been left with no choice but to look for opportunities elsewhere—namely, across the water in mainland Europe. He now accepted almost every offer that crossed his desk, no matter how distasteful, and his killers were regarded as the most reliable and professional on the Continent. In fact, Gabriel was one of only two people ever to survive an Orsati family contract.

Don Anton Orsati lived in the mountains at the center of the island, surrounded by walls of *macchia* and rings of bodyguards. Two stood watch at his gate. Upon seeing Gabriel, they stepped aside and invited him to enter. A dirt road bore him through a grove of van Gogh olive trees and, eventually, to the gravel forecourt of the don's immense villa. More bodyguards waited outside. They gave Gabriel's possessions a cursory search, then one, a dark, pinch-faced killer who looked to be about twenty, escorted him upstairs to the don's office. It was a large space with rustic Corsican furnishings and a terrace overlooking the don's private valley. *Macchia* wood crackled in the stone fireplace. It perfumed the air with rosemary and sage.

In the center of the room was the large oaken table at which the don worked. On it stood a decorative bottle of Orsati olive oil, a telephone he rarely used, and a leather-bound ledger that contained the secrets of his unique business. His *taddunaghiu* were all employees of the Orsati Olive Oil Company, and the murders they carried out were booked as orders for product, which meant that, in Orsati's world, oil and blood flowed together in a single seamless enterprise. All of his assassins were of Corsican descent except one. Owing to his extensive training, he handled only the most difficult assignments. He also served as director of sales for the lucrative central European market.

The don was a large man by Corsican standards, well over six feet tall and broad through the back and shoulders. He was wearing a pair of loose-fitting trousers, dusty leather sandals, and a crisp

white shirt that his wife ironed for him each morning, and again in the afternoon when he rose from
his nap. His hair was black, as were his eyes. His
hand, when grasped by Gabriel, felt as though it
were chiseled from stone.

"Welcome back to Corsica," Orsati said as he relieved Gabriel of the two bottles of rosé. "I knew
you couldn't stay away for long. Don't take this the
wrong way, Gabriel, but I always thought you had a
little Corsican blood in your veins."

"I can assure you, Don Orsati, that's not the case."

"It doesn't matter. You're practically one of us
now." The don lowered his voice and added, "Men
who kill together develop a bond that cannot be
broken."

"Is that another one of your Corsican proverbs?"

"Our proverbs are sacred and correct, which is a
proverb in and of itself." The don smiled. "I thought
you were supposed to be in Venice with your wife."

"I was," replied Gabriel.

"So what brings you back to Corsica? Business or
pleasure?"

"Business, I'm afraid."

"What is it this time?"

"A favor."

"Another one?"

Gabriel nodded.

"Here on Corsica," the don said, frowning in dis-
approval, "we believe a man's fate is written at birth.
And you, my friend, seem fated to be forever solving
problems for other people."

"There are worse fates, Don Orsati."

"Heaven helps those who help themselves."

"How charitable," said Gabriel.

"Charity is for priests and fools." The Corsican looked at the attaché case hanging from Gabriel's hand. "What's in the bag?"

"A million euros in used bills."

"Where did you get it?"

"A friend in Rome."

"An Italian?"

Gabriel nodded.

"At the end of many disasters," said Don Orsati darkly, "there is always an Italian."

"I happen to be married to one."

"Which is why I light many candles on your behalf."

Gabriel tried but failed to suppress a smile.

"How is she?" asked the don.

"I seem to annoy her to no end. Otherwise, she's quite well."

"It's the pregnancy," said the don with a thoughtful nod. "Once the children are born, everything will be different."

"How so?"

"It will be as though you don't exist." The Corsican looked at the attaché case again. "Why are you walking around with a million euros in used bills?"

"I've been asked to find something valuable, and it's going to take a lot of money to get it back."

"Another missing girl?" asked the don.

"No," replied Gabriel. "This."

Gabriel handed Orsati a photograph of an empty frame hanging above the altar of the Oratorio di San Lorenzo. A look of recognition flashed across the heavy features of the Corsican's face.

"The *Nativity*?" he asked.

"I never realized you were a man of the arts, Don Orsati."

"I'm not," he admitted, "but I've followed the case carefully over the years."

"Any particular reason?"

"I happened to be in Palermo the night the Caravaggio was stolen. In fact," Don Orsati added, smiling, "I'm almost certain I was the one who discovered it was missing."

On the terrace overlooking the valley, Don Anton Orsati recounted how, in the late summer of 1969, there came to Corsica a Sicilian businessman named Renato Francona. The Sicilian wanted vengeance for his beautiful young daughter, who had been murdered a few weeks earlier by Sandro di Luca, an important member of the Cosa Nostra. Don Carlu Orsati, then the chief of the Orsati clan, wanted no part of it. But his son, a gifted assassin called Anton, eventually convinced his father to allow him to carry out the contract personally. Everything went as planned that night except for the weather, which made it impossible to leave Palermo. Having nothing better to do, young Anton went in search of a church to confess his sins. The church he entered was the Oratorio di San Lorenzo.

"And this," Orsati said, holding up the photograph of the empty frame, "is exactly what I saw that night. As you might expect, I didn't report the theft to the police."

"Whatever happened to Renato Francona?"

"The Cosa Nostra killed him a few weeks later."

"They assumed he was behind the murder of di Luca?"

Orsati nodded gravely. "But at least he died with honor."

"How so?"

"Because he had avenged the murder of his daughter."

"And one wonders why Sicily isn't the economic and intellectual powerhouse of the Mediterranean."

"Money doesn't come from singing," said the don. "Your point?"

"The vendetta has kept this family in business for generations," answered the don. "And the killing of Sandro di Luca proved we could operate outside Corsica without detection. My father remained opposed to it until his death. But once he was gone, I took the family business international."

"If you're not growing, you're dying."

"Is that a Jewish proverb?"

"Probably," replied Gabriel.

The table was laid with a traditional Corsican lunch of *macchia*-flavored foods. Gabriel helped himself to the vegetables and cheeses but ignored the sausage.

"It's kosher," the don said as he forked several pieces of the meat onto Gabriel's plate.

"I didn't realize there were any rabbis on Corsica."

"Many," the don assured him.

Gabriel moved the sausage aside and asked the don whether he still went to church after taking a life.

"If I did," the Corsican replied, "I'd spend more time on my knees than a washerwoman. Besides, at this point I'm beyond redemption. God can do with me as he wishes."

"I'd love to see the conversation between you and God."

"May it be conducted over a Corsican lunch." Orsati smiled and refilled Gabriel's glass with the rosé. "I'll let you in on a secret," he said, returning the bottle to the center of the table. "Most of the people we kill deserve to die. In our own small way, the Orsati clan has made the world a much better place."

"Would you feel that way if you'd killed me?"

"Don't be silly," answered the don. "Allowing you to live was the best decision I ever made."

"As I recall, Don Orsati, you had nothing to do with the decision to let me live. In fact," added Gabriel pointedly, "you were steadfastly opposed to it."

"Even I, the infallible Don Anton Orsati, make mistakes from time to time, though I've never done anything so foolish as agreeing to find a Caravaggio for the Italians."

"I didn't really have much choice in the matter."

"It's a fool's errand."

"My specialty."

"The Carabinieri have been looking for that painting for more than forty years, and they've never been able to find it. In my opinion, it was probably destroyed a long time ago."

"That's not the word on the street."

"What are you hearing?"

Gabriel answered the question by giving the don

the same briefing he had given to General Ferrari in San Remo. Then he explained his plan for getting the painting back. The don was clearly intrigued.

"What does this have to do with the Orsatis?" he asked.

"I need to borrow one of your men."

"Anyone in particular?"

"The director of central European sales."

"What a surprise."

Gabriel said nothing.

"And if I agree?"

"One hand washes the other," said Gabriel, "and both hands wash the face."

The don smiled. "Maybe you're a Corsican after all."

Gabriel gazed out at the valley and smiled. "No such luck, Don Orsati."

15

CORSICA

A S IT HAPPENED, the man whom Gabriel needed to find the Caravaggio was away from the island on business. Don Orsati would not say where he was or whether his business concerned oil or blood, only that he would return in two days' time, three at most. He gave Gabriel a Tanfoglio pistol and the keys to a villa in the next valley where he would wait in the interim. Gabriel knew the villa well. He had stayed there with Chiara after their last operation and, on its sun-dappled terrace, had learned she was pregnant with his children. There was only one problem with the house; to reach it Gabriel had to pass the three ancient olive trees where Don Casabianca's wretched palomino goat stood its eternal watch, challenging all those who dared to encroach on its territory. The old goat was a malevolent creature in general but seemed to reserve a particular loathing for Gabriel, with whom it had numerous confrontations filled with mutual threats and insults. Don Orsati, at the conclusion of lunch, promised to have a word with Don Casabianca on Gabriel's behalf.

"Perhaps he can reason with the beast," the don added skeptically.

"Or perhaps he could turn the goat into a handbag and a pair of shoes."

"Don't get any ideas," the don cautioned. "If you touch one hair on that miserable goat's head, there'll be a feud."

"What if it just disappears?"

"The *macchia* has no eyes," warned the don, "but it sees all."

With that, the don walked Gabriel downstairs and saw him into his car. He followed the road inland until it turned to dirt, and then he followed it a little farther; and when he came to the sharp left-hand bend he saw Don Casabianca's goat tethered to one of the three ancient olive trees, a look of humiliation on its grizzled face. Gabriel lowered his window and, in Italian, hurled a string of insults at the goat regarding its appearance, its ancestry, and the degradation of its current predicament. Then, laughing, he headed up the slope of the hill toward the villa.

It was small and tidy, with a red-tile roof and large windows overlooking the valley. As Gabriel entered, it was instantly obvious that he and Chiara had been its last occupants. His sketch pad lay on the coffee table in the sitting room, and in the refrigerator he found an unopened bottle of Chablis that had been given to him by Don Orsati's absent director of European sales. The shelves of the pantry were otherwise bare. Gabriel opened the French doors to the afternoon breeze and sat on the terrace, working his way through the general's Caravaggio file, until the cold drove him back inside. By then, it was a few minutes after four o'clock and the sun seemed balanced atop the rim of the valley. He showered quickly, changed into clean clothing, and drove to the village to do a bit of marketing before the shops closed.

There had been a town in this isolated corner of Corsica since the dark days after the fall of the Roman Empire, when the Vandals ravaged the coastlines so ruthlessly that terrified native island-ers had no choice but to take to the hills for survival. A single ancient street spiraled its way past cottages and apartment buildings to a broad square at the highest point of the village. On three sides were shops and cafés; on the fourth was the old church. Gabriel found a parking space and started toward the market but decided he needed the fortification of a coffee first. He entered one of the cafés and took a table where he could watch the men playing *boules* in the square by the light of an iron streetlamp. One of the men recognized Gabriel as a friend of Don Orsati and invited him to join the game. Ga-briel feigned a sore shoulder and, in French, said he would prefer to remain a spectator. He didn't men-tion anything about having to shop. In Corsica, the women still saw to the marketing.

Just then, the bells of the church tolled five o'clock. A few minutes later its heavy wooden door swung open and a priest in a black cassock emerged onto the steps. He stood there smiling benevolently as several parishioners, old women mainly, filed into the square. One of the women, after absently nod-ding good evening to the priest, stopped suddenly, as if she alone had been alerted to the presence of danger. Then she resumed walking and disappeared through the door of a crooked little house adjoining the rectory.

Gabriel ordered another coffee. Then he changed his mind and ordered a glass of red wine instead. The dusk was a memory; lights burned warmly in the shops and in the windows of the crooked little house next to the rectory. A boy of ten with long curly hair was now standing at the door, which was open only a few inches. A small pale hand poked through the breach clutching a slip of blue paper. The boy seized the paper and carried it across the square to the café, where he placed it on Gabriel's table next to the glass of red wine.

"What is it this time?" he asked.

"She didn't say," replied the boy. "She never does."

Gabriel gave the boy a few coins to buy a sweet and drank the wine as night fell hard upon the square. Finally, he picked up the slip of paper and read the single line that had been written there:

I can help you find what you're looking for.

Gabriel smiled, slipped the note into his pocket, and sat there finishing the last of his wine. Then he rose and headed across the square.

She was standing in the doorway to receive him, a shawl around her frail shoulders. Her eyes were bottomless pools of black; her face was as white as

baker's flour. She regarded him warily before finally offering her hand. It was warm and weightless.
Holding it was like cradling a songbird.

"Welcome back to Corsica," she said.

"How did you know I was here?"

"I know everything."

"Then tell me how I arrived on the island."

"Don't insult me."

Gabriel's skepticism was pretense. He had long
ago relinquished any doubts about the old woman's
ability to glimpse both the past and future. She held
his hand tightly and closed her eyes.

"You were living in the city of water with your
wife and working in a church where a great painter
is buried. You were happy, truly happy, for the first
time in your life. Then a one-eyed creature from
Rome appeared and—"

"All right," said Gabriel. "You've proven your
point."

She released Gabriel's hand and gestured toward
the small wooden table in her parlor. On it was a
shallow plate of water and a vessel of olive oil. They
were the tools of her trade. The old woman was a
signadora. The Corsicans believed she had the power
to heal those infected by the *occhju*, the evil eye. Gabriel had once suspected she was nothing more than
a conjurer, but that was no longer the case.

"Sit," she said.

"No," replied Gabriel.

"Why not?"

"Because we don't believe in such things."

"Israelites?"

"Yes," he said. "Israelites."

"But you did it before."

"You told me things about my past, things you couldn't possibly have known."

"So you were curious?"

"I suppose so."

"And you're not curious now?"

The woman sat in her usual place at the table and lit a candle. After a moment's hesitation, Gabriel sat down opposite. He pushed the vessel of oil toward the center of the table and folded his hands obstinately. The old woman closed her eyes.

"The one-eyed creature has asked you to find something on his behalf, yes?"

"Yes," answered Gabriel.

"It's a painting, is it not? The work of a madman, a murderer. It was taken from a small church many years ago, on an island across the water."

"Did Don Orsati tell you that?"

The old woman opened her eyes. "I've never spoken to the don about this matter."

"Go on."

"The painting was stolen by men such as the don, only far worse. They treated it very badly. Much of it has been destroyed."

"But the painting survives?"

"Yes," she said, nodding slowly. "It survives."

"Where is it now?"

"It's close."

"Close to what?"

"It is not in my power to tell you that. But if you will perform the test of the oil and the water," she added with a glance at the center of the table, "perhaps I can be of help."

Gabriel remained motionless.

"What are you afraid of?" the old woman asked.

"You," answered Gabriel truthfully.

"You have the strength of God. Why should you fear someone as frail and old as me?"

"Because you have powers, too."

"Powers of sight," she said. "But not earthly powers."

"The ability to see the future is a great asset."

"Especially for someone in your line of work."

"Yes," agreed Gabriel, smiling.

"So why won't you perform the test of the oil and the water?"

Gabriel was silent.

"You have lost many things," the old woman said kindly. "A wife, a son, your mother. But your days of grief are behind you."

"Will my enemies ever try to kill my wife?"

"No harm will come to her or your children."

The old woman nodded toward the vessel of olive oil. This time, Gabriel dipped his forefinger into it and allowed three drops to fall onto the water. By the laws of physics, the oil should have gathered into a single gobbet. Instead, it shattered into a thousand droplets and soon there was no trace of it.

"You are infected with the *occhju*," the old woman pronounced gravely. "You would be wise to let me draw it from your system."

"I'll take two aspirin instead."

The old woman peered into the plate of water and oil. "The painting for which you are searching depicts the Christ Child, does it not?"

"Yes."

"How curious that a man such as yourself would search for our Lord and savior." Again she lowered her gaze toward the plate of water and oil. "The painting has been moved from the island across the water. It looks different than it did before."

"How so?"

"It has been repaired. The man who did the work is now dead. But you already know this."

"Someday you're going to have to show me how you do that."

"It's not something that can be taught. It is a gift from God."

"Where is the painting now?"

"I cannot say."

"Who has it?"

"It is beyond my powers to give you his name. The woman can help you find it."

"What woman?"

"I cannot say. Do not let any harm come to her, or you will lose everything."

The old woman's head fell toward her shoulder; the prophecy had exhausted her. Gabriel slipped several bills beneath the plate of water and oil.

"I have one more thing to tell you before you go," the old woman said as Gabriel rose.

"What is it?"

"Your wife has left the city of water."

"When?" asked Gabriel.

"While you were in the company of the one-eyed creature in the town near the sea."

"Where is she now?"

"She's waiting for you," the old woman said, "in the city of light."

"Is that all?"

"No," she said as her eyelids closed. "The old man doesn't have long to live. Make peace with him before it's too late."

She was right about at least one thing; it seemed Chiara had indeed left Venice. During a brief call to her mobile phone, she said she was feeling well and that it was raining again. Gabriel quickly checked the weather for Venice and saw that it had been sunny for days. Calls to the phone in their apartment went unanswered, and her father, the inscrutable Rabbi Zolli, seemed to have a list of ready-made excuses to explain why his daughter was not at her desk. She was shopping, she was in the ghetto bookstore, she was visiting the old ones in the rest home. "I'll have her call you the moment she returns. Shalom, Gabriel." Gabriel wondered whether the general's handsome bodyguard was complicit in Chiara's disappearance or whether he had been duped, too. He suspected it was the latter. Chiara was better trained and more experienced than any hunk of Carabinieri muscle.

He went to the village twice each day, once in the morning for his bread and coffee, and again in the evening for a glass of wine at the café near the *boules* game. On both occasions he saw the *signadora* leaving the church after mass. On the first evening, she paid him no heed. But on the second, the boy with curly hair appeared at his table with another note. It seemed the man for whom Gabriel was waiting would be arriving in Calvi by ferry the next day.

Gabriel called Don Orsati, who confirmed it was true.

"How did you know?" he asked.

"The *macchia* has no eyes," said Gabriel cryptically, and rang off. He spent the next morning putting the finishing touches on his plan to find the missing Caravaggio. Then, at noon, he walked to the three ancient olive trees and freed Don Casabianca's goat from its tether. An hour later he saw a battered Renault hatchback coming up the valley in a cloud of dust. As it approached the three ancient olive trees, the old goat stepped defiantly into its path. A car horn blared, and soon the valley echoed with profane insults and threats of unspeakable violence. Gabriel went into the kitchen and opened the Chablis. The Englishman had returned to Corsica.

T WAS NOT often that one had occasion to shake the hand of a dead man, but that is precisely what occurred, two minutes later, when Christopher Keller stepped through the door of the villa. According to British military records, he died in January 1991 during the first Persian Gulf war, when his Special Air Services Sabre squadron came under Coalition air attack in a tragic case of friendly fire. His parents, both respected Harley Street physicians, mourned him as a hero in public, though privately they told each other that his death would never have come to pass had he stayed at Cambridge instead of running off to join the army. To this day, they still did not know that he alone had survived the attack on his squadron. Nor did they know that, after walking out of Iraq disguised as an Arab, he had made his way across Europe to Corsica, where he had fallen into the waiting arms of Don Anton Orsati. Gabriel had forgiven Keller for once trying to kill him. But he could not countenance the fact that the Englishman had allowed his parents to grow old believing their only child was dead.

Keller looked well for a dead man. His eyes were clear and blue, his cropped hair was bleached nearly white from the sea and the sun, his skin was taut and deeply tanned. He wore a white dress shirt, open at the neck, and a business suit weary with travel. When he removed the jacket, the lethality of his physique was revealed. Everything about Keller, from his powerful shoulders to his coiled forearms, seemed to have been expressly designed for the purpose of killing. He tossed the jacket over the back of a chair and glanced at the Tanfoglio pistol resting on the coffee table, next to the general's Caravaggio file.

"That's mine," he said of the gun.

"Not anymore."

Keller walked over to the open bottle of Chablis and poured himself a glass.

"How was your trip?" asked Gabriel.

"Successful."

"I was afraid you were going to say that."

"Better than the alternative."

"What kind of job was it?"

"I was delivering food and medicine to widows and orphans."

"Where?"

"Warsaw."

"My favorite city."

"God, what a dump. And the weather's lovely this time of year."

"What were you really doing, Christopher?"

"Taking care of a problem for a private banker in Switzerland."

"What kind of problem?"

"A Russian problem."

"Did the Russian have a name?"

"Let's call him Igor."

"Was Igor legit?"

"Not even close."

"*Mafiya*?"

"To the core."

"I take it Igor of the *mafiya* entrusted money to the private banker in Switzerland."

"A great deal of money," Keller said. "But he was unhappy with the interest he was earning on his investments. He told the Swiss banker to improve his performance. Otherwise, he was going to kill the banker, his wife, his children, and his dog."

"So the Swiss banker turned to Don Orsati for help."

"What choice did he have?"

"What happened to the Russian?"

"He had a mishap following a meeting with a prospective business partner. I won't bore you with the details."

"And his money?"

"A portion of it has been wired into an account controlled by the Orsati Olive Oil Company. The rest is still in Switzerland. You know how those Swiss bankers are," Keller added. "They don't like to part with money."

The Englishman sat on the couch, opened the general's Caravaggio file, and removed the photograph of the empty frame in the Oratorio di San Lorenzo. "A pity," he said, shaking his head. "Those Sicilian bastards have no respect for anything."

"Did Don Orsati ever tell you that he was the one who discovered the painting had been stolen?"

"He might have mentioned it one night when his well of Corsican proverbs had run dry. It's a shame he didn't arrive at the oratorio a few minutes earlier," added Keller. "He might have been able to prevent the thieves from stealing the painting."

"Or the thieves might have killed him before leaving the church."

"You underestimate the don."

"Never."

Keller returned the photograph to the file. "What does this have to do with me?"

"The Carabinieri have retained me to recover the painting. I need your help."

"What kind of help?"

"Nothing much," answered Gabriel. "I just need you to steal a priceless masterpiece and sell it to a man who's killed two people in less than a week."

"Is that all?" Keller smiled. "I was afraid you were going to ask me to do something difficult."

Gabriel told him the entire story, beginning with Julian Isherwood's star-crossed visit to Lake Como and ending with General Ferrari's unorthodox proposal for recovering the world's most coveted missing painting. Keller remained motionless throughout, his forearms resting on his knees, his hands folded, like a reluctant penitent. His capacity for long periods of complete stillness unnerved even Gabriel. While serving in the SAS in Northern Ireland, Keller had specialized in close observation, a dangerous surveillance technique that required him to spend weeks in cramped "hides" such as attics and haylofts. He had also infiltrated the Irish Republican Army by posing as a Catholic from West Belfast, which was why Gabriel was confident Keller could play the role of an art thief with a hot picture to unload. The Englishman, however, wasn't so sure.

"It's not what I do," he said when Gabriel had finished the briefing. "I watch people, I kill people, I blow things up. But I don't steal paintings. And I don't sell them on the black market."

"If you can pass as a Catholic from the Ballymurphy housing estates, you can pass as a hood from East London. If memory serves," Gabriel added, "you're rather good at accents."

"True," admitted Keller. "But I know very little about art."

"Most thieves don't. That's why they're thieves instead of curators or art historians. But don't worry, Keller. You'll have me whispering in your ear."

"I can't tell you how much I'm looking forward to that."

Gabriel said nothing.

"What about the Italians?" Keller asked.

"What about them?"

"I'm a professional killer who, on occasion, has been known to ply his trade on Italian soil. I won't be able to go back there if your friend from the Carabinieri ever finds out I was working with you."

"The general will never know you were involved."

"How can you be certain?"

"Because he doesn't *want* to know."

Keller didn't appear convinced. He lit a cigarette and blew a cloud of smoke thoughtfully toward the ceiling.

"Must you?" asked Gabriel.

"It helps me think."

"It makes it difficult for me to breathe."

"Are you sure you're Israeli?"

"The don seems to think I'm a closet Corsican."

"Not possible," said Keller. "No Corsican would ever have agreed to find a painting that's been missing for more than forty years, especially for a bloody Italian."

Gabriel went into the kitchen, took a saucer down from the cabinet, and placed it in front of Keller. The Englishman took one final pull at his cigarette before crushing it out.

"What are you planning to use for money?"

Gabriel told Keller about the suitcase filled with a million euros given to him by the general.

"A million won't get you far."

"Do you have any loose change lying around?"

"I might have a bit of pocket money left over from the Warsaw hit."

"How much?"

"Five or six hundred."

"That's very generous of you, Christopher."

"It's my money."

"What's five or six hundred between friends?"

"A lot of money." Keller let out a long breath. "I'm still not sure whether I can pull it off."

"Pull what off?"

"Passing myself off as an art thief."

"You kill people for money," said Gabriel. "I don't think it will be much of a stretch."

Dressing Christopher Keller for the role of an international art thief proved to be the easiest part of his preparation, for in the closet of his villa was a large selection of clothing for any occasion or assassination. There was Keller the wandering bohemian, Keller the jet-setting elite, and Keller the mountain-climbing outdoorsman. There was even Keller the Roman Catholic priest, complete with a breviary and a traveling mass kit. In the end, Gabriel chose the sort of clothing that Keller wore naturally—white dress shirts, tailored dark suits, and fashionable loafers. He accessorized the Englishman's appearance with several gold chains and bracelets, a flashy Swiss wristwatch, blue-tinted spectacles, and a blond wig with a dense forelock. Keller supplied his own false British passport and credit cards in the name of Peter Rutledge. Gabriel thought it sounded a bit too upper-class for a criminal from the East End, but it didn't matter. No one in the art world would ever know the thief's name.

17

RUE DE MIROMESNIL, PARIS

THEY GATHERED IN the cramped back office of Antiquités Scientifiques at eleven the following morning: the art thief, the professional killer, and the once and future operative of the Israeli secret intelligence service. The operative quickly explained to the art thief how he intended to find the long-missing Caravaggio altarpiece. The thief, like the killer before him, was dubious at best.

"I steal paintings," he pointed out, his tone laborious. "I don't *find* them on behalf of the police. In fact, I do my very best to avoid the police altogether."

"The Italians will never know of your involvement."

"So you say."

"Do I need to remind you that the man who acquired the Caravaggio killed your friend and associate?"

"No, Monsieur Allon, you do not."

The buzzer howled. Maurice Durand ignored it.

"What would you need me to do?"

"I need you to steal something no dirty collector could resist."

"And then?"

"When rumors start swirling through the nether regions of the art world that the painting is in Paris, I'll need you to point the vultures in the right direction."

Durand looked at Keller. "Toward him?"

Gabriel nodded.

"And why will the vultures think the painting is in Paris?"

"Because I'm going to tell them it is."

"You do think of everything, don't you, Monsieur Allon?"

"The best way to win at a game of chance is to remove chance from the equation."

"I'll try to remember that." Durand looked at Keller again and asked, "How much does he know about the trade in stolen art?"

"Nothing," admitted Gabriel. "But he's a quick study."

"What does he do for a living?"

"He cares for widows and orphans."

"Yes," said Durand skeptically. "And I'm the president of France."

They spent the remainder of the day working out the details of the operation. Then, as night fell over the Eighth Arrondissement, Monsieur Durand switched the sign in the window from OUVERT to FERMÉ, and they filed into the rue de Miromesnil. The art thief headed to the brasserie across the street for his nightly glass of red wine, the killer took a taxi to a hotel on the rue de Rivoli, and the once and future operative of Israeli intelligence walked to an Office safe flat overlooking the Pont

Marie. He saw a pair of security agents sitting in a parked car outside the entrance of the building; and when he entered the flat, he smelled the aroma of cooking and heard Chiara singing softly to herself. He kissed her lips and led her into the bedroom. He didn't ask her how she was feeling. He didn't ask her anything at all.

"Do you realize," she asked afterward, "this is the first time we've made love since we found out I was pregnant?"

"Is it really?"

"When someone of your intelligence plays dumb, Gabriel, it isn't terribly effective."

He slowly twirled a lock of her hair around his fingertip but said nothing. Her chin was resting against his breastbone. The glow of the Paris streetlamps had turned her skin to gold.

"Why haven't you made love to me until now? And don't tell me you've been busy," she added quickly, "because that never stopped you before."

He released her hair but made no reply.

"You were afraid something might go wrong with the pregnancy again? Is that why?"

"Yes," he answered. "I suppose it was."

"What changed your mind?"

"I spent a few moments with an old woman on the island of Corsica."

"What did she tell you?"

"That no harm would ever come to you and the children."

"And you believe her?"

"She warmed up by telling me several things she couldn't possibly have known. Then she told me that you'd left Venice."

"Did she tell you I was in Paris?"

"Not in so many words."

"I was hoping to surprise you."

"How did you know where to find me?"

"How do you think?"

"You called King Saul Boulevard."

"Actually, King Saul Boulevard called me."

"Why?"

"Because Uzi wanted to know why you were keeping company with a man like Maurice Durand. Obviously, I leapt at the opportunity."

"How did you get away from the general's bodyguard?"

"Matteo? He was easy."

"I never realized you two were on a first-name basis."

"He was very helpful in your absence. And he never once asked me how I was feeling."

"I won't make that mistake again."

Chiara kissed Gabriel's lips and asked him why he had renewed his relationship with the world's most successful art thief. Gabriel told her everything.

"Now I understand why General Ferrari was so eager for you to look into Bradshaw's death."

"He knew all along that Bradshaw was dirty," said Gabriel. "And he'd also heard rumors that his fingerprints were on the Caravaggio."

"I suppose that might explain something peculiar I found in the billing records of the Meridian Global Consulting Group."

"What's that?"

"During the past twelve months, Meridian has done a great deal of work for something called LXR Investments of Luxembourg."

"Who are they?"

"Hard to say. LXR is a rather opaque company, to say the least."

Gabriel gathered up another lock of Chiara's hair and asked what else she had discovered in the electronic debris of Jack Bradshaw.

"During the final few weeks of his life, he sent several e-mails to a Gmail account with an auto-generated user name."

"What did they talk about?"

"Weddings, parties, the weather—all the usual things people discuss when they're actually talking about something else."

"Any idea where his pen pal is based?"

"Internet cafés in Brussels, Antwerp, and Amsterdam."

"But of course."

Chiara rolled onto her back. Gabriel laid his hand upon her abdomen as the rain beat softly against the window.

"What are you thinking?" she asked after a moment.

"I was wondering whether it was real or just my imagination."

"What?"

"Never mind."

She let it drop. "I suppose I'm going to have to say something to Uzi."

"I suppose you are."

"What should I tell him?"

"The truth," replied Gabriel. "Tell him I'm going to steal a painting worth two hundred million dollars and see if I can sell it to Mr. Big."

"What are you going to do next?"

"I have to go to London to start a nasty rumor."

"And then?"

"I'm going to Marseilles to make the nasty rumor come true."

18

HYDE PARK, LONDON

GABRIEL RANG ISHERWOOD Fine Arts the following morning while crossing Leicester Square. He asked to see Isherwood away from the gallery and the usual art world watering holes in St. James's. Isherwood suggested the Lido Café Bar in Hyde Park. No one from the art world, he said, would be caught dead there.

He arrived a few minutes after one o'clock, dressed for the country in a tweed jacket and waterproof shoes. He looked far less hungover than he usually did in the early afternoon.

"Far be it from me to complain," said Gabriel, shaking Isherwood's hand, "but your secretary left me on hold for nearly ten minutes before finally putting me through to you."

"Consider yourself lucky."

"When are you going to fire her, Julian?"

"I can't."

"Why not?"

"It's possible I'm still in love with her."

"She's abusive."

"I know." Isherwood smiled. "If only we were sleeping together. Then it would be perfect."

They sat at a table overlooking the Serpentine. Isherwood frowned at the menu.

"Not exactly Wilton's, is it?"

"You'll survive, Julian."

Isherwood didn't appear convinced. He ordered a prawn sandwich and a glass of white wine for his blood pressure. Gabriel ordered tea and a scone. When they were alone again, he told Isherwood everything that had transpired since he had left Venice. Then he told him what he planned to do next.

"Naughty boy," said Isherwood softly. "Naughty, naughty boy."

"It was the general's idea."

"He's a devious bastard, isn't he?"

"That's why he's so good at his job."

"He has to be. But as the director of the Committee to Protect Art," Isherwood added with a tone of formality, "I would be remiss if I didn't object to one aspect of your rather clever operation."

"There's no other way, Julian."

"And if the painting is damaged during the theft?"

"I'm sure I can find someone to fix it."

"Don't be so glib, my boy. It doesn't suit you."

A heavy silence fell between them.

"It'll be worth it if I can get that Caravaggio back," Gabriel said finally.

"*If*," replied Isherwood skeptically. He let out a long breath. "I'm sorry I got you mixed up in all this. And to think none of it would have happened if it wasn't for bloody Oliver Dimbleby."

"Actually, I've devised a way for Oliver to atone for his sins."

"You're not thinking about using him in some way, are you?"

Gabriel nodded slowly. "But this time, Oliver will never know it."

"Wise move," replied Isherwood. "Because Oliver Dimbleby has one of the biggest mouths in the entire art world."

"Exactly."

"What are you thinking?"

Gabriel told him. Isherwood gave a mischievous smile.

"Naughty boy," he said. "Naughty, naughty boy."

By the time they finished lunch, Gabriel had managed to convince Isherwood of the efficacy of his plan. They worked out the final details as they crossed Hyde Park and then parted company on the crowded pavements of Piccadilly. Isherwood headed back to his gallery in Mason's Yard; Gabriel, to St. Pancras Station, where he boarded a late-afternoon Eurostar to Paris. That evening, in the safe flat overlooking the Pont Marie, he made love to Chiara for the second time since learning she was pregnant with his children.

In the morning they ate breakfast at a café near the Louvre. Then, after walking Chiara back to the safe flat, Gabriel took a taxi to the Gare de Lyon. He boarded a Marseilles-bound train at nine and by 12:45 was coming down the steps of the Gare Saint-Charles. They deposited him at the foot of

the boulevard d'Athènes, which he followed to La
Canebière, the broad shopping street that ran from
the city center down to the Old Port. The fishing boats had returned from their morning runs;
sea creatures of every sort lay atop the metal tables
along the port's eastern flank. At one of the tables
was a gray-haired man in a tattered wool sweater
and a rubber apron. Gabriel paused there briefly to
inspect the man's catch. Then he walked around the
corner to the southern edge of the port and climbed
into the passenger seat of a battered Renault sedan.
Seated behind the wheel, the stub of a cigarette
burning between his fingertips, was Christopher
Keller.

"Must you?" asked Gabriel wearily.

Keller crushed out his cigarette and immediately
lit another.

"I can't believe we're back here again."

"Where?"

"Marseilles," answered Keller. "This is where we
started our search for the English girl."

"And where you needlessly took a life," added Gabriel darkly.

"Let's not relitigate that one."

"That's a rather big word for an art thief, Christopher."

"You don't think it's something of a coincidence
that we're sitting in the same car on the same side of
the Old Port?"

"No."

"Why not?"

"Because Marseilles is where the criminals are."

"Like him." Keller nodded toward the man in the tattered wool sweater standing at a fish table at the edge of the port.

"Know him?"

"Everyone in the business knows Pascal Rameau. He and his crew are the best thieves in the Côte d'Azur. They steal everything. There was a rumor they once tried to steal the Eiffel Tower."

"What happened?"

"The buyer backed out—at least, that's the way Pascal likes to tell the story."

"Ever had any dealings with him?"

"He doesn't need people like me."

"Meaning?"

"Pascal runs a tight ship." Keller exhaled a cloud of cigarette smoke. "So Maurice places an order and Pascal delivers the goods—is that the way it works?"

"Just like Amazon."

"What's Amazon?"

"You need to get out of your valley a little more often, Christopher. The world has changed since you died."

Keller fell silent. Gabriel turned his gaze away from Pascal Rameau, toward the hilly quarter of Marseilles near the basilica. Images of the past flashed in his memory: the door of a stately apartment building on the boulevard Saint-Rémy, a man walking quickly through the cool shadows of morning, an Arab girl with pitiless brown eyes standing atop a flight of stone steps. *Excuse me, monsieur. Are you lost?* He blinked away the memory, reached into his coat pocket for his cell phone, but stopped himself. There was a security team outside the safe flat in Paris. No harm would come to her.

"Something wrong?" asked Keller.

"No," replied Gabriel. "Everything's fine."

"You sure about that?"

Gabriel returned his gaze to Pascal Rameau. Keller smiled.

"It's a bit odd, don't you think?"

"What's that?"

"That a man such as yourself could be associated with an art thief."

"Or a professional killer," Gabriel added.

"What's that supposed to mean?"

"It means that life is complicated, Christopher."

"Tell me about it."

Keller crushed out his cigarette and started to light another.

"Please," said Gabriel quietly.

Keller tapped the cigarette back into its packet. "How much longer do we have to wait?"

Gabriel glanced at his wristwatch. "Twenty-eight minutes."

"How can you be so certain?"

"Because his train gets into Saint-Charles at one thirty-four. The walk from the station to the port will take him twelve minutes."

"What if he makes a stop along the way?"

"He won't," replied Gabriel. "Monsieur Durand is very reliable."

"If he's so reliable, why are we back in Marseilles again?"

"Because he's got a million euros of the Carabinieri's money, and I want to make sure it ends up in the right place."

"In the pocket of Pascal Rameau."

Gabriel made no reply.

"It's a bit odd, don't you think?"

"Life is complicated, Christopher."

Keller lit a cigarette. "Tell me about it."

It was 1:45 when they saw him coming down the slope of La Canebière, which meant he was running a minute ahead of schedule. He wore a flint-gray worsted suit and a neat fedora, and in his right hand carried an attaché case containing one million euros in cash. He walked over to the fishmongers and worked his way slowly along the tables until he was standing in front of Pascal Rameau. Words were exchanged, product was diligently inspected for freshness, and finally a selection was made. Durand handed over a single banknote, collected a plastic bag filled with squid, and set out toward the southern side of the port. A moment later, he passed Gabriel and Keller without a glance.

"Where's he going now?"

"A boat called *Mistral*."

"Who owns the boat?"

"René Monjean."

Keller raised an eyebrow. "How do you know Monjean?"

"Another story for another time."

Durand was now walking along one of the floating docks between the rows of white pleasure craft.

As Gabriel predicted, he boarded a motor yacht called *Mistral* and ducked into the cabin. He remained there for seventeen minutes precisely, and when he reappeared he was no longer in possession of the briefcase or the squid. He walked past Keller's battered Renault and started back toward the train station.

"Congratulations, Christopher."

"For what?"

"You are now the proud owner of a van Gogh masterpiece worth two hundred million dollars."

"Not yet."

"Maurice Durand is very reliable," said Gabriel. "And so is René Monjean."

19

AMSTERDAM

FOR THE NEXT nine days, the art world spun smoothly on its gilded axis, blissfully unaware of the time bomb ticking in its midst. It lunched well, it drank late into the evening, it slid carelessly down the slopes of Aspen and St. Moritz on the last good snow of the season. Then, on the third Friday of April, it woke to the news that a calamity had struck the Rijksmuseum Vincent van Gogh in Amsterdam. *Sunflowers*, oil on canvas, 95 by 73 centimeters, was gone.

The technique employed by the thieves did not match the sublime beauty of their target. They chose the bludgeon over the rapier, speed over stealth. The chief of Amsterdam's police department would later call it the finest display of "smash and grab" he had ever seen, though he was careful not to release too many details, lest he make it easier for the next band of thieves to make off with another iconic and irreplaceable work of art. He was grateful for only one thing: the thieves did not use a razor to remove the canvas from its frame. In fact, he said, they had treated the painting with a tenderness that bordered on reverence. Many experts in the field of art security, however, saw the careful handling of the canvas as a troubling sign. For them, it suggested a commissioned theft carried out by highly competent professional criminals. One retired art sleuth from Scotland Yard was skeptical about the prospects for a successful recovery. In all likelihood, he said, *Sunflowers* was now hanging in the museum of the missing and would never be seen by the public again.

The managing director of the Rijksmuseum went before the media to issue a plea for the painting's safe return. And when that failed to move the thieves, he offered a substantial reward, which forced the Dutch police to waste countless hours chasing down hoaxes and false leads. The mayor of Amsterdam, an unrepentant radical, thought a demonstration was in order. Three days later, several hundred activists of every stripe converged on the Museumplein to demand that the thieves hand over the painting unharmed. They also called for the ethical treatment of animals, an end to global warming, the legalization of all recreational narcotics, the closure of the American detention center at Guantánamo Bay, and an end to the occupation of the West Bank and Gaza Strip. There were no arrests, and a good time was had by all, especially those who availed themselves of the free cannabis and condoms. Even the most liberal Dutch newspapers thought the protest was pointless. "If this is the best we can do," editorialized one, "we should prepare ourselves for the day when the walls of our great museums are bare."

Behind the scenes, however, the Dutch police were engaged in a far more traditional effort to recover what was, arguably, van Gogh's most famous work. They talked to their snitches, tapped the phones and e-mail accounts of known thieves, and kept a watch on galleries in Amsterdam and Rotterdam that were suspected of dealing in stolen goods. But when another week passed with no progress, they decided to open a conduit to their brethren in European law enforcement. The Belgians sent them on a wild goose chase to Lisbon, while the French did little more than wish them well. The most intriguing foreign lead came from General Cesare Ferrari of the Art Squad, who claimed to have heard a rumor that the Russian *mafiya* had engineered the theft. The Dutch made entreaties to the Kremlin for information. The Russians didn't trouble themselves with a reply.

By then, it was early May, and the Dutch police possessed not a single substantive lead on the painting's whereabouts. Publicly, the chief vowed to redouble his efforts. Privately, he admitted that, short of divine intervention, the van Gogh was probably lost forever. Inside the museum, a black shroud was hung in the painting's place. One British columnist sardonically implored the museum's director to increase security. Otherwise, he quipped, the thieves would steal the shroud, too.

There were some in London who found the column in poor taste, but for the most part the art world shrugged its collective shoulders and carried on. The important Old Master auctions were fast approaching, and by all accounts the season would be the most lucrative in years. There were paintings to see, clients to entertain, and bidding strategies to devise. Julian Isherwood was a blur of activity. On the Wednesday of that week, he was spotted in the saleroom at Bonhams pawing an Italianate river landscape attributed to the circle of Agostino Buonamico. The next day he was lunching well at the Dorchester with an expatriate Turk of seemingly limitless means. Then, on the Friday, he stayed after hours at Christie's to perform due diligence on an eighteenth-century *John the Baptist* from the Bolognese School. As a result, the bar at Green's was filled to capacity by the time he arrived. He paused to have a private word with Jeremy Crabbe before settling into his usual table, with his usual bottle of Sancerre. Tubby Oliver Dimbleby was flirting shamelessly with Amanda Clifton, the delectable new head of Sotheby's Impressionist and Modern Art department. He pressed one of his gold-plated business cards into her palm, blew a kiss to Simon Mendenhall, and then walked over to Isherwood's table. "Darling Julie," he said as he plopped into the empty chair. "Tell me something absolutely scandalous. A naughty rumor. A bit of malicious gossip. Something I can dine out on for the rest of the week." Isherwood smiled, poured two inches of wine into Oliver's empty glass, and proceeded to make his evening.

"Paris? Really?"

Isherwood gave a conspiratorial nod.

"Says who?"

"I couldn't possibly say."

"Come on, petal. It's me you're talking to. I have more dirty secrets than MI6."

"Which is why I'm not going to breathe another word about it."

Dimbleby appeared genuinely hurt, which, until that moment, Isherwood wouldn't have thought possible.

"My source is connected to the Paris art scene. That's as far as I can go."

"Well, that's a revelation. I thought you were going to tell me he was a sous-chef at Maxim's."

Isherwood said nothing.

"Is he in the biz, or is he a consumer of the arts?"

"Biz."

"Dealer?"

"Use your imagination."

"And he's actually seen the van Gogh?"

"My source would never be caught dead in the same room as a stolen painting," Isherwood replied with just the right hint of righteous indignation. "But he has it on good authority that several disreputable dealers and collectors have been shown Polaroid photographs."

"I didn't know they still existed."

"What's that?"

"Polaroid cameras."

"Apparently so."

"Why use a Polaroid?"

"They leave no digital footprints that can be traced by the police."

"Good to know," said Dimbleby, with a glance at Amanda Clifton's backside. "So who's flogging it?"

"According to the rumor mill, he's an English-man without a name."

"An Englishman? What a cad."

"Shocking," agreed Isherwood.

"How much is he asking?"

"Ten million."

"For a bloody van Gogh? That's a steal."

"Exactly."

"It won't last long, not at that price. Somebody's going to snatch it up and lock it away forever."

"My source thinks our Englishman might actu-ally have a bidding war on his hands."

"Which is why," Dimbleby said, his tone sud-denly serious, "you have no choice but to go to the police."

"I can't."

"Why not?"

"Because I have to protect my source."

"You're professionally obligated to tell the police. Morally, too."

"I do love it when you lecture me about morality, Oliver."

"No need to get personal, Julie. I was just trying to do you a favor."

"Like sending me on an all-expenses-paid trip to Lake Como?"

"Are we going to have this conversation again?"

"I still have nightmares about his body hanging from that bloody chandelier. It looked like some-thing painted by . . ."

Isherwood's voice trailed off. Dimbleby frowned thoughtfully.

"By whom?"

"Never mind."

"Did they ever find out who killed him?"

"Who?"

"Jack Bradshaw, you dolt."

"I believe it was the butler."

Dimbleby smiled.

"Now remember, Oliver, everything I've told you about the van Gogh being in Paris is *entre nous*."

"It shall never pass my lips."

"Swear to me, Oliver."

"You have my solemn word," said Dimbleby. Then, after finishing his drink, he told everyone in the room.

By lunchtime the following day, it was all anyone at Wilton's was talking about. From there, it made its way over to the National Gallery, the Tate, and lastly to the Courtauld Gallery, which was still smarting over the theft of van Gogh's *Self-Portrait with a Bandaged Ear*. Simon Mendenhall told everyone at Christie's; Amanda Clifton did the same at Sotheby's. Even the normally taciturn Jeremy Crabbe couldn't keep his own counsel. He put it all in a chatty e-mail to someone at the New York office of Bonhams, and before long it was rattling round the galleries of Midtown and the Upper East Side. Nicholas Lovegrove, art consultant to the vastly rich, whispered it into the ear of a reporter at the *New York Times*, but the reporter had already heard it from someone else. She rang the chief of the Dutch police, who'd heard it, too.

The Dutchman called his counterpart in Paris,

who didn't think much of it. Nevertheless, the French police began looking for a well-built Englishman of early middle age with blond hair, blue-tinted eyeglasses, and a faint cockney accent. They found several, though none turned out to be an art thief. Among those swept up in the dragnet was the British home secretary's nephew, whose accent was posh London but hardly cockney. The home secretary called the French interior minister to complain, and the nephew was quietly released.

There was one aspect of the rumor, however, that was unassailably true: *Sunflowers*, oil on canvas, 95 by 73 centimeters, was indeed in Paris. It had arrived there the morning after its disappearance, in the trunk of a Mercedes sedan. It went first to Antiquités Scientifiques, where, rolled in protective glassine paper, it spent two restful nights in a climate-controlled cabinet. Then it was carried by hand to the Office safe flat overlooking the Pont Marie. Gabriel quickly returned the painting to a new stretcher and propped it on an easel in the makeshift studio he had prepared in the spare bedroom. That evening, when Chiara was cooking, he sealed the door with tape to avoid any contamination of the surface. And when they slept, the painting slept next to them, bathed in the yellow glow of the streetlamps along the Seine.

The next morning he went to a small gallery near the Luxembourg Gardens where, posing as a German, he purchased a Paris streetscape by a third-tier Impressionist who used the same type of canvas as van Gogh. Returning to the flat, he stripped away the painting using a powerful solution of solvent and then removed the canvas from its stretcher. After trimming the canvas to the proper dimensions, he attached it to the same type of stretcher on which he placed *Sunflowers*, a stretcher measuring 95 by 73 centimeters. Next he covered the canvas with a fresh coat of ground. Twelve hours later, when the ground had dried, he prepared his palette with chrome yellow and yellow ocher, and began to paint.

He worked as van Gogh had worked, swiftly, wet-in-wet, and with a touch of madness. At times he felt as though van Gogh were standing at his shoulder, pipe in hand, guiding his every brushstroke. At others, he could see him in his studio in the Yellow House in Arles, racing to capture the beauty of the sunflowers on his canvas before they wilted and died. It was August 1888 when van Gogh produced his first studies of sunflowers in Arles; he hung them upstairs in the spare bedroom, into which Paul Gauguin, with many misgivings, settled in late October. The domineering Gauguin and the supplicant Vincent painted together for the remainder of the autumn, often working side by side in the fields around Arles, but they were prone to violent quarrels about God and art. One occurred on the afternoon of December 23. After confronting Gauguin with a razor, Vincent went to the brothel on the rue du Bout d'Aeles and sliced off a portion of his left ear. Two weeks later, following his discharge from the hospital, he returned to the Yellow House, alone and bandaged, and produced three startling repetitions of the sunflowers he had painted for Gauguin's room. Until recently, one of those paintings had hung in the Rijksmuseum Vincent van Gogh in Amsterdam.

Van Gogh had probably painted the Amsterdam *Sunflowers* in a matter of hours, just as he had painted its predecessor the previous August. Gabriel, however, required three days to produce what he would later refer to as the Paris version. With the addition of van Gogh's distinctive signature to the vase, the forgery was identical to the original in every way but one: it had no craquelure, the fine network of surface cracking that appears in paintings over time. To induce craquelure quickly, Gabriel removed the canvas from its stretcher and baked it in a 350-degree oven for thirty minutes. Then, when the canvas had cooled, he held it taut between both hands and dragged it over the edge of the dining room table, first horizontally, then vertically. The result was the appearance of instant craquelure. He returned the canvas to its stretcher, covered it in a coat of varnish, and placed it next to the original. Chiara could not tell one from the other. Neither could Maurice Durand.

"I never would have imagined it was possible," the Frenchman said.

"What's that?"

"That anyone could be as good as Yves Morel." He traced his fingertip gently over Gabriel's impasto brushwork. "It's as if Vincent painted it himself."

"That's the goal, Maurice."

"But not so easy to achieve, even for a professional restorer." Durand leaned a little closer to the canvas. "What technique did you use to produce your craquelure?"

Gabriel told him.

"The van Meegeren method. Very effective, so long as you don't burn the painting." Durand turned his gaze from Gabriel's forgery to van Gogh's original.

"Don't get any ideas, Maurice. It's going back to Amsterdam as soon as we're done with it."

"Do you know how much I could get for it?"

"Ten million."

"Twenty at least."

"But you didn't steal it, Maurice. It was stolen by an Englishman with blond hair and tinted eyeglasses."

"An acquaintance of mine thinks he's actually met him."

"I hope you didn't disabuse him of that notion."

"Not at all," replied Durand. "The dirty side of the trade believes your friend has the painting and that he's already negotiating with several potential buyers. It won't be long before you-know-who throws his hat into the ring."

"Perhaps he needs a bit of encouragement."

"What kind?"

"Fair warning before the gavel comes down. Do you think you can manage that, Maurice?"

Durand smiled. "With a single phone call."

20

GENEVA

THERE WAS ONE aspect of the affair that had been gnawing at Gabriel from the beginning: Jack Bradshaw's secret rooms in the Geneva Freeport. As a rule, a businessman utilized the unique services of the Freeport because he wanted to avoid taxation or because he was hiding something. Gabriel suspected Bradshaw's motives fell into the second category. But how to get inside without a court order and a police escort? The Freeport wasn't the sort of place one could break into with a lock pick and a confident smile. Gabriel would need an ally, someone with the power to quietly open any door in Switzerland. He knew such a man. A bargain would have to be struck, a secret deal made. It would be complicated, but then matters involving Switzerland generally were.

The initial contact was brief and unpromising. Gabriel rang the man at his office in Bern and gave him a wholly incomplete account of what he needed and why. The man from Bern was understandably unimpressed, though he sounded intrigued.

"Where are you now?" he asked.

"Siberia."

"How quickly can you be in Geneva?"

"I can be on the next train."

"I didn't realize there was a train from Siberia."

"It actually runs through Paris."

"Send up a flare when you get into town. I'll see what I can do."

"I can't come all the way to Geneva without assurances."

"If you want assurances, call a Swiss banker. But if you want to have a look inside those rooms, you're going to have to do it my way. And don't even think about going anywhere near the Freeport without me," the man from Bern added. "If you do, you're going to be in Switzerland for a very long time."

Gabriel would have preferred better odds before making the trip, but now seemed as good a time as any. With the copy of the van Gogh complete, the Paris end of the operation was little more than a waiting game. He could spend the day staring at the telephone, or he could use the lull in activity more productively. In the end, Chiara made the decision for him. He locked the two paintings in the bedroom closet, hurried over to the Gare de Lyon, and boarded the nine o'clock TGV. It arrived in Geneva a few minutes after noon. Gabriel rang the man in Bern from a pay phone in the ticket hall.

"Where are you?" the man asked.

Gabriel answered truthfully.

"I'll see what I can do."

The train station was in a section of Geneva that looked like a gritty *quartier* of a French city. Gabriel walked to the lake and crossed the Pont du Mont-

Blanc, to the South Bank. He dawdled over pizza in the Jardin Anglais and then walked through the shadowed streets of the sixteenth-century Old City. By four o'clock the air was cool with the coming evening. Footsore, tired of waiting, Gabriel rang the man from Bern a third time but received no answer. Ten minutes later, while walking past the banks and exclusive shops of the rue du Rhône, he rang him again. This time, the man picked up.

"Call me old-fashioned," said Gabriel, "but I really don't like it when people stand me up."

"I never promised you anything."

"I could have stayed in Paris."

"That would have been a shame. Geneva is lovely this time of year. And you would have missed your chance to have a look inside the Freeport."

"How much longer do you intend to keep me waiting?"

"We can do it now, if you like."

"Where are you?"

"Turn around."

Gabriel did as he was told. "Bastard."

His name was Christoph Bittel—at least, that was the name he had used on the occasion of their one and only previous meeting. He worked, or so he had said at the time, for the counterterrorism division of the NDB, Switzerland's dependable intelligence and internal security service. He was thin and pale, with a large forehead that gave him the appearance, not unwarranted, of high intelligence. His bloodless hand, when offered over the stick shift of a sporty

German sedan, felt as though it had been recently purged of bacteria.

"Welcome back to Geneva," Bittel said as he eased the car into the traffic. "It was good of you to make a reservation for a change."

"The days of my unauthorized operations in Switzerland are over. We're partners now, remember, Bittel?"

"Let's not get carried away, Allon. We wouldn't want to spoil the fun."

Bittel slipped on a pair of wraparound dark glasses, which lent a mantis-like quality to his features. He drove well but cautiously, as though he had contraband in the trunk and was trying to avoid contact with the authorities.

"As you might expect," he said after a moment, "your confession has provided hours of interesting listening for our officers and senior ministers."

"It wasn't a confession."

"How would you describe it?"

"I gave you a thorough debriefing about my activities on Swiss soil," said Gabriel. "In exchange, you agreed not to throw me in prison for the rest of my life."

"Which you deserved." Bittel shook his head slowly as he drove. "Assassinations, robberies, kidnappings, a counterterrorism operation in Canton Uri that left several members of al-Qaeda dead. Have I left anything out?"

"I once blackmailed one of your most prominent businessmen in order to gain access to Iran's nuclear supply chain."

"Ah, yes. How could I forget Martin Landesmann?"

"That was one of my better ones."

"And now you want to gain access to a storage facility in the Geneva Freeport without a court order?"

"Surely you have a friend in the Freeport who's willing to let you have an extrajudicial peek at the merchandise every now and again."

"Surely," agreed Bittel. "But I generally like to know what I'm going to find before I break open the lock."

"Paintings, Bittel. We're going to find paintings."

"Stolen paintings?"

Gabriel nodded.

"And what happens if the owner discovers we've been inside?"

"The owner is dead. He won't complain."

"The storage rooms in the Freeport are registered under the name of Bradshaw's company. And the company lives on."

"The company is a sham."

"This is Switzerland, Allon. Sham companies are what keep us in business."

Ahead a traffic signal changed from green to amber. Bittel had more than enough time to slip through the intersection. Instead, he eased off the throttle and brought the car gently to a stop.

"You still haven't told me what this is all about," he said, picking at the grip of his stick shift.

"With good reason."

"And if I'm able to get you inside? What do I get in return?"

"If I'm right," replied Gabriel, "you and your friends at the NDB will one day be able to announce the recovery of several long-missing works of art."

"Stolen art in the Geneva Freeport. Not exactly a public relations coup for the Confederation."

"You can't have everything, Bittel."

The light changed. Bittel lifted his foot off the brake and accelerated slowly, as though he were trying to conserve fuel.

"We go in, we look around, and then we leave. And everything in the vault stays in the vault. Are we clear?"

"Whatever you say."

Bittel drove silently, smiling.

"What's so funny?" asked Gabriel.

"I think I like the new Allon."

"I can't tell you how much that means to me, Bittel. But can you drive a little faster? I'd like to reach the Freeport before morning."

They glimpsed it a few minutes later, a row of featureless white buildings topped by a red sign that read PORTS FRANCS. In the nineteenth century it had been little more than a granary where agricultural goods were stored on their way to market. Now it was a secure tax-free repository where the global superrich stashed away treasures of every kind: gold bars, jewelry, vintage wine, automobiles, and, of course, art. No one knew exactly how much of the world's great art resided within the vaults of the Geneva Freeport, but it was thought to be enough to create several great museums. Much of it would never again see the light of day; and if it ever changed hands, it would do so in private. It was not art to be viewed and cherished. It was art as a commodity, art as a hedge against uncertain times.

Despite the vast wealth contained within the Freeport, security was conducted with Swiss discretion. The fence surrounding the port was more a discouragement than a barrier, and the gate through which Bittel drove his car was slow in closing. Video cameras sprouted from every building, though, and within seconds of their arrival a customs official emerged from a doorway holding a clipboard in one hand and a radio in the other. Bittel climbed out of the car and spoke a few words to the officer in fluent French. The customs man returned to his office, and a moment later there appeared a shapely brunette in a snug skirt and blouse. She handed Bittel a key and pointed toward the far end of the complex.

"I take it that's your friend," Gabriel said when Bittel returned to the car.

"Our relationship is strictly professional."

"I'm sorry to hear that."

Addresses in the Freeport were a combination of the building, the corridor, and the door of the vault. Bittel parked outside Building 4 and led Gabriel inside. From the entrance foyer stretched a seemingly endless corridor of doors. One was open. Glancing inside, Gabriel saw a small bespectacled man seated behind a lacquered Chinese table, a telephone to his ear. The vault had been turned into an art gallery.

"Several Geneva businesses have moved into the Freeport in recent years," Bittel explained. "The rent is cheaper than the rue du Rhône, and the clients seem to like the Freeport's reputation for intrigue."

"It's well deserved."

"Not anymore."

"We'll see about that."

They entered a stairwell and climbed to the third floor. Bradshaw's vault was located on Corridor 12, behind a gray metal door that bore the number 24. Bittel hesitated before inserting the key.

"It's not going to explode, is it?"

"Good question."

"That's not funny."

Bittel opened the door, threw the light switch, and swore softly. There were paintings everywhere—paintings in frames, paintings on stretchers, paintings rolled like carpets in a Persian bazaar. Gabriel unfurled one onto the floor for Bittel to see. It showed a cottage standing atop a sea cliff ablaze with wildflowers.

"Monet?" asked Bittel.

Gabriel nodded. "It was stolen from a museum in Poland about twenty years ago."

He unrolled another canvas: a woman holding a fan.

"If I'm not mistaken," said Bittel, "that's a Modigliani."

"You're not. It was one of the paintings taken from the Museum of Modern Art in Paris in 2010."

"The heist of the century. I remember it."

Bittel followed Gabriel through a doorway into the inner room of the vault. It contained two large easels, a halogen lamp, flasks of solvent and medium, containers of pigment, brushes, a well-used palette, and a Christie's catalogue from the 2004 London Old Master auction. It was open to a crucifixion attributed to a follower of Guido Reni, competently executed but uninspired, not quite worth the seller's premium.

Gabriel closed the catalogue and looked around the vault. It was the secret workshop of a master forger, he thought, in the art gallery of the missing. But it was obvious that Yves Morel had done more in this room than forge paintings; he had also done a bit of restoration work. Gabriel picked up the palette and ran his fingertip over the swatches of paint that remained on the surface. Ocher, gold, and crimson: the colors of the *Nativity*.

"What is it?" asked Bittel.

"Proof of life."

"What are you talking about?"

"It was here," said Gabriel. "It exists."

There were one hundred and forty-seven paintings in the two rooms of the vault—Impressionist, Modern, Old Master—but not one of them was a Caravaggio. Gabriel photographed each canvas using the camera on his mobile phone. The only other items in the vault were a desk and a small floor safe—too small, thought Gabriel, to contain an Italian altarpiece measuring seven by eight feet. He searched the desk drawers but found they were empty. Then he crouched before the safe and twirled the tumbler between his thumb and forefinger. Two turns to the right, two turns to the left.

"What are you thinking?" asked Bittel.

"I'm wondering how long it would take you to get a locksmith in here."

Bittel smiled sadly. "Maybe next time."

Yes, thought Gabriel. Next time.

They headed back to the train station through what passed for Geneva's evening rush. Crossing the Pont du Mont-Blanc, Bittel pressed Gabriel for a fuller account of the case. And when his questions failed to elicit a response, he insisted on advance notification should Gabriel's itinerary include another visit to Switzerland. Gabriel readily agreed, though both men realized it was a promise in name only.

"At some point," said Bittel, "we're going to have to clean out that vault and return those paintings to their rightful owners."

"At some point," Gabriel agreed.

"When?"

"It's not in my power to tell you that."

"I say you have a month. After that, I'll have to refer the matter to the Federal Police."

"If you do that," said Gabriel, "it will blow up in the press, and Switzerland will get yet another black eye."

"We're used to it."

"So are we."

They arrived at the station in time for Gabriel to make the four thirty train back to Paris. It was dark when he arrived; he climbed into a waiting taxi and gave the driver an address a short distance from the safe flat. But as the car pulled into the street, Gabriel felt his mobile phone vibrate. He answered the call, listened in silence for a moment, and then severed the connection.

"Change in plan," he said to the driver.

"Where to?"

"The rue de Miromesnil."

"As you wish."

Gabriel slipped the phone into his pocket and smiled. They were in play, he thought. They were definitely in play.

21

RUE DE MIROMESNIL, PARIS

A T FIRST, MAURICE Durand tried to claim executive privilege regarding the identity of the caller. Under pressure, though, he admitted it was Jonas Fischer, a wealthy industrialist and well-known collector from Munich who regularly utilized Monsieur Durand's unique services. Herr Fischer made it clear from the outset he was not interested in the van Gogh himself, that he was interceding on behalf of an acquaintance and fellow collector who, for obvious reasons, he could not name. It seemed the second collector had already dispatched a representative to Paris, based on certain rumors swirling around the art world. Herr Fischer was wondering whether Durand could point the representative in the right direction.

"And what did you tell him?" asked Gabriel.

"I told him I didn't know the whereabouts of the van Gogh but that I would make a few phone calls."

"And if you're able to be of service?"

"I'm supposed to call the representative directly."

"I don't suppose he has a name."

"Only a phone number," replied Durand.

"How professional."

"My thoughts exactly."

They were in the small office in the back of Durand's shop. Gabriel was leaning in the doorway; Durand was seated at his Dickensian little desk. On the blotter before him was a brass microscope, late nineteenth century, by Vérick of Paris.

"Is he the one we're looking for?" asked Gabriel.

"A man like Herr Fischer wouldn't be involved with anyone other than a serious collector. He also intimated that his friend had made a number of important acquisitions of late."

"Was one of those acquisitions a Caravaggio?"

"I didn't ask."

"It's probably better you didn't."

"Probably," agreed Durand.

A silence fell between them.

"Well?" asked the Frenchman.

"Tell him to be standing in the forecourt of Saint-Germain-des-Prés at two o'clock tomorrow afternoon, near the red door. Tell him to bring his phone, but no gun. Whatever you do, don't engage him. Just tell him what to do, then hang up."

Durand lifted the receiver of his phone and dialed.

They left the shop five minutes later, the art thief and the once and future operative of the Israeli secret intelligence service, and parted with scarcely a word or glance. The art thief headed to the brasserie across the street; the operative, to the Israeli embassy at 3 rue Rabelais. He entered the building through the back door, made his way down to the secure communications room, and rang the chief of Housekeeping, the division of the Office that managed safe properties. He said he needed something close to Paris but isolated, preferably to the north. It needn't be anything grand, he added. He wasn't planning on doing any entertaining.

"Sorry," said the chief of Housekeeping. "I can allow you to stay in an existing property, but I can't acquire a new one without the approval of the top floor."

"Perhaps you weren't listening when I said my name."

"What am I supposed to tell Uzi?"

"Nothing, of course."

"How soon do you need it?"

"Yesterday."

By nine the following morning, Housekeeping had closed the deal on a quaint holiday farmhouse in the Picardy region of France, just outside the village of Andeville. A towering hedgerow shielded the entrance from view, and from the edge of its pretty rear garden spread a patchwork quilt of flat farmland. Gabriel and Chiara arrived at noon and concealed the two van Goghs in the wine cellar. Then Gabriel immediately drove back to Paris. He left his car in a parking lot near the Odéon Métro station and walked along the boulevard to the Place Saint-Germain-des-Prés. In one corner of the busy square was a café called Le Bonaparte. Seated at a table facing the street was Christopher Keller. Gabriel greeted him in French and sat next to him. He glanced at his wristwatch. It was 1:55. He ordered a coffee and stared at the red door of the church.

It wasn't difficult to spot him; on that perfect spring afternoon, with the sun blazing in a cloudless sky and a soft wind chasing around the crowded streets, he was the only one who came to the church alone. He was average in height, about five ten, and sleek in build. His movements were fluid and assured—like those of a football player, thought Gabriel, or an elite soldier. He wore a lightweight tan sport coat, a white shirt, and gray gabardine trousers. A straw boater shaded his face; dark sunglasses concealed his eyes. He walked over to the red door and pretended to consult a tourist guidebook. Two young girls, one in shorts, the other in a strapless sundress, were seated on the steps, their bare legs stretched before them. Clearly, there was something about the man that made them uncomfortable. They stayed another moment, then rose and headed across the square.

"What do you think?" asked Keller.

"I think that's our boy."

The waiter delivered Gabriel's coffee. He added sugar and stirred it thoughtfully while watching the man standing next to the red door of the church.

"Aren't you going to call him?"

"It's not two o'clock yet, Christopher."

"Close enough."

"It's better not to appear too eager. Remember, we already have a buyer on the hook. Our friend over there raised his paddle very late in the bidding."

Gabriel remained at the table until the clock in the bell tower of the church read two minutes past the hour. Then he rose and walked into the interior of the café. It was deserted except for the staff. He moved close to the window, drew his phone from his coat pocket, and dialed. A few seconds later, the man standing in front of the church answered.

"Bonjour."

"You don't have to speak French just because we're in Paris."

"I prefer French, if you don't mind."

He might have preferred French, thought Gabriel, but it wasn't his native language. He was no longer pretending to look at his guidebook. He was surveying the square, searching for a man with a mobile phone to his ear.

"Did you come alone?" asked Gabriel.

"Since you're watching me right now, you know the answer is yes."

"I see a man standing where he's supposed to be, but I don't know whether he came alone."

"He did."

"Were you followed?"

"No."

"How can you be sure?"

"I'm sure."

"How should I refer to you?"

"You can call me Sam."

"Sam?"

"Yes, Sam."

"Are you carrying a gun, Sam?"

"No."

"Take off your blazer."

"Why?"

"I want to see if there's anything underneath it that's not supposed to be there."

"Is this really necessary?"

"Do you want to see the painting or not?"

The man placed the guidebook and phone on the steps, removed his blazer, and draped it over his arm. Then he picked up the phone again and said, "Satisfied?"

"Turn around and face the church."

The man rotated about forty-five degrees.

"More."

Another forty-five.

"Very good."

The man returned to his original orientation and asked, "What now?"

"You take a walk."

"I don't feel like walking."

"Don't worry, Sam. It won't be a long walk."

"Where do you want me to go?"

"Down the boulevard toward the Latin Quarter. Do you know the way to the Latin Quarter, Sam?"

"Of course."

"You're familiar with Paris?"

"Very."

"Don't look over your shoulder or make any stops. And don't use your phone, either. You might miss my next call."

Gabriel severed the connection and rejoined Keller.

"Well?" asked the Englishman.

"I think we just found Samir. And I think he's a professional."

"Are we in play?"

"We'll know in a minute."

On the other side of the square, Sam was pull-

ing on his sport coat. He slipped the mobile phone
into his breast pocket, dropped the guidebook into a
rubbish bin, and then made his way to the boulevard
Saint-Germain. A right turn would take him in the
direction of Les Invalides; a left, to the Latin Quarter. He hesitated for a moment and then turned to
the left. Gabriel counted slowly to twenty before
rising to his feet and following after him.

If nothing else, he was capable of following instructions. He walked a straight line down the boulevard, past the shops and crowded cafés, never once
pausing or glancing over his shoulder. This allowed
Gabriel to focus on his primary task, which was
countersurveillance. He saw nothing to suggest
that Sam was working with an accomplice. Nor did
it appear as though he were being followed by the
French police. He was clean, thought Gabriel. As
clean as a buyer of stolen art could be.

After ten minutes of steady walking, Sam was
nearing the point where the boulevard met the
Seine. Gabriel, a half-block in his wake, drew his
mobile phone from his pocket and dialed. Again
Sam answered immediately, with the same cordial
"Bonjour."

"Turn left into the rue du Cardinal Lemoine and
follow it to the Seine. Cross the bridge to the Île
Saint-Louis and then keep walking straight until
you hear from me again."

"How much farther?"

"Not far, Sam. You're almost there."

Sam made the turn as instructed and crossed the

Pont de la Tournelle to the small island in the middle of the Seine. A series of picturesque quays ran along the perimeter of the island, but only a single street, the rue Saint-Louis en l'Île, stretched the length of it. With a phone call, Gabriel instructed Sam to turn to the left again.

"How much farther?"

"Just a little more, Sam. And don't look over your shoulder."

It was a narrow street, with tourists wandering aimlessly past shop windows. At the western end was an ice cream parlor, and next to the parlor was a brasserie with a fine view of Notre Dame. Gabriel called Sam and issued his final instructions.

"How long do you intend to keep me waiting?"

"I'm afraid I won't be joining you for lunch, Sam. I'm just the hired help."

Gabriel severed the connection without another word and watched Sam enter the brasserie. A waiter greeted him, then gestured toward a sidewalk table occupied by an Englishman with blond hair and blue-tinted glasses. The Englishman rose and, smiling, extended his hand. "I'm Reg," Gabriel heard him say as he rounded the corner. "Reg Bartholomew. And you must be Sam."

22

ÎLE SAINT-LOUIS, PARIS

WOULD LIKE TO begin this conversation, Mr. Bartholomew, by offering you my congratulations. That was an impressive transaction you and your men carried out in Amsterdam."

"Who's to say I didn't do it alone?"

"It's not the sort of thing one generally does alone. You surely had help," Sam added. "Like your friend who was on the phone with me. He speaks French very well, but he isn't French, is he?"

"What difference does it make?"

"One likes to have a sense of who one is doing business with."

"This isn't Harrods, luv."

Sam surveyed the street with the languor of a tourist who'd visited too many museums in too brief a time. "He's out there somewhere, is he not?"

"I wouldn't know."

"And there are others?"

"Several."

"And yet I was required to come alone."

"It's a seller's market."

"So I've heard."

Sam resumed his study of the street. He was still wearing his boater and his sunglasses, which left only the lower half of his face visible. It was closely shaven and judiciously fragranced. The cheekbones were high and prominent, the chin was notched, the teeth were even and very white. His hands had no scars or tattoos. He wore no rings on his fingers or bracelets on his wrists, only a large gold Rolex to indicate he was a man of means. He had the polished mannerisms of a well-born Arab but with a harder edge.

"One hears other things as well," Sam continued after a moment. "Those who've seen the merchandise say you managed to get it out of Amsterdam with minimal damage."

"None, actually."

"One also hears there are Polaroids."

"Where did you hear that?"

Sam smiled unpleasantly. "This is going to take much longer than necessary if you insist on playing these games, Mr. Bartholomew."

"One likes to have a sense of who one is doing business with," Keller said pointedly.

"Are you asking me for information about the man I represent, Mr. Bartholomew?"

"I wouldn't dream of it."

There was a silence.

"My client is a businessman," Sam said finally. "Quite successful, very wealthy. He is also a lover of the arts. He collects widely, but like many serious collectors he has grown frustrated by the fact there are very few good pictures for sale any longer. He has been interested in acquiring a van Gogh for many years. You are now in possession of a very good one. My client would like it."

"So would a lot of other people."

Sam appeared untroubled by this. "And what about you?" he asked after a moment. "Why don't you tell me a little about yourself?"

"I steal things for a living."

"You're English?"

"I'm afraid so."

"I've always been fond of the English."

"I won't hold that against you."

A waiter appeared and handed them each a menu. Sam ordered a bottle of mineral water; Keller, a glass of wine he had no intention of drinking.

"Let me make one thing clear from the outset," he said when they were alone again. "I'm not interested in drugs, or guns, or girls, or a condominium in Boca Raton, Florida. This is a cash-only proposition."

"How much cash are we talking about, Mr. Bartholomew?"

"I have an offer of twenty million on the table."

"What flavor?"

"Euros."

"Is it a firm offer?"

"I delayed the sale to meet with you."

"How flattering. Why would you do such a thing?"

"Because I hear your client, whoever he is, is a man of deep pockets."

"Very deep." Another smile, only slightly more pleasant than the first. "So how shall we proceed, Mr. Bartholomew?"

"I need to know whether you're interested in beating the offer on the table."

"I am."

"By how much?"

"I suppose I could offer you something trivial, like an additional five hundred thousand, but my client doesn't like auctions." He paused, then asked, "Would twenty-five million be sufficient to take the painting off the table?"

"It would indeed, Sam."

"Excellent," he said. "Perhaps now would be a good time for you to show me the Polaroids."

The Polaroids were in the glove box of a rented Mercedes parked along a quiet street behind Notre Dame. Keller and Sam walked there together and climbed inside, Keller behind the wheel, Sam in the passenger seat. Keller subjected him to a quick but thorough search before popping the hatch of the glove box and fishing out the photos. There were four in all—one full shot, three detail images. Sam leafed through them skeptically.

"It looks a bit like the van Gogh that hangs above the bed in my hotel room."

"It isn't."

He made a face to indicate he wasn't convinced. "The painting in this photograph could be a copy. And you could be a clever con man who's trying to cash in on the theft in Amsterdam."

"Take off your sunglasses and have a better look, Sam."

"I intend to." He handed the pictures back to Keller. "I need to see the real thing, not photographs."

"I'm not running a museum, Sam."

"Your point?"

"I can't show the van Gogh to anyone who wants to see it. I need to know whether you're serious about acquiring it."

"I've offered you twenty-five million euros in cash for it."

"It's easy to *offer* twenty-five million, Sam. Handing it over is quite another thing."

"My client is a man of extraordinary wealth."

"Then I'm sure he didn't send you to Paris empty-handed." Keller returned the photos to the glove box and closed the lid firmly.

"Is this the way your scam works? You demand to see money before showing the painting and then you steal it?"

"If I was running a scam, you and your client would have already heard about it by now."

He had no answer for that.

"I can't get more than ten thousand in cash on such short notice."

"I'll need to see a million."

He snorted, as if to say a million was out of the question.

"If you want to see a van Gogh for less than a million," Keller said, "you can go to the Louvre or the Musée d'Orsay. But if you want to see *my* van Gogh, you're going to have to show me the money."

"It's not safe to walk around the streets of Paris with that kind of cash."

"Something tells me you can look after yourself just fine."

Sam gave a capitulatory exhalation of breath. "Where and when?"

"Saint-Germain-des-Prés, two o'clock tomorrow afternoon. No friends. No guns."

Sam climbed out of the car without another word and walked away.

He crossed the Seine to the Right Bank and walked along the rue de Rivoli, past the northern wing of the Louvre, to the Jardin des Tuileries. He spent much of that time on the telephone, and twice he engaged in rudimentary tradecraft to see whether he was being followed. Even so, he did not appear to notice Gabriel walking fifty meters in his wake.

Before reaching the Jeu de Paume, he cut over to the rue Saint-Honoré and entered an exclusive shop that sold costly leather goods for men. He emerged ten minutes later with a new attaché case, which he carried to a branch of the HSBC Private Bank on the boulevard Haussmann. He remained there twenty-two minutes precisely, and when he reappeared the attaché case looked heavier than when he had entered. He bore it swiftly to the Place de la Concorde and then through the grand entrance of the Hôtel de Crillon. Watching from a distance, Gabriel smiled. Nothing but the best for the representative of Mr. Big. As he walked away, he rang Keller and told him the news. They were in play, he said. They were definitely in play.

23

BOULEVARD SAINT-GERMAIN, PARIS

H E WAS STANDING outside the red door of the church at two the following afternoon, with his hat and sunglasses firmly in place and the new attaché case clutched in his right hand. Gabriel waited five minutes before calling him.

"You again," said Sam glumly.

"I'm afraid so."

"What now?"

"We take another walk."

"Where now?"

"Follow the rue Bonaparte to the Place Saint-Sulpice. Same rules as last time. Don't make any stops and don't look over your shoulder. No phone calls, either."

"How far do you intend to make me walk this time?"

Gabriel hung up without another word. On the other side of the busy square, Sam started walking. Gabriel counted slowly to twenty and then followed after him.

He let Sam walk to the Luxembourg Gardens before ringing him again. From there, they headed southwest on the rue de Vaugirard, then north on the boulevard Raspail, to the entrance of the Hôtel Lutetia. Keller was sitting at a table in the bar, reading the *Telegraph*. Sam joined him as instructed.

"How was he this time?" asked Keller.

"As thorough as ever."

"Can I get you anything to drink?"

"I don't drink."

"What a pity." Keller folded his newspaper. "You'd better take off those sunglasses, Sam. Otherwise, management might get the wrong idea about you."

He did as Keller suggested. His eyes were light brown and large. With his face exposed, he was a much less threatening figure.

"Now the hat," said Keller. "A gentleman doesn't wear a hat in the bar of the Lutetia."

He removed the boater, revealing a full head of hair, brown but not black, with a bit of gray around the ears. If he was an Arab, he wasn't from the Peninsula or the Gulf. Keller looked at the attaché case.

"Did you bring the money?"

"One million, just as you requested."

"Give me a little peek. But be careful," Keller added. "There's a surveillance camera over your right shoulder."

Sam placed the briefcase on the table, popped the latches, and lifted the lid two inches, just enough for Keller to glimpse the tightly packed rows of hundred-euro banknotes.

"Close it," said Keller quietly.

Sam closed and locked the briefcase. "Satisfied?" he asked.

"Not yet." Keller stood.

"Where now?"

"My room."

"Will there be anyone else?"

"It'll just be the two of us, Sam. Very romantic."

Sam rose to his feet and picked up the attaché case. "I think it's important that I make something clear before we go upstairs."

"What's that, Sam?"

"If anything happens to me or my client's money, you and your friend are going to get hurt very badly." He slipped on his sunglasses and smiled. "Just so we understand each other, luv."

In the entrance hall of the room, beyond the prying eyes of the hotel's surveillance cameras, Keller searched Sam for weapons or recording devices. Finding nothing objectionable, he placed the attaché case at the end of the bed and popped the latches. Then he removed three bundles of cash and, from each bundle, a single banknote. He inspected each note with a professional-grade hand lens; then, in the darkened bathroom, he subjected them to Gabriel's ultraviolet lamp. The security strips glowed lime-green; the bills were genuine. He returned the banknotes to their bundles and the bundles to the briefcase. Then he closed the lid and, with a nod, indicated they were ready to go to the next step.

"When?" asked Sam.

"Tomorrow night."

"I have a better idea," he said. "We do it tonight. Otherwise, the deal's off."

Maurice Durand had told them to expect something like this—a small tactical ploy, a token rebellion, that would allow Sam to feel as though he, and not Keller, were in charge of the negotiating process. Keller pushed back gently, but Sam held his ground. He wanted to be standing in front of the van Gogh before midnight; if he wasn't, he and his twenty-five million euros were gone. Which left Keller no option but to accede to his opponent's wishes. He did so with a concessionary smile, as though the change in plan were little more than an inconvenience. Then he quickly laid down the rules for that evening's viewing. Sam could touch the painting, smell the painting, or make love to the painting. But under no circumstances could he photograph it.

"Where and when?" asked Sam.

"We'll call you at nine o'clock and tell you how to proceed."

"Fine."

"Where are you staying?"

"You know exactly where I'm staying, Mr. Bartholomew. I'll be standing in the lobby of the Crillon at nine tonight, no friends, no guns. And tell your friend not to keep me waiting this time."

He left the hotel ten minutes later, wearing his hat and sunglasses, and walked to the HSBC Private Bank on the boulevard Haussmann, where, presumably, he returned the one million euros to his client's safe-deposit box. Afterward, he made his way on foot to the Musée d'Orsay and spent the next two hours studying the paintings of one Vincent van Gogh. By the time he left the museum, it was approaching six. He ate a light supper in a bistro on the Champs-Élysées and then returned to his room at the Crillon. As promised, he was standing in the lobby at nine o'clock sharp, dressed in gray trousers, a black pullover, and a leather jacket. Gabriel knew this because he was sitting a few feet away, in the lobby bar. He waited until two minutes past nine before calling Sam's number.

"Do you know how to use the Paris Métro?"

"Of course."

"Walk to the Concorde station and take the Number Twelve to Marx Dormoy. Mr. Bartholomew will be waiting for you."

Sam walked out of the lobby. Gabriel remained in the bar for another five minutes. Then he collected his car from the valet and headed for the farmhouse in Picardy.

The Marx Dormoy station was located in the Eighteenth Arrondissement, on the rue de la Chapelle. Keller was parked across the street smoking a cigarette when Sam appeared at the top of the steps. He walked over to the car and slid into the passenger seat without a word.

"Where's your phone?" asked Keller.

Sam drew it from his coat pocket and held it up for Keller to see.

"Turn it off and remove the SIM card."

Sam did as he was told. Keller slipped the car into gear and eased into the evening traffic.

He allowed Sam to remain in the passenger seat until they broke free of the northern suburbs.

Then, in a stand of trees near the town of Ézanville, he ordered him into the trunk. He took the long way north to Picardy, adding at least an hour to the journey. As a result, it was approaching midnight by the time he turned into the drive of the farmhouse. When Sam emerged from the trunk, he spotted the silhouette of a man standing in the moonlight at the edge of the property.

"I take it that's your associate."

Keller didn't respond. Instead, he led him through the rear door of the farmhouse and down a flight of stairs to the cellar. Propped against one wall, lit by a bare bulb hanging from a wire, was *Sunflowers*, oil on canvas, 95 by 73 centimeters, by Vincent van Gogh. Sam stood before it for a long moment without speaking. Keller stood next to him.

"Well?" he asked at last.

"In a moment, Mr. Bartholomew. In a moment."

Finally, he stepped forward, picked up the painting by the vertical stretcher bars, and turned it over to examine the museum markings on the back of the canvas. Then he looked at the edges of the painting and frowned.

"Something wrong?" asked Keller.

"Vincent was notoriously careless in the way he handled his paintings. Look here," he added, turning the edges of the stretcher toward Keller. "He left his fingerprints all over it."

Sam smiled, held the painting close to the light, and spent several minutes carefully examining the brushwork. Then he returned it to its original position and stepped back to scrutinize it from a distance. This time, Keller didn't intrude on his silence.

"Spectacular," he said after a moment.

"And quite the real thing," added Keller.

"It could be. Or it could be the work of a highly skilled forger."

"It isn't."

"I'll need to perform a simple test to make certain, a paint chip analysis. If the paint is genuine, we have a deal. If it isn't, you will never hear from me again, leaving you free to foist it onto a less sophisticated buyer."

"How long will it take?"

"Seventy-two hours."

"You have forty-eight."

"I won't be rushed, Mr. Bartholomew. Neither will my client."

Keller hesitated before nodding his head once. Using a surgical scalpel, Sam expertly removed two tiny flakes of paint from the canvas—one from the bottom right, the other from the bottom left—and placed them into a glass vial. Then he slipped the vial into his coat pocket and, with Keller at his back, headed up the stairs. Outside, the silhouetted figure was still standing at the edge of the farmland.

"Do I ever get to meet your associate?" asked Sam.

"I wouldn't advise it," replied Keller.

"Why not?"

"Because his will be the last face you'll ever see."

Sam frowned and climbed into the trunk of the

Mercedes. Keller slammed the lid and drove him back to Paris.

———————

They were all seasoned operatives, each in their own unique way, but they would later say that the next three days passed with the speed of an icebound river. Gabriel's usual forbearance abandoned him. He had engineered the theft of one of the world's most famous paintings as part of a ploy to find another one; and yet it would all come to nothing if the man called Sam walked away from the deal. Only Maurice Durand, perhaps the world's foremost expert on the illicit art trade, remained confident. In his experience, dirty collectors like Mr. Big rarely walked away from a chance to acquire a van Gogh. Surely, he said, the lure of *Sunflowers* would be too powerful to resist. Unless Gabriel had shown Sam the forgery by mistake, which he had not, the paint chip analysis would come back positive, and the deal would go forward.

They had one other option in the event Sam backed out; they could follow him and attempt to establish the identity of his client, the man of great wealth, who was ready to pay 25 million euros for a stolen work of art. It was just one of the reasons why Gabriel and Keller, two of the most experienced man-trackers in the world, monitored Sam's every move during the three days of waiting. They watched him in the morning while he walked the footpaths of the Tuileries, and in the afternoon while he visited the tourist sights for the sake of his cover, and in the evening when he dined, always

alone, along the Champs-Élysées. The impression
he left was one of discipline. At some point in his
life, Keller and Gabriel agreed, Sam had been a
member of the secret brotherhood of spies. Or perhaps, they thought, he still was.

On the morning of the third day, he gave them
a small fright when he failed to appear for his usual
walk. Their alarm increased at four that afternoon
when they saw him emerge from the Crillon with
two large suitcases and climb into the back of a limousine. But their concern quickly dissolved when
the car took him to the HSBC Private Bank on the
boulevard Haussmann. Thirty minutes later, he was
back in his room. There were only two possibilities,
said Keller. Sam had either carried out the quietest
bank robbery in history, or he had just withdrawn
a large sum of cash from a safe-deposit box. Keller
suspected it was the latter. So, too, did Gabriel.
Therefore, there was little suspense when the time
finally came to ring Sam for his answer. Keller did
the honors. When the call was over, he looked at
Gabriel and smiled. "We may never find the Caravaggio," he said, "but we're about to get twenty-five
million euros of Mr. Big's money."

24

CHELLES, FRANCE

B UT THERE WAS one condition: Sam reserved the right to choose the time and place of the exchange of money and merchandise. The time, he said, would be half past eleven the following evening. The place would be a warehouse in Chelles, a drab commune east of Paris. Keller drove there the next morning while the rest of northern France was streaming toward the city center. The warehouse was where Sam had said it would be, on the avenue François Mitterrand, directly across the street from a Renault dealership. A faded sign read EUROTRANZ, though there was no indication of precisely the sort of services the company provided. Pigeons flew in and out of the broken windows; a savanna of weeds flourished behind the bars of the iron fence. Keller climbed out of his car and inspected the automatic gate. It had been a long time since anyone had opened it.

He spent an hour carrying out a routine reconnaissance assessment of the streets surrounding the warehouse and then drove north to the farmhouse at Andeville. When he arrived, he found Gabriel and Chiara relaxing in the sunlit garden. The two van Goghs were propped against the wall in the living room.

"I still don't know how you can tell them apart," Keller said.

"It's rather obvious, don't you think?"

"No, I don't."

Gabriel inclined his head toward the painting on the right.

"You're sure?"

"Those are my fingerprints on the sides of the stretcher bars, not Vincent's. And then there's this."

Gabriel powered on his Office-issued BlackBerry and held it near the top right corner of the canvas. The screen flashed red, indicating the presence of a concealed transmitter.

"You're sure about the range?" asked Keller.

"I tested it again this morning. It's rock solid at ten kilometers."

Keller looked at the genuine van Gogh. "Too bad no one thought to put a tracker in that one."

"Yes," said Gabriel distantly.

"How long do you intend to keep it?"

"Not a day longer than necessary."

"Who's going to hold on to it while we chase the forgery?"

"I was hoping to leave it in the Paris embassy," said Gabriel, "but the station chief won't touch it. So I had to make other arrangements."

"What sort of arrangements?"

When Gabriel answered, Keller shook his head slowly.

"It's a bit odd, don't you think?"

"Life is complicated, Christopher."

Keller smiled. "Tell me about it."

They left the quaint farmhouse for the last time at eight that evening. The copy of *Sunflowers* was in the trunk of Keller's Mercedes; the authentic van Gogh was in Gabriel's. He delivered it to Maurice Durand at his shop on the rue de Miromesnil. Then he dropped Chiara at the safe flat overlooking the Pont Marie and set out for the commune of Chelles.

He arrived a few minutes before eleven and made his way to the warehouse on the avenue François Mitterrand. It was in a section of town where there was little life on the streets after dark. He circled the property twice, looking for evidence of surveillance or anything that suggested Keller was about to walk into a trap. Finding nothing out of the ordinary, he went in search of a suitable observation post where a man sitting alone wouldn't attract the attention of the gendarmes. The only option was a brown park where a dozen local skateboard toughs were drinking beer. On one side of the park was a row of benches lit by yellow streetlamps. Gabriel parked his car on the street and sat on the bench closest to the entrance of Eurotranz. The toughs looked at him quizzically for a moment before resuming their discussion of the day's pressing affairs. Gabriel glanced at his wristwatch. It was five minutes past eleven. Then he consulted his BlackBerry. The beacon was not yet in range.

Looking up again, he saw the headlamps of a car on the avenue. A small red Citroën, it shot past the

entrance of Eurotranz and sped along the edge of
the park, leaving in its wake the throb of French
hip-hop. Behind it was another car, a black BMW,
so clean it looked newly washed for the occasion. It
stopped at the gate and the driver climbed out. In
the darkness it was impossible to see his face, but
in build and movement he was Sam's doppelganger.

He jabbed his forefinger at the keypad a few
times with the confidence of a man who had known
the combination for a long time. Then he climbed
behind the wheel again, waited for the gate to open,
and drove onto the property. He paused while the
gate closed behind him and then approached the entrance of the warehouse. Again, he emerged from
the car and stabbed at the security keypad with a
speed that suggested familiarity. When the door
rolled open, he eased the car inside and disappeared
from sight.

In the little brown park, the arrival of a luxury
automobile at the disused warehouse on the avenue
François Mitterrand went unnoticed by everyone
except for the man of late middle age sitting alone.
The man glanced at his wristwatch and saw that it
was 11:08. Then he looked at his BlackBerry. The
red light was blinking and heading his way.

Keller arrived promptly at eleven thirty. He rang
Sam's mobile and the gate swung open. A patch of
cracked asphalt stretched before him, empty, darkened. He drove across it slowly and, following Sam's
instructions, nosed the car into the warehouse.
At the opposite end of a football-pitch-size space

glowed the parking lamps of a BMW. Keller could make out the figure of a man leaning against the hood, a phone to his ear, two large suitcases at his feet. There was no one else visible.

"Stop there," said Sam.

Keller put a foot on the brake.

"Turn off the engine and switch off your headlamps."

Keller did as instructed.

"Get out of the car and stand where I can see you."

Keller climbed out slowly and stood in front of the hood. Sam reached inside his BMW and switched on the headlamps.

"Take off your coat."

"Is this really necessary?"

"Do you want the money or not?"

Keller removed his coat and tossed it on the hood of his car.

"Turn around and face the car."

Keller hesitated, then turned his back to Sam.

"Very good."

Keller rotated slowly to face Sam again.

"Where's the painting?"

"In the trunk."

"Take it out and put it on the ground twenty feet in front of the car."

Keller opened the trunk using the inside latch release and removed the painting. It was sheathed in a protective layer of glassine paper and concealed by a contractor-grade rubbish bag. He placed it on the concrete floor of the warehouse twenty paces in front of the Mercedes and waited for Sam's next instruction.

"Walk back to your car," came the voice from the opposite end of the space.

"Not a chance," Keller replied into the glare of Sam's headlamps.

A brief impasse occurred. Then Sam came forward through the light. He stopped a few feet away from Keller, looked down, and frowned.

"I need to see it one more time."

"Then I suggest you remove the plastic wrapper. But do it carefully, Sam. If anything happens to that painting, I'm going to hold you responsible."

Sam crouched and removed the canvas from the bag. Then he turned the image toward the headlamps of his car and squinted at the brushwork and the signature.

"Well?" asked Keller.

Sam looked at the fingerprints along the sides of the stretcher bars, then at the museum markings on the back. "In a moment," he said quietly. "In a moment."

Keller's car emerged from the warehouse at 11:40. The gate was open by the time he arrived. He turned to the right and sped past the bench where Gabriel sat. Gabriel ignored him; he was watching the taillights of a BMW moving off along the avenue François Mitterrand. He looked down at his BlackBerry and smiled. They were on, he thought. They were definitely on.

The red light of the beacon blinked with the regularity of a heartbeat. It floated through the remaining Paris suburbs and then raced eastward along the A4 toward Reims. Gabriel followed a kilometer behind, and Keller followed a kilometer behind Gabriel. They spoke on the phone only once, a brief conversation during which Keller confirmed that the deal had gone through without a hitch. Sam had the painting; Keller had Sam's money. It was hidden in the trunk of the car, inside the trash bag that Gabriel had placed around the copy of *Sunflowers*. All except for a single bundle of hundred-euro notes, which was tucked into the pocket of Keller's coat.

"Why is it in your pocket?" asked Gabriel.

"Gas money," replied Keller.

One hundred and twenty kilometers separated the eastern suburbs of Paris from Reims, a distance that Sam covered in little more than an hour. Just beyond the city, the red light came suddenly to a stop along the A4. Gabriel quickly closed the gap and saw Sam filling his car with gas at a roadside service station. He immediately rang Keller and told him to pull over; then he waited until Sam was once again on the road. Within a few moments, the three cars had resumed their original formation: Sam in the lead, Gabriel following a kilometer behind Sam, and Keller following a kilometer behind Gabriel.

From Reims, they pushed farther eastward, through Verdun and Metz. Then the A4 bent to the south and carried them to Strasbourg, the capital of the Alsace region of France and the seat of the European Parliament. At the edge of the city flowed the gray-green waters of the Rhine. A few minutes after sunrise, 25 million euros in cash and a copy of a stolen masterpiece by Vincent van Gogh crossed undetected into Germany.

The first city on the German side of the border
was Kehl, and beyond Kehl was the A5 autobahn.
Sam followed it as far as Karlsruhe; then he turned
onto the A8 and headed toward Stuttgart. By the
time he reached the southeastern suburbs, the
morning rush was at its worst. He crawled into
the city along the Hauptstätterstrasse and made
his way to Stuttgart-Mitte, a pleasant district of
offices and shops at the heart of the sprawling
metropolis. Gabriel sensed that Sam was nearing his final destination, so he closed to within a
few hundred meters. And then the one thing happened that he expected least.

The blinking red light vanished from his screen.

According to Gabriel's BlackBerry, the beacon
transmitted its dying electronic impulse at Böheim-
strasse 8. The address corresponded to a gray stucco
hotel that looked as though it had been imported
from East Berlin during the darkest days of the
Cold War. At the back of the hotel, reached by an
alleyway, was a public parking garage. The BMW
was on the lowest level, in a corner where the overhead light had been smashed. Sam was slumped over
the wheel, eyes frozen open, blood and brain tissue
spattered across the inside of the windshield. And
Sunflowers, oil on canvas, 95 by 73 centimeters, by
Gabriel Allon, was gone.

25

GENEVA

THEY LEFT STUTTGART by the same route they had entered it and crossed back into France at Strasbourg. Keller headed for Corsica; Gabriel, for Geneva. He arrived in midafternoon and immediately rang Christoph Bittel from a public phone along the lakeshore. The secret policeman didn't sound pleased to hear from him again so soon. He was even less pleased when Gabriel explained why he was back in town.

"Out of the question," he said.

"Then I suppose I'll have to tell the world about all those stolen paintings I found in that vault."

"So much for the new Gabriel Allon."

"What time should I expect you, Bittel?"

"I'll see what I can do."

It took Bittel an hour to clear his desk at NDB headquarters and another two hours to make the drive from Bern down to Geneva. Gabriel was waiting for him on a busy street corner along the rue du Rhône. It was a few minutes after six. Tidy Swiss moneymen were spilling from the handsome office blocks; pretty girls and slick foreigners were streaming into the glittering cafés. It was all very orderly. Even mass murderers minded their manners when they came to Geneva.

"You were about to tell me why I'm supposed to open that safe for you," Bittel said as he eased back into the evening traffic with his usual overabundance of caution.

"Because the operation I'm running hit a snag, and for the moment I have nowhere else to turn."

"What kind of snag?"

"A dead body."

"Where?"

Gabriel hesitated.

"Where?" asked Bittel again.

"Stuttgart," replied Gabriel.

"I suppose it was that Arab who was shot in the head this morning in the city center?"

"Who said he was an Arab?"

"The BfV."

The BfV was Germany's internal security service. It maintained close relations with its Alemannic brethren in Bern.

"How much do they have on him?" asked Gabriel.

"Almost nothing, which is why they reached out to us. It seems the killers took his wallet after they shot him."

"That wasn't all they took."

"Were you responsible for his death?"

"I'm not sure."

"Let me put it to you this way, Allon. Did you put a gun to his head and pull the trigger?"

"Don't be ridiculous."

"It's not such a far-fetched question. After all, you do have something of a track record when it comes to dead bodies on European soil."

Gabriel made no reply.

"Do you know the name of the man who was inside the car at the time?"

"He called himself Sam, but I have a feeling his real name was Samir."

"Last name?"

"I never caught it."

"Passport?"

"He spoke French very well. If I had to guess, he was from the Levant."

"Lebanon?"

"Maybe. Or maybe Syria."

"Why was he killed?"

"I'm not sure."

"You can do better than that, Allon."

"It's possible he was in possession of a painting that looked a great deal like *Sunflowers* by Vincent van Gogh."

"The one that was stolen from Amsterdam?"

"Borrowed," said Gabriel.

"Who painted the forgery?"

"I did."

"Why did Sam have it?"

"I sold it to him for twenty-five million euros."

Bittel swore beneath his breath.

"You asked, Bittel."

"Where's the painting?"

"Which painting?"

"The *real* van Gogh," snapped Bittel.

"It's in safe hands."

"And the money?"

"Even safer hands."

"Why did you steal a van Gogh and sell a copy to an Arab named Sam?"

"Because I'm looking for a Caravaggio."

"For whom?"

"The Italians."

"Why is an Israeli intelligence officer looking for a painting for the Italians?"

"Because he finds it hard to tell people no."

"And if I get you into that safe? What do you expect to find?"

"To be honest with you, Bittel, I haven't a clue."

Bittel exhaled heavily and reached for his phone.

He made two calls in rapid succession. The first was to his shapely friend at the Freeport. The second was to a locksmith who occasionally did favors for the NDB in the Geneva area. The woman was waiting at the gate when they arrived; the locksmith appeared an hour after that. His name was Zimmer. He had a round, soft face and the unblinking gaze of a stuffed animal. His hand was so cool and tender that Gabriel released it quickly for fear of injuring it.

He had in his possession a heavy rectangular case of black leather, which he clutched tightly as he followed Bittel and Gabriel through the outer door of Jack Bradshaw's vault. If he was aware of the paintings, he gave no sign of it; he had eyes only for the small floor safe standing next to the desk. It had been built by a German manufacturer from

Cologne. Zimmer was frowning, as though he had been hoping for something a bit more challenging.

The locksmith, like the art restorer, did not like people watching him while he worked. As a result, Gabriel and Bittel were forced to confine themselves in the interior room of the vault that Yves Morel had used as his clandestine studio. They sat on the floor, backs resting against the wall, legs outstretched. It was obvious from the sounds radiating through the open door that Zimmer was using a technique known as weak-point drilling. The air smelled of warm metal. It reminded Gabriel of the smell of a recently fired gun. He looked at his wristwatch and frowned.

"How long is this going to take?" he asked.

"Some safes are easier than others."

"That's why I've always preferred a carefully placed charge of plastic explosive. Semtex is a great equalizer."

Bittel pulled out his phone and scrolled through his e-mail inbox; Gabriel picked absently at the paint on Yves Morel's palette: *ocher, gold, crimson* . . . Finally, an hour after Zimmer commenced work, there came a heavy metallic thump from the next room. The locksmith appeared in the doorway, clutching his black leather bag, and nodded once to Bittel. "I believe I can find my way out," he said. And then he was gone.

Gabriel and Bittel rose to their feet and walked into the next room. The door of the safe was slightly ajar, an inch, no more. Gabriel reached for it, but Bittel stopped him.

"I'll do it," he said.

He motioned for Gabriel to step back. Then he opened the door of the safe and peered into the interior. It was empty except for a white letter-size envelope. Bittel removed it and read the name written across the front.

"What is it?" asked Gabriel.

"It appears to be a letter."

"To whom?"

Bittel held it toward Gabriel and said, "You."

It was more like a memorandum than a letter, an after-action field report written by a fallen spy with a conscience made guilty by treachery. Gabriel read it twice, once while still in Jack Bradshaw's vault, and a second time while seated in the departure lounge of Geneva International Airport. His flight was called a few minutes after nine o'clock, first in French, then in English, and, finally, in Hebrew. The sound of his native language quickened his pulse. He slipped the letter into his overnight bag, rose, and boarded the plane.

PART THREE

THE OPEN WINDOW

26

KING SAUL BOULEVARD, TEL AVIV

THE OFFICE BUILDING that stood at the far end of King Saul Boulevard was drab, featureless, and, best of all, anonymous. No emblem hung over its entrance, no brass lettering proclaimed the identity of its occupant. In fact, there was nothing at all to suggest it was the headquarters of one of the world's most feared and respected intelligence services. A closer inspection of the structure, however, would have revealed the existence of a building within a building, one with its own power supply, its own water and sewer lines, and its own secure communications system. Employees carried two keys. One opened an unmarked door in the lobby; the other operated the lift. Those who committed the unpardonable sin of losing one or both of their keys were banished to the Judean Wilderness, never to be seen or heard from again.

There were some employees who were too senior, or whose work was too sensitive, to show their faces in the lobby. They entered the building "black" through the underground parking garage, as Gabriel did thirty minutes after his flight from Geneva

touched down at Ben-Gurion Airport. His motorcade included an escort vehicle filled with a heavily
armed security team. He supposed it was a sign of
things to come.

Two of the security agents followed him into the
elevator, which shot him to the top floor of the building. From the vestibule he made his way through a
cipher-protected door into an anteroom where a
woman in her late thirties sat behind a modern desk
with a gleaming black surface. The desk had only a
lamp and a secure multiline phone; the woman had
very long suntanned legs. Inside King Saul Boulevard she was known as the Iron Dome because of her
matchless ability to shoot down unwanted requests
for a moment with the boss. Her real name was Orit.

"He's in a meeting," she said, glancing at the
red light glowing over the boss's impressive double
door. "Have a seat. He won't be long."

"Does he know I'm in the building?"

"He knows."

Gabriel lowered himself onto what was quite possibly the most uncomfortable couch in all of Israel
and stared at the red light blazing above the doorway. Then he looked at Orit, who smiled back at
him uneasily.

"Can I get you anything?" she asked.

"A battering ram," replied Gabriel.

Finally, the light changed from red to green. Gabriel rose quickly and slipped into the office as the
participants of the now-adjourned meeting were
filing out a second doorway. Two of them he recognized. One was Rimona Stern, the chief of the Office's Iran nuclear program. The other was Mikhail

Abramov, a field agent and gunman who had worked closely with Gabriel on a number of high-profile operations. The suit he was wearing suggested a recent promotion.

When the door closed, Gabriel turned slowly to face the room's only other occupant. He was standing next to a large desk of smoked glass, an open file folder in his hand. He wore a gray suit that seemed a size too small and a white shirt with a fashionably high collar that left the impression his head was bolted to his powerful shoulders. His spectacles were of the small, rimless variety worn by German business executives who wish to appear youthful and trendy. His hair, or what remained of it, was gray stubble.

"Since when does Mikhail attend meetings in the chief's office?" asked Gabriel.

"Since I promoted him," replied Uzi Navot.

"To what?"

"Deputy chief of Special Ops." Navot lowered the file and smiled insincerely. "Is it all right if I make personnel moves, Gabriel? After all, I'm still the chief for another year."

"I had plans for him."

"What sort of plans?"

"I was actually going to put him in charge of Special Ops."

"Mikhail? He's not ready, not by a long shot."

"He'll be fine, so long as he has an experienced operational planner looking over his shoulder."

"Someone like you?"

Gabriel was silent.

"And what about me?" asked Navot. "Have you decided what you're going to do yet?"

"That's entirely up to you."

"Obviously not."

Navot dropped the file folder onto his desk and pressed a button on his control panel that sent the venetian blinds falling slowly over the floor-to-ceiling bulletproof windows. He stood there for a moment in silence, imprisoned by bars of shadow. Gabriel glimpsed an unappealing portrait of his own future, a gray man in a gray cage.

"I have to admit," Navot said, "I'm deeply envious of you. Egypt is sliding into civil war, al-Qaeda is in control of a swath of land extending from Fallujah to the Mediterranean, and one of the bloodiest conflicts in modern history is raging on our northern border. And yet you have the time to go chasing after a stolen masterpiece for the Italian government."

"It wasn't my idea, Uzi."

"You could have at least shown me the courtesy of seeking my approval when the Carabinieri came to you."

"Would you have given it?"

"Of course not."

Navot walked slowly past his long executive conference table to his cozy executive seating area. The world's television networks played silently on his video wall; the world's newspapers were arrayed neatly on his coffee table.

"The European police have been quite busy of late," he said. "A murdered British expat in Lake Como, a stolen masterpiece by van Gogh, and now this." He picked up a copy of *Die Welt* and held it up for Gabriel to see. "A dead Arab in the middle of Stuttgart. Three seemingly unconnected events with one thing in common." Navot allowed the newspaper to drop onto the table. "Gabriel Allon, the future chief of Israel's secret intelligence service."

"Two things, actually."

"What's the second?"

"LXR Investments of Luxembourg."

"Who owns LXR?"

"The worst man in the world."

"Is he on the Office payroll?"

"No, Uzi," said Gabriel, smiling. "Not yet."

***

Navot knew the broad outlines of Gabriel's search for the missing Caravaggio, for he had watched it from a distance: airline reservations, credit card expenditures, border crossings, requests for safe properties, news accounts of a vanished masterpiece. Now, seated in the office that would soon be his, Gabriel completed the picture, beginning with General Ferrari's summons in Venice and ending with the death of a man called Sam in Stuttgart—a man who had just paid twenty-five million euros for *Sunflowers*, oil on canvas, 95 by 73 centimeters, by Gabriel Allon. Then he held up the three pages of the letter that Jack Bradshaw had left for him in the Geneva Freeport.

"Sam's real name was Samir Basara. Bradshaw first met him when he was working in Beirut. Samir was a classic hustler. Drugs, weapons, girls, all the things that made life interesting in a place like Beirut in the eighties. But it turns out Samir wasn't actually Lebanese. Samir was from Syria, and he was working for Syrian intelligence."

"Was he still working for them when he was killed?"

"Absolutely," replied Gabriel.

"Doing what?"

"Buying stolen art."

"From Jack Bradshaw?"

Gabriel nodded. "Samir and Bradshaw renewed their relationship fourteen months ago over lunch in Milan. Samir had a business proposition. He said he had a client, a wealthy businessman from the Middle East who was interested in acquiring paintings. Within a few weeks, Bradshaw used his contacts in the dark corners of the art world to secure a Rembrandt and a Monet, both of which happened to be stolen. That didn't bother Samir. In fact, he rather liked it. He gave Bradshaw five million dollars and told him to find more."

"How did he pay for the paintings?"

"He funneled the money into Bradshaw's company through something called LXR Investments of Luxembourg."

"Who owns LXR Investments?"

"I'm getting to that," said Gabriel.

"Why did Sam want stolen paintings?"

"I'm getting to that, too." Gabriel looked down at the letter. "At this point Jack Bradshaw went on something of a shopping spree for his new money-eyed client—a couple of Renoirs, a Matisse, a Corot that was stolen from the Montreal Museum of Fine Arts back in 1972. He also acquired several important Italian paintings that weren't supposed to leave the country. Samir still wasn't satisfied. He said his client wanted something big. That's when Bradshaw suggested the holy grail of missing paintings."

"The Caravaggio?"

Gabriel nodded.

"Where was it?"

"Still in Sicily, in the hands of the Cosa Nostra. Bradshaw went to Palermo and negotiated the deal. After all these years, the mafiosi were actually glad to be rid of it. Bradshaw smuggled it into Switzerland in a load of carpets. Needless to say, the altarpiece wasn't in great condition when it arrived. He accepted five million euros as down payment from Samir and hired a French forger to make the *Nativity* presentable again. But something happened before he could complete the sale."

"What's that?"

"He figured out who was really buying the paintings."

"Who was it?"

Before answering, Gabriel returned to a question Navot had posed a few minutes earlier: Why was Samir Basara's wealthy client in the market for stolen paintings? To answer it, Gabriel first explained the four basic categories of art thieves: the penniless art lover, the incompetent loser, the professional, and the organized criminal. The organized criminal, he said, was responsible for most major thefts. Sometimes he had a buyer waiting, but often stolen paintings ended up being used as a form of underworld cash, traveler's checks for the criminal class. A Monet, for example, might be used as collateral for a shipment of Russian arms; a Picasso, for Turkish heroin. Eventually, someone along the chain of possession would decide to cash in, usually with the help of a knowledgeable fence like Jack Bradshaw. A painting worth $200 million on the legitimate market would be worth $20 million on the dirty market. Twenty million that could never be traced, added Gabriel. Twenty million that could never be frozen by the governments of the United States and the European Union.

"Do you see where I'm going with this, Uzi?"

"Who is it?" Navot asked again.

"He's a man who's been presiding over a rather messy civil war, a man who's used systematic torture, indiscriminate artillery barrages, and chemical weapons attacks against his own people. He saw Hosni Mubarak put into a cage and watched Muammar Gaddafi being lynched by a bloodthirsty mob. As a result, he's concerned about what might happen to him if he falls, which is why he asked Samir Basara to prepare a little nest egg for him and his family."

"Are you saying Jack Bradshaw was selling stolen paintings to the president of Syria?"

Gabriel looked up at the images flickering across Navot's video wall. The regime had just shelled a rebel-held neighborhood in Damascus. The number of dead was incalculable.

"The Syrian ruler and his clan are worth billions," said Navot.

"True," replied Gabriel. "But the Americans and the EU are freezing his assets and the assets of his closest aides wherever they can find them. Even Switzerland has frozen hundreds of millions in Syrian assets."

"But most of the fortune is still out there somewhere."

"For now," said Gabriel.

"Why not gold bars or vaults filled with cash? Why paintings?"

"I assume he has gold and cash, too. After all, as any investment adviser will tell you, diversity is the key to long-term success. But if I were the one advising the Syrian president," Gabriel added, "I'd tell him to invest in assets that are easy to conceal and transport."

"Paintings?" asked Navot.

Gabriel nodded. "If he buys a painting for five million on the black market, he can sell it for roughly the same price, minus commission fees for the middleman, of course. It's a rather small price to pay for tens of millions in untraceable cash."

"Ingenious."

"No one ever accused them of being stupid, just ruthless and brutal."

"Who killed Samir Basara?"

"If I had to guess, it was someone who knew him." Gabriel paused, then added, "Someone who was sitting in the backseat of the car when he pulled the trigger."

"Someone from Syrian intelligence?"

"That's the way it usually works."

"Why did they kill him?"

"Maybe he knew too much. Or maybe they were upset with him."

"For what?"

"Letting Jack Bradshaw find out too much about the personal finances of the ruling family."

"How much did he know?"

Gabriel held up the letter and said, "A great deal, Uzi."

27

KING SAUL BOULEVARD, TEL AVIV

WHAT DO YOU suppose Bradshaw did with the Caravaggio?"

"He must have taken it back to his villa on Lake Como," replied Gabriel. "Then he asked Oliver Dimbleby to come to Italy to have a look at his collection. It was a ruse, a clever operation conceived by a former British spy. What he really wanted was for Oliver to deliver a message to Julian Isherwood, who would in turn deliver it to me. But it didn't work out as planned. Oliver sent Julian to Como instead. And by the time he arrived, Bradshaw was dead."

"And the Caravaggio was gone?"

Gabriel nodded.

"Why did Bradshaw want to tell *you* about the connection to the Syrian president?"

"I suppose he thought I would handle the matter with discretion."

"Meaning?"

"I wouldn't tell the British or Italian police that he was a smuggler and a fence," answered Gabriel. "He was hoping to meet with me face-to-face. But he took the added step of putting everything he knew in writing and locking it away in the Freeport."

"Along with a stash of stolen paintings?"

Gabriel nodded.

"Why the sudden change of heart? Why not take the ruler's blood money and laugh all the way to the bank?"

"Nicole Devereaux."

Navot narrowed his eyes thoughtfully. "Why is that name familiar to me?"

"She was the AFP photographer who was kidnapped and killed in Beirut in the eighties," said Gabriel. Then he told Navot the rest of the story: the love affair, the recruitment by the KGB, the half a million in a Swiss bank account. "Bradshaw never forgave himself for Nicole's death," he added. "And he surely never forgave the Syrian regime for killing her."

Navot was silent for a moment. "Your friend Jack Bradshaw did many foolish things during his lifetime," he said finally. "But the dumbest thing he ever did was accepting five million euros from Syria's ruling family for a painting he failed to deliver. There's only one thing the family hates more than disloyalty, and that's people who try to take their money."

Navot watched the images playing out on the video wall. "If you ask me," he said, "that's what this entire exercise in human depravity is all about. A hundred and fifty thousand dead and millions left homeless. And for what? Why is the ruling family hanging on for dear life? Why are they murdering on an industrial scale? For their faith? For the Syrian ideal? There is no Syrian ideal. Quite frankly, there is no Syria any longer. And yet the killing goes on for one reason, and one reason only."

"Money," said Gabriel.

Navot nodded slowly.

"You sound as though you have special insight into the Syria situation, Uzi."

"I happen to be married to the country's preeminent expert on Syria and the Baathist movement." He paused, then added, "But then, you already knew that."

Navot rose, walked over to the credenza, and drew a cup of coffee from the pump-action thermos. Gabriel noted the absence of heavy cream or Viennese butter cookies, two things Navot was powerless to resist. He drank his coffee black now, with no accompaniment other than a white pellet of sweetener, which he fired into his cup from a plastic dispenser.

"Since when do you take cyanide in your coffee, Uzi?"

"Bella's trying to wean me off sugar. Caffeine is next."

"I can't imagine trying to do this job without caffeine."

"You'll know soon enough."

Navot smiled in spite of himself and retook his seat. Gabriel was watching the video screen. The body of a child—boy or girl, it was impossible to tell—was being pulled from the rubble. A woman was wailing. A bearded man was screaming for vengeance.

"How much is there?" he asked.

"Money?"

Gabriel nodded.

"Ten billion is the number that gets thrown about in the press," Navot replied, "but we think the actual number is much higher. And it's all controlled by Kemel al-Farouk." Navot gave Gabriel a sidelong glance and asked, "Know the name?"

"Syria isn't my area of expertise, Uzi."

"It will be soon." Navot gave another faint smile before continuing. "Kemel isn't actually a member of the ruling family, but he's been working in the family business his entire life. He started out as a bodyguard for the ruler's father. Kemel took a bullet for the old man back in the late seventies, and the ruler's father never forgot that. He gave Kemel a big job at the Mukhabarat, where he earned a reputation as a vicious interrogator of political prisoners. He used to nail members of the Muslim Brotherhood to the wall for fun."

"Where is he now?"

"His official title is deputy minister of state for foreign affairs, but in many respects he's running the country and the war. The ruler never makes a decision without first talking to Kemel. And, perhaps more important, Kemel is the one who looks after the money. He's parked some of the fortune in Moscow and Tehran, but there's no way he'd trust it all to the Russians and the Iranians. We think he's got someone working for him in Western Europe who's been busy hiding assets. What we *don't* know," said Navot, "is who that person is or where he's hiding the money."

"Thanks to Jack Bradshaw, we now know that some of it is in LXR Investments. And we can use LXR as a window into the rest of the family's holdings."

"And then what?"

Gabriel was silent. Navot watched another body being pulled from the rubble in Damascus.

"It's hard for Israelis to watch scenes like this," he said after a moment. "It makes us uneasy. It brings back bad memories. Our natural instinct is to kill the monster before the monster can do any more harm. But the Office and the IDF have concluded it is better to leave the monster in place, at least for now, because the alternative could be worse. And the Americans and Europeans have reached the same conclusion, despite all the happy talk about a negotiated settlement. No one wants Syria to fall into the hands of al-Qaeda, but that's what will happen if the ruling family goes."

"Much of Syria is already controlled by al-Qaeda."

"True," agreed Navot. "And the contagion is spreading. A few weeks ago, a delegation of European intelligence chiefs went to Damascus with a list of their Muslim citizens who've gone to Syria to join the jihad. I could have given them a few more names, but I wasn't invited to the party."

"What a surprise."

"It's probably better I didn't go. The last time I was in Damascus, I traveled under a different name."

"Who?"

"Vincent Laffont."

"The travel writer?"

Navot nodded.

"He was always one of my favorites," Gabriel said.

"Mine, too." Navot placed his coffee cup on the

table. "The Office has never been shy about committing the odd crime in the service of an operation that was moral and just. But if we run roughshod over the international banking system, the repercussions could be disastrous."

"The Syrian ruling family didn't come by those assets honestly, Uzi. They've been looting the economy for two generations now."

"That doesn't mean you can just steal them."

"No," said Gabriel with feigned contrition. "That would be wrong."

"So what are you suggesting?"

"We freeze them."

"How?"

Gabriel smiled and said, "Office style."

"What about our friends at Langley?" Navot asked when Gabriel had finished explaining.

"What about them?"

"We can't launch an operation like this without the support of the Agency."

"If we tell the Agency, the Agency will tell the White House. And then it will end up on the front page of the *New York Times*."

Navot smiled. "All we need now is the approval of the prime minister and the money to run the operation."

"We already have money, Uzi. Lots of money."

"The twenty-five million you made on the sale of the forged van Gogh?"

Gabriel nodded. "That's the beauty of this operation," he said. "It funds itself."

"Where's the money now?"

"It might be in the trunk of Christopher Keller's car."

"In Corsica."

"I'm afraid so."

"I'll send a *bodel* to pick it up."

"The great Don Orsati doesn't deal with couriers, Uzi. He would find it terribly insulting."

"What are you suggesting?"

"I'll collect the money as soon as I have the operation up and running, though it's possible I'll have to leave behind a small payment of tribute for the don."

"How small?"

"Two million should keep him happy."

"That's a lot of money."

"One hand washes the other, and both hands wash the face."

"Is that a Jewish proverb?"

"Probably, Uzi."

Which left only the composition of Gabriel's operational team. Rimona Stern and Mikhail Abramov were nonnegotiable, he said. So were Dina Sarid, Yossi Gavish, and Yaakov Rossman.

"You can't possibly have Yaakov at a time like this," objected Navot.

"Why not?"

"Because Yaakov is the one who's tracking all the missiles and other deadly goodies that are flowing from the Syrians to their friends in Hezbollah."

"Yaakov can walk and chew gum at the same time."

"Who else?"

"I need Eli Lavon."

"He's still digging beneath the Western Wall."

"By tomorrow afternoon, he's going to be digging into something else."

"Is that all?"

"No," said Gabriel. "There's one other person I need to do an op like this."

"Who?"

"The country's preeminent expert on Syria and the Baathist movement."

Navot smiled. "Maybe you should take a couple of bodyguards, just to be on the safe side."

28

PETAH TIKVA, ISRAEL

THE NAVOTS LIVED on the eastern fringes of Petah Tikva, on a quiet street where the houses were tucked away behind walls of concrete and bougainvillea. There was a call button next to the metal gate, which buzzed unanswered when pressed by Gabriel. He stared directly into the lens of the security camera and pressed it again. This time, the intercom emitted the sound of a woman's voice.

"Who's there?"

"It's me, Bella. Open the gate."

There was another silence, fifteen seconds, maybe longer, before the lock released with a thump. As the gate yielded, the house appeared, a cubist structure with large shatter-resistant windows and a secure communications aerial sprouting from the roof. Bella stood in the shade of the portico, her arms folded defensively. She wore white silk trousers and a yellow blouse belted at her slender waist. Her dark hair looked newly colored and styled. According to the Office rumor mill, she had a standing appointment each morning at Tel Aviv's most exclusive salon.

"You have a lot of nerve showing your face in this house, Gabriel."

"Come on, Bella. Let's try to be civil."

She held her ground another moment before stepping aside and, with an indifferent movement of her hand, inviting him to enter. She had decorated the rooms of the house as she had decorated her husband: gray, sleek, modern. Gabriel followed her through a kitchen of high-gloss chrome and polished black granite and onto the rear terrace where a light Israeli lunch had been laid. The table was in shadow, but in the garden the sun blazed brightly. It was all pools and gurgling fountains. Gabriel remembered suddenly that Bella had always adored Japan.

"I love what you've done with the place, Bella."

"Sit down," was all she said in response.

Gabriel lowered himself onto a cushioned garden chair. Bella poured a tall glass of citrus juice and placed it decorously in front of him.

"Have you given any thought to where you and Chiara are going to live when you become chief?" she asked.

He couldn't tell whether her question was sincere or malicious. He decided to answer it honestly. "Chiara thinks we need to live close to King Saul Boulevard," he said, "but I'd rather stay in Jerusalem."

"It's a long drive."

"I won't be the one doing the driving."

Her face tightened.

"I'm sorry, Bella. I didn't mean that the way it sounded."

She didn't respond directly. "I've never really liked it up there in Jerusalem. It's a little too close to God for my taste. I like it down here in my little secular suburb."

A silence fell between them. They both knew the real reason Gabriel preferred Jerusalem to Tel Aviv.

"I'm sorry I never sent you and Chiara a note about the pregnancy." She managed a brief smile. "God knows the two of you deserve some happiness after everything you've been through."

Gabriel nodded and murmured something appropriate. Bella had never sent a note, he thought, because her anger wouldn't allow it. She had a vindictive streak. It was one of her most endearing qualities.

"I think we should talk, Bella."

"I thought we were."

"Really talk," he said.

"It might be better if we behaved like characters in one of those drawing-room mysteries on the BBC. Otherwise, I'm liable to say something I'll regret later."

"There's a reason why those programs are never set in Israel. We don't talk like that."

"Maybe we should."

She picked up a plate and began filling it with food for Gabriel.

"I'm not hungry, Bella."

She dropped the plate on the table. "I'm angry with you, damn it."

"I got that impression."

"Why are you stealing Uzi's job?"

"I'm not."

"What would you call it?"

"I didn't have a choice in the matter."

"You could have told them no."

"I tried. It didn't work."

"You should have tried harder."

"It wasn't my fault, Bella."

"I know, Gabriel. Nothing's ever your fault."

She looked out at the waterworks in her garden. They seemed to momentarily calm her.

"I'll never forget the first time I saw you," she said at last. "You were walking alone along a hallway inside King Saul Boulevard, not long after Tunis. You looked exactly the way you look now, those green eyes, those gray temples. You were like an angel, Israel's angel of vengeance. Everyone loved you. Uzi worshipped you."

"Let's not get carried away, Bella."

She acted as though she hadn't heard him. "And then Vienna happened," she resumed after a moment. "It was a cataclysm, a disaster of biblical proportions."

"We've all lost loved ones, Bella. We've all grieved."

"That's true, Gabriel. But Vienna was different. You were never the same after Vienna. None of us were." She paused, then added, "Especially Shamron."

Gabriel followed Bella's gaze into the glare of the garden, but for a moment he was striding across a sun-bleached courtyard at the Bezalel Academy of Art and Design in Jerusalem. It was September 1972, a few days after the murder of eleven Israeli athletes and coaches at the Munich Olympics. Seemingly from nowhere there appeared a small iron bar of a man with hideous black spectacles and teeth like a steel trap. The man didn't offer a name, for none was necessary. He was the one they spoke of only in whispers. The one who had stolen the secrets that led to Israel's lightning victory in the Six-Day War. The one who had plucked Adolf Eichmann, managing director of the Holocaust, from an Argentine street corner.

Shamron . . .

"Ari blamed himself for what happened to you in Vienna," Bella was saying. "And he never quite forgave himself, either. He treated you like a son after that. He let you come and go as you pleased. But he never gave up hope that one day you would come home and take control of his beloved Office."

"Do you know how many times I turned the job down?"

"Enough so that Shamron eventually gave it to Uzi. He got the job as a consolation prize."

"Actually, I was the one who suggested Uzi become the next chief."

"As though the job was yours to bestow." She smiled bitterly. "Did Uzi ever tell you that I advised him not to take the job?"

"No, Bella. He never mentioned it."

"I always knew it would end like this. You should have exited the stage gracefully and stayed in Europe. But what did you do? You inserted a shipment of compromised centrifuges into the Iranian nuclear supply chain and destroyed four secret enrichment facilities."

"That operation occurred on Uzi's watch."

"But it was *your* operation. Everyone at King Saul Boulevard knows it was yours, and so does everyone at Kaplan Street."

Kaplan Street was the location of the prime minister's office. By all accounts, Bella was an all-too-frequent visitor. Gabriel always suspected her influence at King Saul Boulevard went beyond the furnishings in her husband's office.

"Uzi's been a good chief," she said. "A damn good chief. He had only one fault. He wasn't you, Gabriel. He'll *never* be you. And for that, he's being thrown to the side of the road."

"Not if I have anything to say about it."

"Haven't you done enough already?"

From inside the house came the ringing of a telephone. Bella showed no interest in answering it.

"Why are you here?" she asked.

"I want to talk to you about Uzi's future."

"Thanks to you, he doesn't have one."

"Bella . . ."

She refused to be mollified, not yet. "If you have something to say about Uzi's future, you should probably talk to Uzi."

"I thought it would be more productive if I went over his head."

"Don't try to flatter me, Gabriel."

"I wouldn't dream of it."

She clicked the nail of her forefinger against the tabletop. It had a new coat of polish.

"He told me about the conversation you had in London when you were looking for that kidnapped girl. Needless to say, I didn't think much of your proposal."

"Why not?"

"Because there's no precedent for it. Once a chief's term is over, the chief is shown gently into the night, never to be heard from again."

"Tell that to Shamron."

"Shamron is different."

"So am I."

"What exactly are you proposing?"

"We run the Office together. I'll be the chief, and Uzi will be my deputy."

"It'll never work."

"Why not?"

"Because it will leave the impression that you're not quite up to the job."

"No one thinks that."

"Appearances matter."

"You have me confused with someone else, Bella."

"Who's that?"

"Someone who cares about appearances."

"And if he agrees?"

"He'll have an office next door to mine. He'll be involved in every key decision, every important operation."

"What about his salary?"

"He'll keep his full salary, not to mention his car and his security detail."

"Why?" she asked. "Why are you doing this?"

"Because I need him, Bella." He paused, then added, "You, too."

"Me?"

"I want you to come back to the Office."

"When?"

"Tomorrow morning, ten o'clock. Uzi and I are going to run an op against the Syrians. We need your help."

"What kind of op?"

When Gabriel told her, she smiled sadly. "It's too

bad Uzi didn't think of that," she said. "He might still be the chief."

They spent the next hour in Bella's garden negotiating the terms of her return to King Saul Boulevard. Afterward, she saw him outside and into the back of his official car.

"It looks good on you," she said through the open door.

"What's that, Bella?"

She smiled and said, "I'll see you in the morning, Gabriel." Then she turned away and was gone. A bodyguard closed the car door; another climbed into the front passenger seat. Gabriel realized suddenly he was unarmed. He sat there for a moment debating where to go next. Then he glanced into the rearview mirror and gave the driver an address in West Jerusalem. He had one more piece of unpleasant business to attend to before going home. He had to tell a ghost he was going to be a father again.

29

JERUSALEM

T HE TINY CIRCULAR drive of the Mount Herzl Psychiatric Hospital vibrated beneath the weight of Gabriel's three-vehicle motorcade. He alighted from the back of his limousine and, after a terse word with the head of his security detail, entered the hospital alone. Waiting in the lobby was a bearded, rabbinical-looking doctor in his late fifties. He was smiling pleasantly, despite the fact that, as usual, he had been given little warning of Gabriel's pending arrival. He extended his hand and looked out at the commotion in the normally quiet entrance of Israel's most private facility for the long-term mentally disabled.

"It seems your life is about to change again," said the doctor.

"In more ways than one," replied Gabriel.

"For the better, I hope."

Gabriel nodded and then told the doctor about the pregnancy. The doctor smiled, but only for a moment. He had witnessed Gabriel's long struggle over whether to remarry. Fatherhood, he knew, was going to be a mixed blessing.

"And twins, no less. Well," the doctor added, remembering to smile again, "you're certainly—"

"I need to tell her," Gabriel said, cutting him off. "I've put it off long enough."

"It's not necessary."

"It is."

"She won't understand, not fully."

"I know."

The doctor knew better than to pursue the matter further. "It might be better if I stay with you," he said. "For both your sakes."

"Thank you," answered Gabriel, "but I have to do it alone."

The doctor turned without a word and led Gabriel along a corridor of Jerusalem limestone, to a common room where a few of the patients were staring blankly at a television. A pair of large windows overlooked a walled garden. Outside, a woman sat alone in the shade of a stone pine, with the stillness of a gravestone.

"How is she?" asked Gabriel.

"She misses you. It's been a long time since you've come to see her."

"It's hard."

"I understand."

They stood for a moment at the window, not speaking, not moving.

"There's something you should know," the doctor said finally. "She never stopped loving you, even after the divorce."

"Is that supposed to make me feel better?"

"No," said the doctor. "But you deserve to know the truth."

"So does she."

Another silence.

"Twins, eh?"

"Twins."

"Boy or girl?"

"One of each."

"Maybe you could let her spend a little time with them."

"First things first, Doctor."

"Yes," said the doctor as Gabriel entered the garden alone. "First things first."

***

She was seated in her wheelchair with the twisted remnants of her hands resting in her lap. Her hair, once long and dark like Chiara's, was now cut institutional short and shot with gray. Gabriel kissed the cool, firm scar tissue of her cheek before lowering himself onto the bench next to her. She stared sightlessly into the garden, unaware of his presence. She was getting older, he thought. They were all getting older.

"Look at the snow, Gabriel," she said suddenly. "Isn't it beautiful?"

He looked at the sun burning in a cloudless sky. "Yes, Leah," he said absently. "It's beautiful."

"The snow absolves Vienna of its sins," she said after a moment. "The snow falls on Vienna while the missiles rain down on Tel Aviv."

They were some of the last words Leah had spoken to him the night of the bombing in Vienna. She suffered from a particularly acute combination of psychotic depression and post-traumatic stress disorder. At times, she experienced moments of lucidity, but for the most part she remained a prisoner of the past. Vienna played ceaselessly in her mind like a loop of videotape that she was unable to pause: the last meal they shared together, their last kiss, the fire that killed their only child and burned the flesh from Leah's body. Her life had shrunk to five minutes; and she had been reliving it, over and over again, for more than twenty years.

"I thought you'd forgotten about me, Gabriel."

Her head turned slowly, and for now there was a flash of recognition in her eyes. Her voice, when she spoke again, sounded shockingly like the voice he had first heard many years ago, calling to him from across a studio at Bezalel.

"When was the last time you were here?"

"I came to see you on your birthday."

"I don't remember."

"We had a party, Leah. All the other patients came. It was lovely."

"I'm lonely here, Gabriel."

"I know, Leah."

"I have no one. No one but you, my love."

He felt as though he had lost the ability to draw air into his lungs. Leah reached out and placed her hand in his.

"You have no paint on your fingers," she said.

"I haven't worked for a few days."

"Why not?"

"It's a long story."

"I have time," she said. "I have nothing but time."

She turned away from him and stared into the garden. The light was receding from her eyes.

"Don't go, Leah. There's something I have to tell you."

She came back to him. "Are you restoring a painting now?" she asked.

"Veronese," he replied.

"Which one?"

He told her.

"So you're living in Venice again?"

"For a few more months."

She smiled. "Do you remember when we lived in Venice together, Gabriel? It was when you were serving your apprenticeship with Umberto Conti."

"I remember, Leah."

"Our apartment was so small."

"That's because it was a room."

"They were wonderful days, weren't they, Gabriel? Days of art and wine. We should have stayed in Venice together, my love. Things would have turned out differently if you hadn't gone back to the Office."

Gabriel didn't respond. He wasn't capable of speech.

"Your wife is from Venice, is she not?"

"Yes, Leah."

"Is she pretty?"

"Yes, Leah, she's very pretty."

"I'd like to meet her sometime."

"You have, Leah. She's come here to see you many times."

"I don't remember her. Perhaps it's better that way." She turned away from him. "I want to talk to my mother," she said. "I want to hear the sound of my mother's voice."

"We'll call her right away, Leah."

"Make sure Dani is buckled into his seat tightly. The streets are slippery."

"He's fine, Leah."

She turned to face him again. Then, after a moment, she asked, "Do you have children?"

He wasn't certain whether she was in the present or the past. "I don't understand," he said.

"With Chiara."

"No," he answered. "No children."

"Maybe someday."

"Yes," he said, but nothing more.

"Make me a promise, Gabriel."

"Anything, my love."

"If you have another child, you mustn't forget Dani."

"I think about him every day."

"I think of nothing else."

He felt as though the bones of his rib cage were snapping beneath the weight of the stone that God had laid over his heart.

"And when you leave Venice?" Leah asked after a moment. "What then?"

"I'm coming home."

"For good?"

"Yes, Leah."

"What are you going to do? There are no paintings here in Israel."

"I'm going to be the chief of the Office."

"I thought Ari was the chief."

"That was a long time ago."

"Where will you live?"

"Here in Jerusalem so I can be close to you."

"In that little apartment?"

"I've always liked it."

"It's not big enough for children."

"We'll find the room."

"Will you still come to see me after you have children, Gabriel?"

"Every chance I get."

She tilted her face to the cloudless sky. "Look at the snow, Gabriel."

"Yes," he said, weeping softly. "Isn't it beautiful?"

The doctor was waiting for Gabriel in the common room. He spoke not a word until they had returned to the lobby.

"Is there anything you want to tell me?" he asked.

"It went as well as could be expected."

"For her or for you?"

Gabriel said nothing.

"It's all right, you know," the doctor said after a moment.

"What's that?"

"For you to be happy."

"I'm not sure I know how."

"Try," said the doctor. "And if you need someone to talk to, you know where to find me."

"Take good care of her."

"I always have."

With that, Gabriel surrendered himself to the care of his security detail and climbed into the back of the limousine. It was odd, he thought, but he no longer felt like crying. He supposed that was what it meant to be the chief.

30

NARKISS STREET, JERUSALEM

CHIARA HAD ARRIVED in Jerusalem only an hour before Gabriel, and yet their apartment on Narkiss Street already looked like a photograph in one of those glossy home design magazines she was always reading. There were fresh flowers in the vases and bowls of snacks on the end tables, and the glass of wine she placed in his hand was chilled to perfection. Her lips, when kissed, were warm from the Jerusalem sun.

"I expected you sooner," she said.

"I had a couple of errands to run."

"Where have you been?"

"Hell," he answered seriously.

She frowned. "You'll have to tell me about it later."

"Why later?"

"Because we have company coming, darling."

"Do I have to ask who it is?"

"Probably not."

"How did he know we were back?"

"He mentioned something about a burning bush."

"Can't we do it another night?"

"It's too late to cancel now. He and Gilah have already left Tiberias."

"I suppose he's giving you running updates on his location."

"He's called twice already. He's very excited about seeing you."

"I wonder why."

He kissed Chiara again and carried the glass of wine into their bedroom. Its walls were hung with paintings. There were paintings by Gabriel, paintings by his gifted mother, and several paintings by his grandfather, the noted German expressionist Viktor Frankel, who was murdered at Auschwitz in the lethal winter of 1942. There was also a three-quarter-length portrait, unsigned, of a gaunt young man who appeared haunted by the shadow of death. Leah had painted it a few days after Gabriel returned to Israel with the blood of six Black September terrorists on his hands. It was the first and last time he agreed to sit for her.

We should have stayed in Venice together, my love. Things would have turned out differently . . .

He stripped away his clothing under the portrait's pitiless gaze and stood beneath the shower until the last traces of Leah's touch had slipped from his skin. Then he changed into clean clothing and returned to the sitting room, just as Gilah and Ari Shamron were coming through the front door. Gilah was holding a platter of her famous eggplant with Moroccan spice; her famous husband held only an olive wood cane. He was dressed, as usual, in a pair of pressed khaki trousers, a white oxford cloth shirt, and a leather jacket with an unrepaired tear in the left shoulder. It was obvious he was unwell, but the smile he wore was one of contentment. Shamron had spent years trying to convince Gabriel to return to Israel to take his rightful place in the executive suite at King Saul Boulevard. Now, at long last, the task was complete. His successor was in place. The bloodline was secure.

He leaned his cane against the wall of the entrance hall and, with Gabriel following, went out onto the little terrace where two wrought-iron chairs stood beneath the drooping canopy of a eucalyptus tree. Narkiss Street lay still and silent beneath their feet, but in the distance came the faint rush of evening traffic along King George. Shamron lowered himself unsteadily into one of the chairs and motioned for Gabriel to sit in the other. Then he removed a packet of Turkish cigarettes and, with enormous concentration, extracted one. Gabriel looked at Shamron's hands, the hands that had nearly squeezed the life out of Adolf Eichmann on a street corner in northern Buenos Aires. It was one of the reasons Shamron had been given the assignment: the unusual size and power of his hands. Now they were liver-spotted and covered with unhealed abrasions. Gabriel looked away as they fumbled with the old Zippo lighter.

"You really shouldn't, Ari."

"What difference does it make now?"

The lighter flared, acrid Turkish smoke mingled with the sharp scent of the eucalyptus tree. Memories gathered suddenly at Gabriel's feet like floodwaters. He tried to hold them at bay but could not; Leah had shattered what remained of his defenses. He was

driving across a sea of windblown Cornish grass with
Shamron at his side. It was the dawn of the new millennium, the days of suicide bombings and delusion.
Shamron had recently been hauled from retirement
to repair the Office after a string of operational disasters, and he wanted Gabriel's help with the enterprise. The bait he used was Tariq al-Hourani, the
Palestinian master terrorist who had planted the
bomb beneath Gabriel's car in Vienna.

*Maybe if you help me take down Tariq, you can finally
let go of Leah and get on with your life . . .*

Gabriel heard the sound of Chiara's laughter
from the sitting room and the memory dissolved.

"What's wrong now?" he asked gently of Shamron.

"The list of my physical ailments is almost as long
as the list of challenges facing the State of Israel. But
don't worry," he added hastily. "I'm not going anywhere yet. I fully intend to be around to witness the
birth of my grandchildren."

Gabriel resisted the impulse to remind Shamron
that they were not truly father and son. "We're expecting you to be there, Ari."

Shamron smiled. "Have you decided where you're
going to live after they're born?"

"It's funny," replied Gabriel, "but Bella asked me
the same thing."

"I heard it was an interesting conversation."

"How did you know I went to see her?"

"Uzi told me."

"I thought he wasn't taking your calls."

"It seems the great thaw has begun. It's one of the
few advantages of failing health," he added. "All the

petty grievances and broken promises seem to fall away as one gets closer to the end."

The limbs of the eucalyptus tree swayed with the first breeze of the evening. The air was cooling by the minute. Gabriel had always loved the way it turned cold in Jerusalem at night, even in summer. He wished he had the power to freeze this moment a little longer. He looked at Shamron, who was tapping his cigarette thoughtfully against the rim of an ashtray.

"It took a great deal of courage for you to sit down with Bella. And shrewdness, too. It proves I was right about one thing all along."

"What's that, Ari?"

"That you have the makings of a great chief."

"Sometimes I wonder whether I'm about to make my first mistake."

"By keeping Uzi on in some capacity?"

Gabriel nodded slowly.

"It's risky," Shamron agreed. "But if there's anyone who can pull it off, it's you."

"No advice?"

"I'm through giving you advice, my son. I am the worst thing a man can be, old and obsolete. I am a bystander. I am underfoot." Shamron looked at Gabriel and frowned. "Feel free to disagree with me at any time."

Gabriel smiled but said nothing.

"Uzi tells me things got a bit heated between you and Bella," Shamron said.

"It reminded me of the interrogation I went through that night in the Empty Quarter."

"The worst night of my life." Shamron thought

about it for a moment. "Actually," he said, "it was the second worst."

He didn't have to say which night ranked above it. He was talking about Vienna.

"I think Bella is more upset about all this than Uzi is," he continued. "I'm afraid she's grown rather accustomed to the trappings of power."

"Whatever gave you that impression?"

"The way she's clinging to them. She blames me for everything, of course. She thinks I planned this all along."

"You did."

Shamron made a face that fell somewhere between a grimace and a smile.

"No denials?" asked Gabriel.

"None," replied Shamron. "I had my fair share of triumphs, but when all is said and done, yours is the career against which all others will be measured. It's true I played favorites, especially after Vienna. But my faith in you was rewarded with a string of operations that were far beyond the talents of someone like Uzi. Surely even Bella realizes that."

Gabriel made no reply. He was watching a boy of ten or eleven riding a bicycle along the quiet street.

"And now," Shamron was saying, "it appears you may have found a way into the finances of the butcher boy from Damascus. With a bit of luck, it will go down as the first great triumph of the Gabriel Allon era."

"I thought you didn't believe in luck."

"I don't." Shamron ignited another cigarette; then, with a flip of his wrist, he closed his lighter with a sharp snap. "The butcher boy has the cruelty of his father but lacks his father's cleverness, which makes him very dangerous. At this point, it's all about the money. It's what's holding the clan together. It's why the loyalists remain loyal. It's why children are dying by the thousands. But if you could actually get control of the money . . ." He smiled. "The possibilities would be endless."

"Do you really have no advice for me?"

"Keep the butcher boy in power for as long as he remains even remotely palatable. Otherwise, the next few years will be very interesting for you and your friends in Washington and London."

"So this is how the Great Arab Awakening ends?" asked Gabriel. "We cling to a mass murderer because he's the only one who can save Syria from al-Qaeda?"

"Far be it from me to say I told you so, but I predicted the Arab Spring would end disastrously, and it has. The Arabs are not yet ready for true democracy, not at a time when radical Islam is in ascendance. The best we can hope for is *decent* authoritarian regimes in places like Syria and Egypt." Shamron paused, then added, "Who knows, Gabriel? Perhaps you can find some way to convince the ruler to educate his people properly and treat them with the dignity they deserve. Maybe you can compel him to stop gassing children."

"There's one other thing I want from him."

"The Caravaggio?"

Gabriel nodded.

"First you find the money," said Shamron, crushing out his cigarette. "Then you find the painting."

Gabriel said nothing more. He was watching the boy on the bicycle gliding in and out of the long shadows at the end of the street. When the child was gone, he tilted his face toward the Jerusalem sky. Look at the snow, he thought. Isn't it beautiful?

31

JERUSALEM

THE TOLLING OF church bells woke Gabriel from a dreamless sleep. He lay motionless for a moment, not altogether certain where he was. Then he saw Leah's brooding portrait staring down at him from the wall and realized he was in his bedroom in Narkiss Street. He slipped from beneath the sheets, quietly, so as not to wake Chiara, and padded into the kitchen. The only evidence of the previous evening's dinner party was the heavy, sweet smell of flowers wilting in their vases. On the spotless counter stood a French press coffee maker and a tin of Lavazza. Gabriel placed the kettle atop the stove and stood over it while waiting for the water to boil.

He drank his coffee outside on the terrace and read the morning papers on his BlackBerry. Then he crept into the bathroom to shave and shower. When he emerged, Chiara was still sleeping soundly. He opened the closet and stood there for a moment, debating what to wear. A suit, he decided, was inappropriate; it might send the message to the troops that he was already in charge. In the end he settled for his usual attire: a pair of faded blue jeans, a cotton pullover, and a leather jacket. Shamron had had his uniform, he thought, and so would he.

A few minutes after eight o'clock, he heard his motorcade disturb the quiet of Narkiss Street. He kissed Chiara softly and then headed downstairs to his waiting limousine. It bore him eastward across Jerusalem to the Dung Gate, the main entrance to the Jewish Quarter of the Old City. He skirted the metal detectors and, flanked by his bodyguards, set out across the open plaza toward the Western Wall, the much-disputed remnant of the ancient retaining barrier that had once surrounded the great Temple of Jerusalem. Above the Wall, shimmering in the early-morning sunlight, was the golden Dome of the Rock, Islam's third-holiest shrine. There were many aspects to the Israeli-Arab conflict, but Gabriel had concluded it all came down to this—two faiths locked in a death struggle over the same parcel of a sacred land. There could be periods of quiet, months or even years with no bombs or blood; but Gabriel feared there would never be true peace.

The portion of the Western Wall visible from the plaza was 187 feet wide and 62 feet high. The actual western retaining wall of the Temple Mount plateau, however, was much larger, descending 42 feet below the plaza and stretching more than a quarter mile into the Muslim Quarter, where it was concealed behind residential structures. After years of politically and religiously charged archaeological excavations, it was now possible to walk nearly the entire length of the wall via the Western Wall Tunnel, an underground passageway running from the plaza to the Via Dolorosa.

The entrance to the tunnel was on the left side of the plaza, not far from Wilson's Arch. Gabriel slipped through the modern glass doorway and, trailed by his bodyguards, descended a flight of aluminum stairs into the basement of time. A newly paved walkway ran along the base of the wall. He followed it past the massive Herodian ashlars until he arrived at a section of the tunnel complex that was concealed by a curtain of opaque plastic. Beyond the curtain was a rectangular excavation pit where a single figure, a small man of late middle age, picked at the soil in a cone of soft white light. He seemed oblivious to Gabriel's presence, which was not the case. It would be easier to surprise a squirrel than Eli Lavon.

Another moment elapsed before Lavon looked up and smiled. He had wispy, unkempt hair and a bland, almost featureless face that even the most gifted portrait artist would have struggled to capture on canvas. Eli Lavon was a ghost of a man, a chameleon who was easily overlooked and soon forgotten. Shamron had once said he could disappear while shaking your hand. It wasn't far from the truth.

Gabriel had first worked with Lavon on Wrath of God, the secret Israeli intelligence operation to hunt down and kill the perpetrators of the Munich Olympics massacre. In the Hebrew-based lexicon of the team, Lavon had been an *ayin*, a tracker and surveillance artist. For three years he had stalked the terrorists of Black September across Europe and the Middle East, often in dangerously close proximity. The work left him with numerous stress disorders, including a notoriously fickle stomach that troubled him to this day.

When the unit disbanded in 1975, Lavon settled in Vienna, where he opened a small investigative unit called Wartime Claims and Inquiries. Operating on a shoestring budget, he managed to track down millions of dollars' worth of looted Holocaust assets and played a significant role in prying a multibillion-dollar settlement from the banks of Switzerland. The work won him few admirers in Vienna, and in 2003 a bomb exploded in his office, killing two young female employees. Heartbroken, he returned to Israel to pursue his first love, which was archaeology. He now served as an adjunct professor at Hebrew University and regularly took part in digs around the country. He had spent the better part of two years sifting through the soil in the Western Wall Tunnel.

"Who are your little friends?" he asked, glancing at the bodyguards standing along the edge of the excavation pit.

"I found them wandering lost in the plaza."

"They're not making a mess, are they?"

"They wouldn't dare."

Lavon looked down and resumed his work.

"What have you got there?" asked Gabriel.

"A bit of loose change."

"Who dropped it?"

"Someone who was upset by the fact the Persians were about to conquer Jerusalem. It was obvious he was in a hurry."

Lavon reached out and adjusted the angle of his work lamp. The bottom of the trench shone with embedded pieces of gold.

"What are they?" asked Gabriel.

"Thirty-six gold coins from the Byzantine era and a large medallion with a menorah. They prove there were Jews living on this spot before the Muslim conquest of Jerusalem in 638. For most biblical archaeologists, this would be the find of a lifetime. But not for me." Lavon looked at Gabriel and added, "Or you, either."

Gabriel glanced over his shoulder at the ashlars of the Wall. A year earlier, in a secret chamber 167 feet beneath the surface of the Temple Mount, he and Lavon had discovered twenty-two pillars from Solomon's Temple of Jerusalem, thus proving beyond doubt that the ancient Jewish sanctuary, described in Kings and Chronicles, had in fact existed. They had also discovered a massive bomb that, had it detonated, would have brought down the entire sacred plateau. The pillars now stood in a high-security exhibit at the Israel Museum. One had required special cleaning before it could be displayed, for it was stained with Lavon's blood.

"I got a call from Uzi last night," Lavon said after a moment. "He told me you might be stopping by."

"Did he tell you why?"

"He mentioned something about a lost Caravaggio and a company called LXR Investments. He said you were interested in acquiring it, along with the rest of Evil Incorporated."

"Can it be done?"

"There's only so much you can do from the outside. Eventually, you're going to need help from someone who can provide the keys to the kingdom."

"So we'll find him."

"We?" When Gabriel made no reply, Lavon leaned down and began picking at the soil around one of the ancient coins. "What do you need me to do?"

"Exactly what you're doing right now," replied Gabriel. "But I want you to use a computer and a balance sheet instead of a hand trowel and a brush."

"These days, I prefer a trowel and a brush."

"I know, Eli, but I can't do it without you."

"There's not going to be any rough stuff, is there?"

"No, Eli, of course not."

"You always say that, Gabriel."

"And?"

"There's always rough stuff."

Gabriel reached down and disconnected the lamp from its power source. Lavon worked in the darkness for a moment longer. Then he rose to his feet, brushed his hands against his trousers, and climbed out of the pit.

A lifelong bachelor, Lavon kept a small apartment in the Talpiot district of Jerusalem, just off the Hebron Road. They stopped there long enough for him to change into clean clothing and then headed down the Bab al-Wad to King Saul Boulevard. After entering the building "black," they made their way down three flights of stairs and followed a windowless corridor to a doorway marked 456C. The room on the other side had once been a dumping ground for obsolete computers and worn-out furniture, often used by the night staff as a clandestine meeting place for romantic trysts. It was now known throughout King Saul Boulevard only as Gabriel's Lair.

The keyless cipher lock was set to the numeric version of Gabriel's date of birth, reputedly the Office's most closely guarded secret. With Lavon peering over his shoulder, he punched the code into the keypad and pushed open the door. Waiting inside was Dina Sarid, a small, dark-haired woman who carried herself with an air of early widowhood. A human database, she was capable of reciting the time, place, perpetrators, and casualty toll of every act of terrorism committed against Israeli and Western targets. Dina had once told Gabriel that she knew more about the terrorists than they knew about themselves. And Gabriel had believed her.

"Where are the others?" he asked.

"Stuck in Personnel."

"What's the holdup?"

"Apparently, the division heads are in revolt." Dina paused, then added, "That's what happens to an intelligence service when word gets around that the chief isn't long for this world."

"Maybe I should go upstairs and have a word with the division heads."

"Give it a few minutes."

"How bad has it been?"

"I've put together a list of al-Qaeda operatives who've set up shop next door in Syria—serious global jihadists who need to be taken out of circulation permanently. And guess what happens every time I propose an operation?"

"Nothing."

Dina nodded slowly. "We're frozen in place," she said. "We're treading water at a time we can least afford it."

"Not any more, Dina."

Just then, the door swung open, and Rimona Stern entered the room. Mikhail Abramov came loping in next, followed a few minutes later by Yaakov Rossman, who looked as though he hadn't slept in a month. Soon after there appeared a pair of all-purpose field hands named Mordecai and Oded, followed lastly by Yossi Gavish, a tall, balding figure dressed in corduroy and tweed. Yossi was a top officer in Research, which is how the Office referred to its analytical division. Born in the Golders Green section of London, he had studied at Oxford and still spoke Hebrew with a pronounced English accent.

Within the corridors and conference rooms of King Saul Boulevard, the eight men and women gathered in the subterranean room were known by the code name Barak, the Hebrew word for lightning, for their uncanny ability to gather and strike quickly. They were a service within a service, a team of operatives without equal or fear. Throughout their existence, it had sometimes been necessary to admit outsiders into their midst—a British investigative journalist, a Russian billionaire, the daughter of a man they killed—but never before had they allowed another agent of the Office to join their fraternity. Therefore, they were all surprised when, at the stroke of ten, Bella Navot appeared in the doorway. She was dressed for the boardroom in a gray pantsuit and was clutching a batch of files to her breast. She stood in the threshold for a moment, as if waiting for an invitation to enter, before settling wordlessly next to Yossi at one of the communal worktables.

If the team was made uneasy by Bella's presence, they gave no sign of it as Gabriel rose to his feet and walked over to the last chalkboard in all of King Saul Boulevard. On it was written three words: BLOOD NEVER SLEEPS. He erased them with a single swipe of his hand and in their place wrote three letters: LXR. Then he recounted for the team the remarkable series of events that had hastened their reunion, beginning with the murder of a British spy turned art smuggler named Jack Bradshaw and ending with the note Bradshaw had left for Gabriel in his vault at the Geneva Freeport. In death, Bradshaw had tried to atone for his sins by giving Gabriel the identity of the man who was acquiring stolen paintings by the truckload: the murderous ruler of Syria. He had also supplied Gabriel with the name of the front company the ruler had used for his purchases: LXR Investments of Luxembourg. Surely LXR was but a small star in a galaxy of global wealth, much of which was carefully hidden beneath layers of shells and front companies. But a network of wealth, like a network of terrorists, had to have a skilled operational mastermind in order to function. The ruler had entrusted his family's money to Kemel al-Farouk, the bodyguard of the ruler's father, the henchman who tortured and killed at the regime's behest. But Kemel couldn't manage the money himself, not with the NSA and its partners monitoring his every move. Somewhere out there was a man of trust—a lawyer, a banker, a relative—who had the power to move those assets at will. They were going to use LXR as a way to track him down. And Bella Navot was going to guide them every step of the way.

32

KING SAUL BOULEVARD, TEL AVIV

T HEY STARTED THEIR search not with the son but with the father: the man who had ruled Syria from 1970 until his death of a heart attack in 2000. He was born in the Ansariya Mountains of northwestern Syria in October 1930, in the village of Qurdaha. Like the other villages in the region, Qurdaha belonged to the Alawites, followers of a tiny, persecuted branch of Shia Islam whom the majority Sunnis regarded as heretics. Qurdaha had no mosque or church and not a single café or shop, but rain fell upon the land thirty days each year, and there was a mineral spring in a nearby cave that the villagers called 'Ayn Zarqa. The ninth of eleven children, he lived in a two-room stone house with a small front yard of beaten earth and an adjoining mud patch for the animals. His grandfather, a minor village notable who was good with his fists and a gun, was known as al-Wahhish, the Wild Man, because he had once thrashed a traveling Turkish wrestler. His father could put a bullet through a cigarette paper at a hundred paces.

In 1944 he left Qurdaha to attend school in the

coastal town of Latakia. There he became active in politics, joining the new Arab Baath Socialist Party, a secular movement that sought to end Western influence in the Middle East through pan-Arab socialism. In 1951 he enrolled in a military academy in Aleppo, a traditional route for an Alawite trying to escape the bonds of mountain poverty, and by 1964 he was in command of the Syrian air force. After a Baathist coup in 1966, he became Syria's defense minister, a post he held during Syria's disastrous war with Israel in 1967, when it lost the Golan Heights. Despite the catastrophic failure of his forces, he would be the president of Syria just three years later. In a sign of things to come, he referred to the bloodless coup that brought him to power as a "corrective movement."

His rise ended a long cycle of political instability in Syria, but at a high cost to the Syrian people and the rest of the Middle East. A client of the Soviet Union, his regime was among the most dangerous in the region. He supported radical elements of the Palestinian movement—Abu Nidal operated with impunity from Damascus for years—and equipped his military with the latest in Soviet tanks, fighters, and air defenses. Syria itself became a vast prison, a place where fax machines were outlawed and a misplaced word about the ruler would result in a trip to the Mezzeh, the notorious hilltop prison in western Damascus. Fifteen separate security services spied on the Syrian people and on one another. All were controlled by Alawites, as was the Syrian military. An elaborate cult of personality rose around the ruler and his family. His face, with its domed forehead and sickly pallor, loomed over every square and hung on the walls of every public building in the country. His peasant mother was revered almost as a saint.

Within a decade of his ascent, however, much of the country's Sunni majority was no longer content to be ruled over by an Alawite peasant from Qurdaha. Bombs exploded regularly in Damascus, and in June 1979 a member of the Muslim Brotherhood killed at least fifty Alawite cadets in the dining hall of the Aleppo military academy. A year later, Islamic militants hurled a pair of grenades at the ruler during a diplomatic function in Damascus—at which point the ruler's hot-tempered brother declared all-out war on the Brotherhood and its Sunni Muslim supporters. Among his first acts was to dispatch units of his Defense Companies, the guardians of the regime, to the Palmyra desert prison. An estimated eight hundred political prisoners were slaughtered in their cells.

But it was in the town of Hama, a hotbed of Muslim Brotherhood activity along the banks of the Orontes River, that the regime showed the lengths to which it would go to ensure its survival. With the country teetering on the brink of civil war, the Defense Companies entered the city early on the morning of February 2, 1982, along with several hundred agents of the feared Mukhabarat secret police. What followed was the worst massacre in the history of the modern Middle East, a month-long frenzy of killing, torture, and destruction that left at least twenty thousand people dead and a city reduced to rubble. The ruler never denied the massacre, nor did he quibble over the number of dead. In fact, he allowed the city to lie in ruins for months as a reminder of what would happen to those who dared to challenge him. In the Middle East, a new term came into vogue: Hama Rules.

The ruler never again faced a serious threat. Indeed, in a 1991 presidential plebiscite, he earned 99.9 percent of the vote, which prompted one Syrian commentator to note that even Allah would not have performed so well. He hired a famous architect to build him a lavish presidential palace, and as his health deteriorated he gave thought to a successor. The hotheaded younger brother attempted to seize power when the ruler was incapacitated with illness, and was cast into exile. The cherished eldest son, a soldier, a champion equestrian, died violently in an automobile accident. Which left only the soft-spoken middle son, a London-educated eye doctor, to assume control of the family business.

The first years of his rule were filled with hope and promise. He granted his fellow citizens access to the Internet and allowed them to travel outside the country without first securing the government's permission. He dined in restaurants with his fashion-conscious wife and freed several hundred political prisoners. Luxury hotels and shopping malls altered the skyline of drab Damascus and Aleppo. Western cigarettes, banned by his father, appeared on Syrian store shelves.

Then came the great Arab Awakening. The Syrians remained on the sidelines as the old order crumbled around them, as if they had a premonition of what lay ahead. Then, in March 2011, fifteen young boys dared to spray anti-regime graffiti on the wall of a school in Daraa, a small farming town sixty miles south of Damascus. The Mukhabarat quickly took the boys into custody and advised their fathers to go home and produce new children, because they would never see their sons again. Daraa exploded into protests, which quickly spread to Homs, Hama, and, eventually, to Damascus. Within a year, Syria would be engulfed in a full-blown civil war. And the son, like his father before him, would play by Hama Rules.

But where was the money? The money that had been looted from the Syrian treasury for two generations. The money that had been skimmed from state-owned Syrian enterprises and funneled into the pockets of the ruler and his Alawite kin from Qurdaha. A portion of it was hidden within a company called LXR Investments of Luxembourg, and it was there Gabriel and the team made their initial inquiries. They were polite at first and, consequently, wholly unsatisfactory. A simple search of the Internet revealed that LXR had no public Web site and had appeared in no news stories or public relations releases, business-related or otherwise. There was a short entry in the Luxembourg commercial registry, but it contained no names of LXR investors or management—only an address, which turned out to be the premises of a corporation lawyer. It was obvious to Eli Lavon, the team's most experienced financial investigator, that LXR was a classic instrument used by someone who wished to invest his money anonymously. It was a cipher, a ghost company, a shell within a shell.

They broadened their search to commercial registries in Western Europe. And when that failed to produce more than a weak blip on their radar screens, they scoured tax and real estate records in every country where such documents were available. None of the searches produced any matches except in the United Kingdom, where they learned that LXR Investments was the leaseholder of record for a retail building on King's Road in Chelsea, currently occupied by a well-known women's clothing company. The lawyer representing LXR in Britain worked for a small law firm based in Southwark, London. His name was Hamid Khaddam. He was born in November 1964, in the town of Qurdaha, Syria.

He lived in a cottage in the Tower Hamlets section of London with his Baghdad-born wife, Aisha, and three teenage daughters who were far too westernized for his tastes. He traveled to work each morning by Tube, though on occasion, when it was raining or if he was running late, he would grant himself the small luxury of a taxi. The law firm's offices were located in a small brick building on Great Suffolk Street, a long way from the tony addresses of Knightsbridge and Mayfair. There were eight lawyers in all—four Syrians, two Iraqis, an Egyptian, and a flashy young Jordanian who claimed blood links to his country's Hashemite rulers. Hamid Khaddam was the only Alawite. He had a television in his office, which was tuned always to Al Jazeera. He obtained most of his news, however, by reading Arabic-language blogs from the Middle East. All tilted editorially in favor of the regime.

He was careful in his personal and professional life, though not careful enough to realize he was the target of an intelligence assault that was as far-reaching as it was quiet. It began the morning after the team learned his name, when Mordecai and Oded parachuted into London with Canadian passports in their pockets and suitcases filled with the carefully disguised tools of their trade. For two days they watched him from a distance. Then, on the morning of the third, the nimble-fingered Mordecai was able to briefly acquire Khaddam's mobile phone while he was riding a Central Line train between Mile End and Liverpool Street. The software Mordecai inserted into the device's operating system gave the team real-time access to Khaddam's e-mails, text messages, contacts, photos, and voice calls. It also turned the device into a full-time transmitter, which meant that everywhere Hamid Khaddam went, the team went with him. What's more, they were granted entrée into the computer network of the law firm and Hamid Khaddam's personal desktop at home. It was, said Eli Lavon, the gift that kept on giving.

The data flowed from Khaddam's phone to a computer inside London Station, and from London Station it moved securely to Gabriel's Lair in the depths of King Saul Boulevard. There the team pulled it apart, phone number by phone number, e-mail address by e-mail address, name by name.

LXR Investments appeared in an e-mail to a Syrian lawyer in Paris, and a second e-mail sent to an accountant in Brussels. The team pursued both lines of inquiry, but the thread frayed long before it reached Damascus. Indeed, they found nothing in the trove of material to suggest Khaddam was in contact with any elements of the Syrian regime or the extended ruling family. He was a spear-carrier, declared Lavon, a runner of financial errands directed by higher authority. In fact, he said, it was possible the lowly Syrian lawyer from London didn't even realize who he was working for.

And so they burrowed and sifted and argued among themselves while all around them the rest of King Saul Boulevard watched and waited in anticipation. The rules of compartmentalization meant that only a handful of senior officers knew the nature of their work, but the flow of files from Research to Room 456C clearly illuminated the path they were following. It did not take long for word to spread that Gabriel was back in the building. Nor was it a secret that Bella Navot, bride of his vanquished rival, was working faithfully at his side. Rumors flourished. Rumors that Navot was planning to hand over the reins to Gabriel before his term had ended. Rumors that Gabriel and the prime minister were actually trying to hasten Navot's departure. There was even a rumor that Bella was planning to divorce her husband once he had been stripped of the trappings of power. They were all put to rest one afternoon when Gabriel and the Navots were seen lunching pleasantly in the executive dining room. Navot was eating poached fish and steamed vegetables, a sign he was once again adhering to Bella's draconian dietary restrictions. Surely, said the rumors, he would not submit to the will of a woman who was planning to leave him.

But there was no denying the fact that the Office had stirred to life in the days since Gabriel's return. It was as if the entire building was dusting off the cobwebs after a long operational slumber. There was a sense of an imminent strike, even if the troops had no idea where the strike would take place or what form it would take. Even Bella seemed caught up in the change that had come over her husband's service. Her appearance changed markedly. She traded her Fortune 500 suits for jeans and a sweatshirt, and started wearing her hair in a messy undergraduate ponytail. It was the way Gabriel would always think of her, the intense young analyst in sandals and a wrinkled shirt, toiling at her desk long after everyone else had gone home for the night. There was a reason Bella was regarded as the country's top expert on Syria; she worked harder than anyone else and didn't need things like food or sleep. She was also ruthless in her desire to succeed, be it in the academic arena or within the walls of King Saul Boulevard. Gabriel always wondered whether a bit of the Baathists had rubbed off on her over the years. Bella was a natural killer.

Her reputation preceded her, of course, so it was understandable the team kept a polite distance at first. But gradually their walls came down, and within a few days they were treating her as though she had been there with them from the beginning. When the team commenced one of its legendary

quarrels, Bella was invariably on the winning side.
And when they gathered at night for their traditional family dinner, Bella left her husband to his
own devices and joined them. It was their custom to
avoid talking about the case over meals, and so they
debated Israel's place in the changing Arab world
instead. Like the great powers of the West, Israel
had always preferred the Arab strongman to the
Arab street. It had never made peace with an Arab
democrat, only dictators and potentates. For many
decades, the strongmen had provided a modicum of
regional stability, but at a terrible cost to the people
who lived beneath their thumbs. The numbers did
not lie, and Bella, a scholar of the region's cruelest
regime, could recite them by rote. Despite massive
oil wealth, one-fifth of the Arab world survived on
less than two dollars a day. Sixty-five million Arabs,
the majority of them women, could not read or
write, and millions received no schooling at all. The
Arabs, once pioneers in the fields of mathematics
and geometry, had fallen woefully behind the developed world in scientific and technological research.
During the past millennium, the Arabs had translated fewer books than Spain translated in a single
year. In many parts of the Arab world, the Koran
was the only book that mattered.

But how, asked Bella, had it come to this? Radical
Islam had surely played its role, but so had money.
Money that the dictators and potentates spent on
themselves rather than on their people. Money that
flowed out of the Arab world and into the private
banks of Geneva, Zurich, and Liechtenstein. Money
that Gabriel and the team were desperately trying

to find. As the days dragged on, they hit brick walls, dead ends, dry holes, and doors they could not open. And they read the e-mail of a lowly London lawyer named Hamid Khaddam and listened carefully as he went about his day: the Tube rides, the meetings with clients on matters large and small, the petty disagreements with his pan-Arab partners. And they listened, too, as he returned each evening to the cottage in Tower Hamlets where he lived in the company of four women. On one such evening, he had a torrid argument with his eldest daughter over the length of a skirt she was planning to wear to a party where boys would be present. Like the young girl, the team was grateful for the interruption of his mobile phone. The conversation was two minutes and eighteen seconds in length. And when it was over, Gabriel and his team knew they had finally found the man they were looking for.

ONE HUNDRED MILES west of Vienna, the river Danube bends abruptly from the northwest to the southeast. The ancient Romans installed a garrison on the spot; and when the Romans were gone, the people who would one day be known as Austrians built a city they called Linz. The city grew rich from the iron ore and salt that moved along the river, and for a time it was the most important in the Austro-Hungarian Empire—more important, even, than Vienna. Mozart composed his Symphony no. 36 while living in Linz; Anton Bruckner served as the organist in the Old Cathedral. And in the small suburb of Leonding, at Michaelsbergstrasse 16, there stands a yellow house where Adolf Hitler lived as a child. Hitler moved to Vienna in 1905 in hopes of winning admission to the Academy of Fine Arts, but his beloved Linz would never be far from his thoughts. Linz was to be the cultural center of the Thousand-Year Reich, and it was there that Hitler planned to build his monumental Führermuseum of plundered art. Indeed, the very code name of his looting opera-

tion was Sonderauftrag Linz, or Special Operation
Linz. Modern Linz had worked hard to conceal its
links to Hitler, but reminders of the past were everywhere. The city's most prominent firm, the steel
giant Voestalpine AG, was originally known as the
Hermann-Göring-Werke. And twelve miles east of
the city center were the remnants of Mauthausen,
the Nazi camp where inmates were subjected to "ex-
termination through labor." Among those prisoners who lived to see the camp liberated was Simon
Wiesenthal, who would later become the world's
most famous Nazi hunter.

The man who came to Linz on the first Tuesday
of June knew much about the city's dark past. In fact,
for a period of his many-faceted life, it had been his
primary obsession. As he stepped lightly from his
train at the Hauptbahnhof, he wore a dark suit that
suggested he possessed substantial wealth, and a gold
wristwatch that left the impression he had not come
by it altogether honestly, which happened to be true.
He had traveled to Linz from Vienna, and before that
he had been in Munich, Budapest, and Prague. Twice
along his journey he had changed identities. For now,
he was Feliks Adler, a Middle European of uncertain
national origin, a lover of many women, a fighter of
forgotten wars, a man who was more comfortable in
Gstaad and Saint-Tropez than he was in his home-
town, wherever that had been. His real name, however, was Eli Lavon.

From the station he walked along a street lined with
cream-colored apartment houses, until he came to the
New Cathedral, Austria's largest church. By edict, its
soaring spire was ten feet shorter than that of its coun-

terpart in Vienna, the mighty Stephansdom. Lavon went inside to see whether anyone from the street would follow him. And as he walked beneath the soaring nave, he wondered, not for the first time, how such a devoutly Roman Catholic land could have played such an outsize role in the murder of six million. It was in their bones, he thought. They drank it with their mother's milk.

But these were Lavon's judgments, not Feliks Adler's, and by the time he returned to the square he was dreaming only of money. He walked to the Hauptplatz, Linz's most famous square, and performed a last check for surveillance. Then he headed across the Danube and made his way to a streetcar roundabout, where a pair of modern trams baked in the warm sun, looking as though they had been dropped mistakenly in the wrong city, in the wrong century. On one side of the roundabout was a street called the Gerstnerstrasse, and near the end of the street was a stately door with a brass plaque that read BANK WEBER AG: BY APPOINTMENT ONLY.

Lavon reached for the call button, but something made him hesitate. It was the old fear, the fear he had knocked on too many doors and had walked along too many darkened streets behind men who would have killed him, had they known he was there. Then he thought of a camp that lay twelve miles to the east, and of a city in Syria that was nearly erased from the map. And he wondered whether somewhere there was a link, an arc of evil, between the two. A sudden anger rose within him, which he tempered by straightening his necktie and smoothing what remained of his hair. Then he placed his thumb firmly atop the call button and, in a voice not his own, declared that he was Feliks Adler and that he had business within. A few seconds elapsed, which to Lavon seemed like an eternity. Finally, the locks opened and a buzzer jolted him like the starting gun of a race. He drew a deep breath, placed his hand upon the latch, and headed inside.

Beyond the door was a vestibule, and beyond the vestibule was a waiting room where there sat a young Upper Austrian girl who was so pale and pretty she looked scarcely real. The girl was apparently used to unwanted attention from men like Herr Adler, for the greeting she gave him was at once cordial and dismissive. She offered him a chair in her waiting room, which he accepted, and coffee, which he politely declined. He sat with his knees together and his hands folded in his lap, as though he were waiting on the platform of a country rail station. On the wall above his head an American financial news network played silently on a television. On the table at his elbow were copies of the world's important economic journals, along with several magazines extolling the benefits of life in the mountains of Austria.

Finally, the telephone on the young woman's desk chimed, and she announced that Herr Weber—Herr Markus Weber, president and founder of Bank Weber AG—would see him now. He was waiting beyond the next door, an emaciated figure, tall, bald, bespectacled, wearing an undertaker's dark suit and a superior smile. He shook Lavon's hand solemnly, as though consoling him over the death of a distant aunt, and led him along a corridor hung with oil paintings of mountain lakes and meadows in bloom. At the end of the hall was a desk where another woman, older than the first and darker in hair color and complexion, sat peering into the screen of a computer. Herr Weber's office was to the right; to the left was the office that belonged to his partner, Waleed al-Siddiqi. The door to Mr. al-Siddiqi's office was tightly closed. Posted outside it were two matching bodyguards who stood with the stillness of potted palms. Their tailored suits could not conceal the fact that both were armed.

Lavon nodded toward the two men, eliciting not so much as a blink, and then looked at the woman. Her hair was as black as a raven's wing and fell almost to the shoulders of her dark suit jacket. Her eyes were wide and brown; her nose was straight and prominent. The overall impression left by her appearance was one of seriousness and, perhaps, a trace of distant sadness. Lavon glanced at her left hand and saw that the third finger was absent a wedding band or a ring of betrothal. He placed her age at perhaps forty, the danger zone for spinsterhood. She was not unattractive, but she was not quite pretty, either. The subtle arrangement of bones and flesh that comprise the human face had conspired to make her ordinary.

"This is Jihan Nawaz," Herr Weber announced. "Miss Nawaz is our account manager."

Her greeting was only slightly more pleasant than the one Lavon had received from the Austrian receptionist. He released her cool hand quickly and followed Herr Weber into his office. The furnishings were modern but comfortable, and the floor was covered by a lush carpet that seemed to absorb all sound. Herr Weber directed Lavon toward a chair before settling behind his desk. "How may I be of assistance?" he said, suddenly all business.

"I'm interested in placing a sum of money in your care," replied Lavon.

"May I ask how you heard about our bank?"

"A business associate is a client here."

"Might I ask his name?"

"I'd rather not say."

Herr Weber raised a palm, as if to say he understood fully.

"I do have one question," Lavon said. "Is it true the bank had some difficulty a few years back?"

"That's correct," conceded Weber. "Like many European banking institutions, we were hit hard by the collapse of the American real estate market and the ensuing financial crisis."

"And so you were forced to take on a partner?"

"Actually, I was pleased to do it."

"Mr. al-Siddiqi."

Weber nodded carefully.

"He is from Lebanon, I take it?"

"Syria, actually."

"A pity."

"What's that?"

"The war," replied Lavon.

Weber's blank expression made it clear he was not interested in discussing the current state of affairs in his partner's country of origin. "You speak German as though you come from Vienna," he said after a moment.

"I lived there for a period of time."

"And now?"

"I carry a Canadian passport, but I prefer to think of myself as a citizen of the world."

"Money knows no international boundaries these days."

"Which is why I've come to Linz."

"You've been here before?"

"Many times," answered Lavon truthfully.

Weber's phone rang.

"Would you mind?"

"Not at all."

The Austrian lifted the receiver to his ear and stared directly at Lavon while listening to the voice at the other end of the line. The thick carpeting swallowed his murmured response. Then he hung up the phone and asked, "Where were we?"

"You were about to assure me that your bank is solvent and stable and that my money will be safe here."

"Both those things are true, Herr Adler."

"I'm also interested in discretion."

"As you undoubtedly know," Weber replied, "Austria recently agreed to some modifications in our banking system to please our European neighbors. That said, our secrecy laws remain among the strictest in the world."

"It is my understanding you have a ten-million-euro minimum for new clients."

"That is our policy." Weber paused, then asked, "Is there a problem, Herr Adler?"

"None at all."

"I thought that would be your answer. You strike me as a very serious person."

Herr Adler accepted this flattery with a nod of his head. "Who else inside the bank will know that I have an account here?"

"Myself and Miss Nawaz."

"What about Mr. al-Siddiqi?"

"Mr. al-Siddiqi has his clients, I have mine." Weber tapped his gold fountain pen against his leather desk blotter. "Well, Herr Adler, how shall we proceed?"

"It is my intention to place ten million euros under your management. I would like you to hold five million of that in cash. The rest I would like you to invest. Nothing too complicated," he added. "My goal is wealth preservation, not wealth creation."

"You won't be disappointed," replied Weber. "You should know, however, that we charge a fee for our services."

"Yes," said Lavon, smiling. "Secrecy has its price."

Armed with his gold fountain pen, the banker jotted down a few of Lavon's particulars, none of which happened to be true. For his password, he chose "quarry," a reference to the slave labor pit at Mauthausen that went soaring over the shining bald head of Herr Weber, who, as it turned out, had never found the time to visit the Holocaust memorial located a few miles from the town of his birth.

"The password has to do with the nature of my business," explained Lavon through a false smile.

"Your business is mining, Herr Adler?"

"Something like that."

With that, the banker rose and entrusted him

to the care of Miss Nawaz, the account manager. There were forms to be filled out, declarations to be signed, and pledges to be made by both parties regarding secrecy and adherence to tax laws. The addition of ten million euros to Bank Weber's balance sheets did little to soften her standoffish demeanor. She was not naturally cold, Lavon reckoned; it was something else. He looked at the pair of bodyguards posed outside the door of Waleed al-Siddiqi, the Syrian-born savior of Bank Weber AG. Then he looked again at Jihan Nawaz.

"An important client?" he asked.

She stared at him blankly. "How do you wish to fund the account?" she asked.

"A wire transfer would be most convenient."

She handed him a slip of paper on which was written the routing number for the bank.

"Shall we do it now?" asked Lavon.

"As you wish."

Lavon withdrew his mobile phone and rang a reputable bank in Brussels that was not aware of the fact it controlled much of the Office's operational funds for Europe. He informed his banker that he wished to wire ten million euros posthaste to Bank Weber AG of Linz, Austria. Then he hung up the phone and smiled again at Jihan Nawaz.

"You will have the money by midday tomorrow at the latest," he said.

"Shall I call you with confirmation?"

"Please."

Herr Adler handed her a business card. She reciprocated by handing him one of her own.

"If there's anything more you require, Herr

Adler, please don't hesitate to call me directly. I'll help you, if I can."

Lavon slipped the card into the breast pocket of his suit jacket, along with his mobile phone. Rising, he shook the hand of Jihan Nawaz a final time before making his way toward reception, where the pretty young Austrian girl stood waiting for him. As he moved along the carpeted hall, he could feel the eyes of the two bodyguards boring into his back, but he didn't dare look over his shoulder. He was afraid, he thought. And so was Jihan Nawaz.

34

KING SAUL BOULEVARD, TEL AVIV

I T SEEMS DIFFICULT to imagine, but there was once a time when human beings did not feel the need to share their every waking moment with hundreds of millions, even billions, of complete and utter strangers. If one went to a shopping mall to purchase an article of clothing, one did not post minute-by-minute details on a social networking site; and if one made a fool of oneself at a party, one did not leave a photographic record of the sorry episode in a digital scrapbook that would survive for all eternity. But now, in the era of lost inhibition, it seemed no detail of life was too mundane or humiliating to share. In the online age, it was more important to live out loud than to live with dignity. Internet followers were more treasured than flesh-and-blood friends, for they held the illusive promise of celebrity, even immortality. Were Descartes alive today, he might have written: I tweet, therefore I am.

Employers had learned long ago that the online presence of an individual spoke volumes about his character. Not surprisingly, the world's intelligence services had discovered the same thing. In a bygone time, spies had to open mail and rummage through drawers to learn the deepest secrets of a potential target or recruit. Now all they had to do was tap a few keys, and the secrets came spilling into their laps: names of friends and enemies, lost loves and old wounds, secret passions and desires. In the hands of a skilled operative, such details were a veritable road map to the human heart. They allowed him to push any button, tap any emotion, almost at will. It was easy to make a target feel afraid, for example, if the target had already voluntarily handed over the keys to his fear centers. The same was true if the operative wished to make the target feel happy.

Jihan Nawaz, account manager of Bank Weber AG, born in Syria, naturalized citizen of Germany, was no exception. Technologically savvy, she was a Facebook pioneer, an inveterate user of Twitter, and had recently discovered the delights of Instagram. By scouring her accounts, the team learned that she lived in a small apartment just beyond the perimeter of Linz's Innere Stadt, that she had a troublesome cat called Cleopatra, and that her car, an old Volvo, had given her no end of grief. They learned the names of her favorite bars and nightclubs, her favorite restaurants, and the café where she stopped each morning for coffee and bread on the way to work. They learned, too, that she had never been married and that her last serious boyfriend had treated her deplorably. Mainly, they learned that she had never managed to penetrate the innate xenophobia of the Austrians and that she was lonely. It was a story the team understood well. Jihan Nawaz, like the Jews before her, was the stranger.

Curiously, there were two elements of her life about which Jihan Nawaz never spoke online: her place of work or the country of her birth. Nor was there any mention of the bank or Syria in the mountain of private e-mail that the hackers of Unit 8200, Israel's electronic surveillance service, unearthed from her multiple accounts. Eli Lavon, who had experienced the tense atmosphere inside the bank, wondered whether Jihan was only following an edict laid down by Waleed al-Siddiqi, the man who worked behind a locked door, guarded by a pair of armed Alawites. But Bella Navot suspected the source of Jihan's silence resided elsewhere. And so, as the rest of the team sifted through the digital debris, Bella headed to the file rooms of Research and started digging.

The first twenty-four hours of her search produced nothing of value. Then, on a hunch, she dug out her old files on an incident that had occurred in Syria in February 1982. Under Bella's direction, the Office had produced two definitive accounts of the incident—a highly classified document for use inside Israel's intelligence community, and an unclassified white paper that was released to the public through the Foreign Ministry. Both versions of the report contained the eyewitness testimony of a young girl, but Bella had withheld her name in both documents in order to protect her identity. Deep within her personal research files, however, was a transcript of the girl's original statement, and at the end of the transcript was her name. Two minutes later, breathless after sprinting from Research to Room 456C, she placed the document triumphantly in front of Gabriel. "It's Hama," she said. "The poor thing was at Hama."

"How much do we really know about Waleed al-Siddiqi?"

"Enough to know he's the one we're looking for, Uzi."

"Humor me, Gabriel."

Navot removed his eyeglasses and massaged the bridge of his nose, something he always did when he was not certain how to proceed. He was seated at his large glass desk, with one foot resting on the blotter. Behind him an orange sun was sinking slowly toward the surface of the Mediterranean. Gabriel watched it for a moment. It had been a long time since he had seen the sun.

"He's an Alawite," he said at last, "originally from Aleppo. When he was working in Damascus, he billed himself as a relative of the ruling family. As you might expect, there's no mention of his blood ties in any of Bank Weber's brochures."

"How is he related?"

"Apparently, he's a distant cousin of the mother, which is significant. The mother is the one who told her son to come down like a ton of bricks on the protesters."

"Sounds as though you've been hanging around with my wife."

"I have."

Navot smiled. "So Waleed al-Siddiqi is a charter member of Evil Incorporated?"

"That's what I'm saying, Uzi."

"How did he make his money?"

"He started his career in Syria's state-run pharmaceutical industry, which is also significant."

"Because Syria's pharmaceutical industry is an extension of its chemical and biological weapons program."

Gabriel nodded slowly. "Al-Siddiqi made certain that a good portion of the industry's profits flowed directly into the coffers of the family. He also made certain that Western firms wishing to do business in Syria paid for the privilege in the form of bribes and commissions. Along the way al-Siddiqi became very rich." Gabriel paused, then added, "Rich enough to buy a bank."

Navot frowned. "When did al-Siddiqi leave Syria?"

"Four years ago."

"Just as the Arab Spring was in full bloom," Navot pointed out.

"It was no coincidence. Al-Siddiqi was looking for a safe place to manage the family fortune. And he found one when a small bank in Linz got into trouble during the Great Recession."

"You think the money is being held in accounts at Bank Weber?"

"A portion of it," answered Gabriel. "And he's controlling the rest by using Bank Weber as his calling card."

"Is Herr Weber in on it?"

"I'm not sure."

"What about the girl?"

"No," said Gabriel. "She doesn't know."

"How can you be certain?"

"Because a kissing cousin of the Syrian ruler would never trust a girl from Hama to be his account manager."

Navot lowered his feet to the floor and laid his heavy forearms upon the desktop. The glass seemed in danger of shattering beneath the strain of his powerful body.

"So what do you have in mind?" he asked.

"She's looking for a friend," replied Gabriel. "I'm going to give her one."

"Boy or girl?"

"Girl," said Gabriel. "Definitely a girl."

"Who are you planning to use?"

Gabriel answered.

"She's an analyst."

"She speaks fluent German and Arabic."

"What kind of approach are you thinking about?"

"Hard, I'm afraid."

"And the flag?"

"I can assure you it won't be blue and white."

Navot smiled. When he had worked in the field as a *katsa*, false-flag operations were his specialty. He routinely posed as an officer of German intelligence when recruiting spies from Arab countries or from within the ranks of terrorist organizations. Convincing an Arab to betray his country, or his cause, was easier if the Arab didn't know he was working for the State of Israel.

"What are you planning to do with Bella?" he asked.

"She wants to go into the field. I told her it was your decision."

"The wife of the chief doesn't go into the field."

"She's going to be disappointed."

"I'm used to it."

"What about you, Uzi?"

"What about me?"

"I could use your help for the recruitment."

"Why?"

"Because your grandparents lived in Vienna before the war, and you speak German like an Austrian goatherd."

"It's better than that dreadful Berlin accent of yours."

Navot looked up at his video wall, where a family in the besieged city of Homs was preparing a meal of boiled weeds. It was the only thing left in the city to eat.

"There's one other thing you need to think about," he said. "If you make even the smallest mistake, Waleed al-Siddiqi is going to chop that girl to pieces and throw her into the Danube."

"Actually," replied Gabriel, "he'll let the boys have a little fun with her first. Then he'll kill her."

Navot lowered his gaze from the screen and looked at Gabriel seriously. "You sure you want to go through with this?"

"Absolutely."

"I was hoping that would be your answer."

"What are we going to do about Bella?"

"Take her with you. Or better yet, send her straight to Damascus." Navot looked at the video wall again and shook his head slowly. "This damn war would be over in a week."

Later that evening, the *Guardian* of London published a report accusing the Syrian regime of utilizing torture and murder on an industrial scale. The report was based on a trove of photographs that had been smuggled out of Syria by the man whose job it had been to take them. They depicted the bodies of thousands of people, young men mainly, who had died while in the custody of their government. Some of the men had been shot. Some bore the marks of hanging or electrocution. Others had no eyes. Nearly all looked like human skeletons.

It was against this backdrop that the team carried out their final preparations. From Housekeeping they acquired two safe properties—a small apartment in the center of Linz and a large tawny-colored villa on the shore of the Attersee, twenty-five miles to the south. Transport saw to the cars and motorbikes; Identity, to the passports. Gabriel had several from which to choose, but in the end he settled on Jonathan Albright, an American who worked for something called Markham Capital Advisers of Greenwich, Connecticut. Albright was no ordinary financial consultant. He had recently smuggled a Russian spy from St. Petersburg to the West. And before that he inserted a shipment of sabotaged centrifuges into Iran's nuclear supply chain.

When the preparations were complete, the team members left King Saul Boulevard and headed to their assigned "jump sites," a constellation of safe flats in the Tel Aviv area where Office field operatives assumed their new identities before leaving Israel for their missions. As usual, they traveled to their destination at different times, and by different routes, so as not to arouse the suspicion of the local immigration authorities. Mordecai and Oded were the first to arrive in Austria; Dina Sarid, the last. Her passport identified her as Ingrid Roth, a native of Munich. She spent a single night at the villa on the Attersee. Then, at noon the following day, she took possession of the apartment in Linz. That evening, while standing in the window of the cramped sitting room, she saw an old Volvo rattle to a stop outside the building on the opposite side of the street. The woman who emerged from behind the wheel was Jihan Nawaz.

Dina snapped Jihan's photograph and dispatched it securely to Room 465C, where Gabriel was working late, with no company other than Bella's files on the massacre at Hama. He left King Saul Boulevard a few minutes after ten and, bypassing normal Office procedures, returned to his apartment in Narkiss Street to spend his last night in Israel with his wife. She was sleeping when he arrived; he slipped into bed quietly and placed his hand atop her abdomen. She stirred, gave him a drowsy kiss, and then drifted back to sleep. And in the morning, when she woke, he was gone.

35

MUNICH, GERMANY

THE MANY VERSIONS of Gabriel's face were well known to the security services of Austria, so Travel thought it best to route him through Munich instead. He sailed easily through passport control as a smiling, moneyed American and then rode an airport coach to the long-term parking lot, where Transport had left an untraceable Audi A7. The key was hidden in a magnetic box in the left-rear wheel well. Gabriel removed it with a swipe of his hand and, crouching, searched the undercarriage for any evidence of a bomb. Seeing nothing out of the ordinary, he climbed behind the wheel and started the engine. The radio had been left on; a woman with a low, bored voice was reading a news bulletin on Deutschlandfunk. Unlike many of his countrymen, Gabriel did not recoil at the sound of German. It was the language he had heard in his mother's womb, and even now it remained the language of his dreams. Chiara, when she spoke to him in his sleep, spoke in German.

He found the parking chit where Transport had said it would be—in the center console, tucked

inside a brochure for Munich's racier nightclubs—
and drove with a foreigner's caution toward the
exit. The parking attendant examined the chit long
enough to send the first operational charge of elec-
tricity down the length of Gabriel's spine. Then the
arm of the barricade rose, and he made his way to
the entrance of the autobahn. As he drove through
the Bavarian sunlight, memories assailed him at
every turn. To his right, floating above the Munich
skyline, was the space-age Olympic Tower, beneath
which Black September had carried out the attack
that launched Gabriel's career. And an hour later,
when he crossed into Austria, the first town he entered was Braunau am Inn, the birthplace of Hitler.
He tried to keep thoughts of Vienna at bay, but it
was beyond his powers of compartmentalization.
He heard a car engine hesitate to turn over and saw
a flash of fire rising over a graceful street. And he
sat again at Leah's hospital bed and told her that
her child was dead. *We should have stayed in Venice
together, my love. Things would have turned out differently* . . . Yes, he thought now. Things would be
different. He would have a son of twenty-five. And
he would never have fallen in love with a beautiful
young girl from the ghetto named Chiara Zolli.

The house where Hitler was born stood at
Salzburger Vorstadt 15, not far from Braunau's main
shopping square. Gabriel parked across the street
and sat for a moment with the engine idling, wondering whether he had the strength to go through
with it. Then, suddenly, he flung open the door and
propelled himself across the street, as if to remove
the option of turning back. Twenty-five years ear-

lier, Braunau's mayor had decided to place a stone of remembrance outside the house. It had been mined from the quarry at Mauthausen and was carved with an inscription that made no specific mention of the Jews or the Holocaust. Alone, Gabriel stood before it, thinking not of the murder of six million but of the war taking place two thousand miles to the southeast, in Syria. Despite all the books, the documentaries, the memorials, and the declarations regarding universal human rights, a dictator was once again killing his people with poison gas and turning them into human skeletons in camps and prisons. It was almost as if the lessons of the Holocaust had been forgotten. Or perhaps, thought Gabriel, they had never been learned in the first place.

A young German couple—their distinct accents betrayed them as Bavarians—joined him at the stone and spoke of Hitler as though he were a minor tyrant from a distant empire. Dispirited, Gabriel returned to his car and set out across Upper Austria. Snow clung to the highest mountain peaks, but in the valleys, where the villages lay, the meadows burned with wildflowers. He entered Linz a few minutes after two o'clock and parked near the New Cathedral. Then he spent an hour surveying what would soon be the most bucolic battlefield in the Syrian civil war. It was festival season in Linz. A film festival had just ended; a jazz festival would soon begin. Pale Austrians sunned themselves on the green lawns of Danube Park. Overhead, a single cotton wool cloud scudded across the azure sky like a barrage balloon adrift from its moorings.

The last stop on Gabriel's survey was the streetcar

roundabout adjacent to Bank Weber AG. Parked outside the bank's plain entrance, its engine throbbing at idle, was a black Mercedes Maybach limousine. Judging by the way the car was resting low on its wheels, it was heavily armored. Gabriel sat on a bench and allowed two trams to pass. Then, as a third was nearing the stop, he saw an elegantly dressed man emerge from the bank and duck quickly into the back of the car. His face was memorable for its hard cheekbones and unusually small, straight mouth. A few seconds later, the car shot past Gabriel's shoulder in a black blur. The man was now holding a mobile phone tensely to his ear. Money never sleeps, thought Gabriel. Even blood money.

When a fourth tram slithered into the roundabout, Gabriel stepped on board and rode it to the other side of the Danube. He searched the undercarriage of the car a second time to make certain it had not been tampered with in his absence. Then he headed for the Attersee. The safe house was located on the western shore of the lake, near the town of Litzlberg. There was a wooden gate, and beyond the gate stretched a drive lined with pine and flowering vines. Several cars were parked in the forecourt, including an old Renault with Corsican registration plates. Its owner was standing in the open door of the villa, dressed casually in a pair of loose-fitting khaki trousers and a yellow cotton pullover. "I'm Peter Rutledge," he said, extending his arm toward Gabriel with a smile. "Welcome to Shangri-La."

They were supposed to be on holiday, thus the paperback novels lying open on the lounge chairs,

and the badminton birdies scattered across the
lawn, and the gleaming wooden motorboat, rented
for the princely sum of twenty-five thousand a
week, dozing at the end of the long dock. Inside
the villa, however, it was all business. The walls of
the dining room were hung with maps and surveillance photographs, and resting upon the formal
table were several open notebook computers. On
the screen of one was a static shot of a modern
glass-and-steel mansion located in the hills above
Linz. On another was the entrance of Bank Weber
AG. At ten minutes past five, Herr Weber himself emerged from the doorway and climbed into
a sensible BMW sedan. Two minutes later, there
appeared a young girl who was so pale and pretty
she looked scarcely real. And after the young girl
came Jihan Nawaz. She hurried across the little
square and stepped aboard a waiting streetcar. And
though she did not realize it, the man with pockmarked skin seated across the aisle from her was an
Israeli intelligence officer named Yaakov Rossman.
Together they rode the tram to the Mozartstrasse,
each staring into a private space, and then went
their separate ways—Yaakov to the west, Jihan to
the east. When she arrived at her apartment building, she saw Dina Sarid dismounting her shiny blue
motor scooter on the opposite side of the street.
The two women exchanged a fleeting smile. Then
Jihan entered her building and climbed the stairs
to her flat. Two minutes later, a message appeared
on her Twitter feed, stating that she was thinking
about running over to Bar Vanilli for a drink later
that evening. There were no responses.

For the next three days, the two women floated through the tranquil streets of Linz along lines that did not meet. There was a near encounter on the promenade outside the Museum of Modern Art and a brief meeting of their eyes in the stalls of Alter Markt. But otherwise, fate seemed to conspire to keep them apart. They seemed destined to remain neighbors who did not speak, strangers who gazed at one another across a gulf that could not be bridged.

But unbeknownst to Jihan Nawaz, their eventual meeting was preordained. In fact, it was being actively plotted by a group of men and women operating from a beautiful villa along the shore of a lake twenty miles to the southwest. It was not a question of whether the two women would meet, only of when. All the team required was one more piece of evidence.

It arrived at dawn on the fourth day, when they overheard Hamid Khaddam, the London-based lawyer for LXR Investments, opening a pair of accounts at a dubious bank in the Cayman Islands. Afterward, he rang Waleed al-Siddiqi at his home in Linz and told him the accounts were now ready to receive funds. The money arrived twenty-four hours later, in a transaction that was monitored by the computer hackers of Unit 8200. The first account received $20 million in funds that flowed through Bank Weber AG. The second received $25 million.

Which left only the time, place, and circumstances of the meeting between the two women.

The time would be half past five the following afternoon; the place would be the Pfarrplatz. Dina was seated outside at Café Meier, reading a tattered copy of *The Remains of the Day*, when Jihan walked past her table alone, a shopping bag dangling from her hand. She stopped suddenly, turned around, and walked over to the table.

"That's such a coincidence," she said in German.

"What's that?" replied Dina in the same language.

"You're reading my favorite book."

"Whatever you do, don't tell me how it ends." Dina placed the novel on the table and held out her hand. "I'm Ingrid," she said. "I believe I live across the street from you."

"I believe you do. I'm Jihan." She smiled. "Jihan Nawaz."

36

LINZ, AUSTRIA

THEY WALKED TO a small place not far from their apartments where they could get wine. Dina ordered an Austrian Riesling, knowing full well that, like *The Remains of the Day*, Riesling was Jihan's favorite. The waiter filled their glasses and departed. Jihan raised hers and made a toast to a new friendship. Then she smiled awkwardly, as though she feared she had been presumptuous. She seemed eager, nervous.

"You haven't been in Linz long," she said.

"Ten days," replied Dina.

"And where were you before?"

"I lived in Berlin."

"Berlin is very different from Linz."

"Very," agreed Dina.

"So why did you come here?" Jihan gave another awkward smile. "I'm sorry. I shouldn't pry. It's my worst fault."

"Prying into other people's affairs?"

"I'm hopelessly nosy," she replied, nodding. "Feel free to tell me to mind my own business at any time."

"I wouldn't dream of it." Dina stared into her

glass. "My husband and I were divorced recently. I decided I needed a change of pace, so I came here."

"Why Linz?"

"My family and I used to spend summers in Upper Austria on a lake. I've always loved it here."

"Which lake?"

"The Attersee."

The long shadow of a church bell tower was stretching across the street toward their table. Yossi Gavish and Rimona Stern passed through it, laughing, as though sharing a private joke. The recently divorced Ingrid Roth seemed saddened by the sight of a happy couple. Jihan seemed annoyed.

"But you weren't raised in Germany, were you, Ingrid?"

"Why do you ask?"

"You don't sound like a native German speaker."

"My father worked in New York," Dina explained. "I grew up in Manhattan. When I was young, I refused to speak German at home. I thought it was totally uncool."

If Jihan found the explanation suspicious, she gave no sign of it. "Are you working in Linz?" she asked.

"I suppose that depends on how you define working."

"I define it as going to an office each morning."

"Then I'm definitely not working."

"So why are you here?"

I'm here because of you, thought Dina. Then she explained that she had come to Linz to work on a novel.

"You're a writer?"

"Not yet."

"What's your book about?"

"It's a story of unrequited love."

"Like Stevens and Miss Kenton?" Jihan nodded toward the novel that lay on the table between them.

"A little."

"Is the story set here in Linz?"

"Vienna, actually," replied Dina. "During the war."

"World War Two?"

Dina nodded.

"Are your characters Jewish?"

"One is."

"The boy or the girl?"

"The boy."

"And you?"

"What about me?"

"Are you Jewish, Ingrid?"

"No, Jihan," said Dina. "I'm not Jewish."

Jihan's face remained expressionless.

"And what about you?" asked Dina, changing the subject.

"I'm not Jewish, either," answered Jihan with a smile.

"And you're not from Austria."

"I grew up in Hamburg."

"And before that?"

"I was born in the Middle East." She paused, then added, "In Syria."

"Such a terrible war," Dina said distantly.

"If it's all right with you, Ingrid, I'd rather not discuss the war. It depresses me."

"Then we shall pretend the war doesn't exist."

"At least for now." Jihan drew a packet of cigarettes from her handbag; and when she lit one, Dina could see her hand was trembling slightly. The first inhalation of tobacco seemed to calm her.

"Aren't you going to ask *me* what I'm doing in Linz?"

"What are you doing in Linz, Jihan?"

"A man from my country bought a stake in a small private bank here. He needed someone on his staff who spoke Arabic."

"Which bank?"

Jihan answered truthfully.

"I assume the man from your country isn't named Weber," Dina remarked.

"No." Jihan hesitated, then said, "His name is Waleed al-Siddiqi."

"What kind of work do you do?"

Jihan seemed grateful for the change of subject. "I'm the account manager."

"Sounds important."

"I can assure you it isn't. Primarily, I open and close accounts for our clients. I also oversee transactions with other banks and financial institutions."

"Is it as secretive as everyone says?"

"Austrian banking?"

Dina nodded.

Jihan adopted a stern expression. "Bank Weber takes the privacy of its clients very seriously."

"That sounds like a slogan from a brochure."

Jihan smiled. "It is."

"And what about Mr. al-Siddiqi?" asked Dina. "Does he take the privacy of his clients seriously, too?"

Jihan's smile evaporated. She drew on her cigarette and glanced nervously around the empty street.

"I need to ask a favor, Ingrid," she said at last.

"Anything."

"Please don't ask me any questions about Mr. al-Siddiqi. In fact, I would prefer it if you never mention his name again."

Thirty minutes later, in the Attersee safe house, Gabriel and Eli Lavon were seated before a laptop computer, listening as the two women parted in the street outside their opposing apartment buildings. When Dina was safely in her flat, Gabriel slid the toggle bar of the audio player back to the beginning and listened to the entire encounter a second time. Then he listened to it again. He might have replayed it a fourth time had Eli Lavon not reached out and clicked the STOP icon.

"I told you she was the one," Lavon said.

Gabriel frowned. Then he set the toggle bar to 5:47 p.m. and clicked PLAY.

"Are your characters Jewish?"

"One is."

"The boy or the girl?"

"The boy."

"And you?"

"What about me?"

"Are you Jewish, Ingrid?"

"No, Jihan. I'm not Jewish."

Gabriel clicked STOP and looked at Lavon.

"You can't have everything, Gabriel. Besides, this is the important part."

Lavon slid the toggle bar forward and pressed PLAY again.

"I open and close accounts for our clients. I also oversee transactions with other banks and financial institutions."

STOP.

"Do you see my point?" asked Lavon.

"I'm not sure you've made one."

"Flirt with her. Make her feel comfortable. And then bring her in for a landing. But whatever you do," Lavon added, "don't take too long. I wouldn't want Mr. al-Siddiqi to find out that Jihan has a new girlfriend who may or may not be Jewish."

"Do you think he'd mind?"

"He might."

"So how should we proceed?"

Lavon moved the toggle bar forward and clicked PLAY.

"It was a pleasure to meet you, Ingrid. I'm only sorry we didn't get together sooner."

"Let's not let another ten days go by."

"Are you free for lunch tomorrow?"

"I usually work during lunch."

Lavon clicked STOP.

"I think Ingrid's been working too hard, don't you?"

"It might be dangerous to break the rhythm of her writing routine."

"Sometimes a change can help. Who knows? She might be inspired to write a different novel."

"What's the story line?"

"It's about a girl who decides to betray her boss when she finds out he's hiding money for the worst man in the world."

"How does it end?"

"The good guys win."

"Does the girl get hurt?"

"Send the message, Gabriel."

Gabriel quickly dispatched an encrypted e-mail to Dina instructing her to make a lunch date with Jihan Nawaz for the following afternoon. Then he reset the toggle and pressed PLAY a final time.

"And what about Mr. al-Siddiqi? Does he take the privacy of his clients seriously, too?"

"I need to ask a favor, Ingrid."

"Anything."

"Please don't ask me any questions about Mr. al-Siddiqi. In fact, I would prefer it if you never mention his name again."

STOP.

"She knows," said Lavon. "The only question is, how much?"

"I suspect it's just enough to get her killed."

"Hama Rules?"

Gabriel nodded slowly.

"Then I suppose that leaves us with only one option."

"What's that, Eli?"

"We'll have to play by Hama Rules, too."

The two women had lunch the next day at Ikaan, and the evening after that they had drinks at Bar Vanilli. Gabriel allowed two more days to pass without additional contact, in part because he needed to move a certain asset from Israel to the Attersee, namely, Uzi Navot. Then, on the Thursday of that week, Jihan and Dina had an accidental meeting in the Alter Markt that was not an accident at all. Jihan invited Dina for a coffee, but Dina apologized and said she had to get back to her writing.

"But are you doing anything on Saturday?" she asked.

"I'm not sure. Why?"

"Some friends of mine are having a party."

"What kind of party?"

"Food, drinks, boat rides on the lake—the usual thing people do on a Saturday afternoon in the summertime."

"I wouldn't want to be an imposition."

"You won't be. In fact," Dina added, "I'm quite certain my friends will make you the guest of honor."

Jihan smiled. "I'm going to need a new dress."

"And a swimsuit," said Dina.

"Will you come shopping with me now?"

"Of course."

"What about your book?"

"There'll be time for that later."

37

THE ATTERSEE, AUSTRIA

THEY HAD TWO transportation options: Dina's little motor scooter or Jihan's fickle Volvo. They chose the fickle Volvo. It rattled out of the Innere Stadt a few minutes after noon, and by half past they had put the last suburbs of Linz behind them and were speeding through the Salzkammergut on the A1. The weather had conspired to create the illusion of gaiety. The sun shone from a cloudless sky, and the air that flowed through their open windows was cool and soft. Jihan wore the white sleeveless dress that Dina had chosen for her and wide movie-starlet sunglasses that concealed the plainness of her features. Her nails were freshly painted; her scent was warm and intoxicating. It filled Dina with guilt. She had given false happiness to a lonely and friendless woman. It was, she thought, the ultimate feminine betrayal.

She had in her handbag a set of driving instructions, which she removed as they turned off the A1, onto the Atterseestrasse. Gabriel had insisted she carry them, and now, with her conscience in rebellion, she clutched them tightly as she guided

Jihan toward her destination. They passed through a small resort town, then through a checkerboard of cultivated land. The lake lay to their left, deep blue and rimmed by green mountains. Dina, playing the role of tour guide, pointed out the tiny island, reached by a jetty, where Gustav Klimt had painted his renowned Attersee landscapes.

Beyond the island was a marina where white sailboats sparkled at their moorings, and beyond the marina was a colony of lakefront villas. Dina feigned a moment of confusion over which one belonged to their host. Then, suddenly, she pointed toward an open gate, as though surprised they had reached it so quickly. Jihan swung the car expertly to the left and headed slowly up the drive. Dina was grateful for the heavy scent of the pine and the flowering vines, for it temporarily overwhelmed the accusatory aroma of Jihan's perfume. Several cars were parked haphazardly in the shade of the forecourt. Jihan found an empty space and switched off the engine. Then she reached into the backseat to retrieve the flowers and wine she had brought as gifts. As they climbed out of the car, music swelled from an open window: "Trust in Me" by Etta James.

The front door of the villa was open, too. As Dina and Jihan approached, there appeared a man of late middle age with a head of wispy, flyaway hair. He wore a costly dress shirt of French blue, pale linen trousers, and a large gold wristwatch. He was smiling pleasantly, but his brown eyes were watchful, vigilant. Jihan took a few steps toward him and froze. Then her head turned toward Dina, who appeared oblivious to her apprehension. "I'd like you to meet an old friend of my family," she was saying. "Jihan Nawaz, this is Feliks Adler."

Jihan remained motionless, unsure of whether to advance or retreat, as the man she knew as Feliks Adler came slowly down the steps. Still smiling, he relieved her of the flowers and wine. Then he looked at Dina.

"I'm afraid Miss Nawaz and I are already acquainted." His gaze moved from Dina to Jihan. "But she can't tell you that because it would violate the customs of Austrian private banking." He paused long enough to hoist another smile. "Isn't that correct, Miss Nawaz?"

Jihan remained silent. She was staring at the flowers in Herr Adler's hand.

"It's not a coincidence I opened an account at Bank Weber the week before last," he said after a moment. "Nor is it a coincidence you're here today. You see, Miss Nawaz, Ingrid and I are more than old friends. We're colleagues, too."

Jihan shot Dina a dark look of anger. Then she stared again at the man she knew as Herr Adler. When finally she spoke, her voice was hollow with fear.

"What do you want with me?" she asked.

"We have a serious problem," he replied. "And we need your help in solving it."

"What kind of problem?"

"Come inside, Jihan. No one can hurt you here." He smiled and took her gently by the elbow. "Have a glass of wine. Join the party. Meet the rest of our friends."

In the great room of the villa a table had been laid with food and drink. It had not been touched, so the impression was of a celebration canceled, or at least delayed. A gentle wind blew in through the open French doors, bringing with it the occasional grumble of a passing motorboat. At the far end of the room was a dormant fireplace where Gabriel sat peering into an open file. He wore a dark business suit with no necktie, and was unrecognizable in a gray wig, contact lenses, and eyeglasses. Uzi Navot sat next to him in similar attire, and next to Navot was Yossi Gavish. He wore chinos and a rumpled blazer and was staring at the ceiling in the manner of a traveler suffering from terminal boredom.

The arrival of Jihan Nawaz stirred only Gabriel into action. He closed his file, placed it on the coffee table before him, and rose slowly to his feet. "Jihan," he said through a charitable smile. "It was good of you to come." He advanced on her cautiously, an adult approaching a lost child. "Please forgive the unorthodox nature of our invitation, but it was all done for your protection."

He said this in German, in his distinct Berlin dialect. It was not lost on Jihan, the Syrian girl from Hamburg now living in Linz.

"Who are you?" she asked after a moment.

"I'd rather not begin this conversation by lying to you," he said, still smiling, "so I won't bother giving you a name. I am employed by a government department that deals with issues related to taxation and finance." He pointed to Navot and Yossi. "These gentlemen are similarly employed by their respective governments. The large, unhappy-looking fellow is from Austria, and the wrinkled chap sitting next to him is from Great Britain."

"What about them?" Jihan asked with a nod toward Lavon and Dina.

"Ingrid and Herr Adler belong to me."

"They're very good." She glared at Dina through narrowed eyes. "Especially her."

"I'm sorry we deceived you, Jihan, but we had no other choice. It was all done for your safety."

"My safety?"

He took a step closer to her. "We wanted to meet you in a way that wouldn't raise the suspicion of your employer." He paused, then added, "Mr. al-Siddiqi."

She seemed to recoil at the mention of his name. Gabriel pretended not to notice.

"I assume you brought your mobile phone with you?" he asked, as though the thought had just occurred to him.

"Of course."

"Would you give it to Ingrid, please? It is important that we switch off all our mobile devices before we continue this conversation. One never knows who's listening."

Jihan extracted her phone from her handbag and surrendered it to Dina, who switched off the power before slipping silently into the next room. Gabriel returned to the coffee table and retrieved his file. He opened it gravely, as though it contained material he'd rather not air in public.

"I'm afraid the bank for which you work has been under investigation for some time," he said after a moment. "The investigation is international in nature, as you can see by the presence of my counterparts from Austria and the United Kingdom. And it has uncovered substantial evidence to suggest that Bank Weber AG is little more than a criminal enterprise involved in money laundering, fraud, and the illegal concealment of taxable assets and income. Which means that you, Jihan, are in serious trouble."

"I'm just the account manager."

"Exactly." He drew a sheet of paper from the file and held it up for her to see. "Whenever an account is opened at Bank Weber, Jihan, your signature appears on all accompanying documentation. You also handle most of the bank's wire transfers." He drew another sheet of paper from the file, though this time his consultation was private. "For example, you recently wired a rather large sum of money to the Trade Winds Bank in the Cayman Islands."

"How do you know about that transfer?"

"There were two, actually—one for twenty-five million dollars, the other for a paltry twenty million. The accounts where the money was sent are controlled by LXR Investments. A lawyer named Hamid Khaddam opened them on Mr. al-Siddiqi's instructions. Hamid Khaddam is from London. He was born in Syria." Gabriel looked up from the file. "Like you, Jihan."

Her fear was palpable. She managed to lift her chin a little before offering her response.

"I've never met Mr. Khaddam."

"But you're familiar with his name?"

She nodded slowly.

"And you don't dispute the fact that you personally wired the money into those accounts."

"I was only doing what I was told."

"By Mr. al-Siddiqi?"

She was silent. Gabriel returned the documents to the file folder and the file folder to the coffee table. Yossi was staring at the ceiling again. Navot was gazing out the French doors at a passing boat as though he wished he could be on it.

"I seem to be losing my audience," Gabriel said, gesturing toward the two unmoving figures. "I can tell that they'd like me to get to the point so we can move on to more important matters."

"What point is that?" Jihan asked with more calm than Gabriel would have thought possible.

"My friends from Vienna and London aren't interested in prosecuting a lowly bank clerk. And, quite frankly, neither am I. We want the man who pulls the strings at Bank Weber, the man who works behind a locked door, protected by a pair of armed bodyguards." He paused, then added, "We want Mr. al-Siddiqi."

"I'm afraid I can't help you."

"Of course you can."

"Do I have a choice?"

"We all make choices in life," Gabriel replied. "Unfortunately, you decided to take a job at the dirtiest bank in Austria."

"I didn't know it was dirty."

"Prove it."

"How?"

"By telling us everything you know about Mr. al-Siddiqi. And by giving us a complete list of all of Bank Weber's clients, the amount of money they've placed under management there, and the location of the various financial instruments in which the money is invested."

"That's impossible."

"Why?"

"Because it would be a violation of Austrian banking laws."

Gabriel placed a hand on Navot's shoulder. "This man works for the Austrian government. And if he says it isn't a violation of Austrian law, then it isn't."

Jihan hesitated. "There's another reason I can't help you," she said finally. "I don't have complete access to the names of all the account holders."

"Are you not the account manager?"

"Of course."

"And is not the job of the account manager to actually *manage* the accounts?"

"Obviously," she replied with a frown.

"So what's the problem?"

"Mr. al-Siddiqi."

"Then perhaps we should start there, Jihan." Gabriel placed a hand gently on her shoulder. "With Mr. al-Siddiqi."

T HEY SETTLED HER in a place of honor in the sitting room, with Dina, her false friend, on her left, and Gabriel, the nameless tax authority from Berlin, on her right. Uzi Navot offered her food, which she refused, and tea, which she accepted. He served it to her Arab style, in a small glass, medium sweet. She granted herself a small sip, blew gently on the surface, and placed the glass carefully on the table in front of her. Then she described an afternoon in the autumn of 2010, when she noticed an ad in a trade publication for a job opening in Linz. She was working deep within the Hamburg headquarters of an important German bank at the time and, quietly, was exploring other options. She traveled to Linz the following week and interviewed with Herr Weber. Then she walked down the hall, past a pair of bodyguards, for a separate meeting with Mr. al-Siddiqi. He conducted it entirely in Arabic.

"Did he mention the fact he was from Syria originally?" asked Gabriel.

"He didn't have to."

"Syrians have a distinct accent?"

She nodded. "Especially when they come from the Ansariya Mountains."

"The Ansariya are in western Syria? Near the Mediterranean?"

"That's correct."

"And the people who live there are mainly Alawites, are they not?"

She hesitated, then nodded slowly.

"Forgive me, Jihan, but I am a bit of a novice when it comes to the affairs of the Middle East."

"Most Germans are."

He accepted her rebuke with a conciliatory smile and then resumed his line of questioning.

"Was it your impression that Mr. al-Siddiqi was an Alawite?" he asked.

"It was obvious."

"Are you an Alawite, Jihan?"

"No," she answered. "I'm not an Alawite."

She offered no additional biographical details about herself, and Gabriel didn't ask for any.

"The Alawites are the rulers of your country, are they not?"

"I am a citizen of Germany living in Austria," she replied.

"Will you allow me to rephrase my question?"

"Please."

"The ruling family of Syria are Alawites—isn't that correct, Jihan?"

"Yes."

"And Alawites hold the most powerful positions in the military and the Syrian security services."

She gave a brief smile. "Perhaps you're not such a novice after all."

"I'm a quick study."

"Obviously."

"Did Mr. al-Siddiqi tell you he was a relative of the president?"

"He hinted at it," she said.

"Did this concern you?"

"It was before the Arab Spring." She paused, then added, "Before the war."

"And the two bodyguards outside his door?" asked Gabriel. "How did he explain them?"

"He told me he'd been kidnapped in Beirut several years earlier and held for ransom."

"And you believed him?"

"Beirut is a dangerous city."

"You've been?"

"Never."

Gabriel peered into his file again. "Mr. al-Siddiqi must have been very impressed with you," he said after a moment. "He offered you a job on the spot, at twice the salary you were earning at your bank in Hamburg."

"How do you know that?"

"It was on your Facebook page. You told everyone you were looking forward to a fresh start. Your colleagues in Hamburg threw a good-bye party for you at a swanky restaurant along the river. I can show you the photos if you like."

"That won't be necessary," she said. "I remember the evening well."

"And when you arrived in Linz," Gabriel continued, "Mr. al-Siddiqi had an apartment waiting for you, didn't he? It was fully furnished—linens, dishes, pots and pans, even the electronics."

"It was included in my compensation package."

Gabriel looked up from the file and frowned. "Didn't you find it odd?"

"He said he wanted my transition to be as painless as possible."

"That was the word he used? Painless?"

"Yes."

"And what did Mr. al-Siddiqi ask for in return?"

"Loyalty."

"Is that all?"

"No," she said. "He told me I was never to discuss the affairs of Bank Weber with anyone."

"With good reason."

She was silent.

"How long did it take you to realize Bank Weber was no ordinary private bank, Jihan?"

"I had some suspicions early on," she replied. "But by the time spring arrived, I was all but certain of it."

"What happened in the spring?"

"Fifteen boys from Daraa painted graffiti on the wall of a school. And Mr. al-Siddiqi started to get very nervous."

―――――――――――

For the next six months, she said, he was in constant motion—London, Brussels, Geneva, Dubai, Hong Kong, Argentina, sometimes all in the same week. His appearance began to deteriorate. He lost weight; dark circles appeared beneath his eyes. His concerns about security increased dramatically. When he was in his office, which was seldom, the television was tuned constantly to Al Jazeera.

"He was following the war?" asked Gabriel.

"Obsessively," replied Jihan.

"Did he choose sides?"

"What do you think?"

Gabriel made no reply. Jihan sipped her tea thoughtfully before elaborating.

"He was furious at the Americans for calling on the Syrian president to step aside," she said finally. "He said it was Egypt all over again. He said they would rue the day they allowed him to be pushed out."

"Because al-Qaeda would take over Syria?"

"Yes."

"And you, Jihan? Did you take sides in the war?"

She was silent.

"Surely Mr. al-Siddiqi must have been curious about how you felt."

More silence. She glanced nervously around the room, at the walls, at the ceiling. It was the Syrian disease, thought Gabriel. The fear never left them.

"You're safe here, Jihan," said Gabriel quietly. "You're among friends."

"Am I?"

She looked at the faces gathered around her. The client who was not a client. The neighbor who was not a neighbor. The three tax officials who were not tax officials.

"One doesn't voice one's true opinion in front of a man like Mr. al-Siddiqi," she said after a moment. "Especially if one has relatives who still live in Syria."

"You were afraid of him?"

"With good reason."

"And so you told him that you shared his opinion about the war."

She hesitated, then nodded slowly.

"And do you, Jihan?"

"Share his opinion?"

"Yes."

Another hesitation. Another nervous glance around the room. Finally, she said, "No, I do not share Mr. al-Siddiqi's opinion about the war."

"You support the rebels?"

"I support freedom."

"Are you a jihadist?"

She raised her bare arm and asked, "Do I look like a jihadist?"

"No," said Gabriel, smiling at her demonstration. "You look like a thoroughly modern, westernized woman who no doubt finds the conduct of the Syrian regime abhorrent."

"I do."

"So why did you remain in the employ of a man who supports a regime that is murdering its own citizens?"

"I sometimes wonder the same thing."

"Did Mr. al-Siddiqi pressure you to stay?"

"No."

"Then maybe you stayed for the money. After all, he was paying you twice as much as you were earning at your previous job." Gabriel paused and cocked his head thoughtfully to one side. "Or maybe you stayed for another reason, Jihan. Maybe you stayed because you were curious about what was going on behind the locked door and the shield of bodyguards. Maybe you were curious about why Mr. al-Siddiqi was traveling so much and losing so much weight."

She hesitated, then said, "Maybe I was."

"Do you know what Mr. al-Siddiqi is doing, Jihan?"

"He's managing the money of a very special client."

"Do you know the client's name?"

"I do."

"How did you learn it?"

"By accident."

"What sort of accident?"

"I forgot my wallet at work one night," she answered. "And when I went back to get it, I heard something I wasn't supposed to hear."

THE ATTERSEE, AUSTRIA

LATER, WHEN JIHAN thought about that day, she would remember it as Black Friday. Fears of a Greek meltdown had caused stock prices to plummet dramatically in Europe and America, and in Switzerland the Economy Ministry announced it was freezing $200 million worth of assets linked to the Syrian ruling family and their associates. Mr. al-Siddiqi appeared stricken by the news. He remained barricaded in his office most of the afternoon, emerging only twice to shout at Jihan over trivial matters. She spent the last hour of that workday watching the clock, and at the stroke of five she bolted for the door without wishing Mr. al-Siddiqi or Herr Weber a pleasant weekend, as was her custom. It was only later, when she was dressing for dinner, that she realized she had left her wallet at the office.

"How did you get back into the bank?" asked Gabriel.

"With my keys, of course."

"I didn't realize you had your own set."

She dug them from her handbag and held them

up for Gabriel to see. "As you know," she said, "Bank Weber isn't a retail bank. We are a private bank, which means we are primarily a wealth-management firm for high-net-worth individuals."

"Do you keep cash on hand?"

"A small amount."

"Does the bank offer safe-deposit boxes to its clients?"

"Of course."

"Where are they?"

"Below street level."

"Do you have access to them?"

"I'm the account manager."

"Which means?"

"I can go anywhere in the bank, except for the offices of Herr Weber or Mr. al-Siddiqi."

"They're off-limits?"

"Unless I am invited inside."

He paused, as if to digest this information, and then asked Jihan to resume her account of the events of Black Friday. She explained that she returned to the bank in her car and, using her personal keys, admitted herself through the front entrance. Once the door was opened, she had thirty seconds to enter the proper eight-digit number into the security system control panel; otherwise, the alarm would sound and half the police force of Linz would be there in a matter of minutes. But when she went to the panel, she could see that the alarm system had not been activated.

"Which meant someone else was in the bank?"

"Correct."

"It was Mr. al-Siddiqi?"

"He was in his office," she said, nodding slowly. "On the phone."

"With whom?"

"Someone who was unhappy that his assets had just been frozen by the Swiss government."

"Do you know who it was?"

"No," she answered. "But I suspect it was someone powerful."

"Why do you say that?"

"Because Mr. al-Siddiqi sounded frightened." She was silent for a moment. "It was rather shocking. It's not something I'll ever forget."

"Were the bodyguards present?"

"No."

"Why not?"

"I assume he'd sent them away."

He asked what she did next. She answered that she'd collected her wallet and left the bank as quickly as possible. On Monday morning, when she returned to work after the weekend, a note waited on her desk. It was from Mr. al-Siddiqi. He wanted a word in private.

"Why did he want to see you?"

"He said he wished to apologize." She smiled unexpectedly. "Another first."

"Apologize for what?"

"For snapping at me the previous Friday. It was a lie, of course," she added quickly. "He wanted to see whether I'd heard anything when I was inside the bank that evening."

"He knew you'd been there?"

She nodded.

"How?"

"He routinely checks the memory of the surveillance cameras. In fact, they're fed directly into the computer on his desk."

"Did he ask you outright what you'd heard?"

"Mr. al-Siddiqi never does anything outright. He prefers to nibble around the edges."

"What did you tell him?"

"Enough to put his mind at ease."

"And he believed you?"

"Yes," she answered after a moment of thought. "I think he did."

"And that was the end of it?"

"No," she replied. "He wanted to talk about the war."

"What about the war?"

"He asked me whether my relatives still living in Syria were well. He wanted to know whether there was anything he could do to help them."

"Was he being genuine?"

"When a relative of the ruling family offers to help, it usually means the opposite."

"He was threatening you?"

She was silent.

"And yet you stayed," said Gabriel.

"Yes," she said. "I stayed."

"And your relatives?" he asked, consulting his file again. "Are they well, Jihan?"

"Several have been killed or injured."

"I'm very sorry to hear that."

She nodded once but said nothing.

"Where were they killed?"

"In Damascus."

"Is that where you're from, Jihan?"

"I lived there briefly when I was a child."

"But you weren't born there?"

"No," she said. "I was born north of Damascus."

"Where?"

"Hama," she said. "I was born in Hama."

A SILENCE FELL OVER the room, heavy and foreboding, like the silence that follows hard upon a suicide bombing in a crowded marketplace. Bella crept into it without introduction and settled herself in an empty chair directly across from Jihan. The two women stared at each other, as if they alone were privy to a terrible secret, while Gabriel leafed distractedly through his file. When finally he spoke again, he adopted a tone of clinical detachment, a doctor conducting a routine physical on an otherwise healthy patient.

"You're thirty-eight years old, Jihan?" he asked.

"Thirty-*nine*," she corrected him. "But has no one ever told you that it's terribly impolite to ask a woman her age?"

Her remark produced tepid smiles around the room, which faded as Gabriel posed his next question.

"Which means you were born in . . ." His voice trailed off, as though he were trying to work out the calculation. Jihan supplied the date for him without further prompting.

"I was born in 1976," she said.

"In Hama?"

"Yes," she answered. "In Hama."

Bella looked at her husband, who was looking elsewhere. Gabriel was again leafing through his file with a tax collector's devotion to printed matter.

"And when did you move to Damascus, Jihan?" he asked.

"It was the autumn of 1982."

He looked up suddenly and wrinkled his brow. "Why, Jihan?" he asked. "Why did you leave Hama in the autumn of 1982?"

She returned his gaze silently. Then she looked at Bella, the newcomer, the woman with no apparent job or purpose, and delivered her response. "We left Hama," she said, "because in the autumn of 1982 there was no Hama. The city was gone. Hama had been wiped from the face of the earth."

"There was fighting in Hama between the regime and the Muslim Brotherhood?"

"It wasn't fighting," she replied. "It was a massacre."

"And so you and your family moved to Damascus?"

"No," she said. "I went by myself."

"Why, Jihan?" he asked, closing the file. "Why did you go to Damascus by yourself?"

"Because I didn't have a family anymore. No family, no town." She looked at Bella again. "I was alone."

To understand what happened in Hama, Jihan resumed, it was necessary to know what had come before. The city was once regarded as the most beautiful in Syria, noted for the graceful water-wheels along the Orontes River. It was also known for the unique fervor of its Sunni Islam. The women of Hama wore the veil long before it was fashionable in the rest of the Muslim world, especially in the old neighborhood of Barudi, where the Nawaz family lived in a cramped apartment. Jihan was one of five children, the youngest, the only girl. Her father had no formal education and worked odd jobs in the old souk on the other side of the river. Mainly, he studied the Koran and railed against the Syrian dictator, whom he regarded as a heretic and a peasant who had no right to rule over Sunnis. Her father was not a full-fledged member of the Muslim Brotherhood, but he supported the Brotherhood's goal of turning Syria into an Islamic state. Twice he was arrested and tortured by the Mukhabarat, and once he was forced to dance in the street while singing the praises of the ruler and his family. "It was the ultimate insult," Jihan explained. "As a devout Sunni Muslim, my father did not listen to music. And he *never* danced."

Her personal memories of the troubles leading up to the massacre were gauzy at best. She recalled some of the Brotherhood's bigger terrorist bombings—in particular, an attack in Damascus that killed sixty-four innocent people—and she remembered bullet-riddled bodies in the alleys of Barudi, victims of summary executions carried out by agents of the Mukhabarat. But like most Hamawis, she had no premonition of the calamity that was about to befall the beautiful city along the banks of the Orontes. Then, on a wet, cold night in early February, word spread that units of the Defense Companies had quietly slipped into the city. They attempted to stage their first raid in Barudi, but the Brotherhood was lying in wait. Several of the regime's men were cut down in a hail of gunfire. Then the Brotherhood and their supporters launched a series of murderous attacks against members of the Baath Party and the Mukhabarat across the city. From the minarets came the same exhortation: "Rise up and drive the unbelievers from Hama!" The battle for the city had begun.

As it turned out, the Brotherhood's initial successes would unleash the fury of the regime as never before. For the next three weeks, the Syrian army used tanks, attack helicopters, and artillery to turn Hama into a pile of rubble. And when the military phase of the operation was complete, Syrian demolition experts dynamited any building left standing and steamrolled the debris. Those who managed to survive the onslaught were rounded up and put into detention centers. Anyone suspected of having links to the Brotherhood was brutally tortured and killed. The corpses were buried in mass graves and paved over with asphalt. "To walk the streets of Hama today," said Jihan, "is to walk over the bones of the dead."

"But you survived," said Gabriel quietly.

"Yes," she replied. "I survived."

A tear spilled onto her cheek and left a trail that stretched to her chin. It was her first. She brushed it away abruptly, as though she were afraid of showing emotion in front of strangers, and then straightened the hem of her sundress.

"And your family?" asked Gabriel, intruding on her silence. "What happened to them?"

"My father and brothers were killed during the fighting."

"And your mother?"

"She was killed a few days later. She had given birth to four enemies of the regime. She could not be allowed to live."

Another tear escaped her eye. This time she ignored it.

"And you, Jihan? What was your fate?"

"I was sent to a camp along with the other children of Hama. It was somewhere in the desert, I'm not sure where. A few months later, the Mukhabarat allowed me to go to Damascus to live with a distant cousin. He never liked me much, so he packed me off to Germany to live with his brother."

"In Hamburg?"

She nodded slowly. "We lived on the Marienstrasse. Number Fifty-Seven." She paused, then asked, "Have you ever heard of this street? The Marienstrasse?"

Gabriel said he hadn't. It was yet another lie.

"There were some boys who lived across the street at Number Fifty-Four. Muslim boys. Arabs. I thought one of the boys was quite handsome. He was quiet, intense. He never looked me in the eye when we passed in the street because I didn't wear the veil." Her gaze moved from face to face. "And do you know who that boy turned out to be? He was Mohamed Atta." She shook her head slowly. "It was almost as if I'd never left Barudi. I'd traded one Muslim Brotherhood neighborhood for another."

"But you weren't interested in Middle East politics?"

"Never," she said, shaking her head resolutely. "I tried my best to be a good German girl, even if the Germans didn't like me very much. I went to school, I went to university, and then I got a job at a German bank."

"And then you came to Linz," said Gabriel. "And you took a job working for a man who was related to the people who murdered your family."

She was silent.

"Why?" asked Gabriel. "Why did you go to work for a man like Waleed al-Siddiqi?"

"I don't know." She looked at the faces gathered around her. The client who was not a client. The neighbor who was not a neighbor. The three tax officials who were not tax officials. "But I'm glad I did."

Gabriel smiled. "So am I."

THE ATTERSEE, AUSTRIA

B Y THEN, IT was late afternoon. Outside, the wind had died and the surface of the lake looked like a sheet of tinted glass. Jihan appeared suddenly exhausted; she was staring through the open French doors with the blank eyes of a refugee. Gabriel quietly packed away his files and removed his bureaucrat's suit coat. Then, alone, he led Jihan across the garden to the wooden motorboat tied to the end of the long dock. He boarded first and, taking Jihan's hand, helped her into the aft seating area. She slipped on her movie-starlet sunglasses and arranged herself carefully, as though she were about to have her photograph taken. Gabriel started the engine, untied the lines, and set them adrift. He eased away from the dock slowly, so as to leave no wake, and turned the boat to the south. The sky was still clear, but the mountain peaks at the end of the lake had snared a few strands of a passing cloud. The Austrians called the mountains the Höllengebirge: the Mountains of Hell.

"You handle a boat very well," Jihan said to his back.

"I used to do a bit of sailing when I was younger."

"Where?"

"The Baltic," he answered. "I spent my summers there when I was a boy."

"Yes," said Jihan distantly. "And I hear Ingrid used to spend her summers here on the Attersee."

They were alone in the center of the lake. Gabriel killed the engine and swiveled his chair round to face her.

"You know everything about me now," she said, "and yet I know nothing about you. Not even your name."

"It's for your own protection."

"Or maybe it's for yours." She lifted her dark glasses so he could see her eyes. The late-afternoon sun lightened them. "Do you know what will happen to me if Mr. al-Siddiqi ever learns that I've told you these things?"

"He'll kill you," replied Gabriel flatly. "Which is why we'll make certain he never knows."

"Maybe he already knows." She regarded him seriously for a moment. "Or maybe you work for Mr. al-Siddiqi. Maybe I'm already dead."

"Do I look like I work for Mr. al-Siddiqi?"

"No," she admitted. "But you don't look much like a German tax collector, either."

"Looks can be deceiving."

"So can German tax collectors."

A breath of wind blew across the boat and made ripples on the surface of the lake.

"Do you smell that?" asked Jihan. "The air smells of flowers."

"They call it the Rosenwind."

"Really?"

He nodded. Jihan closed her eyes and inhaled the scent.

"My mother always wore a bit of rose oil on the side of her neck and on the hem of her hijab. When the Syrians were shelling Hama, she would hold me tightly so I wouldn't be afraid. I used to press my face against the side of her neck so I could smell roses instead of the smoke from the fires."

She opened her eyes and looked at Gabriel. "Who are you?" she asked.

"I'm the man who's going to help you finish what you started."

"What does that mean?"

"You stayed at Bank Weber for a reason, Jihan. You wanted to know what Mr. al-Siddiqi was doing. And now you know that he's been hiding money for the regime. Billions of dollars that should have been spent to educate and care for the Syrian people. Billions of dollars now sitting in a network of bank accounts scattered around the world."

"What do you intend to do about it?"

"I'm going to turn the Syrian ruling family into peasants from the Ansariya Mountains again." He paused, then added, "And you're going to help me."

"I can't."

"Why not?"

"Because I can't get the information you're looking for."

"Where is it?"

"Some of it is on the computer in Mr. al-Siddiqi's office. It's very secure."

"Computer security is a myth, Jihan."

"Which is why he doesn't keep the truly important information stored there. He knows better than to trust it to any electronic device."

"Are you telling me it's all in his head?"

"No," she replied. "It's here."

She placed her hand over her heart.

"He carries it with him?"

"In a small leather notebook," she answered, nodding. "It's either in the breast pocket of his jacket or in his briefcase, but he *never* lets it out of his sight."

"What's in the book?"

"A list of account numbers, institutions, and current balances. Very simple. Very straightforward."

"You've seen it?"

She nodded. "It was on his desk once when he called me into his office. It's written in his own hand. Accounts that have been terminated or changed are crossed out by a single line."

"Are there any other copies?"

She shook her head.

"You're sure?"

"Absolutely," she answered. "He keeps only one copy so he'll know if anyone has had access to it."

"And if he suspects that someone has seen it?"

"I suppose he has a way to lock down the accounts."

A faint breeze made it seem as though a bouquet of roses had been laid between them. She slipped on her sunglasses and trailed a fingertip over the surface of the water.

"There is one other problem," she said after a moment. "If several billion dollars in Syrian assets disappears, Mr. al-Siddiqi and his friends in Damascus are going to start looking for it." She paused, then added, "Which means you're going to have to make me disappear, too." She withdrew her hand from the water and looked at Gabriel. "Can you do that?"

"In the blink of an eye."

"Will I be safe?"

"Yes, Jihan. You'll be safe."

"Where will I live?"

"Wherever you want—within reason, of course."

"I like it here," she said, looking around at the mountains. "But it might be too close to Linz."

"So we'll find somewhere like it."

"I'll need a house. And a bit of money. Not much," she added quickly. "Just enough to live."

"Something tells me money isn't going to be a problem."

"Make sure it isn't the ruler's money." She dipped her fingertip into the lake again. "It's covered in blood."

She seemed to be writing something on the surface of the water. Gabriel was tempted to ask her what it was, but he left her in peace. A strand of cloud had broken free of the Mountains of Hell. It floated over their heads, so close, it seemed, that Gabriel had to resist the urge to reach out and grasp it.

"You never explained how you found me," Jihan said suddenly.

"You wouldn't believe me if I told you."

"Is it a good story?"

"I hope so."

"Maybe Ingrid will write it instead of the story she's working on now. I've never liked stories about

Vienna during the war. They're too much like Hama."

She lifted her gaze from the water and settled it on Gabriel. "Are you ever going to tell me who you are?"

"When it's over."

"Are you telling me the truth?"

"Yes, Jihan. I'm telling you the truth."

"Tell me your name," she insisted. "Tell it to me now and I'll write it on the lake. And when it's gone, I'll forget it."

"I'm afraid it doesn't work that way."

"Will you at least let me drive the boat back to the house?"

"Do you know how?"

"No."

"Come here," he said. "I'll show you."

***

She remained at the villa on the Attersee long after dark; then, with Dina at her side, she drove her fickle Volvo back to Linz. She spent much of the trip trying to learn the name and affiliation of the man who was going to steal the ill-gotten fortune of the Syrian ruling family, but Dina was having none of it. She spoke only of the party they had not attended, of a handsome young architect who had seemed particularly fond of Jihan, and of the beguiling smell of roses that arrived on the night wind. By the time they reached the outskirts of the city, even Jihan seemed to have temporarily purged the events of the afternoon from her memory. "Do you think he'll really call me?" she asked of Dina's imaginary architect. "Yes," said Dina, as the guilt settled once more on her shoulders. "I think he will."

It was a few minutes after midnight when they turned into their quiet little street near the Innere Stadt. They parted with formal kisses on the cheek and headed upstairs to their apartments. As Dina entered hers, she saw the silhouette of a powerfully built man seated rigidly in the window. He was peering through a slit in the blinds. Lying on the floor at his feet was an HK 9mm.

"Anything?" she asked.

"No," replied Christopher Keller. "She's clean."

"Can I make you some coffee?"

"I'm good."

"Something to eat?"

"I brought my own."

"Who's going to relieve you?"

"I'm flying solo for the foreseeable future."

"But you have to sleep sometime."

"I'm Regiment," said Keller as he stared into the darkness. "I don't need sleep."

PART FOUR

THE SCORE

B UT HOW TO take possession of the notebook long enough to steal its contents? And
how to do it in a way that Waleed al-Siddiqi
would never realize the notebook was missing?
Those were the questions the team wrestled with
in the hours after Jihan's departure from the Attersee safe house. The most obvious solution was the
Office equivalent of a smash and grab, but Gabriel
rejected the proposal outright. He insisted the operation be conducted without bloodshed and in a
way that would not alert the Syrian ruling clan that
something was amiss with their money. Nor did he
rise to Yaakov's tepid suggestion of a honey trap. By
all appearances, Mr. al-Siddiqi was a man without
personal vice, other than the fact he managed the
plundered wealth of a mass murderer.

There was an Office maxim, conceived by Shamron and chiseled into stone, that a simple problem
sometimes had a simple solution. And the solution
to their problem, said Gabriel, had but two compo-
nents. They had to compel Waleed al-Siddiqi to get
on an airplane, and they had to force him to cross

a friendly border. What's more, he added, the team had to have advance warning of both occurrences.

Which explained why early the following morning, having slept fitfully if at all, Gabriel hauled himself into his rented Audi and departed Austria along the same route by which he had entered it. Germany had never seemed so beautiful to him. The green farmland of Bavaria was his Eden; Munich, with the spire of the Olympic Tower floating above the summer haze like a minaret, was his Jerusalem. He left the car in the long-term parking lot at Munich's airport and hurried aboard the ten thirty British Airways flight to London. His seatmate was a morning alcoholic from Birmingham; and Gabriel, just a few hours removed from Jihan's presence, was once again Jonathan Albright of Markham Capital Advisers. He had come to Munich, he explained, to explore the possibility of acquiring a German tech firm. And yes, he added sheepishly, it promised to be highly lucrative.

It was raining in London, a low, black gale of a storm that had cast Heathrow Airport into a state of permanent evening. Gabriel shot through passport control and followed the yellow signs to the arrivals hall, where Nigel Whitcombe stood in a drenched mackintosh, looking like a colonial governor in a distant corner of the Empire. "Mr. Baker," he said as he shook Gabriel's hand limply. "So good to see you again. Welcome back to England."

Whitcombe owned a Vauxhall Astra, which he drove very fast and with an indolent skill. He headed into

London along the M4. Then, at Gabriel's request, he took a few countersurveillance laps through Earl's Court and West Kensington before finally making his way to a mews cottage in Maida Vale. It had a front door the color of a lemon rind and a welcome mat that read BLESS ALL THOSE WHO ENTER THIS HOUSE. Graham Seymour sat in the library, a volume of Trollope open on his knee. As Gabriel entered alone, the MI6 chief closed the book slowly and, rising, returned it to its place on the shelf.

"What is it now?" he asked.

"Money," replied Gabriel.

"Who does it belong to?"

"The Syrian people. But for the moment," Gabriel added, "it's in the hands of Evil Incorporated."

Seymour raised a baronial eyebrow. "How did you find it?" he asked.

"Jack Bradshaw pointed me in the right direction. And a woman named Jihan told me how to get my hands on the treasure map."

"And you, I assume, intend to dig it up."

Gabriel was silent.

"What do you need from Her Majesty's Secret Service?"

"Permission to conduct an operation on British soil."

"Will there be any dead bodies?"

"I shouldn't think so."

"Where will it take place?"

"The Tate Modern, if it's still available."

"Anywhere else?"

"Heathrow Airport."

Seymour frowned. "Maybe you should start from

the beginning, Gabriel. And this time," he added, "it might be a good idea if you told me everything."

It was Jack Bradshaw, the fallen British spy turned art smuggler, who had brought Gabriel and Graham Seymour together in the first place, and so it was with Bradshaw that Gabriel began his account. It was thorough but, by necessity, heavily redacted. For example, Gabriel did not mention the name of the art thief who had told him the long-missing Caravaggio had recently been sold. Nor did he identify the master art forger he had found dead in his Paris studio, or the thieves who had plucked *Sunflowers* from the Rijksmuseum Vincent van Gogh in Amsterdam, or the name of the Swiss secret policeman who had given him access to Jack Bradshaw's gallery of the missing at the Geneva Freeport. It was the letter found in Bradshaw's safe that led Gabriel to LXR Investments and, eventually, to a small private bank in Linz, though Gabriel neglected to point out that the trail had passed through a pan-Arab law firm based in Great Suffolk Street.

"Who was the chap who took your forged version of the van Gogh to market in Paris?" asked Seymour.

"He was Office."

"Really?" said Seymour dubiously. "Because the word on the street was that he was British."

"Who do you think put the word on the street, Graham?"

"You do think of everything, don't you?" Seymour was still standing before the bookshelves.

"And the *real* van Gogh?" he wondered. "You do intend to return it, don't you?"

"As soon as I get my hands on Waleed al-Siddiqi's notebook."

"Ah, the notebook." He pulled down a volume of Greene and sliced it open with his forefinger. "Let us assume that you succeed in getting access to that list of accounts. Then what?"

"Use your imagination, Graham."

"Steal it? Is that what you're suggesting?"

"Steal is an ugly word."

"Does your service have that sort of capability?"

Gabriel gave a wry smile. "After all we've done together," he said, "I'm surprised you would even ask that question."

Seymour returned the volume of Greene to its original place. "I'm not opposed to having a look at a bank's ledgers every now and again," he said after a moment, "but I do draw the line at theft. After all, we're British. We believe in fair play."

"We don't have that luxury."

"Don't play the victim, Gabriel. It doesn't suit you." Seymour plucked another book from the shelf but this time didn't bother to open the cover.

"Something bothering you, Graham?"

"The money."

"What about the money?"

"There's a good chance that some of it is held by British financial institutions. And if several hundred million pounds were to suddenly vanish from their balance sheets . . ." His voice trailed off, the thought unfinished.

"They shouldn't have accepted the money in the first place, Graham."

"The accounts were undoubtedly opened by a cutout," Seymour countered. "Which means the banks have no idea who the money really belongs to."

"They will soon."

"Not if you want my help."

A silence fell between them. It was broken eventually by Graham Seymour.

"Do you know what will happen if it ever becomes public that I helped you rob a British bank?" he asked. "I'll be standing in Leicester Square with a paper cup in my hand."

"So we'll do it quietly, Graham, the way we always do."

"Sorry, Gabriel, but British banks are off-limits."

"What about branches of British banks on foreign soil?"

"They're still British banks."

"And banks in British overseas territories?"

"Off-limits," Seymour repeated.

Gabriel made a show of deliberation. "Then I suppose I'll have to do it without your help." He rose to his feet. "Sorry to have dragged you away from the office, Graham. Tell Nigel I can find my way back to Heathrow."

Gabriel started toward the door.

"You're forgetting one thing," Seymour said.

Gabriel turned.

"All I have to do to stop you is tell Waleed al-Siddiqi to burn that notebook."

"I know," replied Gabriel. "But I also know that you would never do that. Your conscience wouldn't allow it. And deep down, you want that money just as badly as I do."

"Not if it's deposited in a British bank."

Gabriel looked at the ceiling and in his head counted to five. "If the money is in the Cayman Islands, Bermuda, or any other British territory, I get it. If it's here in London, it stays in London."

"Deal," said Seymour.

"Provided," added Gabriel quickly, "that HMG puts those assets in a deep freeze."

"The prime minister would have to make a decision like that."

"Then I'm quite confident the prime minister will see it my way."

This time, it was Graham Seymour who looked at the ceiling in exasperation. "You still haven't told me how you intend to get the notebook."

"Actually," said Gabriel, "you're going to do it for me."

"I'm glad we cleared that up. But how are we going to get al-Siddiqi to come to Britain?"

"I'm going to invite him to a party. With any luck," Gabriel added, "it will be the last one he ever attends."

"Better make it a good one, then."

"I intend to."

"Who's throwing it?"

"A friend of mine from Russia who doesn't care for dictators who steal money."

"In that case," said Seymour, smiling for the first time, "it promises to be a night to remember."

CHELSEA, LONDON

A FALLEN BRITISH SPY, a one-eyed Italian policeman, a master art thief, a professional assassin from the island of Corsica: this was the menagerie of characters through which the affair had flowed thus far. And so it was only fitting that the next stop along Gabriel's unlikely journey was 43 Cheyne Walk, the London home of Viktor Orlov. Orlov was a bit like Julian Isherwood; he made life more interesting, and for that Gabriel adored him. But his affection toward the Russian was rooted in something far more practical. Were it not for Orlov, Gabriel would be lying dead in a Stalin-era killing field east of Moscow. And Chiara would be lying next to him.

It was said of Viktor Orlov that he divided people into two categories: those willing to be used and those too stupid to realize they were being used. There were some who would have added a third: those willing to let Viktor steal their money. He made no secret of the fact he was a predator and a robber baron. Indeed, he wore those labels proudly, along with his ten-thousand-dollar Italian suits and his trademark striped shirts, specially made by a man in Hong Kong. The dramatic collapse of Soviet communism had presented Orlov with the opportunity to earn a great deal of money in a brief period of time, and he had taken it. Orlov rarely apologized for anything, least of all the manner in which he had become rich. "Had I been born an Englishman, my money might have come to me cleanly," he told a British interviewer shortly after taking up residence in London. "But I was born a Russian. And I earned a Russian fortune."

Raised in Moscow during the darkest days of the Cold War, Orlov had been blessed with a natural facility with numbers. After completing his secondary education, he studied physics at the Leningrad Institute of Precision Mechanics and Optics and then disappeared into the Russian nuclear weapons program, where he worked until the day the Soviet Union breathed its last. While most of his colleagues continued to work without pay, Orlov quickly renounced his membership in the Communist Party and vowed to become rich. Within a few years, he had earned a sizable fortune importing computers, appliances, and other Western goods into the nascent Russian market. Later, he used that fortune to acquire Russia's largest state-owned steel company along with Ruzoil, the Siberian oil giant, at bargain-basement prices. Before long Viktor Orlov, a former government physicist who once had to share an apartment with two other Soviet families, was a billionaire many times over and the richest man in Russia.

But in post-Soviet Russia, a land with no rule of

law and rife with crime and corruption, Orlov's fortune made him a marked man. He survived at least three attempts on his life and was rumored to have ordered several men killed in retaliation. But the greatest threat to Orlov would come from the man who succeeded Boris Yeltsin as president of Russia. He believed that Viktor Orlov and the other oligarchs had stolen the country's most valuable assets, and it was his intention to steal them back. After settling into the Kremlin, the new president summoned Orlov and demanded two things: his steel company and Ruzoil. "And keep your nose out of politics," he added ominously. "Otherwise, I'm going to cut it off."

Orlov agreed to relinquish his steel interests, but not Ruzoil. The president was not amused. He immediately ordered prosecutors to open a fraud-and-bribery investigation, and within a week Russian prosecutors had issued a warrant for Orlov's arrest. Faced with the prospect of a long, cold stay in the neo-gulag, he wisely fled to London, where he became one of the Russian president's most vocal critics. For several years Ruzoil remained legally icebound, beyond the reach of both Orlov and the new masters of the Kremlin. Finally, Orlov agreed to surrender the company in what was effectively history's largest payment of hostage ransom—$12 billion in exchange for the release of three kidnapped Office agents. For his generosity, Orlov received a British passport and a very private meeting with the Queen. Afterward, he declared it the proudest day of his life.

It had been more than five years since Viktor

Orlov had come to financial terms with the Kremlin, yet he remained at the top of the Russian hit list. As a result, he moved about London in an armored limousine, and his house in Cheyne Walk looked a bit like the embassy of an embattled nation. The windows were bulletproof, and parked at the curb was a black Range Rover filled with bodyguards, all of whom were former members of Christopher Keller's old regiment, the Special Air Service. They paid Gabriel little heed as he arrived at the appointed time of half past four and, after slipping through the wrought-iron gate, presented himself at Orlov's stately front door. The bell, when pressed, produced a maid in a starched black-and-white uniform, who escorted Gabriel up a flight of wide, elegant stairs to Orlov's office. The room was an exact replica of the Queen's private study in Buckingham Palace except for the giant plasma media wall behind Orlov's desk. Usually, it flickered with financial data from around the world, but on that afternoon it was the crisis in Ukraine that held Orlov's attention. The Russian army had invaded the Crimean Peninsula and was now threatening to push into other regions of eastern Ukraine. The Cold War was officially on again, or so declared the commentariat. Their logic had but one glaring flaw. In the mind of the Russian president, the Cold War had never ended in the first place.

"I warned this would happen," Orlov said after a moment. "I warned that the tsar wanted his empire back. I made it very clear that Georgia was just the appetizer and that Ukraine, the breadbasket of the old union, would be the main course. And now it's playing out live on television. And what do the Europeans do about it?"

"Nothing," answered Gabriel.

Orlov nodded slowly, his eyes fixed on the screen. "And do you know why the Europeans are doing nothing while the Red Army runs roughshod over yet another independent nation?"

"Money," replied Gabriel.

Again Orlov nodded. "I warned them about that, too. I told them not to grow dependent on trade with Russia. I pleaded with them not to become addicted to cheap Russian natural gas. No one listened to me, of course. And now the Europeans can't bring themselves to impose meaningful sanctions on the tsar because it will hurt their economies too much." He shook his head slowly. "It makes me sick to my stomach."

Just then, the Russian president strode across the screen, one hand rigidly at his side and the other swinging like a scythe. His face had been recently put to the knife again; his eyes were stretched so tight he looked as though he were a man of the Central Asian republics. He might have appeared a comical figure were it not for the blood on his hands, some of which belonged to Gabriel.

"At last estimate," Orlov was saying, his eyes fixed on his old enemy, "he was worth about a hundred and thirty billion dollars, which would make him the richest man in the world. How do you suppose he got all that money? After all, he's spent his entire life on the government payroll."

"I suppose he stole it."

"You think?"

Orlov turned away from the video wall and faced Gabriel for the first time. He was a small, agile man of sixty, with a head of gray hair that had been coaxed and gelled into a youthful, spiky coif. Behind his rimless spectacles his left eye twitched nervously. It usually did when he was speaking about the Russian president.

"I know for a fact he pocketed a large portion of Ruzoil after I surrendered it to the Kremlin to get you out of Russia. It was worth about twelve billion dollars at the time. Rather small beer in the grand scheme of things," Orlov added. "He and his inner circle are growing vastly rich at the expense of the Russian people. It's why he'll do whatever it takes to stay in power." Orlov paused, then added, "Just like his friend in Syria."

"So why don't you help me do something about it?"

"Steal the tsar's money? I'd love nothing more. After all," Orlov added, "some of it is mine. But it's not possible."

"I agree."

"So what are you suggesting?"

"That we steal his Syrian friend's money instead."

"Have you found it?"

"No," Gabriel answered. "But I know who's controlling it."

"That would be Kemel al-Farouk," said Orlov. "But the man who's actually managing the investment portfolio is Waleed al-Siddiqi."

Gabriel was too stunned to offer a reply. Orlov smiled.

"You should have come to me a long time ago," he said. "I could have saved you a lot of trouble."

"How do you know about al-Siddiqi?"

"Because you're not the only one searching for the money." Orlov looked over his shoulder at the video wall, where the Russian president was now receiving a briefing from his generals. "The tsar wants it, too. But that's hardly surprising," he added. "The tsar wants everything."

At the stroke of five, the maid appeared with a bottle of Château Pétrus, the legendary Pomerol wine that Orlov drank as though it were Evian.

"Care for a glass, Gabriel?"

"No, thanks, Viktor. I'm driving."

Orlov gave a dismissive wave of his hand and dumped several inches of the dark red wine into a large goblet.

"Where were we?" he asked.

"You were about to tell me how it is you know about Waleed al-Siddiqi."

"I have sources in Moscow. Very good sources," he added with a smile. "I would think you'd know that by now."

"Your sources are the best, Viktor."

"Better than MI6's," he said. "You should tell your friend Graham Seymour to take my calls every now and again. I can be of great help to him."

"I'll mention it the next time I see him."

Orlov settled at one end of a long brocaded couch and invited Gabriel to sit at the other. On the other side of the bulletproof windows, evening traffic flowed along the Chelsea Embankment and across the Albert Bridge to Battersea. In Viktor Orlov's world, however, there was only the faintly comedic figure striding across the screens of his video wall.

"Why do you suppose he rose to the Syrian president's defense when the rest of the civilized world was ready to use military force against him? Was it because he wanted to protect Russia's only friend in the Arab world? Did he want to keep his naval base at Tartus? The answer to both questions is yes. But there's another reason." Orlov looked at Gabriel and said, "Money."

"How much?"

"Half a billion dollars, payable directly into an account controlled by the tsar."

"Says who?"

"Says I'd rather not say."

"Where did the half a billion come from?"

"Where do you think?"

"Since there was nothing left in the Syrian treasury, I'd say it came directly from the ruler's pocket."

Orlov nodded and looked at the screen again. "And what do you think the tsar did after he received confirmation that the money had been deposited into his account?"

"Since the tsar is a greedy bastard, I suppose he ordered his old colleagues at the SVR to find the rest of it."

"You know the tsar well."

"And I have the scars to prove it."

Orlov smiled and drank some of his wine. "My sources tell me the search was conducted by the SVR *rezident* in Damascus. He already knew about Kemel al-Farouk. It took all of five minutes for him to come up with al-Siddiqi's name."

"Does al-Siddiqi control the entire fortune?"

"Not even close," replied Orlov. "If I had to guess, I'd say about half of the ruler's money is under his management."

"So what's the tsar waiting for?"

"He's waiting to see whether the ruler survives or whether he ends up like Gaddafi. If he survives, he gets to keep his money. But if he ends up like Gaddafi, the SVR is going to grab that list of accounts that al-Siddiqi carries around in his pocket."

"I'm going to beat them to it," said Gabriel. "And you're going to help me."

"What exactly do you need me to do?"

Gabriel told him. Orlov twirled his eyeglasses by the stem, something he always did when he was thinking about money.

"It's not going to be cheap," he said after a moment.

"How much, Viktor?"

"Thirty million, bare minimum. Maybe forty when everything's said and done."

"What do you say we go Dutch treat this time?"

"How much can you spare?"

"I might have ten million lying around," said Gabriel. "But I'd have to give it to you in cash."

"Is it real?"

"Absolutely."

Orlov smiled. "Then cash would be fine."

THERE WAS A spirited debate over what to call it. Orlov demanded that his name be associated with the venture—hardly surprising, for he was footing the lion's share of the bill. "The Orlov name stands for quality," he argued. "The Orlov name stands for success." True, said Gabriel, but it also stood for corruption, double-dealing, and rumors of violence, charges Orlov didn't bother to deny. In the end, they settled on the European Business Initiative: stoic, solid, and without a hint of controversy. Orlov was grudging in defeat. "Why don't we call it twelve hours of unmitigated boredom," he muttered. "That way we can be certain that no one will bother to attend."

They announced the venture the following Monday in the pages of the *Financial Journal*, the venerable London business daily that Orlov had acquired for a song a few years earlier, when it was on the verge of insolvency. The stated goal of the gathering, he said, was to bring together the brightest minds in government, industry, and finance to produce a set of policy recommendations that would lift the European economy out of its post-recession doldrums. The initial reaction was tepid at best. One commentator called it Orlov's Folly. Another christened it Orlov's *Titanic*. "With one critical difference," he added. "This ship will sink before it ever leaves port."

There were still others who dismissed the conference as yet another in a long line of Orlov publicity stunts, an accusation he denied repeatedly during a daylong blitz of interviews on the business news networks. Then, as if to prove his critics wrong, he embarked on a quiet tour of Europe's capitals to build support for his endeavor. His first stop was Paris, where, after a marathon negotiating session, the French finance ministry agreed to send a delegation. Then he was off to Berlin, where he won a commitment from the Germans to attend. The rest of the Continent soon followed suit. The Low Countries fell in an afternoon, as did Scandinavia. The Spanish were so desperate to attend that Orlov didn't bother to make the trip to Madrid. Nor was it necessary for him to go to Rome. Indeed, the Italian prime minister said he would attend personally— provided, of course, he was still in office at the time.

Having won the commitment of European governments, Orlov next went after the stars of business and finance. He snared the titans of the German auto industry, and the manufacturing giants from Sweden and Norway. Big Shipping wanted in on the fun, as did Big Steel and Big Energy. The Swiss banks were initially reluctant, but agreed after Orlov assured them they would not be crucified for past sins. Even Martin Landesmann, the Swiss private-equity king and international doer of good deeds, announced that he would make time in his busy schedule, though he implored Orlov to devote at least some of the program to issues he held dear, such as climate change, Third World debt, and sustainable agriculture.

And so it was that, within a few short days, the conference once dismissed as folly was now the business world's hottest ticket. Orlov was besieged with requests for invitations. There were the Americans, who wondered why they weren't invited in the first place. There were the fashion models, rock stars, and actors who wanted to rub shoulders with the rich and powerful. There was a former British prime minister, disgraced by personal scandal, who wanted a chance at redemption. There was even a fellow Russian oligarch who maintained uncomfortably close ties with Orlov's enemies in the Kremlin. He offered the same reply to each. The invitations would be issued via overnight mail on the first day of July. RSVPs were due back in forty-eight hours. The press would be allowed to view Orlov's introductory remarks, but all other proceedings, including the gala dinner, would be closed to the media. "We want our participants to feel free to speak their minds," said Orlov. "And they won't be able to do that if the press are hanging on their every word."

All of which seemed to matter little in the enchanted Austrian city located along an unusually sharp bend in the river Danube. Yes, the chairman of Voestalpine AG, the Linz-based steel giant, had received feelers from Orlov about attending the London conference, but otherwise life went on as normal. A pair of summer festivals came and went, the cafés filled and emptied twice each day, and in the little private bank located near the street-car roundabout, a child of Hama went about her daily routine as if nothing unusual had transpired. Owing to her compromised mobile phone, which was now acting as a full-time transmitter, Gabriel and the rest of the team were able to listen to her every move. They listened as she opened accounts and moved money. They listened to her meetings with Herr Weber and with Mr. al-Siddiqi. And late at night, they listened as she dreamed of Hama.

They listened, too, as she renewed her friendship with an aspiring novelist, recently divorced and living alone in Linz, named Ingrid Roth. They lunched together, they shopped together, they visited museums together. And on two occasions they returned to the pretty yellow villa on the western shore of the Attersee, where Jihan was briefed and prepared by a man she had been led to believe was German. At the end of the first session, he asked her for a detailed description of Mr. al-Siddiqi's office. And when she returned for the second session, a replica of the office had been created in one of the rooms of the villa. It was a perfect forgery in every detail: the same desk, the same computer, the same telephone, even the same surveillance camera overhead and the same numeric keypad on the door.

"What's it for?" asked Jihan, amazed.

"Practice," said Gabriel with a smile.

And practice they did, for three hours without a break, until she could carry out her assignment without showing a trace of fear or tension. Then she did it in the pitch-dark, and with an alarm sounding, and with Gabriel shouting at her that Mr. al-Siddiqi's men were coming for her. He did not tell Jihan that the training she was undergoing had been created by the secret intelligence service of the State of Israel. Nor did he mention the fact that, on several occasions, he had endured similar periods of training himself. In her presence, he was never Gabriel Allon. He was a dull German tax collector without a name who just happened to be very good at his job.

The deception of Jihan seemed to weigh heavily upon Gabriel's conscience as the day of the operation drew nearer. He reminded the team at every turn that their opponents would be playing by Hama Rules—and perhaps Moscow Rules as well—and he fretted over the smallest details. As his mood worsened, Eli Lavon took the liberty of acquiring a small wooden sloop, just to get Gabriel out of the safe house for a few hours each afternoon. He would sail it downwind toward the Mountains of Hell and then expertly tack his way home again, always trying to better his time of the previous day. The smell of the Rosenwind made him think of a terrified child clinging to her mother—and, sometimes, of the warning the old mystic had whispered into his ear on the island of Corsica.

Do not let any harm come to her, or you will lose everything . . .

But his primary obsession during those last days of June was with Waleed al-Siddiqi, the Syrian-born banker who went everywhere with a black leather notebook in his pocket. He traveled frequently during this period and, as was his custom, with only a few hours' advance booking. There was a day trip to Brussels, an overnight jaunt to Beirut, and, lastly, a quick visit to Dubai, where he spent a great deal of time at the headquarters of the TransArabian Bank, an institution the Office knew well. He returned to Vienna at one p.m. on the first day of July, and by three that afternoon he was striding through the door of Bank Weber AG, trailed as usual by his bookend Alawite bodyguards. Jihan greeted him cordially in Arabic and handed him a stack of mail that had arrived in his absence. It included a DHL envelope, inside of which was a glossy invitation to something called the European Business Initiative. He carried it unopened into his office and quietly closed the door.

It was a Wednesday, which meant he had until five p.m. Friday to deliver his RSVP via electronic mail. Gabriel had braced himself for a long wait, and unfortunately Waleed al-Siddiqi did not disappoint. The remainder of Wednesday passed without a response, as did Thursday morning and Thursday afternoon. Eli Lavon saw the delay as a positive sign. It meant, he said, that the banker was flattered by the invitation and was deliberating over whether to attend. But Gabriel feared otherwise. He had invested heavily in time and money to lure the Syrian banker to Britain. And now it seemed he might have nothing to show for his efforts other than a glitzy gabfest for Euro-businessmen. Improving Europe's anemic economy was a noble endeavor, he told Lavon, but it was hardly one of his top priorities.

By Friday morning, Gabriel was brittle with worry. He phoned Viktor Orlov in London at the top and bottom of every hour. He paced the floor of the great room. He muttered at the ceiling in whatever language suited his ever-shifting mood. Finally, at two that afternoon, he flung open the door of al-Siddiqi's mock office and shouted at him in Arabic to make up his mind. It was at this point that Eli Lavon intervened. He took Gabriel gently by the elbow and walked him to the end of the long dock. "Go," he said, pointing to the distant end of the lake. "And don't come back a minute before five."

Gabriel reluctantly climbed aboard the sloop and sailed downwind toward the Mountains of Hell, wing and wing, trailed by the heady scent of roses. It took him only an hour to reach the southern end of the lake; he dropped his sails in a sheltered cove and warmed himself in the sun, all the while resisting the urge to reach for his mobile phone. Finally, at half past three, he raised his mainsail and jib and beat his way northward. He reached the town of Seeberg at ten minutes to five, tacked one final time to starboard, and powered up for the straight run to the safe house on the opposite side of the lake. As he drew near, he spotted the diminutive figure of Eli Lavon standing at the end of the dock, one arm raised in a silent salute.

"Well?" asked Gabriel.

"It seems Mr. al-Siddiqi would be honored to attend the European Business Initiative."

"Is that all?"

"No," said Lavon, frowning. "He'd also like a word with Miss Nawaz in private."

"About what?"

"Come inside," Lavon replied. "We'll know in a minute."

45

LINZ, AUSTRIA

S HE HAD REQUESTED a reprieve of five minutes. Five minutes to lock away the last of her account files. Five minutes to tidy up her already tidy desk. Five minutes to return her chaotic heartbeat to something like normal. Her allotted time was now over. She rose to her feet, a little more abruptly than normal, and smoothed the front of her skirt. Or was she wiping the dampness from the palms of her hands? She checked to make sure she hadn't left a streak of moisture on the fabric and then glanced at the bodyguards standing outside Mr. al-Siddiqi's door. They were watching her intently. She supposed Mr. al-Siddiqi was watching her, too. Smiling, she walked the length of the corridor. Her knock was falsely decisive: three sharp blows that made her knuckle sting. "Come in," was all he said.

She kept her eyes straight ahead as the bodyguard to her right—the tall one called Yusuf—punched the access code into the keypad on the wall. The deadbolts opened with a snap, and the door yielded silently to her touch. The room she entered was in semidarkness, illuminated only by a single halogen desk lamp. She noticed that the lamp had been moved slightly, but otherwise the desk was arranged in its typical fashion: the computer on the left, the leather blotter in the center, the multiline telephone on the right. Presently, the receiver was pressed tightly to the ear of Mr. al-Siddiqi. He wore a charcoal-gray suit, a white shirt, and a dark tie that shone like polished granite. His small dark eyes were focused at some point above Jihan's head; his forefinger lay contemplatively along the side of his aquiline nose. He removed it long enough to aim it pistol-like at an empty chair. Jihan sat and arranged herself primly. She realized she was still smiling. Looking down, she checked her e-mail on her mobile phone and tried hard not to wonder who was on the other end of Mr. al-Siddiqi's call.

Finally, he murmured a few words in Arabic and returned the receiver to its cradle. "Forgive me, Jihan," he said in the same language, "but I'm afraid that couldn't wait."

"A problem?"

"Nothing beyond the usual." He bunched his hands thoughtfully beneath his chin and looked at her seriously for a moment. "I have something I wish to discuss with you," he said at last. "It is both personal and professional. I hope you will allow me to speak freely."

"Is there something wrong?"

"You tell me, Jihan."

The back of her neck felt as though it were on fire. "I don't understand," she said calmly.

"May I ask you a question?"

"Of course."

"Are you happy here in Linz?"

She frowned. "Why would you ask such a thing?"

"Because you don't always seem terribly happy." His small, hard mouth formed into something like a smile. "You strike me as a very serious person, Jihan."

"I am."

"And honest?" he asked. "Do you consider yourself an honest person?"

"Very."

"You would never violate the privacy of our clients?"

"Of course not."

"And you would never discuss our affairs with anyone outside the bank?"

"Never."

"Not with a member of your family?"

"No."

"Not with a friend?"

She shook her head.

"You're sure, Jihan?"

"Yes, Mr. al-Siddiqi."

He looked at the television. It was tuned, as usual, to Al Jazeera. The volume was muted.

"And what about loyalty?" he asked after a moment. "Do you consider yourself to be a loyal person?"

"Very."

"To what are you loyal?"

"I've never really thought about it."

"Think about it now, please." He glanced at his computer screen as if to give her a moment of privacy.

"I suppose I'm loyal to myself," she said.

"Interesting answer." His dark eyes moved from

the computer screen to her face. "In what way are you loyal to yourself?"

"I try to live by a certain code."

"Such as?"

"I would never intentionally try to hurt someone."

"Even if he hurt you?"

"Yes," she said. "Even if he hurt me."

"And what if you suspected someone had done something wrong, Jihan? Would you try to hurt him then?"

She managed to smile in spite of herself. "Is this the personal part or the professional part of what you wanted to discuss?" she asked.

Her question seemed to throw him off balance. His gaze wandered to the silent television. "And what about your country?" he asked. "Are you loyal to your country?"

"I'm very fond of Germany," she replied.

"You carry a German passport and speak the language like a native, Jihan, but you are not a German. You are Syrian." He paused, then added, "Like me."

"Is that why you hired me?"

"I hired you," he said pointedly, "because I needed someone with your linguistic ability to help me function here in Austria. You've proven to be very valuable to me, Jihan, which is why I'm considering creating a new position for you."

"What sort of position?"

"You would work directly for me."

"In what capacity?"

"In whatever capacity I require."

"I'm not a secretary, Mr. al-Siddiqi."

"Nor would I treat you as one. You would help me

manage the investment portfolios of my clients." He scrutinized her for a moment as if trying to read her thoughts. "Would that be of interest to you?"

"Who would serve as the account manager?"

"Someone new."

She lowered her gaze and delivered her response to her hands. "I'm very flattered you would consider me for such a position, Mr. al-Siddiqi."

"You don't seem terribly excited about the idea. In fact, Jihan, you seem rather uncomfortable."

"Not at all," she replied. "I'm just wondering why you would want someone like me in such an important position."

"Why *not* you?" he countered.

"I have no experience managing assets."

"You have something far more valuable than experience."

"What's that, Mr. al-Siddiqi?"

"Loyalty and honesty, the two qualities I value most in an employee. I need someone I can trust." He made a steeple of his long, slender fingers and braced it against the tip of his nose. "I *can* trust you, can't I, Jihan?"

"Of course, Mr. al-Siddiqi."

"Does that mean you're interested?"

"Very," she said. "But I'd like a day or two to think about it."

"I'm afraid I can't wait that long for an answer."

"How long do I have?"

"I'd say you have about ten seconds." Again he smiled. It looked as though he had taught himself the expression by practicing in front of a mirror.

"And if I say yes?" asked Jihan.

"I'll need to perform a background check on you before proceeding." He was silent for a moment. "You wouldn't have a problem with that, would you?"

"I assumed I underwent a background check before you hired me."

"You did."

"Then why must there be another?"

"Because this one will be different."

He made it sound as though it were a threat. Perhaps it was.

———————————

In the sitting room of the Attersee safe house, Gabriel had unwittingly adopted the same pose as Waleed al-Siddiqi: fingertips pressed to the tip of his nose, eyes staring straight ahead. They were fixed not on Jihan Nawaz but on the computer that was emitting the sound of her voice. Eli Lavon was seated next to him, gnawing at something on the inside of his cheek. And next to Lavon sat Yaakov Rossman, the team's most accomplished speaker of Arabic. As usual, Yaakov appeared to be contemplating an act of violence.

"It could be a coincidence," Lavon said without conviction.

"It could be," repeated Gabriel. "Or it's possible Mr. al-Siddiqi doesn't like the company Jihan has been keeping."

"It's not against the rules for her to have a friend."

"Unless the friend works for the intelligence service of the State of Israel. Then I suspect he'd have a problem with it."

"Why would he assume Dina is Israeli?"

"He's Syrian, Eli. He automatically assumes the worst."

From the computer came the sound of Jihan departing Mr. al-Siddiqi's office and returning to her desk. Gabriel set the toggle bar to 5:09 and clicked PLAY.

"Do you consider yourself an honest person?"

"Very."

"You would never violate the privacy of our clients?"

"Of course not."

"And you would never discuss our affairs with anyone outside the bank?"

"Never."

"Not with a member of your family?"

"No."

"Not with a friend?"

Gabriel clicked the STOP icon and looked at Lavon.

"Let us stipulate it doesn't sound encouraging," Lavon said.

"How about this?"

Gabriel clicked PLAY.

"In what way are you loyal to yourself?"

"I try to live by a certain code."

"Such as?"

"I would never intentionally try to hurt someone."

"Even if he hurt you?"

"Yes. Even if he hurt me."

"And what if you suspected someone had done something wrong, Jihan? Would you try to hurt him then?"

STOP.

"If he suspects her of disloyalty," said Lavon,

"why is he offering her a promotion? Why not show her the door?"

"Keep your friends close and your enemies closer."

"Did Shamron say that?"

"He might have."

"Your point?"

"Al-Siddiqi can't fire her because he's afraid she knows too much. So he's using the promotion as an excuse to vet her all over again."

"He doesn't need an excuse. All he needs to do is make a couple of phone calls to his friends in the Mukhabarat."

"How long do we have, Eli?"

"Hard to say. After all, they're rather busy at the moment."

"How long?" Gabriel pressed him.

"A few days, maybe a week."

Gabriel increased the volume on the live feed from Jihan's phone. She was packing her handbag and bidding a good evening to Herr Weber.

"There's no harm in bringing her in and calling it a day," said Lavon quietly.

"There's no money, either."

Lavon was chewing at the inside of his cheek again. "What are we going to do?" he asked finally.

"We're going to make sure nothing happens to her."

"Let us hope Mr. al-Siddiqi's friends in the Mukhabarat are too busy to take his call."

"Yes," said Gabriel. "Let us hope."

It was a few minutes after five o'clock when Jihan Nawaz stepped from the premises of Bank Weber

AG. A streetcar was waiting in the roundabout; she rode it across the Danube to the Mozartstrasse and then walked through the quiet streets of the Innere Stadt, humming softly to herself to hide her fear. It was a song that had been playing on the radio all summer, the kind Jihan had never heard when she was a child. In the Barudi neighborhood of Hama, there had been no music, only the Koran.

As she turned into her street, she noticed a tall, lanky man with bloodless skin and gray eyes walking along the opposite pavement. She had seen him a number of times during the past few days; in fact, he had been sitting behind her on the streetcar that morning on the way to work. On the previous morning, it was the one with pockmarked cheeks who had followed her. And the day before that it had been a small, square man who looked as though he could bend a tire iron. Her favorite, though, was the man who had come to the bank as Herr Feliks Adler. He was different from the others, she thought. He was a true artist.

The fear released her long enough for her to collect the post from her mailbox. The floor of the foyer was scattered with flyers; she stepped over them, climbed the stairs to her apartment, and let herself inside. The sitting room was precisely as she had left it, as was the kitchen and her bedroom. She sat down at her computer and checked her Facebook page and her Twitter feed, and for a few minutes she managed to convince herself that the conversation with Mr. al-Siddiqi had been a normal workplace exchange. Then the fear returned and her hands began to shake.

And what if you suspected someone had done something wrong, Jihan? Would you try to hurt him then?

She reached for her phone and dialed the woman she knew as Ingrid Roth.

"I don't feel like being alone right now. Any chance I can come over?"

"It might be better if you didn't."

"Is there a problem?"

"Just trying to get some work done."

"Is everything all right?"

"Everything's fine."

"You sure, Ingrid?"

"I'm sure."

The call dropped away. Jihan placed the phone next to the computer and walked over to the window. And for an instant she glimpsed the face of a man watching her from across the street. Maybe you work for Mr. al-Siddiqi, she thought as the man's face vanished. Maybe I am already dead.

46

HEATHROW AIRPORT, LONDON

THE DELEGATION FROM the German ministry was the first to arrive. Viktor Orlov found this fitting, for he had always regarded the Germans as expansionist by nature. They were eased through passport control with the help of an official British minder and shepherded to the arrivals hall, where a pretty young woman—Russian, but not blatantly—stood behind a makeshift kiosk that read THE EUROPEAN BUSINESS INITIATIVE. The girl checked off their names and directed them to a waiting luxury coach, which ferried them to the Dorchester Hotel, the official hotel of the conference. Only one member of the delegation, a deputy who did something involving trade, complained about his accommodations. It was an otherwise fine beginning.

The Dutch came next, followed by the French, and the Italians, and the Spaniards, and a group of Norwegians who looked as though they had come to London for a funeral. Then it was German steel, followed by German auto, and German home appliances. The delegation from the Italian fashion industry made the splashiest arrival, and the quietest went to the Swiss bankers, who somehow managed to slip into town unnoticed. The Greeks sent a single deputy minister whose job it was to ask for money. Orlov referred to him as Minister Cap in Hand.

The next to arrive was the delegation from Maersk, the Danish shipping and energy conglomerate. Then, on a midafternoon British Airways flight from Vienna, there came a man named Waleed al-Siddiqi, formerly of Damascus, lately of Linz, where he had a stake in a small private bank. Curiously, he was the only invitee who arrived with bodyguards other than the Italian prime minister, whom no one wanted dead. The girl at the kiosk struggled for a moment to find him on her list, for his name was missing the definite article *al*. It was a small mistake, quite intentional, that the Office regarded as the hallmark of any well-planned operation.

Looking mildly annoyed, al-Siddiqi and his bodyguards headed outside, where a courtesy Mercedes limousine idled curbside. The car belonged to MI6, as did its driver. Some fifty meters behind the limousine was a red Vauxhall Astra. Nigel Whitcombe sat behind the wheel; Gabriel sat in the passenger seat, wearing a miniature earpiece. The earpiece, along with the concealed transmitter to which it was connected, proved to be unnecessary, for Waleed al-Siddiqi passed the entire journey into London in complete and utter silence. It was, thought Gabriel, an otherwise fine beginning.

They followed him to the Dorchester; then Whitcombe dropped Gabriel at a not-so-safe Office

safe flat on Bayswater Road. Its sitting room overlooked Lancaster Gate and Hyde Park, and it was
there he established his modest command post. He
had a secure telephone and two laptop computers,
one tied into MI6's network, the other connected
to the team in Linz. The MI6 computer allowed
him to monitor the feed from the transmitter that
had been placed in al-Siddiqi's hotel room; the feed
from Jihan's compromised mobile phone played on
the other. At that moment, she was walking along
the Mozartstrasse, humming softly to herself. According to the accompanying watch report, Mikhail
Abramov was walking behind her, and Yaakov Rossman was walking along the opposite pavement. No
sign of the opposition. No sign of trouble.

And so it was that Gabriel passed that long night,
listening to other lives, reading the terse stream of
watch reports, wandering through operations past.
He paced the floor of the sitting room, he fretted
over a hundred details, he thought about his wife
and his unborn children. And at two a.m., when
Jihan woke herself with a scream of terror, he briefly
considered making her disappear. But it wasn't possible, not yet. He needed more than Waleed al-
Siddiqi's notebook; he needed the contents of his
private computer as well. And for that he needed the
child of Hama.

Finally, as the sky was beginning to lighten in the
east, he lay on the couch and slept. He woke three
hours later to an Al Jazeera report on the latest
atrocity in Syria, followed by the splash of water in
Waleed al-Siddiqi's luxury Jacuzzi bath. The private
banker emerged from his room at half past eight

and, accompanied by his bodyguards, partook of the Dorchester's lavish buffet. While he was reading the morning papers, an MI6 team checked his room to see if, by any chance, he'd forgotten his notebook. He hadn't.

He emerged from the hotel's entrance without his bodyguards at twenty minutes past nine, a set of credentials suspended from his neck by a blue-and-gold ribbon. Gabriel knew this because an MI6 surveillance photo appeared on his computer screen two minutes later. The next photo showed al-Siddiqi giving his name to the same Russian girl who had met him at the airport. And in the next he was stepping aboard a luxury coach that bore him eastward across London, to the entrance of Somerset House. Another MI6 operative snapped his photo as he stepped from the bus and walked wordlessly past a small knot of reporters. His eyes blazed with arrogance—and perhaps, thought Gabriel, a trace of mislaid pride. It seemed that Waleed al-Siddiqi had reached the summit of Europe's business world. His stay there would not be long, thought Gabriel. And his fall would be harder than most.

When next Gabriel saw the private banker, he was crossing the cobbled expanse of the Fountain Courtyard. Then, two minutes after that, he was settling into his seat in a glorious, high-ceilinged event room overlooking the Thames. To his left, dressed in varying shades of gray, was Martin Landesmann, the Swiss private equity billionaire. Their greeting—which Gabriel was able to overhear, thanks to a concealed MI6 transmitter—was restrained but cordial. Landesmann quickly fell

into conversation with one of the executives from
Maersk, leaving al-Siddiqi with a moment to review
the stack of printed material that had been left at
his place. Bored, he made a quick phone call, to
whom Gabriel could not tell. Then there came a
sharp pounding that sounded like nails being hammered into a coffin. But it wasn't a coffin; it was only
Viktor Orlov, gaveling the European Business Initiative to order.

It was at times like these that Gabriel was glad
he had been born into a family of artists and not
businessmen. Because for the next four hours he
was made to endure a mind-numbing discussion of
European consumer confidence, before-tax profit
margins, standardized value, debt-to-income ratio,
Eurobonds, Eurodollar bonds, and Euroequity
issues. He was grateful for the midday break; he
spent it listening to Jihan and Dina, who lunched
in the Hauptplatz under the watchful gaze of Oded
and Eli Lavon.

The afternoon session of the conference commenced at two and was promptly hijacked by Martin
Landesmann, who made an impassioned speech
about global warming and fossil fuels that caused
much eye rolling and head shaking among the men
from Maersk. At four, a hastily drafted statement
of policy recommendations passed by a unanimous
voice vote, as did a secondary motion calling for
another gathering in London the following year.
Afterward, Viktor Orlov appeared before the press
in the Fountain Courtyard and declared the con-

ference an overwhelming success. Alone in the safe
flat, Gabriel withheld judgment.

With that, the delegates returned to the Dorchester for a bit of downtime. Al-Siddiqi made two telephone calls from his room, one to his wife, and the
other to Jihan. Then he boarded a coach for dinner
in the Turbine Hall of the Tate Modern. He was
seated between a pair of Swiss bankers who spent
most of the evening complaining about new European banking regulations that were threatening
their business model. Al-Siddiqi blamed it on the
Americans. Then, beneath his breath, he said something about Jews that caused the Swiss bankers to
chortle with laughter. "Listen, Waleed," said one of
the gnomes, "you really should come see us the next
time you're in Zurich. I'm sure we can be of help to
you and your clients."

The Swiss bankers claimed to have an early call
and departed before dessert was served. Al-Siddiqi
spent a few minutes chatting with a man from Lloyds
about the risk of doing business with Russians and
then called it an evening himself. He slept well that
night, as did Gabriel, and they woke together the next
morning to the news that Syrian government forces
had won an important victory over the rebels in the
city of Homs. Al-Siddiqi bathed and breakfasted in
luxury; Gabriel showered quickly and swallowed
a cup of double-strength Nescafé. Then he headed
down to Bayswater Road and climbed into the passenger seat of a waiting Vauxhall Astra. Behind the
wheel, dressed in the blue uniform of an airport security officer, was Nigel Whitcombe. He eased into
the morning traffic and they headed for Heathrow.

A gentle rain was falling at 8:32 a.m. as Waleed al-Siddiqi stepped from the grand entrance of the Dorchester Hotel, a bodyguard at each shoulder. His MI6 courtesy limousine waited in the drive, along with his MI6 driver, who was standing next to the open boot, hands clasped behind his back, bouncing slightly on the balls of his feet. "Mr. Siddiqi," he called, deliberately removing the definite article from his client's name. "Let me help you, gentlemen." And he did just that, placing the bags in the boot and their owners in the car: one bodyguard in the front passenger seat, the other in the rear driver's side, and "Mr. Siddiqi" in the rear passenger seat. At 8:34 the car turned into Park Lane. SUBJECT UNDER WAY read the message that appeared on the MI6 communications net. PHOTOS UPON REQUEST.

The drive to Heathrow Airport took forty-five minutes and was made easier by the fact that al-Siddiqi's car was part of a clandestine MI6 motorcade consisting of six vehicles. His flight, British Airways 700 bound for Vienna, departed from Terminal 3. The driver removed the bags from the boot, wished his client a pleasant journey, and received a blank stare in return. Because the Syrian banker was flying first class, the check-in process consumed just ten minutes. The girl at the counter circled the gate number on his boarding pass and pointed him to the appropriate security area. "Just there," she said. "You're in luck, Mr. al-Siddiqi. The lines aren't too horrific this morning."

It was impossible to tell whether Waleed al-

Siddiqi considered himself lucky, because the expression he wore as he crossed the glittering hall of lights and flight-status boards was that of a man wrestling with weightier matters. Trailed by his bodyguards, he presented his passport and boarding document to the security screener for one final inspection and then joined the shortest of the three lines. An experienced traveler, he disrobed without haste and removed the required electronics and liquids from his briefcase and carry-on. Shoeless and in shirtsleeves, he watched the conveyor belt suck his possessions into the belly of the X-ray machine. Then, when instructed, he stepped into the millimeter wave scanner and wearily raised his arms as though he were surrendering after a long siege.

Having been found to be in possession of nothing restricted or remotely dangerous, he was invited to take his place at the end of the conveyor belt. An American couple, young and prosperous looking, waited in front of him. When their bins came trundling off the belt, they collected their things in a rush and hurried into the concourse. Waleed al-Siddiqi gave a superior frown and stepped forward. Absently, he patted the front of his shirt. Then he looked down at the motionless conveyor belt, and he waited.

For thirty long seconds, three security officers frowned at the screen of the X-ray machine as though they feared the patient did not have long to live. Finally, one of the officers detached himself and, plastic bin in hand, walked over to the spot where al-Siddiqi stood. The nameplate on the officer's breast pocket read CHARLES DAVIES. His real name was Nigel Whitcombe.

"Are these your things?" inquired Whitcombe.

"Yes, they are," replied al-Siddiqi curtly.

"We need to do a bit of additional screening. It won't be but a minute," Whitcombe added genially, "and then we'll have you on your way."

"Would it be possible for me to have my suit jacket?"

"Sorry," said Whitcombe, shaking his head. "Is there a problem?"

"No," said Waleed al-Siddiqi, smiling in spite of himself. "No problem at all."

———————————

Whitcombe invited the banker and his bodyguards to have a seat in the waiting area. Then he carried the plastic bin behind a barrier and placed it on the inspection table, next to al-Siddiqi's briefcase and carry-on garment bag. The small leather notebook was exactly where Jihan Nawaz had said it would be, in the left breast pocket of his suit jacket. Whitcombe quickly handed it to a young MI6 operative called Clarissa, who carried it a short distance to a door that opened as she approached. On the other side of the door was a small room with blank white walls occupied by two men. One of the men was her director-general. The other was a man with brilliant green eyes and gray temples whose exploits she had read about in the newspapers. Something made her hand the notebook to the man with green eyes instead of her DG. Accepting it without a word, he opened it to the first page and placed it beneath the lens of a high-resolution document camera. Then he pressed his eye to the viewfinder and snapped the first photo.

"Turn the page," he said quietly, and when the director-general of MI6 turned the page, he took another photo.

"Again, Graham."

Click . . .

"Next."

Click . . .

"Faster, Graham."

Click . . .

"Again."

Click . . .

47

LINZ, AUSTRIA

THE TEXT MESSAGE appeared on Jihan's mobile phone at half past ten Austrian time: I'M FREE FOR LUNCH. FEEL LIKE FRANZESCO? The subject matter was innocuous. The choice of restaurants, however, was not. It was a prearranged signal. For a few seconds, Jihan felt as though she were incapable of drawing a breath; Hama, it seemed, had taken hold of her heart. It took several attempts before she was able to successfully type a three-word response: ARE YOU SURE? The reply came back with the speed of a rifle shot: ABSO-LUTELY! CAN'T WAIT.

Her hand shaking, Jihan placed the mobile device on her desk and then lifted the receiver of her multi-line office phone. Several numbers were programmed into her speed-dial buttons, including one that was labeled MR. AL-SIDDIQI MOBILE. She rehearsed her scripted lines one final time. Then she reached out and pressed the button. The call received no answer, and for that Jihan was momentarily relieved. She hung up without leaving a message. Then she drew another breath and dialed the number again.

Jihan's first call to Waleed al-Siddiqi received no response because at that moment his mobile phone was
still in the possession of a Heathrow Airport security
officer named Charles Davies, otherwise known as
Nigel Whitcombe. By the time the second call came
through, he had regained control of his device but was
too preoccupied to answer; he was checking to see if
his leather notebook was still in the left breast pocket
of his suit jacket, which it was. The third call found
him in the duty-free area of the terminal and in a foul
mood. He answered with little more than a grunt.
"Mr. al-Siddiqi," exclaimed Jihan, as though she were
pleased to hear the sound of his voice. "I'm so glad I
was able to reach you before you boarded your flight.
I'm afraid we have a small problem in the Cayman Islands. May I have a moment of your time?"

The problem, she said, were the notarized letters
of incorporation for a company called LXR Investments of Luxembourg.

"What about them?" asked Mr. al-Siddiqi.

"They're missing."

"What are you talking about?"

"I just received a phone call from Dennis Cahill
at the Trade Winds Bank in Georgetown."

"I know the name."

"Mr. Cahill says he can't find the documents of
registry for the firm."

"I happen to know that my representative gave
him those letters personally."

"Mr. Cahill doesn't dispute that."

"So what's the problem?"

"I got the impression they were shredded by mistake," Jihan said. "He'd like us to send a new set."

"How soon?"

"Immediately."

"What's the rush?"

"Apparently, it has something to do with the Americans. He didn't go into details."

Beneath his breath, al-Siddiqi muttered an old Syrian curse about donkeys and distant relatives. Jihan smiled. Her mother had used the same expression on the rare occasions she lost her temper.

"I believe I have copies of those documents on the computer in my office," he said after a moment. "In fact, I'm sure of it."

"What would you like me to do, Mr. al-Siddiqi?"

"I'd like you to send them to this idiot at the Trade Winds Bank, of course."

"Would it be all right if I called you back on my mobile? It might be easier that way."

"Quickly, Jihan. My flight is boarding."

Yes, she thought, as she hung up the phone. Let's do it quickly.

———

She opened the top drawer of her desk and removed two items: a black leather folio case and an external hard drive, also black, about three inches by five inches in size. The hard drive was beneath the folio case, so that it was invisible to the overhead security cameras. She clutched both items tightly to the front of her blouse, rose, and started down the short corridor to the door of Mr. al-Siddiqi's office. She dialed his number as she walked. He answered at the instant of her arrival.

"Ready," she said.

"The code is eight, seven, nine, four, one, two. Did you get that?"

"Yes, Mr. al-Siddiqi. One moment, please."

Using the same hand that held the phone, she quickly punched in the correct six digits and pressed ENTER. The deadbolts opened with a snap that was audible at the other end of the call.

"Go inside," said Mr. al-Siddiqi.

Jihan pushed open the door. A midnight gloom greeted her. She did nothing to extinguish it.

"I'm here," she said.

"Turn on the computer."

She sat down in his executive leather chair. It was warm, as if he had just risen from it. The computer monitor, darkened, was on the left, the keyboard a few inches in front of it, the CPU on the floor beneath the desk. She reached down and flawlessly carried out the same maneuver she had practiced so many times at the house on the Attersee—the maneuver she had practiced in the dark, and with the nameless German shouting that Mr. al-Siddiqi was coming to kill her. But he wasn't coming to kill her; he was on the other end of the phone, calmly telling her what to do.

"Ready?" he asked.

"Not yet, Mr. al-Siddiqi."

There was a moment of silence. "Now, Jihan?"

"Yes, Mr. al-Siddiqi."

"Do you see the log-in box?"

She said that she did.

"I'm going to give you another six-digit number. Are you ready?"

"Ready," she repeated.

He recited six numbers. They took Jihan to the main menu of Mr. al-Siddiqi's hidden world. When she spoke again, she managed to sound calm, almost bored.

"It worked," she said.

"Do you see my main documents file?"

"Yes, I think so."

"Click on it, please."

She did. The computer asked for another password.

"It's the same as the last," he said.

"I'm afraid I've forgotten it, Mr. al-Siddiqi."

He repeated the number. When typed into the log-in box, the file folder opened. Jihan saw the names of dozens of companies: investment companies, holding companies, real estate development companies, import-export firms. Some of the names she recognized, for she had blindly handled transactions related to them. Most, however, were unknown to her.

"Enter LXR Investments into the search box, please."

She did. Ten folders appeared.

"Open the one labeled Registry."

She tried. "It's asking for another password."

"Try the same one."

"Can you repeat it again, please?"

He did. But when Jihan entered it, the folder remained locked, and a message appeared, warning against unauthorized entry.

"Hold on a minute, Jihan."

She pressed the phone tightly to her ear. She could hear a final boarding announcement for a flight to Vienna and the rustle of turning pages.

"Let me give you another number," al-Siddiqi said at last.

"Ready," she said.

He recited six new numbers. She entered them into the box and said, "I'm in."

"Do you see the PDF file for the letters of incorporation?"

"Yes."

"Attach them to an e-mail and send them to that idiot at Trade Winds. But do me one favor," he added quickly.

"Of course, Mr. al-Siddiqi."

"Send them from your account."

"Certainly."

She attached the document to a blank e-mail, typed in her address, and clicked SEND.

"Done," she said.

"I have to hang up now."

"Have a safe flight."

The line went dead. Jihan placed her phone on Mr. al-Siddiqi's desk next to the keyboard and walked out of the office. The door, when closed, locked automatically behind her. Jihan walked calmly back to her desk, six numbers running through her memory: *eight, seven, nine, four, one, two . . .*

Behind an unmarked door deep within Terminal 3 of London's Heathrow Airport, Gabriel sat staring at an open laptop computer, Graham Seymour at his side. In his hand was a flash drive containing the contents of Mr. al-Siddiqi's notebook; and on the computer screen was a live video image of Mr. al-Siddiqi's private bank in Linz, courtesy of Yossi Gavish, who was sitting in a parked Opel outside. The watch report indicated no sign of the opposition, no sign of trouble. Next to it was a countdown clock: *8:27, 8:26, 8:25, 8:24 . . .* It was the time remaining for the download of the material from Mr. al-Siddiqi's computer.

"So what happens next?" asked Seymour.

"We wait until all the numbers are zero."

"And then?"

"Jihan remembers that she left her phone on Mr. al-Siddiqi's desk."

"Let's hope that al-Siddiqi doesn't have a way to remotely change the entry code for his office door."

Gabriel looked at the clock: *8:06, 8:05, 8:04 . . .*

Seven minutes later, Jihan Nawaz began looking for her mobile phone. It was a pretense, a lie, performed for the benefit of Mr. al-Siddiqi's surveillance cameras and, perhaps, for her own nerves. She searched the top of her desk, the drawers, the floor around it, her wastepaper basket. She even searched the restroom and the break room, though she was quite confident she had visited neither since using her phone last. Finally, she dialed her number from the hard-line phone on her desk and heard it pinging softly on the other side of Mr. al-Siddiqi's door. She swore softly, again for the benefit of Mr. al-Siddiqi's cameras, and called his mobile phone to request permission to enter his office. There was no answer. She rang it again with the same result.

She returned the receiver to its cradle. Surely, she thought, again for her own benefit, Mr. al-Siddiqi would not mind if she entered his office to retrieve her phone. After all, he had just granted her access to his most private files. She checked the time and saw that ten minutes had elapsed. Then she picked up a black leather folio case and rose. She forced herself to walk unhurriedly to his door; her hand felt numb as she entered the six numbers into the cipher keypad: *eight, seven, nine, four, one, two* . . . The deadbolt opened instantly with a sharp snap. She imagined it was the firing pin of the pistol that would fire the fatal bullet into her head. She pushed open the door and went inside, humming softly to herself to hide her fear.

The darkness was impenetrable, absolute. She walked over to the desk and placed her right hand on her mobile phone. Then, with her left, she reached down and placed the folio case atop the identical case she had left there ten minutes earlier—the case that was shielding the external hard drive from the view of Mr. al-Siddiqi's cameras. In a swift, practiced move, she pulled the drive from its USB port and lifted the three items—the hard drive and the two identical folio cases—to the front of her blouse. Then she walked out and closed the door behind her. The deadbolts rammed home with another pistol shot. As she returned to her desk, numbers again filled her thoughts. They were the number of days, the number of hours, she had left to live.

At one o'clock that afternoon, Jihan informed Herr Weber she was going to lunch. She collected her handbag and slipped on her movie-starlet sunglasses. Then, with a curt nod to Sabrina, the receptionist, she went into the street. A tram was waiting in the roundabout; she stepped aboard quickly, followed a few seconds later by the tall one with bloodless skin and gray eyes. He sat closer to Jihan than he usually did, as if he were trying to reassure her; and when she got off at the Mozartstrasse, the one with pockmarked cheeks was waiting to walk her to Franzesco. The woman she knew as Ingrid Roth was reading D. H. Lawrence at a table in the sun. As Jihan sat down opposite, she lowered the book and smiled.

"How was your morning?" she asked.

"Productive."

"Is it in your bag?"

Jihan nodded.

"Shall we order?"

"I can't eat."

"Eat something, Jihan. And smile," she added. "It's important that you smile."

El Al Flight 316 departs Heathrow daily at 2:20 p.m. from Terminal 1. Gabriel boarded with a few minutes to spare, placed his luggage in the overhead bin, and took his seat in first class. The seat next to him was unoccupied. A moment later, Chiara settled into it.

"Hello, stranger," she said.

"How did you manage this?"

"Friends in high places." She smiled. "How did it go in there?"

Wordlessly, he held up the flash drive.

"And Jihan?"

He nodded.

"How long do we have to find the money?"

"Not long," he said.

48

KING SAUL BOULEVARD, TEL AVIV

T HE UNIT THAT toiled in Room 414C of King Saul Boulevard had no official name because, officially, it did not exist. Those who had been briefed on its work referred to it only as the Minyan, for the unit was ten in number and exclusively male in gender. They knew little of pure espionage or special combat operations, though their terminology borrowed much from both disciplines. They penetrated networks by slipping through back doors or with brute force attacks; they made use of Trojan horses, time bombs, and black hats. With but a few keystrokes, they could darken a city, blind an air traffic control network, or make the centrifuges of an Iranian nuclear-enrichment plant spin wildly out of control. In short, they had the ability to turn the machines against their masters. Privately, Uzi Navot referred to the Minyan as ten good reasons why no one in his right mind would ever use a computer or a mobile phone.

They were waiting at their terminals, a motley crew in blue jeans and sweatshirts, when Gabriel returned to King Saul Boulevard, bearing the contents of Waleed al-Siddiqi's notebook and computer. They probed first at the Trade Winds Bank in the Cayman Islands, an institution they had visited on several prior occasions, and there they made their first significant discovery. The numbers for the two recently opened accounts for LXR Investments did not match the numbers al-Siddiqi had entered in his notebook; he had written them in a crude code, an inversion of numerals, that they quickly rendered useless. It seemed he was fond of Trade Winds, for he had opened ten other holding accounts there under various fronts and shells. All totaled, the small bank in the Cayman Islands held more than $300 million in Evil Incorporated assets. In addition, the notebook and computer files revealed that five other banks in the Cayman Islands held accounts for LXR Investments or other shell companies. The grand total in a single offshore banking center was $1.2 billion. And that was just the beginning.

They worked geographically, methodically, and with Gabriel peering over their shoulders every step of the way. From the Cayman Islands, they moved north to Bermuda, where three more banks held in excess of $600 million. Then they made a flying visit to the Bahamas before traveling to Panama, where they unearthed another half a billion stashed away in fourteen accounts listed in al-Siddiqi's notebook. Their tour of the Western Hemisphere concluded in Buenos Aires, the city of scoundrels and war criminals, where they discovered another $400 million sitting in a dozen accounts. At no stop along their journey did they remove a single cent. They merely put in place the trapdoors and invisible routing circuits that would allow them, at the time of their choosing, to carry off the biggest bank robbery in recorded history.

But the money was not Gabriel's only concern. And so, as the hackers expanded their search to the offshore banking center of Hong Kong, he wandered down the hall to his empty lair to review the latest batch of watch reports from Linz. It was late morning in Upper Austria; Jihan was at her desk, Waleed al-Siddiqi was typing rapidly on his desktop computer. Gabriel knew this because he had done more at Heathrow Airport than photograph the pages of al-Siddiqi's secret notebook. He had also compromised the banker's mobile phone. Like Jihan's device, it was now acting as a full-time audio transmitter. In addition, the team had the ability to read al-Siddiqi's e-mail and text messages and to take photographs and video with the phone's camera at will. Waleed al-Siddiqi, private banker to Syria's ruling family, belonged to the Office now. They owned him.

When Gabriel returned to the hackers' workshop, he brought with him his old wooden chalkboard. The cyberspies thought it a curious object; in fact, most had never seen such a contraption before. Gabriel wrote a number on it: $2.9 billion, the total value of the accounts identified and isolated thus far. And when the hackers had finished their work in Hong Kong, he changed the number to $3.6 billion. Dubai raised it to $4.7 billion; Amman and Beirut, to $5.4 billion. Liechtenstein and France added another $800 million, and, not surprisingly, the banks of Switzerland contributed a whopping $2 billion, bringing the grand total to $8.2 billion. The banks of London held another £600 million. On Gabriel's orders, the hackers built their trapdoors and invisible routing circuits in the unlikely event Graham Seymour reneged on his deal to freeze the money.

By then, another thirty hours had elapsed, thirty hours during which Gabriel and the hackers had not slept or consumed anything other than coffee. It was late afternoon in Upper Austria; Jihan was preparing to take her leave, Waleed al-Siddiqi was again hammering on his desktop computer. Bleary-eyed, Gabriel instructed the hackers to create a ceremonial button that, when pressed, would make more than $8 billion in assets disappear in the blink of an eye. Then he headed upstairs to the executive suite. The light over the door shone green. Uzi Navot was reading a file at his desk.

"How much?" he asked, looking up.

Gabriel told him.

"If it were less than eight billion," Navot said sardonically, "I'd be willing to authorize it on my own. But under these circumstances, I'd like to have a quiet word with the prime minister before anyone touches that button."

"I agree."

"Then maybe you should be the one to talk to the prime minister. After all," Navot added, "it's probably time for you two to get better acquainted."

"There'll be plenty of time for that later, Uzi."

Navot closed the file and gazed through the slats of his venetian blinds toward the sea. "So how does it work?" he asked after a moment. "We grab the money, then we grab the girl?"

"Actually," replied Gabriel, "I intend to make them vanish at the same instant."

"Is she ready?"

"She's been ready for a while."

"A mysterious disappearance? Is that how you intend to play it?"

Gabriel nodded. "No luggage, no travel bookings, nothing to suggest she was planning a trip. We take her by car to Germany and then bring her back to Israel from Munich."

"Who gets the unenviable assignment of telling her that she's been working for us?"

"I was hoping to do it myself."

"But?"

"I'm afraid Jihan's good friend Ingrid Roth is going to have to do it for me."

"You want to grab the money tonight?"

Gabriel nodded.

"Then I'd better have that word with the prime minister."

"I suppose you should."

Navot shook his head slowly. "Eight billion dollars," he said after a moment. "That's a lot of money."

"And I'm sure there's more out there somewhere."

"Eight billion is plenty. Who knows?" Navot added. "It might even be enough to buy back that Caravaggio."

Gabriel made no reply.

"So who gets to push the button?" asked Navot.

"It's a job for the chief, Uzi."

"It wouldn't be right."

"Why not?"

"Because it was your operation from beginning to end."

"How about a compromise candidate?" asked Gabriel.

"Who do you have in mind?"

"The country's preeminent expert on Syria and the Baathist movement."

"She might like that." Navot was looking out his window again. "I wish you could be the one to tell Jihan that she's been working for us."

"So do I, Uzi. But there isn't time."

"What if she doesn't get on the plane?"

"She will."

"How can you be so sure?"

"Because she has no other choice."

"I'd like to put Waleed al-Siddiqi on a plane, too," Navot said. "Preferably in a wooden box."

"Something tells me Evil Incorporated will take care of Waleed for us when they discover eight billion dollars of their money is missing."

"How long do you think he has left to live?"

Gabriel looked at his watch.

———

It did not take long for word to spread through Israel's close-knit security and defense fraternity that an event of great magnitude was about to occur. The uninitiated could only guess at what it was. The initiated could only shake their heads in wonder. It was, they declared, an achievement of Shamronian proportions, perhaps the finest of his career. Surely it was time to put poor Uzi Navot out of his misery and make the change at King Saul Boulevard that everyone knew was coming.

If Navot was aware of such talk, he gave no sign

of it during his meeting with the prime minister. He was brisk, authoritative, and sober about the implications of what it would mean to make $8 billion vanish into thin air. It was a bold move, he said, that would surely invite retaliation if it ever became known who was behind the operation. He advised the prime minister to place the IDF's Northern Command on heightened alert and to tighten security at all Israeli embassies worldwide, especially those in cities where Hezbollah and Syrian intelligence were most active. The prime minister agreed to both steps. He also ordered an increase of security at all essential Israeli computer and communications networks. Then, with little more than a nod, he gave his final approval.

"Would you like to be the one to push the button?" asked Navot.

"It's tempting," replied the prime minister with a smile, "but probably unwise."

By the time Navot returned to King Saul Boulevard, Gabriel had issued his final set of instructions to the team. It was his intention to seize the assets at nine p.m. Linz time, ten p.m. in Tel Aviv. Once the money had arrived at its final destination, a process that was expected to take just five minutes, he would send a flash message to Dina and Christopher Keller instructing them to take Jihan into their possession. Housekeeping and Transport would quietly clean up the mess.

By nine p.m. Tel Aviv time, there was nothing left to do but wait. Gabriel spent that final hour locked away in Room 414C, listening to the hackers explain for the twentieth time how $8 billion was going to move from dozens of accounts around the globe into a single account at the Israel Discount Bank, Ltd., without leaving so much as a puff of digital smoke. And for the twentieth time, he pretended to comprehend what they were telling him, when all the while he was wondering how such a thing was truly possible. He did not understand the language the hackers spoke, nor did he particularly want to. He was only glad they were on his side.

The work that took place in Room 414C was so sensitive that even the director of the Office did not know the cipher code that opened the door. As a result, Uzi Navot had to knock in order to gain admittance. Accompanied by Bella and Chiara, he entered the room at 9:50 Tel Aviv time and was given the same briefing that Gabriel had received a few minutes earlier. Unlike Gabriel, who regarded himself as a man of the sixteenth century, Navot actually knew how computers and the Internet functioned. He posed several insightful questions, asked for one final set of assurances regarding deniability, and then formally issued the order to seize the assets.

Bella sat down at the designated computer and waited for Gabriel's command to press the button. It was 9:55 p.m. in Tel Aviv, 8:55 p.m. in Linz. Jihan Nawaz was alone in her apartment, humming softly to herself to hide her fear. Two minutes later, at 8:57 local time, she received a telephone call from Waleed al-Siddiqi. The conversation that followed was ten minutes in length. And even before it had ended, Gabriel issued the order to stand down. No one would be pushing any buttons, he said. Not tonight.

49

THE ATTERSEE, AUSTRIA

L ATER THAT EVENING, another civil war erupted in the Middle East. It was smaller than the others, and fortunately there were no bombings or bloodshed, for this war was a war of words, fought among people of the same faith, children of the same God. Even so, the battle lines were stark and clearly drawn. One side wanted to cash out while they were still playing with house money. The other wanted one more roll of the dice, one more glimpse into Evil Incorporated. For better or worse, the leader of this faction was Gabriel Allon, the future chief of Israel's secret intelligence service. And so, after a quarrel lasting the better part of the night, he boarded El Al Flight 353 bound for Munich, and by early afternoon he was once again in the sitting room of the Attersee safe house, dressed as a nameless tax collector from Berlin. A laptop computer stood open on the coffee table, its speakers emitting the distinct sound of Waleed al-Siddiqi speaking in Arabic. He lowered the volume only slightly as Jihan and Dina entered.

"Jihan," he called out, as though he had not been expecting her so soon. "Welcome home. It's good to see you looking so well. You've succeeded beyond our wildest expectations. Truly. We can't thank you enough for everything you've done."

He had given this speech in his Berlin-accented German, through a hotelier's vacant smile. Jihan glanced at Dina, then at the laptop computer. "Is that why you brought me here again?" she asked finally. "Because you wanted to thank me?"

"No," was all he said.

"Then why am I here?"

"You're here," he said, approaching her slowly, "because of the phone call you received at eight fifty-seven last evening." He cocked his head inquisitively to one side. "You do remember the phone call you received last night, don't you?"

"It was impossible to forget."

"We feel the same way." His head was still tilted to one side, though now his right hand was pressed thoughtfully to his chin. "The timing of the call was remarkable, to say the least. Had it arrived a few minutes later, you would have never received it."

"Why not?"

"Because you would have been gone. And so would a great deal of money," he added quickly. "Eight-point-two billion dollars, to be precise. All because of the brave work you've done."

"Why didn't you seize it?"

"It was very tempting," he replied. "But if we had, it would have made it impossible to consider the opportunity Mr. al-Siddiqi has presented."

"Opportunity?"

"Were you listening to the things he said to you last night?"

"I tried not to."

Gabriel appeared genuinely perplexed by her answer. "Why is that?"

"Because I can't stand the sound of his voice any longer." She paused, then added, "There's no way I can walk through the doors of that bank again. Please make the money disappear. And then make me disappear as well."

"Let's listen to the recording of the conversation together, shall we? And if you still feel the same way, we'll leave Austria together this afternoon, all of us, and never come back."

"I haven't packed."

"You don't need to. We'll take care of everything."

"Where are you planning to take me?"

"Somewhere safe. Somewhere no one will find you."

"Where?" she asked again, but Gabriel made no response other than to sit down in front of the computer. With a click of the mouse, he silenced the voice of Waleed al-Siddiqi. Then, with another click, he opened an audio file labeled INTERCEPT 238. It was 8:57 p.m. the previous evening. Jihan was alone in her apartment, humming softly to herself to hide her fear. And then her phone began to ring.

It rang four times before she answered, and when she did she sounded slightly out of breath.

"*Hello.*"

"*Jihan?*"

"*Mr. al-Siddiqi?*"

"*I'm sorry to call you so late. Am I catching you at a bad time?*"

"*No, not at all.*"

"*Is there something wrong?*"

"*No, why?*"

"*You sound as though you're upset about something.*"

"*I had to run for the phone, that's all.*"

"*You're sure? You're sure there's nothing wrong?*"

Gabriel clicked the PAUSE icon.

"Is he always so concerned about your well-being?"

"It is a recent obsession of his."

"Why did you allow the phone to ring so many times?"

"Because when I saw who was calling, I didn't want to answer."

"You were afraid?"

"Where are you going to take me?"

Gabriel clicked PLAY.

"*I'm fine, Mr. al-Siddiqi. How can I help you?*"

"*I have something important to discuss with you.*"

"*Of course, Mr. al-Siddiqi.*"

"*Would it be possible for me to stop by your apartment?*"

"*It's late.*"

"*I realize that.*"

"*I'm sorry, but it's really not a good time. Can it wait until Monday?*"

Gabriel clicked PAUSE.

"I wish to congratulate you on your tradecraft. You managed to put him off quite easily."

"Tradecraft?"

"It is a term of art from the world of intelligence."

"I didn't realize this was an intelligence operation. And it wasn't tradecraft," she added. "A Sunni Muslim girl from Hama would never allow a married man to come to her apartment unaccompanied, even if the married man also happened to be her employer."

Gabriel smiled and clicked PLAY.

"*I'm afraid it can't wait until Monday. I need you to take a trip for me on Monday.*"

"*Where?*"

"*Geneva.*"

STOP.

"Has he ever asked you to travel on his behalf?"

"Never."

"Do you know what else is happening in Geneva on Monday?"

"Everyone in the world knows that," she answered. "The Americans, the Russians, and the Europeans are going to attempt to broker a peace agreement between the regime and the Syrian rebels."

"A milestone, yes?"

"It will be a dialogue of the deaf."

Another smile.

PLAY.

"*Why Geneva, Mr. al-Siddiqi?*"

"*I need you to collect some documents for me. You'll only be there for an hour or two. I'd do it myself, but I have to be in Paris that day.*"

STOP.

"For the record," said Gabriel, "Mr. al-Siddiqi hasn't purchased an airline ticket for a flight to Paris on Monday."

"He always does it at the last minute."

"And why do the documents have to be collected by hand?" asked Gabriel, ignoring her. "Why not ship them by overnight delivery service? Why not transmit them via electronic mail?"

"It's not unusual for confidential financial records to be delivered by hand."

"Especially when they're being given to a man like Waleed al-Siddiqi."

PLAY.

"*What exactly do you need me to do?*"

"*It's quite simple, really. I just need you to meet a client at the Hotel Métropole. He'll give you a packet of documents, and you'll carry those documents back to Linz.*"

"*And the client's name?*"

"*Kemel al-Farouk.*"

STOP.

"Who is he?" asked Jihan.

Gabriel smiled. "Kemel al-Farouk holds the keys to the kingdom," he said. "Kemel al-Farouk is the reason you have to go to Geneva."

50

THE ATTERSEE, AUSTRIA

T HEY ADJOURNED TO the terrace and sat beneath the shade of a parasol. A passing motorboat opened a wound in the lake; then the boat was gone and they were alone again. It might have seemed possible that they were the last two people in the world were it not for the sound of Waleed al-Siddiqi's voice streaming from the laptop computer in the drawing room.

"I see you've acquired another boat," Jihan said, nodding toward the sloop.

"Actually, my colleagues acquired it on my behalf."

"Why?"

"I was driving them crazy."

"Over what?"

"You, Jihan. I wanted to make sure we were doing everything possible to keep you safe."

She was silent for a moment. "The sailing must be very different here than it is on the Baltic." She looked at him and smiled. "That *is* where you did your sailing, isn't it? The Baltic?"

He nodded slowly.

"I never liked it," she said.

"The Baltic?"

"Sailing. I don't like the feeling of not being in control."

"I can go anywhere in that little sailboat."

"Then you must be good at controlling things."

Gabriel made no reply.

"Why?" Jihan asked after a moment. "Why is it so important that we get those documents from Kemel al-Farouk?"

"Because of his relationship to the ruling family," answered Gabriel. "Kemel al-Farouk is Syria's deputy foreign minister. In fact, he'll be seated at the negotiating table when the talks convene Monday afternoon. But his title belies the scope of his influence. The ruler never makes a move without first talking to Kemel, political or financial. We believe there's more money out there," Gabriel added. "Much more. And we believe Kemel's documents can show us the way."

"Believe?"

"There are no guarantees in this business, Jihan."

"And what business is that?"

Again Gabriel was silent.

"But why does Mr. al-Siddiqi want *me* to collect the documents?" Jihan asked. "Why not do it himself?"

"Because once the Syrian delegation arrives in Geneva, they're going to be under constant surveillance by Swiss intelligence, not to mention the Americans and their European allies. There's no way al-Siddiqi can go near that delegation."

"I don't want to go near them, either. They are the same people who destroyed my town, the same people who murdered my family. I am speaking to you in German because of men like them."

"So why not join the Syrian rebellion, Jihan? Why not avenge the murder of your family by bringing us those documents?"

From the drawing room came the sound of Waleed al-Siddiqi laughing.

"Isn't eight billion dollars enough?" she asked after a moment.

"It's a great deal of money, Jihan, but I want more."

"Why?"

"Because it will allow us to have more influence over his actions."

"The ruler's?"

He nodded.

"Forgive me," she said with a smile, "but that doesn't sound like something a German tax collector would say."

He gave an evasive smile but said nothing.

"How would it work?" she asked.

"You'll do everything Mr. al-Siddiqi asks," Gabriel replied. "You'll fly to Geneva early Monday morning. You'll take a chauffeured car from the airport to the Hotel Métropole and collect the documents. And then you'll go back to the airport and return to Linz." He paused, then added, "And at some point along the way, you'll photograph the documents with your mobile phone and send them to me."

"Then what?"

"If, as we suspect, those documents are a list of additional accounts, we'll attack them while you're in the air. By the time your plane touches down in

Vienna, it will be over. And then we'll make you disappear."

"Where?" she asked. "Where are you going to take me?"

"Somewhere safe. Somewhere no one can hurt you."

"I'm afraid that's not good enough," she said. "I want to know where you intend to take me when this is over. And while you're at it, you can tell me who you really are. And this time, I want the truth. I'm a child of Hama. I don't like it when people lie to me."

They boarded the motorboat with the strained civility of a quarreling couple and headed southward down the lake. Jihan sat rigidly in the aft, her legs crossed, her arms folded, her eyes boring two holes into the back of his neck. She had absorbed his confession in an enraged silence, a wife listening to a husband's admission of an infidelity. For now, he had nothing more to say. It was her turn to speak.

"You bastard," she said at last.

"Do you feel better now?"

He spoke these words without turning to face her. Apparently, she didn't find them worthy of a reply.

"And what if I had told you the truth in the beginning?" he asked. "What would you have done?"

"I would have told you to go straight to hell."

"Why?"

"Because you're just like they are."

He allowed a moment to pass before responding. "You have a right to be angry, Jihan. But don't you dare compare me to the butcher boy of Damascus."

"You're worse!"

"Spare me the bumper-sticker slogans. Because if the conflict in Syria has proven anything, it is that we truly are different from our adversaries. A hundred and fifty thousand dead, millions turned into refugees, all at the hands of brother Arabs."

"You did the same thing!" she shot back.

"Bullshit." He still hadn't turned to face her. "You might find this hard to believe," he said, "but I want the Palestinians to have a state of their own. In fact, I intend to do everything in my power to make that a reality. But for the moment, it's not possible. It takes two sides to make peace."

"You're the ones occupying their land!"

He didn't bother to offer a reply, for he had learned long ago that such debates almost always assumed the quality of a cat chasing its own tail. Instead, he switched off the engine and swiveled his chair around to face her.

"Take off that disguise," she said. "Let me see your face."

He removed the false eyeglasses.

"Now the wig."

He did as she asked. She leaned forward and stared into his face.

"Take out those contact lenses. I want to see your eyes."

He removed the lenses in turn and flicked them into the lake.

"Satisfied, Jihan?"

"Why do you speak German so well?"

"My ancestors were from Berlin. My mother was the only one to survive the Holocaust. When she arrived in Israel, she didn't speak Hebrew. German was the first language I ever heard."

"What about Ingrid?"

"Her parents had six children, one for each million murdered in the Holocaust. Her mother and two of her sisters were killed by a Hamas suicide bomber. Ingrid was severely wounded. That's why she walks with a limp. That's why she never wears shorts or a dress."

"What's her real name?"

"It's not important."

"What's yours?"

"What difference does it make? You hate me because of who I am. You hate me because of *what* I am."

"I hate you because you lied to me."

"I had no choice."

The wind stirred and brought with it the scent of roses.

"Did you really never suspect we were from Israel?"

"I did," she admitted.

"Why didn't you ask?"

She made no reply.

"Maybe you didn't ask because you didn't want to know the answer. And maybe now that you've had a chance to yell at me and call me names, we can get back to work. I'm going to turn the butcher of Damascus into a pauper. I'm going to see to it he never uses poison gas against his own people again, that he never turns another city into rubble. But I can't do it alone. I need your help." He paused, then asked, "Will you help me, Jihan?"

She was trailing her hand, childlike, in the water. "Where will I go when it's over?"

"Where do you think?"

"I couldn't possibly live there."

"It's not as bad as you've been led to believe. In fact, it's rather nice. But don't worry," he added, "you won't have to stay long. As soon as it's safe to leave, you can live wherever you want."

"Are you telling me the truth this time, or is this another one of your lies?"

Gabriel said nothing. Jihan scooped water from the lake and allowed it to run through her fingers. "I'll do it," she said at last, "but I need something from you in return."

"Anything, Jihan."

She looked at him for a moment in silence. Then she said, "I need to know your name."

"It's not important."

"It is to me," she replied. "Tell me your name, or you can find someone else to collect those documents in Geneva."

"It's not the way things are done in our business."

"Tell me your name," she said again. "I'll write it in the water, and then I'll forget it."

He smiled at her and spoke his name.

"Like the archangel?" she asked.

"Yes," he said. "Like the archangel."

"And your last name?"

He told her that, too.

"It's familiar to me."

"It should be."

She leaned over the side of the boat and carved his name into the black surface of the lake. Then a gust of wind swept down from the Mountains of Hell and it was gone.

51

THE ATTERSEE—GENEVA

W<small>HEN IT WAS</small> over, Gabriel would be able to recall little of the next twenty-four hours, for they were a whirlwind of planning, heated family quarrels, and tense conversations carried out over secure channels. At King Saul Boulevard, his emergency demand for additional safe properties and clean transport caused a brief rebellion, which Uzi Navot managed to suppress with a hard glare and a few stern words. Only Banking did not bristle at Gabriel's request for more funding. His operation was already running at a substantial profit, with windfall earnings expected in the fourth quarter.

Jihan Nawaz would know nothing of the internecine battles raging within the Office, only the requirements of her last assignment on its behalf. She returned to the Attersee safe house Sunday afternoon for a final preoperational briefing, and to rehearse photographing documents under Gabriel's unique brand of simulated pressure. Afterward, she gathered with the team for a luncheon on the lawn overlooking the lake. The false flag they had flown since her recruitment had been lowered and packed away for good. They were Israelis now, operatives of an intelligence service that most Arabs regarded with a paradoxical mixture of hatred and awe. There was the bookish Yossi, the false bureaucrat from Britain's Revenue and Customs service. There was the rumpled little figure who had first come to her as Feliks Adler. There were Mikhail, Yaakov, and Oded, her three guardians on the streets of Linz. And there was Ingrid Roth, her neighbor, her confidante, her wounded secret sharer, who had suffered a loss that Jihan understood only too well.

And at the far end of the table, silent and watchful, was the green-eyed man whose name she had written on the water. He was not the monster the Arab press had made him out to be; none of them were. They were charming. They were witty. They were intelligent. They loved their country and their people. They were deeply sorry for what had happened to Jihan and her family at Hama. Yes, they admitted, Israel had made mistakes since its founding, terrible mistakes. But it wanted nothing more than to live in peace and to be accepted by its neighbors. The Arab Spring had briefly held the promise of change in the Middle East, but sadly it had reverted into a death struggle between Sunni and Shiite, between the global jihadists and the old order of Arab strongmen. Surely, they agreed, there was a middle ground, a modern Middle East where religious and tribal ties were less important than decent governance and progress. For a few hours that afternoon on the shores of the Attersee, it seemed anything was possible.

She left them for the last time in early evening and,

accompanied by her friend Ingrid, returned to her apartment. Keller alone watched over her that night, for the rest of the team had commenced a hurried battlefield transition that one Office wit would later refer to as the great westward migration. Gabriel and Eli Lavon traveled by car together, Gabriel driving, Lavon fretting and worrying, the same way they had done it a thousand times before. But that night was different. Their target was not a terrorist with Israeli blood on his hands; it was billions of dollars that rightfully belonged to the people of Syria. Lavon the asset hunter could scarcely contain his excitement. Control the butcher's money, he said, and they could bend him to their will. They could *own* him.

They arrived in Geneva in the uncertain hour between darkness and dawn and made their way to an old Office safe flat on the boulevard de Saint-Georges. Mordecai had been there before them, and in the sitting room he had constructed a command post, complete with computers and a secure radio. Gabriel sent a brief activation message to the Ops Center at King Saul Boulevard. Then, shortly before seven, he listened to a weary-sounding Waleed al-Siddiqi boarding Austrian Air Flight 411 at Vienna's Schwechat Airport. As his plane was passing over Linz, a black sedan eased to the curb outside an apartment house on the fringes of the Innere Stadt. And five minutes after that, Jihan Nawaz, the child of Hama, stepped into the street.

For the next three hours, Gabriel's world shrank to the fifteen luminous inches of his computer screen.

There was no war in Syria, no Israel, no Palestine. His wife was not pregnant with twins. In fact, he did not have a wife. There were only the winking red lights depicting the positions of Jihan Nawaz and Waleed al-Siddiqi, and the winking blue lights depicting the positions of his team. It was ordered, sanitary, a world without danger. It seemed nothing could go wrong.

At eight fifteen, Jihan's red light arrived at Vienna's Schwechat Airport, and at nine it went dark as she dutifully obeyed the flight attendant's instructions to switch off all electronic devices. Gabriel then turned his full attention to Waleed al-Siddiqi, who at that moment was entering the Paris offices of a prominent French bank where he had secretly deposited several hundred million dollars in Syrian assets. The bank was located along an elegant stretch of the rue Saint-Honoré, in the First Arrondissement. Al-Siddiqi's black Mercedes sedan remained parked outside in the street. An Office surveillance team from Paris Station had identified the driver as an asset of Syrian intelligence in France—security, mainly, but occasionally rough stuff, too. Gabriel requested a photo and was rewarded five minutes later with a shot of a thick-necked man grimly clutching a luxury steering wheel.

At ten minutes past nine Paris time, al-Siddiqi entered the office of Monsieur Gérard Beringer, one of the bank's vice presidents. The Syrian did not remain there for long, because at 9:17 he received a call on his mobile phone that took him into the corridor in search of privacy. The call was from a number in Damascus; the baritone voice at the other end was male, a person of authority. At the conclusion of the conversation—which was just twenty seconds in length and conducted in the Alawite dialect of Syrian Arabic—al-Siddiqi switched off his phone, and his red light disappeared from the computer screen.

Gabriel listened to the recording of the conversation five times and was unable to determine exactly what was being said. Then he asked King Saul Boulevard for a translation and was told that the baritone caller had instructed al-Siddiqi to ring him back on another device. Voice analysis turned up no matches on the caller's identity. The eavesdroppers at Unit 8200 were trying to pinpoint the location of the number in Damascus.

"People turn off their cell phones all the time," said Eli Lavon. "Especially people like Waleed al-Siddiqi."

"True," replied Gabriel. "But they generally do it when they fear someone is listening."

"Someone *is* listening."

Gabriel said nothing. He was staring at the computer screen as if he were trying to will al-Siddiqi's light back into life.

"The call probably had something to do with the man sitting in the Hotel Métropole," Lavon said after a moment.

"That's what concerns me."

"It's not too late to cash out, Gabriel. You can make eight billion dollars disappear. And you can make the girl disappear, too."

"What if there's another eight billion out there, Eli? What if there's *eighty* billion?"

Lavon said nothing for a moment. Then, finally, he asked, "What are you going to do?"

"I'm going to consider all the reasons why Waleed al-Siddiqi might have just turned off his phone. And then I'm going to make a decision."

"I'm afraid there isn't time for that."

Gabriel looked at the computer again. The child of Hama had just arrived in Geneva.

The arrivals hall at Geneva Airport was more crowded than usual: diplomats, reporters, extra police and security, a knot of Syrian exiles singing the song of protest that was written by a man whose throat had been cut out by the secret police. As a result, it took Jihan a moment to spot her driver. He was in his mid-thirties, dark-haired and olive-skinned, a bit too intelligent-looking to be working as a chauffeur. His gaze turned toward her as she approached—he had obviously been shown her photograph—and he flashed a smile, exposing a row of even white teeth. He spoke to her in Arabic, with a Syrian accent.

"I hope you had a good flight, Miss Nawaz."

"It was fine," she replied coolly.

"The car is outside. Follow me, please."

He raised a manicured hand toward the appropriate door. Their route took them past the protesters, who were still singing their song of defiance, and past the small square Israeli who looked as though he could bend steel bars. Jihan looked through him as though he were invisible and stepped outside. A black Mercedes S-Class sedan with heavily tinted windows and diplomatic plates idled curb-side. When the driver opened the rear passenger-side door, Jihan hesitated before climbing inside. She waited until the door was closed again before turning her head and looking at the man seated next to her. He was several years older than the driver, with thinning black hair, a heavy mustache, and the hands of a bricklayer.

"Who are you?" asked Jihan.

"Security," he answered.

"Why do I need security?"

"Because you are about to meet with an official of the Syrian foreign ministry. And because there are many enemies of the Syrian government in Geneva at the moment, including that rabble inside," he added with a sidelong nod toward the terminal building. "It is important that you reach your desti-nation safely."

The driver climbed behind the wheel and closed his door. "*Yallah*," said the one in the backseat, and the car shot forward.

It was not until they had left the airport that he bothered to offer a name. He called himself Mr. Omari. He worked, or so he said, as a senior secu-rity officer for Syrian diplomatic posts in Western Europe—a difficult job, he added with a burdened nod, given the political tensions of the time. It was clear from his accent he was an Alawite. It was also clear that the driver, who seemed to have no name at all, was taking anything but the direct route into central Geneva. He wandered through an estate of low-rise industrial buildings for several minutes, glancing constantly into his rearview mirror, before finally making his way to the route de Meyrin. It bore them through a leafy residential quarter and, eventually, to the shore of the lake. As they sped across the Pont du Mont-Blanc, Jihan realized she was clutching her handbag so tightly her knuckles had gone white. She forced herself to relax her hand and to smile slightly as she looked out her window at the beautiful sunlit city. The sight of Swiss policemen lining the ramparts of the bridge gave her a moment of comfort; and when they reached the opposite shore of the lake, she saw the Israeli with pockmarked cheeks peering through the window of an Armani boutique on the Quai du Général-Guisan. The car slid past him and stopped outside the gray-green facade of the Métropole. Mr. Omari waited a moment before speaking.

"I assume Mr. al-Siddiqi told you the name of the man waiting for you upstairs?"

"Mr. al-Farouk."

He nodded gravely. "He's staying in Room 312. Please go directly to his room. Do not talk to the concierge or anyone else in the hotel. Is that clear, Miss Nawaz?"

She nodded.

"Once you have the documents, you are to leave his room and return directly to this car. Do not make any stops along the way. Do not speak to anyone. Understood?"

Another nod. "Is there anything else?" she asked.

"Yes," he said, holding out his hand. "Please give

me your mobile phone, along with any other electronic device you might have in your bag."

Ten seconds later, the red light from Jihan's phone vanished from Gabriel's computer screen. He immediately radioed Yaakov, who had followed her into the hotel, and ordered him to abort the operation. But by then it was too late; Jihan was marching across the crowded lobby at a parade-ground clip, her chin raised defiantly, her handbag over one shoulder. Then she slipped between a pair of closing elevator doors and was gone from his sight.

Yaakov quickly boarded the next elevator and pressed the call button for the third floor. The journey seemed to take an eternity; and when the doors finally opened he saw a Syrian security man standing in the vestibule, hands clasped, feet shoulder-width, as though he were bracing himself for a frontal assault. The two men exchanged a long, cold stare. Then the doors rattled shut, and the elevator sank slowly toward the lobby.

52

HOTEL MÉTROPOLE, GENEVA

S HE KNOCKED LIGHTLY—too lightly, it seemed, because for several long seconds no one answered. Then the door retreated a few inches, and a pair of dark eyes regarded her warily over the security bar. The eyes belonged to yet another security man. He was more like Jihan's driver than the implacable Mr. Omari, young, immaculately groomed and attired, a killer in a presentable wrapper. In the entrance hall he ransacked her handbag to make certain she hadn't brought a pistol or a suicide vest. Then he invited her to follow him into the sitting room of the luxurious suite. There were four more security men just like him scattered about the perimeter; and seated on the couch was Kemel al-Farouk, deputy minister of foreign affairs, former officer of the Mukhabarat, friend and trusted adviser of the ruler. He was balancing a cup and saucer in one hand and shaking his head at something a reporter from Al Jazeera was saying on the television. Files lay scattered about him on the couch and the coffee table. Jihan could only wonder at the contents. Position papers regarding the upcoming peace talks? An account of recent battlefield victories? A list of newly dead opposition figures? Finally, he swiveled his head a few degrees and, with a nod, invited her to sit. He neither stood nor offered his hand. Men like Kemel al-Farouk were too powerful to worry about good manners.

"Your first time in Geneva?" he asked.

"No," she answered.

"You've come here before on behalf of Mr. al-Siddiqi?"

"On holiday, actually."

"When did you come here on holiday, Jihan?" He smiled suddenly and asked, "Is it all right if I call you Jihan?"

"Of course, Mr. al-Farouk."

His smile faded. He asked again about the circumstances of her holiday in Geneva.

"I was a child," she said. "I really don't remember much about it."

"Mr. al-Siddiqi tells me you were raised in Hamburg."

She nodded.

"It is one of the great tragedies of our country, the great Syrian diaspora. How many of us have been scattered to the four winds? Ten million? Fifteen million? If only they would come home again. Syria would be a truly great nation."

She wanted to explain to him that the diaspora would never return as long as men like him were running the country. Instead, she nodded thoughtfully, as though he had spoken words of great insight. He was seated in the manner of the ruler's father, with his feet resting flat on the floor and his palms on his knees. His cropped hair had a reddish tint to it, as did his neatly trimmed beard. In his tailored suit and restrained necktie, it was almost possible to imagine he was truly a diplomat and not a man who used to crucify opponents for fun.

"Coffee?" he asked, as though suddenly aware of his ill manners.

"No, thank you," she answered.

"Something to eat, perhaps?"

"I was told to collect the documents and leave, Mr. al-Farouk."

"Ah, yes, the documents." He laid his hand on a manila envelope lying next to him on the couch. "Did you enjoy growing up in Hamburg, Jihan?"

"Yes, I suppose I did."

"There were many other Syrians there, yes?"

She nodded.

"Enemies of the Syrian government?"

"I wouldn't know."

His smile said he didn't quite believe her.

"You lived on the Marienstrasse, did you not?"

"How did you know that?"

"These are difficult times," he said after a moment, as though Syria were experiencing a spell of inclement weather. "My security men tell me you were born in Damascus."

"That's correct."

"In 1976."

She nodded slowly.

"Also difficult times," he said. "We saved Syria from the extremists then, and we'll save Syria once again now." He looked at her for a moment. "You do want the government to prevail in this war, don't you, Jihan?"

She raised her chin a little and looked him directly in the eye. "I want peace for our country," she said.

"We all want peace," he replied. "But it is impossible to make peace with monsters."

"I couldn't agree more, Mr. al-Farouk."

He smiled and placed the manila envelope on the table in front of her.

"How long until your flight leaves?" he asked.

She glanced at her wristwatch and said, "Ninety minutes."

"Are you sure you won't have coffee?"

"No, thank you, Mr. al-Farouk," she said primly.

"How about some food?"

She forced herself to smile. "I'll eat something on the plane."

For a few minutes that glorious Monday morning in Geneva, it seemed the stately old Hotel Métropole was the center of the civilized world. Black motorcars came and went from her entrance; gray diplomats and bankers flowed in and out of her doors. A famous reporter from the BBC used her as a backdrop for a live report. A band of protesters shouted at her for allowing murderers to sleep peacefully beneath her roof.

Inside the hotel, all was quiet bedlam. After his brief visit to the third floor, Yaakov had pounced upon the last open table at the Mirror Bar and was staring at the elevators over a lukewarm café crème. At 11:40 one set of doors rattled open and Jihan suddenly appeared. When she had entered the hotel a few minutes earlier, she had carried her handbag over her right shoulder. Now it was over her left. It was a prearranged signal. Left shoulder meant she had the documents. Left shoulder meant she was safe. Yaakov quickly radioed Gabriel for directions. Gabriel told Yaakov to let her run.

The team had the hotel surrounded on four sides, but no one had bothered with photographic coverage. It didn't matter; as Jihan stepped from the front entrance, she passed through the camera shot of the BBC. The image, beamed live around the world and stored to this day in the broadcaster's digital archives, was the last ever made of her. Her face appeared calm and resolute; her walk was swift and determined. She paused, as though confused about which of the Mercedes sedans parked outside the hotel was hers. Then a man in his mid-thirties gestured to her, and she disappeared into the backseat of a car. The man in his mid-thirties glanced toward the upper floors of the hotel before climbing behind the wheel. The car lurched from the curb, and the child of Hama was gone.

Among the many aspects of Jihan's departure not captured by the BBC's camera was the silver Toyota sedan that followed her. Kemel al-Farouk did notice the car, however, because at that moment he was standing in the window of his room on the hotel's third floor. A former intelligence officer, he couldn't help but admire the manner in which the driver of the Toyota pulled into traffic with no sense of haste or urgency. He was a professional; Kemel al-Farouk was certain of it.

He drew a mobile phone from his pocket, dialed, and murmured a few coded words that informed the man at the other end of the call that he was being followed. Then he rang off and watched the Jet d'Eau blasting a stream of water high above the lake. His thoughts, however, were on the events that would transpire next. First Mr. Omari was going to make her talk. Then Mr. Omari was going to kill her. It promised to be an entertaining afternoon. Kemel al-Farouk only wished that he could make time in his busy schedule to do it himself.

In the safe flat on the boulevard de Saint-Georges, Gabriel stood before the computer, one hand resting on his chin, head tilted to one side, transfixed. Eli Lavon paced slowly behind him, a mug of tea in hand, a writer searching for the perfect verb. The secure radio told them everything there was to know; the computer provided only corroborating evidence. Jihan Nawaz was safely back in the car, and the car was bound for Geneva International Airport. Mikhail Abramov was two hundred meters behind them on the route de Meyrin, with Yossi serving as his navigator and trusted second pair of eyes. Oded and Rimona Stern were covering the terminal. The rest of the team was en route. Everything was unfolding according to plan, with one small exception.

"What's that?" asked Eli Lavon.

"Her phone," replied Gabriel.

"What about it?"

"I'm just wondering why Mr. Omari hasn't given it back to her."

Another minute passed and still her winking red light did not appear on the screen. Gabriel raised the radio to his lips and ordered Mikhail to close the gap.

Later, during the secret inquest that followed the events in Geneva, there would be some question as to precisely when Mikhail and Yossi received Gabriel's order. Eventually, all agreed it was 12:17. There was no question as to their location at the time; they were driving past Les Asters bar and restaurant at 88 route de Meyrin. A woman with dark hair was standing on the apartment balcony just above the café. A streetcar was snaking toward them. It was the Number 14. Of this Mikhail and Yossi were certain.

They were certain, too, that the Mercedes sedan carrying Jihan Nawaz was one hundred meters in front of them and moving at a considerable rate of speed. So considerable, in fact, that Mikhail admittedly found it difficult to make much of a dent in the interval separating the two cars. He blew through the red light at the avenue Wendt and nearly ran down a daredevil pedestrian, but it was no use. The driver of the Mercedes was tearing hell-for-leather up the boulevard as though he feared Jihan might miss her flight.

Finally, at the edges of Geneva's compact city center, Mikhail was able to press the accelerator to the floor. And that was when the white commercial van, very new, no markings, came careening out of a narrow side street. Mikhail had less than a second to consider evasive action, and in that time determined that no options were available. There was a streetcar stop in the center of the boulevard, and heavy traffic streaming toward him in the opposing lanes. Which left no alternative but to slam hard on the brakes while simultaneously turning the wheel to the left, a maneuver that placed the car in a controlled power skid.

The driver of the van braked, too, thus blocking both lanes of the boulevard. And when Mikhail waved at him to move, the driver climbed out of the van and began ranting in a language that sounded like a cross between French and Arabic. Mikhail climbed out, too, and for an instant considered drawing his concealed weapon. But it wasn't necessary; after making one final lewd gesture, the driver of the van retreated to his cockpit and, smiling, inched slowly out of the way. The Mercedes was gone, and Jihan Nawaz had officially vanished from their radar screens.

The mobile phone belonging to Mr. Omari, first name unknown, rang twice after their departure from the Hotel Métropole, once as they were crossing the Pont du Mont-Blanc and again as they were approaching the airport. During the first call he said nothing; during the second he emitted little more than a grunt before killing the connection. Jihan's phone lay next to him on the center console. Thus far, he had given no indication he planned to return it, now or ever.

"You must be curious about the nature of those documents," he said after a moment.

"Not at all," she replied.

"Really?" He turned and looked at her. "I find that difficult to believe."

"Why?"

"Because most people are naturally curious when it comes to the financial affairs of powerful people."

"I deal with powerful people all the time."

"Not like Mr. al-Farouk." He smiled unpleasantly. Then he said, "Go ahead. Have a look."

"I was told not to."

Jihan remained motionless. His smile disappeared.

"Look at the documents," he said again.

"I can't."

"Mr. al-Farouk just told me that he wanted you to open the envelope before you get on the plane."

"Unless he tells me himself, I can't."

"Look at them, Jihan. It's important."

She removed the manila envelope from her purse and offered it to him. He raised his hands defensively, as though she were offering him a venomous snake.

"I'm not allowed to see them," he said. "Only you."

She released the metal tab, lifted the flap, and removed the sheaf of documents. It was a half-inch thick and bound by a metal clasp. The top page was blank.

"There," she said. "I've looked at them. Can we go to the airport now?"

"Look at the next page," he said, smiling again.

She did. It was blank as well. So was the third. And the fourth. Then she looked up at Mr. Omari and saw the gun in his hand, the gun that was pointed at her chest.

AT TWO O'CLOCK that afternoon, the Geneva Conference on Syria convened at the lakefront headquarters of the United Nations. The dour American secretary of state called for an orderly transition from the regime to democracy, something the Syrian foreign minister said would never happen. Not surprisingly, his position won the support of his Russian counterpart, who warned that the Kremlin would veto any attempt, military or diplomatic, to force its only ally in the Arab world from power. At the conclusion of the session, the UN secretary-general meekly declared the negotiations "a promising start." The global media disagreed. They characterized the entire episode as a monumental waste of time and money, mainly theirs, and went in search of a real story to cover.

Elsewhere in the enchanted little city, life went on as normal. The bankers plied their trade along the rue du Rhône, the cafés of the Old City filled and emptied, white jetliners rose into the clear skies above Geneva International Airport. Among the flights that departed that afternoon was Austrian Airlines 577. Its only irregularity was the absence of a single passenger, a female, age thirty-nine, born in Syria and raised on a street in Hamburg that would be forever linked to Islamic terrorism. Given the woman's unusual background and the events taking place in Geneva that day, the airline forwarded a report to the Swiss aviation authority, which in turn sent the information to the NDB, the Swiss intelligence and security service. Eventually, it crossed the desk of Christoph Bittel, who, coincidentally, had been placed in command of security for the Syrian peace talks. He made a routine request for information from his brethren in Berlin and Vienna and was told in short order that they had nothing to report. Even so, he sent a copy of her file and photo to the Geneva police, to the American and Russian diplomatic security services, and even to the Syrians. And then he moved on to more pressing matters.

The failure of the woman to board her Vienna-bound flight was of significantly more concern to the two men in the safe flat on the boulevard de Saint-Georges. In the span of a few minutes, their mood had swung wildly from one of quiet confidence to quiet desperation. They had recruited her, lied to her, and then revealed themselves to her. They had promised to protect her, promised to give her a new life in a place where the monsters who had murdered her family would never find her. And now, in the blink of an eye, they had lost her. But why had the monsters brought her to Geneva in the first place? And why had they allowed her to enter a hotel room where Kemel al-Farouk, Syria's deputy foreign minister and trusted adviser of the ruler, was present?

"Obviously," said Eli Lavon, "it was a trap."

"Obviously?" asked Gabriel.

Lavon looked at the computer screen. "Do you see a red light?" he asked. "Because I don't."

"That doesn't mean it was a trap."

"What does it mean?"

"Why take her here during the peace conference? Why didn't they take her in Linz?"

"Because they knew we were watching her, and they didn't think they could get her cleanly."

"So they created an excuse to bring her to Geneva? Something we couldn't resist? Is that what you're saying, Eli?"

"Sound familiar?"

"What's your point?"

"That's exactly the way we would have done it."

Gabriel wasn't convinced. "Did you happen to notice any agents of Syrian intelligence when we were in Linz?"

"That doesn't mean they weren't there."

"Did you, Eli?"

"No," Lavon said, shaking his head. "I can't say that I did."

"Neither did I," replied Gabriel. "And that's because Waleed al-Siddiqi and Jihan Nawaz were the only Syrians in town. She was clean until her plane landed in Geneva."

"What happened?"

"This happened." Gabriel pressed the PLAY icon on the computer and a few seconds later came the sound of Waleed al-Siddiqi murmuring in Arabic.

"The phone call from Damascus?" asked Lavon.

Gabriel nodded. "If I had to guess," he said, "it was someone from the Mukhabarat telling Waleed that he'd hired a woman from Hama to serve as his account manager."

"Big mistake."

"Which is why Waleed then called Kemel al-Farouk at the Hotel Métropole and told him to cancel the meeting."

"But al-Farouk had a better idea?"

"Maybe it was al-Farouk's idea. Or maybe it was Mr. Omari's. The point is," Gabriel added, "they've got nothing on her other than the fact that she lied about her place of birth."

"Something tells me it won't take them long to discover the truth."

"I agree."

"So what are you going to do?"

"Make a deal, of course."

"How?"

"Like this." Gabriel typed a three-word message to King Saul Boulevard and pressed SEND.

"That should get their attention," said Lavon. "All we need now is someone to negotiate with."

"We have someone, Eli."

"Who?"

Gabriel turned the computer around so Lavon could see the screen. A red light was winking on the rue Saint-Honoré, in the First Arrondissement of Paris. Waleed al-Siddiqi had finally switched on his phone.

Uzi Navot had a body built for leverage, not speed. Even so, all those who witnessed his headlong dash from the Ops Center to Room 414C would later say they had never seen a chief move so quickly. He hammered so hard on the door it seemed he was trying to break it down, and once inside he made straight for the computer terminal that had been reserved for the heist. "Is it still ready to go?" he asked of no one in particular, and from somewhere in the room came the reply that everything was in order. Navot leaned down and, with far more force than was necessary, pressed the button. It was 4:22 p.m. in Tel Aviv, 3:22 p.m. in Geneva. And all around the world, trapdoors were swinging open and money was beginning to flow.

Approximately five minutes after crossing the French border, Mr. Omari dragged Jihan screaming into the trunk of the car. The lid closed upon her with a heavy thud of finality, and her world turned to black. It was like Hama during the siege, she thought. But here in the trunk of the car, there were no explosions or screams to pierce the darkness, only the maddening drone of the tires over pavement. She imagined she was in her mother's arms again, clinging to her hijab. She even imagined she could smell her mother's rose-scented perfume. Then the stench of petrol overwhelmed her, and the memory of her mother's embrace slipped from her grasp, leaving only the fear. She knew what fate awaited her; she had seen it all before, during the dark days that followed the siege. She would be interrogated. Then she would be killed. There was nothing to be done. It was God's will.

The darkness made it impossible for Jihan to see her wristwatch and therefore to keep track of the passage of time. She hummed to herself to hide her fear. And, briefly, she thought about the Israeli intelligence officer whose name she had written on the surface of the Attersee. He would never abandon her; she was certain of it. But she had to somehow keep herself alive long enough for him to find her. Then she remembered a man she had met in Hamburg when she was a university student, a Syrian dissident who had been tortured by the Mukhabarat. He had survived, he said, because he had told the interrogators things he thought they wanted to hear. Jihan would do the same thing— not the truth, of course, but a lie so irresistible they would want to hear every last word of it. She had no doubts about her ability to deceive them. She had been deceiving people her entire life.

And so, as she lay in the darkness, the road rushing beneath her, she wrote the story she hoped would save her life. It was the story of an unlikely alliance between a powerful man and a lonely young woman, a story of greed and deception. She recast the beginning, did a bit of editing and rewriting here and there, and by the time the car finally came to a stop, it was finished. When the lid of the trunk rose, she glimpsed the face of Mr. Omari before he jammed a black hood over her head. She had been expecting the hood. The Syrian dissident had told her about the Mukhabarat's fondness for sensory deprivation.

She was lifted from the trunk and led across an expanse of gravel. Then they forced her down a flight of stairs that were so steep they eventually gave up and carried her. A moment later they dropped her onto a concrete floor like war dead. Then she heard a door slam shut, followed by the sound of male footfalls receding into silence. She lay motionless for several seconds before finally tearing away the hood and discovering she was once again in a place of total darkness. She tried not to shiver but couldn't help it. She tried not to cry but tears soon stained her face. Then she thought about her story. It was Mr. al-Siddiqi's fault, she told herself. None of this would have happened if Mr. al-Siddiqi hadn't offered her a job.

54

TEL AVIV—HAUTE-SAVOIE, FRANCE

A S IT TURNED out, the ten computer geniuses known collectively as the Minyan had been wrong about how long it would take. The process lasted not five minutes but slightly more than three. As a result, at 4:25 p.m. Tel Aviv time, $8.2 billion of the Syrian ruler's assets were under Office control. A minute later, Uzi Navot sent a flash message to Gabriel at the Geneva safe flat confirming the transfer was complete. At which point Gabriel ordered a second transaction: the transfer of $500 million to an account at the TransArabian Bank in Zurich. The money arrived at 3:29 p.m. local time, as the holder of the account, Waleed al-Siddiqi, was stuck in the Paris afternoon rush. Gabriel dialed the number for the banker's mobile phone but received no answer. He severed the connection, waited another minute, and dialed again.

They did not make her wait long, five minutes, no more. Then Jihan heard a fist pounding on the door, and a male voice instructed her to put on her hood. It was the one who had been waiting for her at Geneva Airport; she recognized his voice and the smell of his wretched cologne a moment later when he hauled her to her feet. He guided her up the flight of steep stairs, then across a marble floor. She reckoned it was a large institutional space of some sort because the echoes of her footsteps seemed to travel back to her from a long way off. Finally, he jerked her to a stop and forced her onto a hard wooden chair. And there she was made to sit for several moments, blinded by the hood and by an all-consuming fear of what would come next. She wondered how long she had to live. Or perhaps, she thought, she was already dead.

Another minute crawled past. Then a hand tore away the hood, taking a lock of Jihan's hair with it. Mr. Omari stood before her in his shirtsleeves, a rubber truncheon in his hand. Jihan looked away from him and surveyed her surroundings. They were in the ornate great room of a large château. Not a château, she thought suddenly, but a palace. It seemed newly decorated, unlived in.

"Where am I?" she asked.

"What difference does it make?"

She looked around the room again and asked, "Who does this belong to?"

"The president of Syria." He paused, then added, "Your president, Jihan."

"I am a citizen of Germany. You have no right to hold me."

The two men smiled at each other. Then Mr. Omari placed his mobile phone on the small, decorative table next to Jihan's chair. "Call your ambassador, Jihan. Or better yet," he added, "why don't you call the French police? I'm sure they'll be along in a moment or two."

Jihan was motionless.

"Call them," he demanded. "The emergency number in France is one, one, two. Then you dial seventeen for the police."

She reached out for the phone, but before she could grasp it the truncheon came crashing onto the back of her hand like a sledgehammer. Instantly, she folded in half and clutched her shattered hand as though it were a broken-winged bird. Then the truncheon fell upon the back of her neck, and she crumpled to the floor. She lay there in a defensive ball, unable to move, unable to make any sound other than a deep sob of agony. So here is where I'll die, she thought. In the palace of the ruler, in a land not my own. She waited for the next blow, but it didn't come. Instead, Mr. Omari gathered up a handful of her hair and twisted her face toward his.

"If we were in Syria," he said, "we would have many devices at our disposal to make you talk. But here we have only this," he added, waving the rubber truncheon. "It might take a while, and you surely won't be much to look at when I'm finished, but you'll talk, Jihan. Everyone talks."

For a moment she was incapable of offering any response. Then, finally, she summoned the ability to speak.

"What do you want to know?"

"I want to know who you're working for."

"I work for Waleed al-Siddiqi at Bank Weber AG in Linz, Austria."

The truncheon fell against the side of her face. It seemed to blind her.

"Who followed you to the hotel in Geneva this morning?"

"I didn't know I was being followed."

This time, the truncheon landed against the side of her neck. She would not have been at all surprised to see her head rolling across the ruler's marble floor.

"You're lying, Jihan."

"I'm not lying! Please," she pleaded, "don't hit me again."

He was still holding a fistful of her hair. His face was reddened with anger and exertion.

"I'm going to ask you a simple question, Jihan. Trust me when I tell you that I know the answer to this question. If you tell me the truth, nothing will happen to you. But if you lie to me, there won't be much left of you when I'm finished." He gave her head a violent shake. "Do you understand me, Jihan?"

"Yes."

"Tell me where you were born."

"Syria."

"Where in Syria, Jihan?"

"Hama," she answered. "I was born in Hama."

"What was your father's name?"

"Ibrahim Nawaz."

"He was a member of the Muslim Brotherhood?"

"Yes."

"He was killed during the uprising in Hama in February 1982?"

"No," she said. "He was murdered by the regime in 1982, along with my brothers and my mother."

Clearly, Mr. Omari was not interested in quibbling over the past. "But not you," he pointed out.

"No," she said. "I survived."

"Why didn't you tell Mr. al-Siddiqi any of this when he hired you to work at Bank Weber?"

"What do you mean?"

"Don't play games with me, Jihan."

"I'm not," she answered.

"Did you tell Mr. al-Siddiqi that you were born in Hama?"

"Yes."

"Did you tell Mr. al-Siddiqi that your family was killed during the uprising?"

"Yes."

"Did you tell him your father was a Muslim Brother?"

"Of course," she said. "I told Mr. al-Siddiqi everything."

———

It took four attempts before Waleed al-Siddiqi finally answered his phone. For several seconds he said nothing, the red light beating like a nervous heart on the screen of Gabriel's computer. Then in Arabic he asked, "Who is this?"

"I'm calling about a problem with one of your accounts," said Gabriel calmly. "Actually, several of your accounts."

"What are you talking about?"

"If I were you, Waleed, I'd call Dennis Cahill at the Trade Winds Bank in the Cayman Islands and ask him about some recent activity regarding the accounts of LXR Investments. And while you're at

it, I'd call Gérard Beringer, the man you just met
with at Société Générale. And then I'd like you to
call me back. You have five minutes. Hurry, Waleed.
Don't keep me waiting."

Gabriel rang off and set down the phone.

"That should get his attention," said Eli Lavon.

Gabriel looked at the computer screen and smiled.
It already had.

He called Trade Winds and Société Générale. Then
he called UBS, Credit Suisse, the Centrum Bank of
Liechtenstein, and the First Gulf Bank of Dubai. At
each institution, he received the same story. Finally,
ten minutes behind schedule, he called Gabriel.

"You'll never get away with this," he said.

"I already have."

"What have you done?"

"I haven't done anything, Waleed. *You* were the
one who took the ruler's money."

"What are you talking about?"

"I think you should make one more phone call,
Waleed."

"Where?"

Gabriel told him. Then he severed the connec-
tion and turned up the volume on the computer.
Ten seconds later, a phone was ringing at the Trans-
Arabian Bank in Zurich.

55

HAUTE-SAVOIE, FRANCE

T HEY BROUGHT HER a bowl of ice water for her hand. The bowl was large and silver; her hand was a bloody, swollen mess. The shock of the cold did much to dull the pain but not the rage burning within her. Men such as Mr. Omari had taken everything from her—her family, her life, her town. Now, at long last, she had a chance to confront him. And perhaps, she thought, to beat him.

"Cigarette?" he asked, and she replied that, yes, she would accept another tender mercy from the murderer. He placed a Marlboro between her parted lips and lit it. She drew upon it, then, awkwardly, removed it with her left hand.

"Are you comfortable, Jihan?"

She lifted her right hand from the ice water but said nothing.

"It wouldn't have happened if you'd told me the truth."

"You didn't give me much of a chance."

"I am now."

She decided to play slow to his haste. She drew

upon the cigarette again and exhaled a cloud of smoke toward the ruler's ornate ceiling.

"And if I tell you what I know? What then?"

"You will be free to go."

"Go where?"

"That is your choice."

She returned her hand slowly to the water. "Forgive me, Mr. Omari," she said, "but as you might imagine, I don't put much stock in anything you say."

"Then I suppose I'll have no choice but to break your other hand." Another cruel smile. "And then I'll break your ribs and every bone in your face."

"What do you want from me?" she asked after a moment.

"I want you to tell me everything you know about Waleed al-Siddiqi."

"He was born in Syria. He made a great deal of money. He bought a stake in a small private bank in Linz."

"Do you know why he bought the bank?"

"He uses it as a platform to invest money and conceal assets for powerful clients in the Middle East."

"Do you know any of their names?"

"Only one," she replied, looking around the room.

"How did you learn the client's identity?"

"Mr. al-Siddiqi told me."

"Why would he tell you such a thing?"

"I suppose he wanted to impress me."

"Do you know where the money is invested?"

"Zurich, Liechtenstein, Hong Kong, Dubai—all the usual places."

"What about the account numbers? Do you know those, too?"

"No," she said, shaking her head. "Only Mr. al-Siddiqi knows the account numbers." She placed her hand over her heart. "He carries the information here, in a black leather notebook."

At that same moment, the man at the center of Jihan's remarkable narrative was seated alone in the back of his car, debating his next move—or, as Christopher Keller would later put it, trying to decide how to kill himself with as little pain as possible. Finally, al-Siddiqi rang Gabriel back and capitulated.

"Who are you?" he asked.

"You'll know soon enough."

"What do you want from me?"

"I want you to call Kemel al-Farouk and tell him how you managed to misplace eight billion dollars of the ruler's money. Then I want you to tell him how a significant portion of those assets ended up in an account under your name."

"And then?"

"I'm going to offer you an amazing investment opportunity," said Gabriel. "It's a can't-lose proposition, a once-in-a-lifetime chance to make a great deal of money very quickly. Are you listening, Waleed? Do I have your full attention now?"

Mr. Omari was about to ask Jihan about the nature of her relationship with Waleed al-Siddiqi when his telephone vibrated softly. He listened in silence for a moment, emitted a grunt, and terminated the call. Then he nodded to his young driver and accomplice, who placed the black hood over Jihan's head and led her downstairs to her cell. And there they left her in pitch-darkness, her hand throbbing, her mind racing with fear. Perhaps she was already dead. Or perhaps, she thought, she had beaten them after all.

GABRIEL AND ELI Lavon took one last drive together, Gabriel behind the wheel, Lavon in the passenger seat, fretting and worrying as usual. They headed westward across the French border, then southward through the countryside of the Haute-Savoie, to Annecy. It was nearly dusk when they arrived; Gabriel dropped Lavon near the prefecture and parked the car near the Church of Saint-François de Sales. A pretty white structure on the embankment of the river Thiou, it reminded Gabriel of the Church of San Sebastiano in Venice. He peered inside, wondering if he would see a restorer standing alone before a Veronese, and then walked to a nearby café called the Savoie Bar. It was a nothing place with a simple menu and a few tables arrayed beneath a burgundy awning. At one of the tables sat Christopher Keller. He was once again wearing the lush blond wig and blue-tinted eyeglasses of Peter Rutledge, the master art thief who never was. Gabriel sat across from him and placed his BlackBerry on the table; and when a waiter finally wandered over, he ordered a café crème.

"I have to admit," Keller said after a moment, "I didn't expect this one to end this way."

"How were you hoping it would end, Christopher?"

"With you holding the Caravaggio, of course."

"We can't have everything. Besides, I found something much better than the Caravaggio. And more valuable, too."

"Jihan?"

Gabriel nodded.

"The eight-billion-dollar girl," murmured Keller.

"Eight-point-two," replied Gabriel. "But who's counting?"

"No second thoughts?"

"About what?"

"Making a deal."

"None whatsoever."

Just then, Eli Lavon walked past them in the square and joined Yaakov at the café next door. Mikhail and Yossi were parked along a narrow street called the rue Grenette. Oded was watching the car from a table at the obligatory kebab joint.

"They're good lads," said Keller as he surveyed the square. "All of them. This wasn't their fault. You ran a good operation in Linz, Gabriel. Something must have gone wrong at the end."

Gabriel made no reply other than to look at his BlackBerry.

"Where is he?" asked Keller.

"A mile north of town and closing hard."

"I think I'm going to enjoy this."

"Something tells me Waleed isn't going to feel the same way."

Gabriel returned the BlackBerry to the table, looked

at Keller, and smiled. "I'm sorry I got you mixed up in all this," he said.

"Actually, I wouldn't have missed it for the world."

"Maybe there's hope for you after all, Christopher. You actually managed not to kill anyone this time."

"Are you sure we didn't kill anyone?"

"Not yet."

Gabriel glanced at the BlackBerry again. The blinking red light had moved within the city limits of Annecy.

"Still headed our way?" asked Keller.

Gabriel nodded.

"Maybe you should let me handle the negotiations."

"Why would I do that?"

"Because it might not be a good idea to let them see your face. After all," Keller added, "as of this moment, they don't know that the Office was involved in any way."

"Unless they've beaten it out of Jihan."

Keller was silent.

"I appreciate the offer, Christopher, but this is something I have to do myself. Besides," Gabriel added, "I want the butcher boy and his henchmen to know I was behind it. Something tells me it will make my job easier when I take over the Office."

"You're not really going to go through with it, are you?"

"I don't have much of a choice in the matter."

"We all choose the life we lead." Keller paused, then added, "Even me."

Gabriel allowed a silence to fall between them. "My offer still stands," he said finally.

"Work for you at the Office?"

"No," said Gabriel. "You can work for Graham Seymour at MI6. He'll give you a new identity, a new life. You can go home again. And, more important, you can tell your parents you're still alive. It's a terrible thing you've done to them. If I didn't like you so much, I'd think you were a real—"

"Do you think it would work?" asked Keller, cutting him off.

"What's that?"

"Me as an MI6 officer?"

"Why wouldn't it?"

"I like living on Corsica."

"So you'll keep a place there."

"The money wouldn't be nearly as good."

"No," agreed Gabriel, "but you have plenty of money already."

"It would be a big change."

"Sometimes a change is good."

Keller made a show of thought. "I've never really enjoyed killing people, you know. It's just something I'm good at."

"I know exactly how you feel, Christopher." Gabriel looked at his BlackBerry again.

"Where is he?"

"Close," said Gabriel. "Very close."

"Where?" asked Keller again.

Gabriel nodded toward the rue Grenette. "Right there."

ANNECY, FRANCE

IT WAS THE same Mercedes that had taken him to his appointment at Société Générale, driven by the same Paris operative of Syrian intelligence. Mikhail slid into the backseat and, with a gun pointed at the driver's spine, gave Waleed al-Siddiqi a thorough and invasive search. When it was complete, the two men climbed out and stood on the pavement while the car moved off along the street. Then Mikhail escorted al-Siddiqi across the empty church square and deposited him at the table of the Savoie Bar where Gabriel and Keller sat waiting. The Syrian was not looking particularly well, but that wasn't surprising. Bankers who lost $8 billion in a single afternoon rarely did.

"Waleed," said Gabriel brightly. "Good of you to come. Sorry to drag you all the way down here, but these things are best done face-to-face."

"Where's the money?"

"Where's my girl?"

"I don't know."

"Wrong answer."

"It's the truth."

"Give me your phone."

The Syrian banker surrendered it. Gabriel opened the directory of recent calls and saw the numbers al-Siddiqi had been dialing frantically since discovering that $8 billion belonging to the ruler of Syria was suddenly missing.

"Which one?" asked Gabriel.

"That one," replied the banker, touching the screen.

"Who's going to answer?"

"A gentleman called Mr. Omari."

"What does this gentleman do for a living?"

"Mukhabarat."

"Did he hurt her?"

"I'm afraid that's what he does."

Gabriel dialed the number. Two rings, then a male voice.

"Mr. Omari, I presume?"

"Who is this?"

"My name is Gabriel Allon. Perhaps you've heard of me."

There was silence.

"I'll take that as a yes," said Gabriel. "Now if you'll be kind enough to give the phone to Jihan for a moment. I want to make sure you've really got her."

There was a brief silence. Then Gabriel heard the sound of Jihan's voice.

"It's me," was all she said.

"Where are you?"

"I'm not sure."

"Did they hurt you?"

"It wasn't too bad."

"Stay with me, Jihan. You're almost home."

The phone changed hands. Mr. Omari came back on the line.

"Where do you want us to go?" he asked.

"The rue Grenette in the center of Annecy. There's a place near the church called Chez Lise. Park outside and wait for my call. And don't you dare so much as touch her again. If you do, I'm going to make it my life's work to find you and kill you. Just so we're clear."

Gabriel severed the connection and returned the phone to al-Siddiqi.

"I thought you looked familiar," the Syrian said. Then he glanced at Keller and added, "Him, too. In fact, he looks a great deal like a man who was trying to sell a stolen van Gogh in Paris a few weeks ago."

"And you were stupid enough to buy it. But don't worry," Gabriel added. "It wasn't the real thing."

"And the European Business Initiative in London? I suppose that was a forgery, too."

Gabriel said nothing.

"My compliments, Allon. I'd always heard you had a creative streak."

"How many have you got, Waleed?"

"Paintings?"

Gabriel nodded.

"Enough to fill a small museum."

"Enough to keep the ruling family in the style to which they are accustomed," said Gabriel coldly, "just in case someone ever found the bank accounts."

"Yes," the Syrian said. "Just in case."

"Where are the paintings now?"

"Here and there," al-Siddiqi answered. "Bank vaults mainly."

"And the Caravaggio?"

"I wouldn't know."

Gabriel leaned menacingly across the table. "I consider myself a reasonable fellow, Waleed, but my friend Mr. Bartholomew is known for the shortness of his fuse. He also happens to be one of the few people in the world who's more dangerous than I am, so this is no time to play dumb."

"I'm telling you the truth, Allon. I don't know where the Caravaggio is."

"Who had it last?"

"That's hard to say. But if I had to guess, it was Jack Bradshaw."

"Which is why you had him killed."

"Me?" Al-Siddiqi shook his head. "I had nothing to do with Bradshaw's death. Why would I kill him? He was my only link to the dirty end of the art world. I was planning to use him to dispose of the paintings if I ever needed to raise cash in a hurry."

"So who killed him?"

"It was Mr. Omari."

"Why would a mid-level Mukhabarat man kill someone like Jack Bradshaw?"

"Because he was ordered to."

"By whom?"

"The president of Syria, of course."

Gabriel did not want Jihan to remain in the hands of the murderers for a minute longer than was necessary, but there was no turning back now; he had to know. And so, as the evening gathered around them and bells tolled in the church towers, he listened as the banker explained that the Caravaggio was never to be used as a stash of underworld cash. It was to be smuggled back to Syria, restored, and hung in one of the ruler's palaces. And when the painting disappeared, the ruler flew into a violent rage. Then he ordered Mr. Omari, a respected officer of the Mukhabarat and trusted former bodyguard of his father, to find out where the painting had gone. He started his search at the Lake Como residence of Jack Bradshaw.

"It was Omari who killed Bradshaw?" asked Gabriel.

"And his forger, too," replied al-Siddiqi.

"What about Samir?"

"He'd outlived his usefulness."

So have you, thought Gabriel. Then he asked, "Where's the Caravaggio now?"

"Omari was never able to find it. The Caravaggio is gone. Who knows?" al-Siddiqi added with a shrug. "Maybe there never was a Caravaggio."

Just then, a car drew to a stop on the rue Grenette, a black Mercedes, tinted windows. Gabriel picked up al-Siddiqi's phone and dialed. Omari answered immediately. Gabriel told him to hand the phone to Jihan.

"It's me," she said again.

"Where are you?" asked Gabriel.

"Parked on a street in Annecy."

"Are you near a restaurant?"

"Yes."

"What's it called?"

"Chez Lise."

"A couple more minutes, Jihan. Then you can come home."

The line went dead. Gabriel handed the phone to al-Siddiqi and told him the terms of the deal.

They were quite simple: $8.2 billion for one woman, minus $50 million to cover resettlement and security costs for the remainder of her life. Al-Siddiqi agreed without negotiation or equivocation. Frankly, he was astonished at the generosity of the offer.

"Where would you like me to send the money?" asked Gabriel.

"Gazprombank in Moscow."

"Account number?"

Al-Siddiqi handed Gabriel a slip of paper with the number written on it. Gabriel forwarded it to King Saul Boulevard and instructed Uzi Navot to push the button a second time. Ten seconds was all it took. Then the money was gone.

"Call your man at Gazprombank," said Gabriel. "He'll tell you the bank's assets have just increased by a rather large amount."

It was midnight in Moscow, but al-Siddiqi's contact was at his desk waiting for the call. Gabriel could hear the excitement in his voice through al-Siddiqi's phone. He wondered how much of the money the Russian president would take before the Syrian managed to move it to more reliable shores.

"Satisfied?" asked Gabriel.

"Very impressive," said the banker.

"Spare me the compliments, Waleed. Just call Mr. Omari and tell him to open the damn door."

———————

Thirty seconds later, the door swung open and a sensible pump reached down toward the street. Then she emerged in a blur, her movie-starlet sunglasses covering the bruises on her face, her handbag over her shoulder. It was her left shoulder, Gabriel noticed, because her right hand was too heavily bandaged to be of any use. She started across the church square, her heels clattering over the paving stones, but Mikhail quickly led her to a waiting car, and she disappeared from view. A moment later, al-Siddiqi took her place in the Mercedes, and then he was gone, too, leaving Gabriel and Keller alone in the café.

"Do you think they run operations like this at MI6?" asked Keller.

"Only when we're involved."

"No second thoughts?"

"About what, Christopher?"

"Eight billion dollars for a single life."

"No," said Gabriel, smiling. "Best deal I ever made."

PART FIVE

ONE LAST WINDOW

F OR THE NEXT nine days, the art world spun smoothly on its gilded axis, blissfully unaware of the lost riches that would soon be flowing its way. Then, on a sultry afternoon in early August, the managing director of the Rijksmuseum Vincent van Gogh announced that *Sunflowers*, oil on canvas, 95 by 73 centimeters, was home again. The director refused to say precisely where the missing masterpiece had been found, though later it would emerge that it had been left in an Amsterdam hotel room. The painting had suffered no damage during its long stay in captivity; in fact, said the managing director, it looked better than it had at the time of the theft. The chief of the Dutch police publicly took credit for the recovery, even though he'd had nothing at all to do with it. Julian Isherwood, chairman of the Committee to Protect Art, released a hyperbolic statement in London calling it "a great day for mankind and all that is decent and beautiful in this world." That evening he was spotted at his usual table at Green's Restaurant, accompanied by Amanda Clifton of Sotheby's. All those present would later describe the expression on her face as one of enchantment. Oliver Dimbleby was said to have been seething with jealousy.

Only Julian Isherwood, the secret helper of spies, one spy in particular, knew there were more riches to come. Another week would pass, long enough, it was said later, for the euphoria over *Sunflowers* to die down. Then, in a cream-colored palazzo in the center of Rome, General Cesare Ferrari of the Art Squad unveiled three paintings, long missing, now recovered: *The Holy Family* by Parmigianino, *Young Women in the Country* by Renoir, and Klimt's *Portrait of a Woman*. But the general was not finished. He also announced the recovery of *Beach in Pourville* by Monet and *Woman with a Fan* by Modigliani, along with works by Matisse, Degas, Picasso, Rembrandt, Cézanne, Delacroix, and something that may or may not have been a Titian. The press conference was conducted with all the flair and drama for which General Ferrari was known, yet it was perhaps most memorable for what the Italian art sleuth did *not* say—specifically, where and how any of the works had been found. He hinted at a large, highly sophisticated network of thieves, smugglers, and fences and suggested there were more paintings to come. Then, hiding behind the shield of a continuing investigation, he made for the door, pausing long enough to field the obligatory question about the prospects for finding the Art Squad's number-one target: the *Nativity with St. Francis and St. Lawrence*, by Caravaggio. "One hates to use the word *never*," he said sadly, and then he was gone.

The events in Amsterdam and Rome stood in

stark contrast to the news from Austria, where authorities were attempting to solve a mystery of a different sort: the disappearance of two people, a man in his early fifties and a woman of thirty-nine, from the ancient Danube trading town of Linz. The man was Waleed al-Siddiqi, a minority partner in a small private bank. The woman was Jihan Nawaz, the bank's account manager. The fact that both were originally from Syria fueled speculation of foul play, as did Jihan Nawaz's movements on the day of her disappearance. She had traveled from Linz to Geneva, according to the authorities, where security cameras of the Hotel Métropole had photographed her entering the room of Kemel al-Farouk, Syria's deputy foreign minister and a close aide and adviser to the country's president. Inevitably, this led to speculation that Miss Nawaz was an agent of the Syrian government; indeed, a once-reputable magazine from Germany published a lengthy article accusing her of being a spy for the Syrian intelligence service. The story collapsed two days later when a relative from Hamburg admitted that the missing woman's German immigration forms were not entirely accurate. She had not been born in Damascus, as previously stated, but in the town of Hama, where regime forces had slaughtered her entire family in February 1982. Jihan Nawaz was not an agent of the regime, said the relative, but a committed opponent.

The development quickly gave rise to speculation that Jihan Nawaz had been operating on behalf not of the Syrian government but of a Western intelligence service. The theory gained traction as additional biographical information about her missing employer leaked slowly into the press, information that suggested he had been involved in concealing and managing financial assets of the Syrian ruler. Then came a report from a respected computer security firm regarding a series of financial transactions it had detected during routine monitoring of the Internet. It seemed that several billion dollars had been plucked from prominent banks around the world and moved to a single location in an unusually short period of time. The firm was never able to produce an accurate estimate of the amount of money involved, nor was it able to identify those responsible. It did, however, manage to find traces of code scattered around the world. All those who analyzed the code were shocked by its sophistication. It was not the work of ordinary hackers, they said, but of professionals working on behalf of a government. One expert compared it to the Stuxnet computer worm that had been inserted into the computer network of the Iranian nuclear weapons program.

It was at this point that the glare of an unwanted spotlight fell upon the intelligence service headquartered within an anonymous office block in Tel Aviv. The experts saw a smoking gun, a perfect nexus of capability and motive, and for once the experts were right. But none of them would ever link the suspicious movement of money to the recent recovery of several stolen masterworks, or to the man of medium height and build, the sun amid small stars, who returned to a church in Venice on the third Wednesday of August. The wooden platform atop his scaffolding was precisely as he had left it several months earlier: flasks of chemicals, a wad of cotton wool, a bundle of dowels, a magnifying visor, two powerful halogen lamps. He slipped a copy of *La Bohème* into the paint-smudged portable stereo and began to work. *Dip, twirl, discard . . . Dip, twirl, discard . . .*

There were days when he couldn't wait to finish, and days when he hoped it would never end. His capricious state of mind played out before the canvas. At times, he worked with Veronese's slowness; at others, with Vincent's reckless haste, as though he were trying to capture the essence of his subject matter before it wilted and died. Fortunately, there was no one to witness his pendulum-like swings of mood. The other members of the team had all completed their work during his long absence. He was alone in the house of another faith, another people.

The operation rarely left his thoughts for long. He saw it in his mind as a cycle of still lifes, landscapes, and portraits: the fallen spy, the art thief, the assassin for hire, the child of Hama writing his name on the surface of a lake. *The eight-billion-dollar girl . . .* He never once regretted his decision to surrender the money in exchange for her freedom. Money could be made and lost, found and frozen. But Jihan Nawaz, the only surviving member of a murdered family, was irreplaceable. She was an original. She was a masterpiece.

The Church of San Sebastiano was scheduled to reopen to the public on the first day of October, which meant that Gabriel had no choice but to work from dawn until dusk without a break. On most days, Francesco Tiepolo stopped by at midday with a bag of *cornetti* and a flask of fresh coffee. If Gabriel was feeling charitable, he would allow Tiepolo to do a bit of inpainting, but most days the Italian would simply hover over Gabriel's shoulder and plead with him to work faster. And, invariably, he would gently interrogate Gabriel over his plans for the future.

"We're about to get a commission for something good," he said one afternoon as a thunderstorm pelted the city. "Something important."

"How important?" asked Gabriel.

"I'm not at liberty to say."

"Church or *scuola*?"

"Church," said Tiepolo. "And the altarpiece has your name on it."

Gabriel smiled and painted in silence.

"Not even tempted?"

"It's time for me to go home, Francesco."

"This is your home," Tiepolo replied. "You should raise your children here in Venice. And when you die, we'll bury you beneath a cypress tree on San Michele."

"I'm not that old, Francesco."

"You're not so young, either."

"Don't you have anything better to do?" asked Gabriel, as he moved the brush from his right hand to his left.

"No," said Tiepolo, smiling. "What could possibly be better than to watch you paint?"

The days were still warm and thick with humidity, but in the evening a breeze from the lagoon made the city tolerable. Gabriel would collect Chiara at her office and take her to dinner. By mid-September, she was six months along, past the point where it was possible to keep her pregnancy a secret from the rest of Venice's small but talkative Jewish community. Gabriel thought she had never looked so beautiful. Her skin glowed, her eyes sparkled like gold dust, and even when she was uncomfortable, she seemed incapable of any expression other than a wide smile. She was a planner by nature, a maker of lists, and at dinner each night she talked incessantly of all the things they needed to do. They had decided to remain in Venice until the last week of October, the first week of November at the latest. Then they would return to Jerusalem to prepare the apartment in Narkiss Street for the birth of the children.

"They'll need names, you know," Gabriel said one evening as they were strolling along the Zattere at dusk.

"Your mother had a beautiful name."

"She did," replied Gabriel. "But Irene isn't really a proper name for a boy."

"So maybe we should call the girl Irene instead."

"Good idea."

"And the boy?"

Gabriel was silent. It was too soon to start choosing a name for the boy.

"I spoke to Ari this morning," Chiara said after a moment. "As you might expect, he's a bit anxious for us to come home."

"Did you tell him I have to finish the Veronese first?"

"I did."

"And?"

"He doesn't understand why an altarpiece should keep the two of you apart at a time like this."

"Because the altarpiece might be the last one I ever get to restore."

"Maybe," said Chiara.

They walked in silence for a moment. Then Gabriel asked, "How did he sound?"

"Ari?"

He nodded.

"Not good, actually." She looked at him seriously and asked, "Do you know something I don't know?"

"The *signadora* told me he doesn't have long."

"Did she tell you anything else I should know?"

"Yes," he said. "She told me it was close."

By then, it was late September, and Gabriel was running hopelessly behind schedule. Tiepolo graciously offered him a brief extension, but Gabriel stubbornly refused it; he did not want the last restoration in his beloved city of water and paintings to be remembered only for the fact that he had failed to complete it in the time allotted. And so he barricaded himself in the church with no distractions and worked with a stamina and speed he would not have thought possible. He retouched the Virgin and the Christ Child in a single day, and on the final afternoon he repaired the face of a curly-haired boy angel who was peering over a heavenly cloud, toward the earthly suffering below. The boy looked too much like Dani, and Gabriel, as he worked, wept softly. When he was finished, he dried his brushes and his face, and stood motionless before the towering canvas, a hand to his chin, his head tilted slightly to one side.

"Is it finished?" asked Francesco Tiepolo, who was watching him from the base of the scaffolding.

"Yes," said Gabriel. "I think it is."

VENICE

N THE NORTHWEST corner of the Campo di Ghetto Nuovo is a small, stark memorial to the Jews of Venice who, in December 1943, were rounded up, interned in concentration camps, and murdered at Auschwitz. General Cesare Ferrari was standing before it when Gabriel entered the square at half past six that evening. His ruined right hand was stuffed into the pocket of his trousers. His harsh gaze seemed more judgmental than usual.

"I never knew it happened here in Venice," he said after Gabriel had joined him. "The Rome roundup was different. Rome was far too big to ever be forgotten. But here . . ." He looked around the tranquil square. "It doesn't seem possible."

Gabriel was silent. The general stepped slowly forward and ran his damaged hand over one of the seven bas-relief plaques. "From where were they taken?" he asked.

"There," said Gabriel.

He pointed toward the three-story building to their right. The sign above the door read CASA ISRA-ELITICA DI RIPOSO. It was a rest home for aged members of the community.

"By the time the roundup finally took place," Gabriel said after a moment, "most of the remaining Jews of Venice had gone into hiding. The only ones left in the city were the old and sick. They were dragged from their beds by the Germans and their Italian helpers."

"How many live there now?" the general asked.

"Ten or so."

"Not many."

"There aren't many left."

The general looked at the memorial again. "I don't know why you live in a place like this."

"I don't," said Gabriel. Then he asked the general why he was back in Venice.

"I had to do a bit of housekeeping at the Art Squad's field office here. I also wanted to attend the reopening of the Church of San Sebastiano." The general paused, then added, "I hear the main altarpiece looks quite amazing. You obviously managed to finish it."

"With a few hours to spare."

"Mazel tov."

"Grazie."

"And now?" asked the general. "What are your plans?"

"I'm going to spend the next month trying to be the best husband I can. And then I'm going to go home again."

"The children are coming soon, yes?"

"Soon," said Gabriel.

"As the father of five, I can assure you that your life will never be the same."

In the far corner of the square, the door of the community office swung open and Chiara emerged into the shadows. She glanced at Gabriel and then disappeared again into the entrance of the ghetto museum. The general seemed not to have noticed her; he was frowning at the green metal structure next to the memorial where a uniformed Carabinieri man sat behind bulletproof glass.

"It's a shame we have to put a security post in the middle of this beautiful place."

"I'm afraid it comes with the territory."

"Why this eternal hatred?" the general asked, shaking his head slowly. "Why does it never end?"

"You tell me."

Greeted by silence, Gabriel again asked the general why he had come back to Venice.

"I've been looking for something for a long time," the Italian said, "and I was hoping you could help me find it."

"I tried," said Gabriel. "But it seems to have slipped through my fingers."

"I hear you actually came close." The general lowered his voice and added, "Closer than you realized."

"How did you hear that?"

"The usual ways." The general looked at Gabriel seriously and asked, "Is there any chance you would agree to a debriefing before you leave the country?"

"What do you want to know?"

"Everything that happened after you stole *Sunflowers*."

"I didn't *steal* it. I borrowed it at the suggestion of the commander of the Art Squad. And so the answer is no," Gabriel added, shaking his head. "I won't be sitting for any debriefings, now or at any time in the future."

"Then perhaps we can quietly compare notes instead."

"I'm afraid my notes are classified."

"That's good," said the general, smiling. "Because mine are, too."

They headed across the square to the kosher café next to the community center and shared a bottle of pinot grigio as the darkness gathered around them. Gabriel began by swearing the general to an omertà and threatening him with reprisals if the oath of silence were ever broken. Then he told him everything that had transpired since their last meeting, beginning with the death of Samir Basara in Stuttgart and ending with the discovery, and eventual surrender, of $8 billion in assets belonging to the president of Syria.

"I suppose this has something to do with those two Syrian bankers who went missing in Austria," the general said when Gabriel had finished.

"What Syrian bankers?"

"I'll take that as a yes." The general drank some of his wine. "So Jack Bradshaw refused to deliver the Caravaggio because the Syrians killed the only woman he ever loved? Is that what you're telling me?"

Gabriel nodded slowly and watched a pair of black-coated yeshiva students making their way across the square.

"Now I know why you made me swear not to mention Bradshaw's name during my press conference," the general was saying. "You didn't want me to posthumously drag his name through the mud."

He paused, then added, "You wanted him to rest in peace."

"He deserves it."

"Why?"

"Because they tortured him mercilessly, and he didn't tell them what he did with the painting."

"Do you believe in redemption, Allon?"

"I'm a restorer," said Gabriel.

The general smiled. "And the paintings you discovered in the Geneva Freeport?" he asked. "How did you get them out of Switzerland so quietly?"

"With the help of a friend."

"A Swiss friend?"

Gabriel nodded.

"I didn't know such a thing was possible."

This time, it was Gabriel who smiled. The yeshiva students entered a *sottoportego* and disappeared from sight. The square was now empty except for two young children, a boy and girl, who were bouncing a ball back and forth under the watchful gaze of their parents.

"The question is," said the general, peering into his wineglass, "what did Jack Bradshaw do with the Caravaggio?"

"I suppose he put it somewhere he thought no one would ever find it."

"Maybe," replied the general. "But that's not the talk on the street."

"What are you hearing?"

"That he gave it to someone for safekeeping."

"Someone at the dirty end of the business?"

"It's hard to say. But as you might expect," the general added quickly, "other people are now looking for it. Which means it's imperative we find it before they do."

Gabriel was silent.

"Not even tempted, Allon?"

"My involvement in this affair is now officially over."

"It sounds as though you actually mean it this time."

"I do."

The family of four quietly departed, leaving the *campo* deserted. The heavy silence seemed to disturb the general. He looked at the lights burning in the windows of the Casa Israelitica di Riposo and shook his head slowly.

"I don't understand why you choose to live in a ghetto," he said.

"It's a nice neighborhood," replied Gabriel. "The nicest in Venice, if you ask me."

FOR THE NEXT several days, Gabriel rarely strayed far from Chiara's side. He made her breakfast each morning. He spent afternoons with her at the office of the Jewish community. He sat at the kitchen counter in the evening and watched over her as she cooked. At first, she was charmed by the attention, but gradually the sheer weight of his ceaseless affections began to grate upon her. It was, she would say later, a little too much of a good thing. She briefly considered asking Francesco Tiepolo for a painting to restore—something small and not too damaged—but decided that they should take a trip instead. Nothing too extravagant, she said, and nowhere that would require air travel. Two days, three at the most. Gabriel had an idea. That evening, he rang Christoph Bittel and requested permission to enter Switzerland; and Bittel, who knew well the reason why his newfound friend and accomplice wanted to return to the Confederation, readily agreed.

"It might be better if I meet you," he said.

"I was hoping you'd say that."

"Do you know the area?"

"Not at all," said Gabriel, lying.

"There's a hotel just outside of town called the Alpenblick. I'll be waiting for you there."

And so it was that, early the following morning, Gabriel and Chiara left their beloved city of water and paintings and set out for the landlocked little country of wealth and secrets that had played such a prominent role in their lives. It was mid-morning when they crossed the border at Lugano and started northward into the Alps. Snow flurries blew through the high passes, but by the time they reached the shores of the Interlaken the sun was shining brightly from a cloudless sky. Gabriel refilled his tank with gas and then set out up the valley to Grindelwald. The Alpenblick Hotel was a rustic building standing alone at the edge of town. Gabriel left the car in the hotel's small parking lot and, with Chiara at his side, climbed the stairs to the terrace. Bittel was drinking coffee and gazing upward at the looming peaks of the Monch and the Eiger. Rising, he shook Gabriel's hand. Then he looked at Chiara and smiled.

"You surely have a very beautiful name, but I won't make the mistake of asking it." He glanced at Gabriel and said, "You never told me you were about to be a father again, Allon."

"Actually," said Gabriel, "she's just my food taster."

"I'm sorry to hear that."

Bittel sat down and waved away an approaching waiter. Then he pointed across a green meadow, toward the base of the mountains.

"The chalet is right over there," he said to Gabriel. "It's a nice place, good views, very clean and comfortable."

"You have a future as an estate agent, Bittel."

"I like protecting my country better."

"I assume you have a static watch post somewhere?"

"We're renting the chalet next door," said Bittel. "We keep two officers here full-time, and others cycle in and out as needed. She never goes anywhere without an escort."

"Any suspicious visitors?"

"Of the Syrian variety?"

Gabriel nodded.

"You get all kinds here in Grindelwald," Bittel responded, "so it's a little hard to tell. But so far, no one's gone anywhere near her."

"How's her mood?"

"She seems lonely," said Bittel seriously. "The guards spend as much time with her as possible, but . . ."

"But what, Bittel?"

The Swiss policeman smiled sadly. "I could be wrong," he said, "but I think she could use a friend."

Gabriel rose to his feet. "I can't thank you enough for agreeing to take her, Bittel."

"It was the least we could do to repay you for cleaning up the mess at the Geneva Freeport. But you should have requested our permission before running that operation at the Hotel Métropole."

"Would you have given it?"

"Of course not," replied Bittel. "Which means you'd still have eight billion dollars in Syrian money in your bank account."

Eight-point-two, thought Gabriel as he headed toward his car. But who was counting?

Gabriel left Chiara and Bittel behind at the hotel and drove into the meadow alone. The house was at the end of a lane, a small, tidy structure of dark timber with a steeply pitched roof and flowerpots lining the balcony. Jihan Nawaz appeared there as Gabriel eased into the grassy drive and switched off the engine. She was wearing blue jeans and a thick woolen sweater. Her hair was longer and lighter; a plastic surgeon had altered the shape of her nose, her cheekbones, and her chin. She was not quite pretty, but she was no longer ordinary looking, either. A moment later, when she came spilling out of the front door, she brought with her the faint scent of roses. She flung her arms around his neck, embraced him tightly, and kissed him on each cheek.

"Am I allowed to call you by your real name?" she whispered in his ear.

"No," he replied. "Not here."

"How long can you stay?"

"As long as you like."

"Come," she said, taking him by the hand. "I've made us something to eat."

The interior of the chalet was warm and comfortable, but it contained not a trace of evidence the person who lived there had a family or a past of any kind. Gabriel felt a stab of regret. He should have left her alone. Waleed al-Siddiqi would still be managing the money of the worst man in the world, and Jihan would be living quietly in Linz. And yet she had known the name of al-Siddiqi's special client, he thought. And she had stayed at the bank for a reason.

"I've seen that look on your face before," she said, watching him intently. "It was in Annecy, as I was coming out of the back of the car. I saw you sitting in the café on the other side of the square. You looked . . ." She left the thought unfinished.

"How?" he asked.

"Guilty," she said without an instant of hesitation.

"I was guilty."

"Why?"

"I never should have let you walk into that hotel."

"My hand healed nicely," she said, holding it up as though to prove the point. "And my bruises have healed, too. Besides, it was nothing compared to what most Syrians have suffered since the war began. I'm only sorry I couldn't do more."

"Your war is over, Jihan."

"You were the one who urged me to join the Syrian rebellion."

"And our rebellion failed."

"You paid too much to get me back."

"I wasn't in the mood for a prolonged negotiation," said Gabriel. "It was a take-away offer."

"I only wish I could have seen Mr. al-Siddiqi's face when he found out you'd taken the money."

"I must admit I enjoyed his suffering a little too much," said Gabriel, "but yours was the only face I wanted to see at that moment."

With that, she turned and led him into the garden. A small table had been laid with coffee and Swiss chocolates. Jihan sat facing her chalet; Gabriel, the towering gray massif. When they were settled, he asked her about her stay in Israel.

"I spent the first two weeks locked away in an apartment in Tel Aviv," she said. "It was dreadful."

"We do our utmost to make visitors feel welcome."

Jihan smiled. "Ingrid came to see me a few times," she said, "but not you. They refused to tell me where you were."

"I'm afraid I had other business to attend to."

"Another operation?"

"In a manner of speaking."

She filled their cups with coffee. "Eventually," she resumed, "they allowed Ingrid and me to take a trip together. We stayed in a hotel on the Golan Heights. At night, we could hear the shelling and the airstrikes on the other side of the border. All I could think about is how many people were being killed each time the sky filled with light."

To that, Gabriel offered no reply.

"I read in the newspapers this morning that the Americans are reconsidering military strikes against the regime."

"I read the same thing."

"Do you think he'll do it this time?"

"Attack the regime?"

She nodded her head. Gabriel didn't have the heart to tell her the truth, so he told her one last falsehood instead.

"Yes," he said. "I think they will."

"And will the regime fall if the Americans attack it?"

"It might."

"If it did," she said after a moment, "I would go back to Syria and help rebuild the country."

"This is your home now."

"No," she said. "This is the place where I hide from butchers. But Hama will always be my home."

A sudden gust of wind blew a lock of her newly lightened hair across her face. She brushed it away and looked across the meadow, toward the massif. Its base was in deep shadow, but the snow-capped peaks were rose-tinted with the setting sun.

"I love my mountain," she said suddenly. "It makes me feel safe. It makes me feel as though nothing can happen to me."

"Are you happy here?"

"I have a new name, a new face, a new country. It is my fourth. That is what it means to be a Syrian."

"And a Jew," said Gabriel.

"But the Jews have a home now." She raised her hand toward the meadow. "And I have this."

"Can you be happy here?"

"Yes," she answered after a long moment. "I think I can. But I did enjoy the time we spent together on the Attersee, especially the boat rides."

"So did I."

She smiled, then asked, "And what about you? Are you happy?"

"I wish they hadn't hurt you."

"But we beat them, didn't we? At least for a little while."

"Yes, Jihan, we beat them."

The last light leaked from the mountain peaks, and evening fell like a curtain upon the valley.

"There's one thing you never told me."

"What's that?"

"How did you find me?"

"You wouldn't believe me."

"Is it a good story?"

"Yes," he said. "I think it is."

"How does it end?"

He kissed her cheek and left her alone with her past.

61

LAKE COMO, ITALY

G ABRIEL AND CHIARA spent the next two nights at a small resort on the shores of the Interlaken and then departed Switzerland by the same route they had entered it. In the mountain passes, Gabriel received a secure text message from King Saul Boulevard instructing him to turn on the radio; and as they crossed the Italian border at Lugano, he learned that Kemel al-Farouk, deputy minister of foreign affairs, former officer of the Mukhabarat, friend and trusted adviser of the Syrian president, had been killed in a mysterious explosion in Damascus. It had been Uzi Navot's operation, but in many respects it was the first killing of the Allon era. Somehow, he suspected it wouldn't be the last.

It was raining by the time they reached Como. Gabriel should have taken the autostrada down to Milan, but instead he followed the winding road above the lake until he arrived once more at the leaden gate of Jack Bradshaw's villa. The gate was tightly closed; next to it was a sign stating the property was for sale. Gabriel sat there for a moment, hands atop the steering wheel, debating what to do. Then he rang General Ferrari in Rome, asked for the security code, and punched it into the keypad. A few seconds later, the gate swung open. Gabriel slipped the car into gear and headed down the drive.

The door was locked, too. Gabriel quickly unbuttoned it with a thin metal tool he carried habitually in his wallet and led Chiara into the entrance hall. A heavy smell of disuse hung on the air, but the blood had been scrubbed from the marble floor. Chiara tried the light switch; the chandelier from which Jack Bradshaw had been hung burst into life. Gabriel closed the door and headed toward the great room.

The walls had been stripped of artwork and freshly painted; some of the furniture had been removed to create the illusion of greater space. But not Bradshaw's pretty antique writing desk. It stood in the same place where it had been before, though the two photographs of Bradshaw before the fall had been removed. His multiline telephone remained, covered in a fine layer of dust. Gabriel lifted the receiver to his ear. There was no dial tone. He returned it to its cradle and looked at Chiara.

"Why are we here?" she asked.

"Because *it* was here."

"Maybe," she said.

"Maybe," he conceded.

In the days after Gabriel's initial discovery, General Ferrari's Art Squad had torn Jack Bradshaw's villa to pieces looking for additional stolen paintings. It was unlikely a canvas measuring seven feet by eight feet had somehow escaped their notice. Even so, Gabriel wanted to have one final look for himself, if only to put his mind at ease. He had spent the last several months of his life in pursuit of the world's most famous lost masterpiece. And thus far all he had to show for it was a few stolen paintings and a dead Syrian thug.

And so, as the daylight faded that autumn afternoon, he searched the home of a man he had never met, with his pregnant wife at his side—room by room, closet by closet, cupboard by cupboard, drawer by drawer, crawl spaces, air ducts, the attic, the cellar. He searched the walls for newly spread plaster. He searched the floorboards for clean nail heads. He searched the gardens for freshly turned earth. Until finally, fatigued, frustrated, and smudged with dirt, he found himself standing again at Bradshaw's writing desk. He lifted the telephone to his ear, but not surprisingly there was still no dial tone. Then he drew his BlackBerry from his coat pocket and dialed a number from memory. A few seconds later, a male voice answered in Italian.

"This is Father Marco," he said. "How can I help you?"

62

BRIENNO, ITALY

THE CHURCH OF San Giovanni Evangelista was small and white and set hard against the street. To the right stretched a wrought-iron fence, behind which was the small garden of the rectory. Father Marco was waiting at the gate when Gabriel and Chiara arrived. He was young, thirty-five at most, with a full head of neatly combed dark hair and a face that seemed eager to forgive all sins. "Welcome," he said, shaking their hands in turn. "Please follow me."

He led them along the garden walk and into the kitchen of the rectory. It was a tidy space with whitewashed walls, a rough-hewn wooden table, and tins of food arrayed upon open shelving. The one luxury was an automatic espresso machine, which Father Marco used to produce three cups of coffee. "I remember the day you telephoned me," he said, as he placed a coffee before Gabriel. "It was two days after Signor Bradshaw was killed, was it not?"

"Yes," said Gabriel. "And for some reason, you hung up on me twice before taking my call."

"Have you ever received a phone call from a man

who was just brutally murdered, Signor Allon?" The priest sat down opposite Gabriel and spooned sugar into his coffee. "It was an unsettling experience, to say the least."

"It seemed you were in contact with him a great deal around the time of his death."

"Yes."

"Before and after."

"Judging from what I read in the newspapers," the priest said, "I probably called the villa while he was hanging dead from the chandelier. It is a terrible image."

"Was he a parishioner here?"

"Jack Bradshaw wasn't a Catholic," said the priest. "He was raised in the Church of England, but I'm not at all sure he was actually a believer."

"You were friends?"

"I suppose we were. But mainly I acted as his confessor. Not in the true sense of the word," the priest added quickly. "I couldn't actually grant him absolution for his sins."

"He was troubled at the time of his death?"

"Deeply."

"Did he tell you why?"

"He said it had something to do with his business. He was a consultant of some sort." The priest gave an apologetic smile. "I'm sorry, Signor Allon, but I'm not terribly sophisticated when it comes to matters of business and finance."

"That makes two of us."

The priest smiled again and stirred his coffee. "He used to sit where you're seated now. He would bring a hamper of food and wine, and we would talk."

"About what?"

"His past."

"How much did he tell you?"

"Enough to know he was involved in secret work of some sort for his government. Something happened many years ago when he was in the Middle East. A woman was killed. I believe she was French."

"Her name was Nicole Devereaux."

The priest looked up sharply. "Did Signor Bradshaw tell you that?"

Gabriel was tempted to answer in the affirmative but had no desire to lie to a man in a Roman collar and a cassock.

"No," he said. "I never met him."

"I think you would have liked him. He was very smart, worldly, funny. But he also carried a heavy burden of guilt about what happened to Nicole Devereaux."

"He told you about the affair?"

The priest hesitated, then nodded. "Apparently, he loved her very much, and he never forgave himself for her death. He never married, never had children. In a way, he lived the life of a priest." Father Marco glanced around the spare room and added, "But in much grander fashion, of course."

"You've been to the villa?"

"Many times. It was very beautiful. But it didn't say much about what Signor Bradshaw was really like."

"And what was he really like?"

"Generous to a fault. He single-handedly kept this church going. He also gave freely to our schools, hospitals, and programs to feed and clothe

the poor." The priest smiled sadly. "And then there was our altarpiece."

Gabriel glanced at Chiara, who was picking absently at the surface of the table as though she weren't listening. Then he looked at the young priest again and asked, "What about the altarpiece?"

"It was stolen about a year ago. Signor Bradshaw spent a great deal of time trying to get it back for us. More time than the police," the priest added. "I'm afraid our altarpiece had little artistic or monetary value."

"Was he ever able to find it?"

"No," said the priest. "So he replaced it with one from his personal collection."

"When did this happen?" asked Gabriel.

"Sadly, it was a few days before his death."

"Where's the altarpiece now?"

"There," said the priest, inclining his head to the right. "In the church."

They entered through a side door and hurried across the nave to the chancel. A stand of votive candles threw a flickering red light upon the niche containing a statue of Saint John, but the altarpiece was invisible in the gloom. Even so, Gabriel could see the dimensions were approximately correct. Then he heard the snap of a light switch, and in the sudden burst of illumination he saw a crucifixion in the manner of Guido Reni, competently executed but rather uninspired, not quite worth the seller's premium. His heart gave a sideways lurch. Then, calmly, he looked at the priest and asked, "Do you have a ladder?"

At a chemical supply company in an industrial quarter of Como, Gabriel purchased acetone, alcohol, distilled water, goggles, a glass beaker, and a protective mask. Next he stopped at an arts-and-crafts shop in the center of town where he picked up wooden dowels and a packet of cotton wool. By the time he returned to the church, Father Marco had located a twenty-foot ladder and had erected it in front of the painting. Gabriel quickly mixed a basic solution of solvent and, clutching a dowel and a wad of cotton wool, scaled the ladder. With Chiara and the priest watching from below, he opened a window at the center of the painting and saw an angel's hand, heavily damaged, clutching a ribbon of white silk. Next he opened a second window, approximately a foot lower on the canvas and a few inches to the right, and saw the face of a woman exhausted by childbirth. The third window revealed yet another face—the face of a newborn child, a boy, illuminated by a heavenly light. Gabriel placed his fingertips gently to the canvas and, much to his surprise, began to weep uncontrollably. Then he closed his eyes tightly and gave a shout of joy that echoed through the empty church.

The hand of an angel, a mother, a child . . .

It was the Caravaggio.

AUTHOR'S NOTE

THE HEIST IS a work of entertainment and should be read as nothing more. The names, characters, places, and incidents portrayed in the story are the product of the author's imagination or have been used fictitiously. Any resemblance to actual persons, living or dead, businesses, companies, events, or locales is entirely coincidental.

There is indeed a Church of San Sebastiano in the *sestiere* of Dorsoduro—it was consecrated in 1562 and is considered one of the five great plague churches of Venice—and Veronese's main altarpiece, *Virgin Assumed with Saints,* is accurately described. Visitors to the city will search in vain for the restoration firm owned by Francesco Tiepolo, nor will they find a certain Rabbi Zolli in the ancient Jewish ghetto. There are several small limestone apartment houses on Narkiss Street in Jerusalem, but to the best of my knowledge no one by the name of Gabriel Allon lives in any of them. The headquarters of the Israeli secret service is no longer located on King Saul Boulevard in Tel Aviv. I have chosen to keep the headquarters of my fictitious service there, in part, because I have always liked the name of the street.

There are many fine antique shops and art galleries on rue de Miromesnil in Paris, but Antiquités Scientifiques is not one of them. Maurice Durand has now appeared in three of the Gabriel Allon novels, and yet he still does not exist. Neither does Pascal Rameau, his accomplice from the criminal underworld of Marseilles. The Carabinieri's Division for the Defense of Cultural Patrimony, better known as the Art Squad, is in fact headquartered in a graceful palazzo on Rome's Piazza di Sant'Ignazio. Its chief is the able Mariano Mossa, not the one-eyed Cesare Ferrari. Deepest apologies to the Rijksmuseum Vincent van Gogh in Amsterdam for borrowing *Sunflowers* from its magnificent collection, but sometimes the best way to find a stolen masterpiece is to steal another one.

There is no Church of San Giovanni Evangelista in Brienno, Italy. Therefore, Caravaggio's glorious *Nativity*, stolen from Palermo's Oratorio di San Lorenzo in October 1969, could not have been discovered hanging above its altar, disguised as a crucifixion in the manner of Guido Reni. The account of Caravaggio's turbulent life contained in *The Heist* is wholly factual, though some may disagree with choices I made regarding the dates and details of certain events, as they occurred four centuries ago and, as a result, are open to interpretation. Even now, the exact circumstances of Caravaggio's death are shrouded in mystery. So, too, are the whereabouts of the *Nativity*. With each passing year, the chances of finding the large canvas intact grow more remote. The impact of its loss cannot be overstated. Caravaggio lived just thirty-nine years and left behind fewer than a hundred works that can be firmly attributed to his hand. The disappearance of even a single painting would leave a hole in the Western canon that can never be refilled.

There is no Luxembourg-registered firm called LXR Investments, nor is there a private bank in Linz, Austria, known as Bank Weber AG. The banks of Austria were once among the most secretive in the world—more secretive, even, than the banks of Switzerland. But in May 2013, under pressure from the European Union and the United States, Austrian banks agreed to begin sharing information on their depositors with the tax authorities of other countries. For better or worse, institutions such as Bank Weber—family-owned boutique-style banks that cater to the very wealthy—are fast becoming a dying breed. At the time of this writing, Switzerland's ledger of private banks had shrunk to just 148 institutions, with further consolidation and attrition expected to reduce that number even further in the future. Clearly, the days of the gnome seem numbered, as American and European governments engage in ever more aggressive measures to combat tax evasion.

There was indeed a massacre in the Syrian city of Hama in 1982, and, using numerous sources, I have tried to render its horror accurately. The man who ordered the city's destruction, and the murder of more than twenty thousand of its residents, was not the nameless dictator portrayed in *The Heist*. He was Hafez al-Assad, ruler of Syria from 1970 until his death in 2000, when his middle son, the London-educated Bashar, assumed control. There were some Middle East experts who mistook Bashar for a reformer. But in March 2011, when the so-called Arab Spring finally came to Syria, he responded with a savagery that included the use of poison gas against women and children. More than 150,000 people have been killed in the Syrian civil war, and another two million have been left homeless or have fled to neighboring countries, mainly Lebanon, Jordan, and Turkey. The number of Syrians living as refugees is soon expected to surpass four million, which would make it the largest refugee population in the world. Such is the legacy of four and a half decades of Assad family rule. If the slaughter and dislocation continues apace, the Assads might one day be rulers of a land without people.

But why do the Assads fight on when a majority of their people clearly want to be done with them? And why with such wanton disregard for civilized norms? Surely, it must have something to do with money. "It's a typical family business," Jules Kroll, the international corporate investigator and asset-recovery specialist, told CNBC in September 2013. "Except the family business is a country." Published estimates of the Assads' wealth range wildly. Bashar is reportedly worth in excess of $1 billion, though experts estimate the total family fortune at about $25 billion. The case of Egypt is illustrative. Former president Hosni Mubarak, a recipient of American taxpayer largesse for more than thirty years, is estimated to have acquired a fortune of perhaps $70 billion—this in a country where the average citizen subsists on just eight dollars a day.

A tiny fraction of Syrian regime assets has been frozen by the United States and its European allies, but billions of dollars remain carefully hidden. At the time of this writing, professional asset hunters were busy searching for the money. So, too, was Steven Perles, a Washington, DC, lawyer who represents victims of Syrian-sponsored terrorism. Experts agree the asset hunters will likely need the help of someone inside Assad Incorporated if their efforts are to prove successful. Perhaps that person has bought a stake in a small private bank in Austria. And perhaps there is a brave young woman, a child of Hama, watching his every move.

ACKNOWLEDGMENTS

THIS NOVEL, LIKE the previous thirteen books in the Gabriel Allon series, could not have been written without the assistance of David Bull, who truly is among the finest art restorers in the world. Each year, David gives up many hours of his valuable time to advise me on technical matters related to the craft of restoration and to review my manuscript for accuracy. His knowledge of art history is exceeded only by the pleasure of his company, and his friendship has enriched our family in ways large and small.

I spoke to numerous Israeli and American intelligence officers and policymakers while preparing this manuscript, and I thank them now in anonymity, which is how they would prefer it. Also, a very special thanks to the brilliant Patrick Matthiesen, who owns an enchanted Old Master art gallery in Mason's Yard, very near Julian Isherwood's. The only other trait they have in common is decency—decency being in short supply these days, in London or anywhere else.

I am indebted to T, an international investor and businessman with wide experience in the Middle

East, who told me about the quiet helpers of the dictators who walk around with lists of bank accounts in their pockets. Louis Toscano, my dear friend and longtime personal editor, made countless improvements to my manuscript, as did my copy editor, Kathy Crosby. Obviously, responsibility for any mistakes or typographical errors that find their way into the finished book falls on my shoulders, not theirs.

I consulted hundreds of books, newspaper and magazine articles, and Web sites while preparing this manuscript, far too many to name here. I would be remiss, however, if I did not mention the extraordinary scholarship of Andrew Graham-Dixon, Helen Langdon, Edward Dolnick, Peter Watson, Patrick Seale, Thomas L. Friedman, Francine Prose, Jonathan Harr, Simon Houpt, and Fouad Ajami. Also, a respectful thanks to the reporters and photojournalists who have courageously ventured into Syria during this time of war and destruction. They are a powerful reminder of why the world still needs quality journalism.

We are blessed with many friends who fill our lives with love and laughter at critical junctures during the writing year, especially Betsy and Andrew Lack, Andrea and Tim Collins, Enola and Stephen Carter, Stacey and Henry Winkler, Mirella and Dani Levinas, Elsa Walsh and Bob Woodward, Jane and Burt Bacharach, Nancy Dubuc and Michael Kizilbash, Joy and Jim Zorn, Caryn and Jeff Zucker, Elliott Abrams, and Fred Zeidman. A heartfelt thanks to Michael Gendler and Linda Rappaport for all their support and wise counsel. Also, to the remarkable team of professionals at HarperCollins, especially Jonathan Burnham, Brian Murray, Michael Morrison, Jennifer Barth, Josh Marwell, Tina Andreadis, Leslie Cohen, Leah Wasielewski, Mark Ferguson, Kathy Schneider, Brenda Segel, Carolyn Bodkin, Doug Jones, Karen Dziekonski, David Watson, Shawn Nicholls, Amy Baker, Mary Sasso, David Koral, Leah Carlson-Stanisic, and Archie Ferguson.

Finally, I wish to extend my deepest gratitude and love to my children, Nicholas and Lily, and to my wife, Jamie Gangel, who listened patiently while I constructed my plot and then skillfully edited my manuscript. Were it not for her patience and attention to detail, *The Heist* would not have been completed by its deadline. My debt to her is immeasurable, as is my love.